GERALD SEYMOUR

KINGFISHER

HODDER

First published in Great Britain in 1977 by Collins

This paperback edition first published in 2013

1

Copyright © Gerald Seymour 1977

Book ISBN 978 1 444 76005 7
eBook ISBN 978 1 444 76006 4

Printed and bound by Clays Ltd, St Ives plc

Hodder & Stoughton policy is to use papers that are natural, renewable
and recyclable products and made from wood grown in sustainable
forests. The logging and manufacturing processes are expected to
conform to the environmental regulations of the country of origin.

Hodder & Stoughton Ltd
338 Euston Road
London NW1 3BH

www.hodder.co.uk

THE JOURNEYMAN TAILOR

There is a rumour of an informer within the Provisional IRA's most active Brigade. But to collaborate with British Intelligence means certain death. If identified, he will be ruthlessly interrogated, tortured and executed. The MI5 agents running the informer must protect their man at all costs, even if that means innocent people will die.

ABOUT THE AUTHOR

Gerald Seymour spent fifteen years as an international television news reporter with ITN, covering Vietnam and the Middle East, and specialising in the subject of terrorism across the world. Seymour was on the streets of Londonderry on the afternoon of Bloody Sunday, and was a witness to the massacre of Israeli athletes at the Munich Olympics.

Gerald Seymour is now a full-time writer, and six of his novels have been filmed for television in the UK and US. KINGFISHER is his third novel.

For more information about Gerald Seymour and his books, visit his Facebook page at
www.facebook.com/GeraldSeymourAuthor

To Gillian, Nicholas and James

I

News of the arrest spread fast.

There had been, of course, nothing of it in the Party newspapers, nor on the radio, nor on the television news programmes, but then they were not the tried and tested sources. News moved in a different and more circuitous way, a constant process of dissemination. In the queues they heard of it while the sun was climbing high over the monuments and parks and lofty buildings that were the achievement of the regime. Queues waiting for the buses, queues at the food store where there was the delay in the arrival of the fresh baked loaves of the day, queues at the bank before it opened.

The talk of the arrest was neither loud nor furtive – just a subject of conversation amongst a bored and tired people – so that it rippled their lives momentarily, spreading the tedium of the day a little less harshly, easing the personal load because of the knowledge that somewhere in the city there was a being in great trouble, someone with a problem more real and more acute than any that the mass would face that morning, or that afternoon, or that night. And the thought of it sent an eddy of apprehension through those that knew.

There were a few who had seen him taken, seen the cruising black car of the militia come to a sudden halt in the midst of the traffic, the rear doors snap open and the men in the pale-brown uniforms weave a path through the other cars till they had reached the pavement and were sprinting for their quarry. He had walked casually and unaware of the risk till they were on him. There had been one at his legs, pitching him forward, another to spread out his arms on the pavement, so that if he had had a gun secreted on his person, hidden impossibly beneath his trousers or his light summer shirt, he would not have been able to take advantage from it. A third had stood above him, looming and huge, right arm extended with the cocked pistol aimed into the small of the boy's back. And then they had gone, even as the crowd, unsure and hesitant, had circled to watch. They had bundled him towards the car, its rear door open and spanning the gutter, dragged him so that his torso was far in front of his feet. There was no siren, no flashing light, and the curious waited till the accelerating car was again engulfed and lost in the traffic. Others looked on as the vehicle spun hard, tyres fighting for a grip, and disappeared into the shadowed entrance of the militia station. The noise attracted them, and because of the loss of speed of the car they had had the opportunity to notice for a fraction of a second a face half-buried amongst the uniforms. A face that was white, eyes staring, and with the hair already dishevelled. That there was fear in the boy was clear for all to see, however short the opportunity. A deep animal fear, and word of it had passed through the city that night, and spread further the following morning.

There were some who conjectured and said that they knew why he had been held. Those that knew of the shooting had heard of the wounding of the policeman far out in the industrial suburbs to the west across the river.

The principal headquarters of the security police in Kiev, capital town of the Ukraine, is a formidable construction. Built close to the seat of power, it is adjacent to Party offices, and within a short walk of the administration centre. There is a wedding-cake decor on the front façade, and it has columns and gently sloping steps and statues, all maintained in a bright and soft-coloured stone by the regular spray of water jets. The legacy of Stalinist post-war rebuilding: but for all that the interior does not match the finery of the façade. Behind the walls no allowance has been made for aesthetics: a functional honeycomb of rooms and corridors and narrow staircases, while deep in the basements are located the prisoners' cells.

At the far end of the buried passage, devoid of natural light, and behind a door numbered '38', Moses Albyov now lay. He rested on a mattress of straw held together by rough farm sack-cloth that rustled with each shift of his weight. A slightly-built figure, he had a pinched and concerned face, and dark, straight hair that had been thrown haphazardly in all directions and that needed the attentions of comb or brush. They had taken his shoes and his belt, and his hands held the waist of his trousers – not that he was about to rise and move, but simply through some vague fantasy of protection. His glasses, too, had gone – left on the pavement where they had spilled from his face at the moment they had taken him, probably broken in the short scuffle, certainly abandoned. Without them his sight was reduced, blending the hard lines of the cell walls, causing them to be softer, less cruel. Not that there was much for him to focus on. A door to the front, steel-faced and scratched where others had attempted to achieve a pathetic immortality by carving their names and the date; fearful perhaps of entering and leaving the cell in total anonymity. Only a spy hole, small, circular and reflecting the light of the room, interrupted the smooth surface of the door. No natural light was permitted to enter the cell: illumination was from a low-powered bulb recessed into the ceiling and covered by what Moses presumed was toughened glass embedded with wire mesh. The floor was of roughened cement, as though the workers had wished to be rid of their job and had hurried their work, leaving it pitted and lined like a ploughed field when the winter frosts have come. Nothing to call furniture, no table, no chair, no cupboard, no shelves. Only the mattress and a bucket that he had moved away to the furthest point from him because of its smell, the odour of vomit and urine and faeces. In the corner, behind the door – it was not far, perhaps seven feet – not far enough to divorce its presence from him, not far enough to shut out the taste that swelled in his mouth.

For company there were the cockroaches. They came fearless

and exploratory, and because of the quietness of the cell he believed he could hear their legs, brushing in a gentle passage across the floor towards him. He had thought that the light that burned through the night would have frightened them, and could not believe that creatures so devoid of intellect could recognize his helplessness, but some instinct told them that they had nothing to fear. Once he had brushed two away with his hand and his whole body had trembled in the aftermath of the contact. He could not touch them again, and they had come, sometimes singly, sometimes in their cohorts, to examine him, to ponder their visitor. And as if bored and disinterested they had gone on their way. It is because there is no food, he thought.

His right shoulder still hurt, ached where the bruising had now won through and discoloured the pale skin into a kaleidoscope of blue and mauve and yellow. On the final flight of stairs, and he had not been ready for it. Already down two flights while they held his arms above the elbows, squeezing and firm, and then on the last leg, without warning, the hands had gone and the knee was in the small of his back and he was away, arms flailing in the vacuum, seeking to break his fall against the cement steps that rushed to meet him. Toes in his ribs, a fist in his hair, and he had risen to walk the rest of the passage, stayed on his own feet while they produced the keys to the cell door, made his entry without interference, and stood stock-still in the centre of the floor as the door had shut behind him. That was all the violence they had shown him. Just the once, reckoning in their trained minds what was sufficient to inculcate a message, insufficient to harden his resistance. The footsteps and the casual conversation of the guards had faded, become immersed in the silence around him, and since then, nothing. Not a door slammed, not a raised voice. As if he were immured, cemented away, forgotten.

He could understand what they were doing. Simple if you examined it, applied logic. The process of vegetation, that is what it was all about. They wouldn't talk to him yet; they would wait until they had assembled the dossier, hardened the evidence. When they were ready and not before, that was when interrogation would begin. Stupid if they rushed it. So he knew what they were at, why they were taking their time. And he knew what they would be asking of him when finally they had prepared themselves.

It had been decided in the group that he would be the first, because it had been he who had drawn the short straw.

All four had known their rôle in the attack. Rebecca from the front, asking the policeman for directions and fumbling in her bag for the map, holding his attention. David from behind, his clenched fist landing on the tunic cloth of the man's right shoulder, enough to fell him. Isaac springing from the shadow, hands at the holster flap to prise away the precious pistol, drawing it clear and throwing it abruptly to where Moses stood. When the gun was in his hand the others had run off, deserting the stage.

Moses's hand had been shaking, and the barrel waving, dancing in the air. And all the time the elephantine form of the policeman had convulsed as semi-stunned he had tried to rise from his knees and make his escape. Bewilderment and pain were etched on the policeman's features, as he struggled to make some sense from the previous moments of confusion. And as Moses had looked down at the barrel, fascinated by its movements, the identity-protecting balaclava had slipped and obscured his vision. He had pulled at it, ripped it across his face, over his head, clear of his hair. A distant scream from David for him to hurry, in concert with a sharper growl, Isaac's. When he fired the policeman was gazing at him, the trained bovine mind eating into the description that he sought to remember, conjuring the facial features even as the bullet struck his chest. From the way the policeman fell Moses had known it was not a fatal shot. That was the moment that he needed to root his feet to the pavement and finish what he had started. But he was running and panting and sobbing to get air in his lungs, frantic to create distance between himself and the man he had failed to kill. The others were at the corner, and when he had come they had all run together till they had not the strength to sprint any further.

It was only after he had vomited the early supper his mother had prepared for him, spewed it out behind the bus shelter, that he had felt in his pockets, one after the other, and realized that he no longer had the balaclava.

The importance of the loss had been demonstrated to him with brutal clarity within minutes of entering the militia headquarters. They'd sat him in a chair, in a room at the back and on the ground floor, and a man in a white coat had come forward with a shined and scrubbed steel comb and had run it through his hair and looked with pleasure at the hairs he extracted. There would be a match: they had the skill to do that. It would be no problem for them, to marry what they found embedded in the wool of the balaclava with the hairs that lay between the teeth of the comb. The man in the white coat had said nothing, just placed the comb in a plastic bag. Too simple, and damning, confirmation of what they would already have obtained from the injured policeman. Sitting in his bed he'd be, with the men around him who make up the photographic imitations of people they are hunting. Moses's 'face' would have been circulated, and the militia men who had come from behind him as he walked must have seen the features that the experts had recreated and assimilated them sufficiently for them to act. When they'd walked inside the headquarters with him they'd shown their pleasure in the knowledge that there was no mistake, that they had the one they wanted. Before, they had been in the realm of belief; now they had the evidence to swing their opinion to certainty. Two follicles of hair, that was all they needed. So silly. Two strands, nothing, till there was a microscope. But they would have a microscope, and scientists to use it, and a laboratory for them to work in.

Yet wasn't it still too easy, Moses, to rely just on their luck? Go deeper, hunt for the source of identification, the factor that isolated him from the mass of youths that paraded the streets of the city . . . Remember the balaclava, remember the campus shop, at the north side of the university, remember the label of sale. They would have stored the information, cared and gloated over it while the bed-ridden pig put together the description of the man that had shot him. Then treasured and coveted the two. The militia would have seen the shoulder satchel, worn carelessly and without concern; emblem of the university emblazoned on its flap. You did it for them, Moses. Performed their work. A student with the features to match – what more could they have asked of you? So forget about photo-fits and laboratories and the magnification of hair roots. There was nothing that should minimize his stupidity. He had given it to them – all they needed for suspicion. He'd left them only to supply the proof. And their technology would be massive, equal to that, hugely excessive for the task.

So how many hours more, how long till the report was typed and the knot tied, till they were ready for him?

It was cold in the cell, and the memory of the warmth as he had been walking in the street, wrapped in his own thoughts, was fading. There was a chill and sort of dampness that he could not identify, for the walls showed no rivulets of moisture. As if water had once been there and had strangely found no route of escape.

There was no escape. He sat up sharply, disturbing the straw underneath him. What would they do to him? It would be easier for him if he knew – he would know then whether he could counter it or not. But he had no answers; all outside his experience. Drugs – perhaps they would use drugs? That would be painless and would remove the stigma of confession, at least. But what if it were to be pain? What if that were the instrument they should use? They'd break him, not because he was special, or different: they'd break anyone with pain . . . David and Isaac as well, and Rebecca quicker than all of them. Everyone has a limit, and they'd push you right through it till you were screaming, shrieking, till the names came tumbling out so fast that they couldn't write them down, and the addresses and the rendezvous. Everything they wanted and much more, only stop, stop and no more! Please, not again, please! He was stirring on the mattress, his body squirming, compressing the flesh together. Pain was what frightened him, the pain of a beating from the truncheons, from the electrodes they would wire to his limbs. And they'd have a place to do that, somewhere in the building, that too was a certainty. If it were to be drugs then you were helpless, unable to summon resistance. But what was the antidote to pain? Moses tossed and heaved now, his mind taking control and leading him along a course from which he could not deflect it. Perhaps it was courage? Not really important for how long. For a few hours, a day perhaps. To give the others time – had to give them time to go. And what if they didn't know that he had been taken? He wondered how long he had been in the cell, but realized he had lost any sense of time after they'd taken his watch. Would have heard by now, wouldn't they? Must have done. And they should be running, dispersing, because he wasn't strong, wasn't ready for the pain, could not give them much time. He sagged back, flattening the harder lumps of the straw, and turned his body so that he lay on his stomach with his face buried in the sacking, and with his arms clasped around his head to shut out the light. There were tears that he could not control, that came without noise, and that ran a little way over his upper cheek before falling on the sacking, staining momentarily, then disappearing.

There was the opportunity now to think: just what they wanted him to do. He had to put it together in his mind, sort out where it had started, and why, and what were their aims and intentions. Quicker for them that way – they'd get their answers faster. And be easier for him, too – he'd suffer less. Have it all ready when they come for you, then they won't need to hurt you so much. The awful fear of waiting – but this would be only the start of it. First the waiting for the time when they were ready to take the confession. Then the waiting for the trial. And after that more waiting. Waiting for sentence, waiting for execution. Be from a cell like this that they'd take you out. Still dark before the creep of dawn, and floodlights playing on the high walls, and somewhere in the yard they'll trip you over, Moses, then jerk you down to your knees, and there'll be a hand to hold your head steady, and then the grip will loosen from the hair and there will be the noise of the pistol being cocked. That's what you're going to wait for, Moses, that's the future, that's eternity.

They'd grown up together, the four of them. The war was long over when they were born, and the fighting finished, but nothing changed in the lot of the Ukrainian Jew. Second-class people, on the outside, without benefit or recognition. They didn't live in a ghetto – that was not the way the housing was allocated – but they'd learned to fall in together because that was survival in an alien world. Taught to be quiet, taught not to answer back, taught not to risk provocation, to ride a jibe or an insult, and to be better and fitter and stronger and more able, because those were the necessities of equality.

As children David had been their leader, the one who knew the answers and understood the struggle. It had been David who told them of Babi Yar, and none of them past eleven years of age. It was not a place their parents spoke of, not talked about by the rabbi, but David had led them to the ravine on the edge of the city's suburbs and told them what had happened there, of the machine-gunning of the Jews, told them there was no monument to commemorate the place because those who had died there had been Jewish. David had pointed to where the Germans had set up their machine-gun tripods, marked the spot for them, explained how the columns of the condemned came without thought of flight or resistance, spoken of the meek and pallid acceptance of the orders to wait patiently, to file forward, to kneel down, not to move, not to obstruct the soldiers' aim. Then he had shown them the refuse of the suburb that had been thrown into this place, and walked with them to the broken jars in which the brave placed flowers at night, when they were safe from view, and which were destroyed in the morning by the boots of those on their way to the trams and the buses. The trio listened as David explained their position in life, their heritage. For a boy of his years he knew so much, had the patience to tell them, when they wanted to play the games of children, the matters with which they should concern themselves.

9

The group had become inseparable. At school they had sat together, at home they had worked together – because David said they must be cleverer, with better grades, better diplomas than those they sought to emulate. But they were being prepared for a life of conformity and inaction, inevitable in its way, until the day that David had come to Rebecca's house with the radio set. They were teenagers now, but isolated from the outside world until the radio flitted into their lives. The Voice of America, the World Service of the BBC, Radio Liberty broadcast by an émigré staff in Munich and beamed from a massive transmitter across Central Europe. The curtain was pulled back, a shaft of sunlight brought in. There was contact with the forbidden, excitement and stimulation at the illegality of it all. David said he'd purchased the radio, and smiled. They knew it was beyond his means, and he'd also said they had no need to learn more of its acquisition, only to listen and to understand.

It became a secret thing, special and precious with its expanded short-wave band, and a door through which they followed the June War of 1967, and the War of Atonement of 1973. They heard of the tribulations endured by those of their faith who sought to emigrate from Russia to the State of Israel, were told of the trials of those not permitted to leave the Motherland that they wanted to forsake. They knew of international protest at the lot of Soviet Jewry, they suckled themselves on what they believed to be the strength of world opinion. Heady and intoxicating drink for the four teenagers . . .

And David was their leader.

Nothing had ever been formally decided. It had never been talked over, but the time came when he made all the decisions for the group. At first there had been discussions, followed always by inevitable agreement to David's point of view, till within the last two years the pros and cons were no longer argued. David announced what they would do, and there was immediate concurrence. And as he assumed command so David's personality seemed to grow, and he took on a mantle in the minds of the other three of new strength, new influence. Yet when Moses submitted to the men in khaki, with their instruments and their drugs, when he gave the names, then David would follow to an identical cell, a fashioned and geometric imitation of the one that Moses lay in now, and his future would be as strongly etched as was that of Moses. The torture would be the same as he would have endured, and the culmination too – perhaps the same dawn, perhaps the same prison yard. All of this would be David's if Moses talked when his interrogators came for him, all of this and an equation of betrayal. Was he any more fitted, better equipped, to confront them in the interrogation basements? David with his smiling face, who could conjure up passion into his words, communicate the life in his eyes. Did he possess a threshold that would protect him from the fear and terror of pain? And Moses realized that he had never known David to experience helpless and uncontrollable stress, had never seen anguish screw up his cheeks, or known him exchange his confidence for confusion and hurt. It hastened a chilling shudder through him; what if David were no better, no stronger, no more resolute than he, Moses, the follower? He clasped his arms across his chest, digging his uncut finger-nails through the fabric of his shirt. What if the leader were no better able to withstand the pigs, had no defiance, no arrogant obscenities? That would be betrayal too: to expose him to them, to leave him weak and vulnerable and screaming.

How many months ago it had been that David had found the woodman's hut amongst the birch forest near the 'dachas' north of the city Moses could not remember. Time had travelled fast since then, much had been compressed into the days till they had seemed to run together without shape or pattern because of the new stimulus of what they called the 'programme'. Moses had allowed his work at the new chemical factory near his home to become subordinate to the meetings that the group held inside the darkened and damp shack, which they reached separately, making their own way at David's behest. Bare walls, only the rough-cut timbers to shield them from the spring rain that followed the snow and that preceded the summer heat and the flies. It was here that David had talked and the others had listened. The irony was – and it was not lost on them – that the doctrine he preached was available for all in the Ukraine to find; there were histories, tomes of them, of the partisan warfare against the Germans who had occupied the area, and treatises of the tactics of Guevara, and for those who had stored them and who had not thrown them away when they were suppressed there were the works of Mao, and there were the thoughts of Giap who had conquered the invincible Americans. That was what David talked to them of. On one fundamental only did he depart from the text and bible of the guerrilla fighter. There would be no 'first stage', there would be no 'infrastructure period', no creation of an 'indoctrinated population base'. They took too long, took too many people, and the circumstances in which they found themselves could not be likened to the paddy fields of Asia. The Jews of Russia had spoken of the ills so often they had no need for more words, only for action. And if the action were successful then his movement would develop as a sapling does under the spring light, but first there must be the root, deep in fertile soil. He told them of the revolutionary warfare that would hit back at the oppressors of the Jewish people. 'Like a flea-bite at first,' he had said. 'But a flea that cannot be found, that cannot be hunted out, that comes back and wants more. That turns what is first an irritation to anger. When their anger is aroused then we know that we are hurting them, then we know that we have vengeance. There has been a great wrong here, too great a wrong for us alone to erode. But it is a gesture that is needed. How many walked in submission to the German shower chambers? How many now walk in submission to the camps at Potma and Perm?'

David had been persuasive, but there was no necessity for it. All in the group knew the fighting ground. Isaac said that he had met a youth who had met once with Yuri Vudka who had seven years at Potma to think on his application for leave to emigrate to Israel. David had chipped in, not allowing him to finish – but then he seldom did, and it was not resented – 'Vudka from our

12

own Kiev, and seven years to think of his city, and his crime that he had wanted to leave, and had written things down, that he had books from the West and in the Hebrew language.' David had talked of the new Jews of Israel, hardened and fashioned in their own sun by the rigours of their own land and their own freedom. He called them 'sabras', men who had washed away the placidity of the former generation that had marched to the cattle trucks with not an arm upraised. So how placid, docile, unquestioning were their people? There was enough evidence to make him believe it, enough that he had heard to verify the belief that they were supine, incapable of self-help. But often they had wondered whether there were other groups that met in bare and shadowed rooms, that came to darkened and pathless woods, that sought shelter in the same nameless anonymity and that talked of a struggle, of hope and revenge, however trivial. David had heard on the radio of the bomb detonated on the Moscow Inner Underground, and had told them of protest and disobedience among their people in Novosibirsk – and in the main square at that – and of a man who was executed in the prison at Tbilisi and who had set off six explosive devices. He had heard it on the radio, where the word carried biblical validity. Not all Jews, he had said, and smiled, but at least others of different faith and aspiration who were burrowing at the edifices, chipping and hacking. Others who rejected the required submission as totally as they, and who stood back from the fly-swat resistance of the press conference, and the smuggled letter to the West, and the complaint to the Foreign Power. 'Words, words, stupid and ineffective,' David had said. 'As valuable as lying in the sand in the path of a steamroller. It is action that will change them, that will achieve something.' They had wondered how many other tribes shared their jungle and ate the same fruit, but they had no way of knowing. As the group became more daring and more cohesive so too their dread of breaking the precious security was augmented. There was no consideration given to widening the size of the cell – too dangerous. Heighten the walls, strengthen the locks, repel recruits even should they be found. An island, aloof in a battle sea, that was how they had decided they should remain.

They had followed David through each step as he prepared the ground for the movement that lifted their course from the level of conspiracy to action, accepting every stage of his logic, not disputing his argument. Moses thought of the long weekend days and the mid-week summer evenings they had spent, the four of them, in the hut. How they had talked of what they would do, sometimes all shouting together and laughing and hanging on to each other's shoulders and imagining how a grateful people would bow to their courage, acknowledge the standard-bearers, feel a pride in their bravery. David had decided when they were ready, and none had queried him, only become quiet in the elation of knowing that the moment had arrived. They had talked in whispers that evening, subdued to the droned harassment of the mosquitoes, and clung to each other before the time to go to their homes, and memorized the route to the rendezvous the next evening. It had been wonderful for Moses as they had held each other close, the male smells unable to counter the softer, more gentle trace of the girl's scent. So much strength, so much power, nothing they could not do because they were together. Later had come the chilling loneliness for the boy, when he left the warmth of the group, to walk back on his own on the forest path towards the road. David had said he would be the first to kill, Isaac had argued till Rebecca had found the compromise. None should claim the privilege by right, in the cell they were as one, she had said, and seemed to mock at David. The leader had rejected her, demanded it for himself, the prerogative of the front runner, but Isaac would not yield. Rebecca had spoken again, chided David. Were they not all capable? It was a simple thing, was it not? She had opened the door, disappeared for a minute, not more, and when she returned there were four twigs in her fist, their tips arranged in line, their length hidden in her closed palm. David had drawn first, expressionless, watching and waiting, then Isaac with a smile lightening his features because his was shorter, Moses third, and the winced sigh of disappointment from the other two men when they saw the stubbed length of the one which he had chosen. A protest from Isaac, a taunt from Rebecca that already they would divide themselves – officers and men, commissars and proletariat – a shrug from David. No remark from the boy himself. Again and again in his mind Moses had worked over the plan, digesting the part that he would play, remembering the details. The first blow they would strike, and Moses Albyov had been chosen; not David who was their leader, not Isaac who fancied and believed in his fitness, but Moses, the last of the recruits to arrive before the cell had been sealed. To curse Rebecca or to love her for the chance she had wished on him – he had not known the answer as he stumbled from the shadows of the wood to the roadside.

But his hand had shaken, and the wool had drifted across his eyes. The mistakes of Moses Albyov. Errors that the others would not have made. And if he now collapsed, if he buckled, then all would pay the penalties for the faults that were his alone.

If there could only be someone to speak to, or just the sound of a human voice, however distant . . .

No food, and his belly aching with the deprivation and bowels grinding an extract from the last meal, God knows how many hours before.

Pray God let it finish.

Those were the thoughts of Moses Albyov. And they stayed with him till the moment he was roused by the sounds of keys turning in the lock of the door and of the bolt being withdrawn from its socket.

Four men for the escort. Not gentle, yet not brutal. Guiding him uncomfortably down the darkened passageway. His arms were pinioned and the men's fingers dug hard down into his muscles, and the manacles that they had put on his wrists were set tight so that the encompassing steel bit into his flesh. He was classified as 'political terrorist', 'enemy of the people', one who had sought to kill a guardian of the State; and Moses knew that there was no possibility of sympathy. No words as they moved and their feet were rubber-shod so that the party – more like a cortège, he thought – went silently on its way. That was why he hadn't heard them, but they must have come, every few minutes, must have come to the door to spy at him, only he had not been aware of it.

Fear now. A horrible, clinging terror, something that was new and that he had not experienced before, compressing the muscles of his stomach and leaving his throat parched and dry.

More doors and more guards and more keys. Out into a brighter corridor where men sat at a low wooden table with a radio playing light music, men who interrupted their card game to stare at him, the look that men have for a fellow creature that is not a part of them, contaminated, condemned. Fit and strong men who were taking him, not tolerating his weakness of step as they bustled their way up the flights of stairs, down the lengths of the passageways. Another door, another lock, another staircase, and they were half pulling him with them. His lagging was not a conscious decision; if anything he wanted to please, like a dog about to be beaten that nestles against its master's legs. But he could not follow at their speed, so they dragged and pushed him to maintain their momentum.

The cold of the cell was gone, replaced by the warmth of midday, a fierce summer's day. There was sweat on the faces of the men that took him, struggling on the corners of the staircase landings, then flattening themselves and their prisoner against the wall to allow free passage for a senior officer in his pressed trousers and tailored tunic, the medal ribbons of his service on his chest. Seven flights they climbed, then a closed and polished door in front and the respectful knock of the *starshina* with the stripes on his arm, and the command, distant but impatient, for them to enter.

One on each arm, one behind and the sergeant in front. Through the outer door and across the outer office, then the inner room, and the door open. Moses could see three men at a desk facing him as he was propelled forward. His trousers were sagging, still held up by his hands, his stockinged feet bruised and chafed from the stair surface of concrete and stone. Cold eyes, looking at him, boring into him, examining and stripping him. The sanctum of the enemy. There was a breeze now on his face, soft and winnowing against his cheeks, playing on his hair, cooling at his chest. On the left the source of the draught, an opened window, double-glazed for winter but pulled back now to permit the free flow of air.

No bar, no impediment.

If they saw him look at it . . . if they gauged his intention . . . These were the ones who would bend and break it out of him, who would make him tell them of David and Isaac, and Rebecca with the black hair and the dark eyes and the breasts that he was afraid of and the waist that he yearned to encircle . . . Moses's eyes were riveted to the front, locked on the man who sat at the central chair of the table.

The guards, preoccupied with delivering their charge to such august company – a full colonel of militia, the KGB major and the major of police – did not detect the flexing of his arm muscles, the bow-string tightness of his legs.

Moses Albyov closed his eyes, closed his mind at the moment that he catapulted himself the 7 feet from where he stood to the window-sill. There was a delay as he scrabbled, impeded by the handcuffs, to swing the weight of his torso out into the void, and for a brief second one of the guards was able to claw at his trousers, now flapping and loose at his knees. If his ankle had been held they might perhaps have been able to arrest his fall, but the fingers of the guard were clamped only onto the cotton cloth of the trousers; it was not enough for him to grip at when he took the full weight of the diving Jew.

As he fell there was a sudden clarity in his mind, and an image of a group, of young faces that were laughing together and smiling, and their arms were all around him, and their voices pealed as bells for him . . .

All ended by the sledgehammer impact on to the tarmac of the headquarters car park.

*　*　*

Hot water into an ants' nest. Men running and shouting and reacting to orders, forming excited, shifting patterns around the broken figure in their midst. From high above the colonel of militia, sharing the seventh-floor vantage-point of the window with the police major, surveyed the chaos below. Alone among them the man from KGB remained at the interrogation table.

It was he who broke the shocked silence of the room.

'Dead?' he asked.

From the window the reply, muffled because the head was still craning outwards. 'There is no possibility of survival, not from such a height.'

'And no preliminary interrogation, no initial questioning?'

'There had been none, as you requested. As you had asked. Just the forensic on the hair and the photograph. You were specific: there were to be no questions until he had cooled. Not even his name and his address, not even why he did not carry the card. You were specific.'

A nodded head, enough of the games, enough of the point-scoring. Wouldn't bring him back, didn't matter now. The KGB man made a gesture of dismissal to the four guards.

'So we have just a photograph. No address, not even a name . . .'

'You had said there should be no questioning.'

'I am aware of what I said. So we take again our starting-point. We have the photograph. He is—' and the dry smile, the suggestion of humour – 'he *was* Jewish. The forensic have confirmed that the hair textures matched. It becomes a job for policemen. It will not be difficult to identify him – many ways – and once we have achieved that then the associates will be easy. We shall have them in a few days. It will take that time, a few days, but less than a week, and then we shall have the little bastards. And we have saved ourselves a bullet. Perhaps that is the way we should look on it: we have saved Mother Russia the price of a bullet.'

2

Early that morning, many hours before Moses had died, his mother had bicycled to where David lived. It was a long journey in the fast-forming heat for a woman suffering the first pangs of arthritis, and the fact that she attempted it indicated the anxiety she held for the overnight absence of her only son. When she arrived it was David who answered her knock, and they had talked at the front door, David blocking her from going inside, determined once he had heard the germ of the news that she carried that she should not meet his own parents.

'He had spoken of taking some food in the city, then going to the library, then he said he would be with you and with the others – with Isaac and Rebecca. He had said he would not be late home. His bed hadn't been disturbed, and he has never before been out the whole night.'

David had half listened and half wondered to himself what had caused the delay. He was aware that only Rebecca and Isaac had joined him the previous evening, and remembered the talk that there had been among the three of them as they considered where Moses might be.

'Always he has been home for the night. And when he went out yesterday he had not taken his police book – his card was at home. That is wrong – not allowed. And without it, if he is in trouble, if he is in the hospital and hurt and cannot speak, then how will they . . . ?'

So Moses had acted as instructed – acted as David had told them they all should. He could imagine Moses's mother rummaging in his drawers looking for a clue to his whereabouts and finding no satisfaction, only the card with its cellophane wrapper with the head-and-shoulders photograph and the official stamp set across it. David had never explained the motive for his order, leaving the others to think for themselves: that if they were taken in – casually, without the link being forged between their activities and the police inquiry in hand – then it would be easier to explain away the absence of identification as a careless lapse. It was usual for the police to pick the Jewish boys off the streets, if they found them out late, if they were in a group – even if they just cared to exist. Not that there had ever been talk among the four of questioning, arrest, imprisonment. It was not a subject David would have tolerated: too chilling, too personal. And therefore it was not considered by the others.

It was impossible for it to happen if they were careful, and they had been careful – except for the balaclava and the policeman who had not died. Isaac had noticed, abrasively and impervious to feelings, as soon as they had gathered again with their breath still coming in a streaming torrent, and while Moses had hung his head, and while David had quietened him. And it was beyond the character of Moses to be away through the night. A steady boy, not likely to panic, not one to sleep in the park, not one for the girls, and David knew all their friends outside the cell.

'. . . without his card if he is injured no-one will know to tell us . . .'

'I will see Isaac and Rebecca, and I will ask them what they know,' said David. He was kindly and reassuring, sufficient to mask from the old lady the drumming fever he felt. Not fear, nothing as defensive as that, and not as strong an emotion as excitement, just a feeling that at last real battle was joined. The skirmishing was over. The patrol cars would be out. Guns issued, semi-automatic to augment the readily carried sidearms. Control rooms perspiring with the effort of pursuit. The beast had been angered and sought to retaliate. The wounds had gone to the quick, as had been intended. But it was not the time that David would have chosen, and his jaw stiffened, and his mouth quivered and he sought to hide it, and to play again the rôle of command and competence. Little to practise his mood on. Only an old woman who showed fear and confusion and who had come to him for help; whose darned stockings were twisted and sagging, and who had missed her place in the queues to seek him out, and who did not know where her son lay. From his own instinct David had already decided that Moses had been taken, arrested, even as the woman had spoken.

He sent her on her way, and closed the door after her, and told his own mother that it was just a friend who had called and that he was going out to walk and that he did not have to be at the plant for the afternoon shift. He needed to be alone, to think, to have a plan to put before the others. It was expected of him now, that he could produce an instant solution, but the initiative was absent. Perhaps it was they, the pigs, that held the high ground? It was not a dimension of the battle that he had ever considered. But what if they were consigned forever to the valleys? It was immaterial. A battle there would be, and he must find the solution.

There was no pavement; he walked on the unmade road, rutted and pitted from the winter's ice, forsaken by workmen in the summer, and never adequately finished when they built the flats. Further out of town were the show blocks of the Krushchev days, when accommodation rose to impress the people that they were at last remembered. But that was not where the Jews lived. Mean little premises, these, that he walked past, where the rent racketeering was fiercer than in the capitalist West that he knew of from his radio. When you were Jewish, how could you get your name high on the housing list? That was the problem, and when you couldn't then you were in the hands of the landlords. Life was a shared bathroom and a shared kitchen and a shared toilet. Inside what passed as the privacy of a front door were three rooms, and his mother and his father and his three sisters to share them with. Nearer into town there would be flowers in front of the small houses, but nobody bothered out here. There seemed no point; they would be covered with dust when the bus came down the road, suffocated, and the water pressure was too low to run a hose . . . and for what, anyway? It would take more than colour and the scent of pollen to brighten these homes.

So perhaps the bastards had Moses. Down in the town, that's where he'd be. Hadn't his card with him, which meant he'd have to talk for them to know who he was. And when he told them that then the short-cuts would begin – names of associates, addresses, rendezvous locations, dates. Identification? Not a difficult task, not for a body so efficient as the militia. How soon would he talk? That was the only question he needed to answer now. How soon? What was the boy made of? How much spunk, how much balls? The same courage as Israel had when the Syrians were traversing the Golan? Did Moses have the courage of the Israeli tank commanders? But it was one thing to fight with your friends around you, on your own side. But what did Moses have now, in a police cell with the electric wires and the batons and the impatience of the questioners? David shivered in the sunlight. Not much that he would have going for him. Just loyalty – and what would that mean when the pain was intense?

Isaac was coming towards him down the road, hot and red in the face. He had been running, and there were stains under his armpits. He was shorter than David, and not so muscled, his face strained and the sinews of his neck bulging.

He was blurting incoherently, so that David embraced him and quietened the boy and told him to get his breath and to begin again.

'It's all around the University. I heard it first in the canteen before classes, then again in the lecture room before the professor came. Everyone is talking of it. They say there has been an attack on a policeman, and that last night the militia took a man, right in the centre of the city, and they say he is a Jew. One of the chemistry students started it – his uncle works there, in the files section – and he told the boy's mother last night, and there were celebrations last night in the headquarters – vodka in all the offices. And you remember that Moses failed to meet up with us last night.'

'He did not come home at all last night. His mother has been round to see us and asked for information.'

'Has nothing been said on the radio?'

'Nothing. How would they? It is not their way.'

'What to do, David?'

'To be calm and to think, and then to fight them . . .'

'With what? How can we fight them? They will do things to Moses, things so that he will talk, and then they will come for us. How long will he last, if he can resist them at all? Not longer than this evening – and that's a whole day, a whole twenty-four hours – and they will come.'

Isaac had no more to say. Through all the time he had run from the bus that had carried him away from the University the thought of the four o'clock awakening, the time the militia always came, had buffeted and pummelled him. The boots, the guns, the hammering, the axes in the door timbers, the bed-clothes wrenched back. Now he could wash it from his system. He had demonstrated his fear, exposed it in the street to David.

'Where is Rebecca?' David asked.

'Still at the University. Botany is an earlier start than chemis-try. She won't come out till eleven, perhaps later if she has work in the library . . .'

'Get her,' said David. 'Meet her and take her to the woods. To the hut. We will meet there, at two . . . you can get there by then . . . and do not be late.' And then the smile that the others so coveted. 'And don't worry: they won't touch us. Moses hasn't talked or they would be here by now. We have some time yet.'

He slapped Isaac on the back, and turned towards his home. There were creases of concentration and worry on his forehead, and his eyes were staring down at the stones and debris of the road. A mystery, and a confusion for him – if Moses had been taken, why were they not here? How much more time could the boy buy for them . . . ?

There was only one certainty. They were not going to be

lying in their beds waiting for the police to come, rubbing the sleep from their eyes as they pulled on the bare essentials of clothing at gun-point. Anything rather than that.

But if they ran how far could they go, and was there anywhere that was safe? And if they hid, for how long and with what future?

Rebecca and Isaac would come to the hut in the afternoon and expect him to lead them, would anticipate that he knew the solution. How to explain there was none, that he was incapable of providing an inspired answer? Rebecca would not see the weakness, would follow where she was taken, but Isaac would see, would strip away the camouflage. And there was nothing in Mao, or Giap, or Guevara, nothing that offered solace, nothing relevant. David watched Isaac's long walk, rolling and round-shouldered, away down the street. A lone figure that skirted the few parked cars, a gesture once to a passing cyclist. David regretted his going, resented that there was no opportunity for Isaac to stay longer, to talk, to discuss, to share.

But you knew it would happen like this, David.

Not so soon, not at this time.

If anything it has been slow coming, David.

But we are not prepared . . .

If you shoot policemen, David . . .

We are in confusion, we do not hold any initiative.

Did you expect them to wait for your readiness, David?

Long strides, adrenaline spurred, he ran towards home.

At first the road followed the west bank of the Dnieper. That was the route out of the city. Then a left turn and the wide tarmac ran far and straight across the agricultural plain, passing by the occasional clusters of homes for the collective workers till the cultivated ground gave way to the forests. A dozen miles later was the bus halt to which each made their separate way. From the roadside they walked along the dirt path through the woods to the place where David had first taken them many months before.

The path led to the 'dacha' complex – neat log cabins built after the war for the Party bourgeoisie. The homes fronted on to a small lake, idyllic and beautiful and unlike anything the group had seen before; another world opened to them after the pretentiousness of the new building in Kiev.

The hut was short of the complex, reached only on foot and from a diversion from the main path, 500 yards along an overgrown trail. Too far from the summer residences for the children of the privileged to stray upon it, and the undergrowth too thick for the adults to push their way to it in search of a remote picnic spot. Because of the density of the trees and the saplings and the bushes it would have been easy to walk straight past the single-storey building and not have noticed it.

There was no key to the door, just a piece of wood that they had propped against it and dug into the ground as a buttress to prevent the weather forcing a way in. David kicked it clear when he arrived, a savage and impatient gesture. First there, as he had wanted, and the others not due for ninety minutes, perhaps more.

This was where they had kept the policeman's pistol, up on a shelf, in a biscuit tin, but closely wrapped against the damp in a plastic bag from the vegetable market. David paced across the lone room, extracted the bag from the tin, the gun from the bag, and checked the mechanism to be certain there was no bullet in the breach. Satisfied that the gun was safe he removed the magazine from the butt. Six rounds only there. There was also the other magazine placed separately in a paper bag – thoughtful of Isaac to grab that, too: seven more shots. That meant thirteen shots in all, and a pistol with an effective range of twenty metres. He should not have allowed Moses to be nominated – himself or Isaac, only they would have been capable. The girl had willed it, and he had listened to her, he did not know why. Should have ignored her, followed his instinct. He wondered why she had called for the game of chance to determine who went first, to give herself the possibility? You, Rebecca, you wanted it, sought the medal? And now catastrophe. No plan yet, only the unfamiliar feeling of helplessness, of near despair, that they had no power and that such an awesome strength was gathering its weapons with which to strike them. He thought of Moses – a cheerful, honest boy, a follower, without a mind of his own, who craved the companionship and the strength of the others, who had been asked to do one thing himself and who had not succeeded. A weak link in the chain he had set himself to forge, and when the chain snapped how long till the dogs were barking, the sirens crying in pursuit?

Isaac was next. He had travelled on the same bus as Rebecca, he in the front, she in the back, not acknowledging each other. He had hurried along the path closely flanked by the tall trees, she had dawdled. Isaac was 22 years old, studying chemistry. Quick, logical in his approach to problems – a 'good pupil' his professors had said when they offered him a place with a future in a government laboratory if he could acquire the right marks at the autumn examinations. He was pleased to be in front because that entitled him to hurry, and he was anxious to reach the hut because he believed he knew the solution to their problem. He had carved and chiselled it against his own self-appointed objections while scurrying across the white stone flags of the University's central precinct. As he approached the hut, using the codes of habitual caution and wariness, he thought of the reaction he would gain from David. Rarely that he was listened to. Not that it was David's fault, only that he seldom offered his opinions. He stepped on a dry branch and as the noise cracked in his ears he cursed the momentary carelessness. It was a good plan and carried the possibility of success. But he would not be the first to speak, he would hear what David had to say. He would evaluate that, and then if his own equation seemed better he would offer it. He was pleased with himself and hoped the others would be too. Not that he minded an existence in the shadow of David, not that he felt the requirement to assert himself, just that on this occasion and after his street meeting with David he had thought on the options, weighed them and was satisfied.

Rebecca came more slowly. Her flat soft-soled shoes were unsuitable for the pitfalls of the path, and her print dress caught in the brambles that trailed across the way. She had little regard for them; she too was thinking of Moses, and it was an effort for her to walk along the path such was the vividness of her image of the surroundings in which her friend was held. And he had been the nervous one, who would have wanted to be the last to shoot, and who would have fulfilled his wish if she had held her silence.

Her dark hair was swept back to the sides of her high-boned face, and pulled to the back by an elastic band before spilling pony-style to below her neck. Attractive lines on her body, small but firm breasts developed beyond the point of adolescence, tight waist, hips that swung as she walked, but all masked by the cut of the GUM store dress. But it had been cheap, and money mattered more than appearance; and since she had met David, and also Isaac and Moses, it was not appearances that were important. When David found her the 'Voice of Israel' on the radio she had listened to the programmes from the kibbutzim and thought to herself, 'Why should one need such sillinesses? The stupidity of frocks and dresses with raised and lowered hems and flowered prints, and waists that hug and hips that fall in flared lines: do they need those to pull a plough across new land?' A quiet and solitary person she had been before the spell of David wove close around her. He had taught her much, she believed, of the Nation State of the Jews, leaving her unaware of the vacuums of her learning. No word of those who came from Russia to the railway stations of Vienna and Amsterdam and Rome, who had won their freedom with a promise that they travelled south to Tel Aviv and instead headed west for the new frontiers of the United States. That there were Jews who left Russia and who then refused to make the final journey to Israel would have dumbfounded her. That emigration from Israel was a subject covered by rigorous censorship laws passed by the Knesset in Jerusalem would have confused her. Sheltered and suppressed, devoid of the trappings of sophistication. A product of the undrawn but actual perimeters of the Kiev ghetto. Twenty years old, she was like the others a Jew without the faith of Judaism, taking only that part of the heritage that imbued the separateness of the race, the pride of a wandering people, and the stubbornness not to falter again as in the past. She did not attend the synagogue for the Feast of Tabernacles, nor on the Kol Nidrei night. Too great a burden her people had stumbled under, she thought, for there to be a faith that she could follow.

David had taken her from the botany classroom, transported her to a battlefield where she herself could fight alongside her kith from the kibbutzim, and it had seemed brave and worthwhile, and the danger had seemed remote. It had hurt her to squash a spider on the kitchen floor, swat a fly on the plaster wall above her bed. She could not have endured the misery of the sight of a snared rabbit. Yet he had turned her, moulded her and guided her arm, caused it to rise, rigid and clamped on the pistol's handle, and influenced the squeeze of the trigger finger as he lectured her in the mechanism and technique of the one, taken weapon on the afternoon after they had possessed it. A terrible and beautiful and desperate secret he had given to her; a secret to be shared by only three others. And he had nurtured her strength, watering and feeding it over the years, till she was capable of participation. No boy, neither with love nor lust, could hold her as the other three had in the hut before they went to search out the policeman. Impossible to match and measure any sensation against the supreme shared orgasm of the cell at that moment of firing. And never a conversation, nor a moment, nor an occasion when she believed she had taken the supreme step over the abyss. Just a logical progression. Then Isaac, standing outside her classroom door, arresting her as she hurried for the next lecture, waiting for her, waiting with the unspoken news. But in his eyes the message that there was catastrophe.

The three of them were together now, sitting cross-legged or sprawled on the bare boards of the floor. David was talking.

'We must continue the fight, we must not give way to them.

Whatever they do to us we must not allow them to destroy the group. If we have to go underground then that is what it shall be. If we have to try to go abroad then we must attempt it, through Czechoslovakia or Rumania. We must not lie down . . .' Rebecca had not heard him talk in this way before, realized that he had no plan, nothing to offer. There was a strain in his voice, and he spoke louder than the level to which she was accustomed, his words coming staccato as if only through speech could he believe in himself. And Isaac was fidgeting and restless, unable to hide his frustration.

'We have not the wherewithal to fight – no equipment,' said Isaac. 'They would hunt us till we were run down. Always they would be after us. We could not strike back.'

'It is certain they have Moses?' asked Rebecca, seeking the consolation that would come if there were any hesitation in the reply, and knowing from the way David ignored her that there could be none.

'We cannot just surrender,' said David. 'Not just because they have taken Moses . . .'

'Forget Moses, obliterate Moses. He's in a cell now, screaming to them, and it was he who lost his clothing, the one that could not hold the gun . . .' Isaac was shouting. And David shouting louder.

'You cannot say that. How can you say that?'

'Because it is true. Because he has no further part to play with us. Because it is as if he had never been part of us.' Isaac steadied, swept the control back through himself. He had no wish to launch his idea in controversy; he wanted their minds receptive. 'We could fly out,' he spoke with great deliberation. 'We could take a plane. We have a gun. It has happened before . . .'

'Impossible, we could never . . .'

'Where would we go? . . .'

'. . . and it has been successful, and . . .'

'How to get abroad? You cannot just carry guns . . .'

'We have no time to plan . . .'

'. . . we could do it. Don't you see the possibility, don't you see the opportunity?'

They had all shouted together, each seeking to denounce the words of the other, their minds racing with objections, clarifications. And then silence. Isaac, his mouth closed, but smiling and knowing that by accident he had chosen his moment well. David blinking and trying to think through the turmoil in his mind. Rebecca shuffling on the boards, wanting to speak again, not knowing what to say.

When Isaac spoke again it was still slowly, demanding no interruption, asserting his right to be heard out. 'We can take a plane. Fly it out. To the West. Then on to Israel. All of us together we can go to Israel. We have not much time, and we would have much to do in preparation, but it could be done. And none of us has another thought, any other prospect.'

It seemed an age to David since he had listened to the ideas of another member of the group. He was strained, choked with the words that were hard to enunciate, and bowing his head in a gesture of deference.

'We are listening. We want to know what you have thought of. Tell us.'

There was a hesitation, then Isaac began to speak.

'We have to take a plane. Divert it from an internal flight, because it is easier for us to buy the tickets for a flight inside Russia. We have to find one that has the range to take us to the West. To the BDR, or to Greece, or to Italy – it is not important. There are many places. Once we have landed and we are beyond their reach it does not matter. From there we can go to Israel. We should not fly directly there. Two reasons. It would be hard to find a plane with the necessary fuel, and too long we would spend over our airspace, and that of our friends and comrades.' Sarcasm and confidence, Isaac blossoming at his opportunity of holding the ring. 'First to the West, the nearest frontier, the nearest landfall, reach it while they are still confused, and there we will find petrol and friendship. We already have the gun, and one gun is enough if it is in the cockpit, beside the pilot. They cannot risk anything, not with the passengers to think of. They must follow our instructions. And we must go tomorrow. It will involve other people. All our parents have their savings and we will need those. We must have that money for the tickets. They are all good people – David's, Rebecca's, mine . . . if we ask they will not query, they will know there is necessity, they need not know the reason. David, it was you that said we cannot just remain here, waiting for them to come for us. We are agreed on that. We have to go, and this is the way to go.'

'I have never been in a plane,' Rebecca said. And the two men laughed at the innocence of the remark, breaking the tension.

'We must have tickets. There is no other way,' Isaac went on. 'I have been to the airport at Kiev twice to fly when we have had holidays, student holidays on the southern coast. It would not be possible just to run to a boarding plane and climb aboard. Too many guards, and all armed, and there is no access to the place where the planes are parked. We would have to board as normal passengers. No other option. But there will be no problem, not if the destination of the plane is far from the frontiers. And if there is suspicion then a bribe will see us through.

'We let the plane get airborne, let the pilot start his journey, then we rush the cockpit. After that it is simple.' He paused, looking from David to Rebecca, stared hard at their eyes, burning the doubt from them. 'That is my plan. And what else can we achieve? Surely this is the gesture, on the grand scale, beyond the life of a mere policeman. Beyond the lives of a hundred policemen. People in many countries will know that the Jews of Russia are not dead and lifeless people, that we have something left to offer.'

'We would need more guns,' said David, pensive now and far away. The primary decision had been taken and he was seeking the answers to the questions of detail.

'We have one gun . . .' resentment from Isaac.

'We do not attack you, Isaac.' David was quick to calm him. 'I think I know where, and without risk. But we must have more. I think I know where it is possible.'

31

'In the West they have checks and searches – we have heard that on the radio. Because of the Palestinians they take precautions that people do not carry guns on to the planes. And it is the same here.' Her first intervention, and Rebecca hacking at the artery of the plan, where Isaac had been vague, because he did not possess the answer.

'They have checks,' Isaac conceded.

'How do we get past them?'

Isaac paused, aggression pushing out his jaw, hardening it. 'I don't know. I have not had time to think of the small points.'

David smiled, as if he were the old one among them, and solutions were more simple to him than the others. Not that there was any significant age difference, just that he was accustomed to taking control and the uncertainties of the last few minutes were banished. 'There was a report on the BBC many months ago. One of the planes, a British one, was taken by the Arab terrorists. There had been great security at the airport, all the passengers were thoroughly searched, and yet they had their guns when it came to the moment of taking the plane. The way they did it was simple. They had a friend, a friend who worked at the airport, and was therefore outside suspicion. It was he who placed the guns on board and hid them, all long before the passengers boarded. What had the Arabs to do? Only to go to a prearranged seat and find the bags. It was all on the BBC. And there is a man who is known to us, isn't there? Yevsei Allon, isn't that the name of the boy, Rebecca? In your class in ninth and tenth year. He is at the airport at Kiev . . .'

'But he is in the freight and the cargo. He would not have access to the cabins of planes.' An interruption, as if she were willing the project not to work. For it was out of the fantasy stage now and becoming something sharper, keener, more dangerous.

'He will have to find a way, Rebecca, and it is you that must persuade him. You are the one that knew him best. You are the one that he will listen to.'

'We rely on you.' Isaac was close beside her, hand on her

shoulder where it had not rested before. 'And we must rely on your friend. Otherwise we will not board the plane, and if we do not then we shall be taken. That is certain.'

David rose from the floor, dusting the dirt from the seat of his trousers, pushing away the coil of hair that had slipped on his forehead. 'Rebecca, you will see Yevsei. Do not hurry yourself, or rush him, but put him in debt to you. Make him a favour that he must repay, and then arrange a rendezvous again tomorrow morning. By then I will have the guns. Isaac, you must go to the Aeroflot booking centre, the big one on Kreshchatik where they will be busiest. A flight tomorrow afternoon that goes far into the interior. A four-hour flight we will want, not less, so we have sufficient fuel. It is for you to decide where we go, and the way you will purchase the tickets. But it must be in the afternoon – if that is not too late.'

'Where do we sleep tonight?' Rebecca asked.

'You, I don't know,' and David laughed, a twist in his lips. 'Isaac and I, we sleep here, and this is where you should come when you have finished with Yevsei. If they have broken Moses then they will come in the morning for us . . . to our homes. Rebecca, you understand what confronts us? You know what is the future if they take us? Basement cells and interrogations, and then they will shoot us or hang us, as the will takes them. There is no mercy, no clemency to those who seek to kill the pigs, not if one is on his back in the hospital and perhaps about to die. Yevsei is important to us, do not forget that. If you want to grow old, to bear children, if you want to know the breadth of Israel – then Yevsei must help you.'

They were all on their feet and moving towards the door. He put out his arms and took her, lightly holding her shoulders and urged her towards him, so that her forehead was against his mouth, and he kissed her gently, just below the hairline and for the first time. 'Tomorrow night we will sleep in the West. Do not forget that. Tomorrow we go.'

The two men watched her as she broke away and went down the path towards the track that would take her to the main road.

She did not look back and her shoulders were hunched except when they straightened and rose in small convulsions, the action of one who is crying. Then she was gone, lost in the trees. Neither boy looked at the other, avoiding a meeting of their eyes and feelings. Had chosen the easier road, both of them. Had given themselves tasks that were not comparable to hers, and felt a clutch of guilt, shared and unspoken. The clinging silence of the forest spread across them when her footsteps had died and faded. Brave little girl, Isaac thought, if she will do this for us, brave little girl, not that he'll have an easy time of it, old Yevsei, not that the winning and wooing would be simple, or painless.

'Will it work, Isaac?' asked David, staring beyond him into the undergrowth.

'There is no alternative. This way offers us a chance. Not a good chance, but something. Without it we are condemned.'

3

It was two years since they had given Charlie Webster a room of his own.

He hadn't really known whether to be flattered or grateful or what. It gave him a certain importance to be able to turn a key in the door when he went off for lunch, leaving an empty desk behind him as he headed for the lift and the fifteen-floor descent in the tower block that overlooked the Thames. Not that many of the deskmen for the 'Firm' enjoyed the privilege of only themselves for company. Trouble was that he could never quite satisfy himself as to whether the room was in recognition of the work he now did or simply a reward for services rendered.

'Foreign Office', Charlie called himself to those who asked but who did not know him. 'Well, not exactly Foreign Office,' his wife would say, 'but something like it, to do with Foreign Affairs anyway.' Fact was he never went near Whitehall. Too public. You couldn't be certain there wouldn't be some of those bloody agency photographers hanging about waiting for an ambassador or something, and he didn't want his photograph plastered all over the front pages just because he happened to be following a Venezuelan or a Zambian diplomat into the place. But since they came under the Foreign Office wing, and that was where the Under-Secretary who now headed the Department had worked before his transfer, it was most convenient for members of the Secret Intelligence Service to bracket themselves with the herd of diplomats and civil servants who ran the public side of Britain's dealings with overseas governments.

Charlie worked at the Soviet Desk. Nine of them in all, answerable to Cecil Parker Smith, OBE MC, and most of them concerned with things military. That put four in the same room where they fiddled in each other's hair and didn't get much done, and thought they were the cream for the cat. Two more on politics, the heavy fellows who spent their time reading the speeches of the Kremlin men, poor buggers. One for economics: he had a room to himself, and needed it, kept him going flat out, flogging his way through text books and brochures and progress reports. Then there was the one they called the Real Estate Man; he was the speculator, and his job was to predict long-range changes in Soviet attitudes and postures; worked to the letter of his brief and kept his thinking right in the far term, to the extent of sitting most of the day with his pipe in his mouth watching the pleasure boats negotiating Lambeth Bridge.

And there was Charlie, the ninth.

Last Christmas party, all a bit drunk, they'd christened him 'Double Diamond' – seen it as a hell of a laugh – and he'd looked blank, and they'd explained. 'DD' – those were the initials for his work. He'd still looked vacant and wondered why grown men always spent the last two days before the holidays dropping everything to gum paper streamers together to drape across the ceiling, and they'd shouted, 'sub-Desk Dissidents'. They'd all thought it hilarious, falling about over themselves. But that was his charge – sub-Desk Dissidents.

There was something to find out: couldn't doubt that. There were groups, cells, sections – call them what you want – that were alive and well and kicking faintly inside the womb of the big red monolith. Not as many as there had been a decade before, but certainly some still there. Problem was that Charlie's job was to put them in perspective, extract any relevance from them. Much of his material came from émigré groups either in London or scattered across the cities of Western Europe, hopelessly unreliable people who would have you believe the whole bloody place was on the point of mass insurrection if you could only drop a Hercules load of Stirlings and FNs and grenades into People's Square, Novosibirsk. You had to weed and prune. Use the cosmetics to brighten the façade, and then search the cross-references and the files. Slowly, patiently – that's the way you touched on the subtle signs that pointed the way to the trends so beloved by his masters. Ukraine was usually fertile. There were bits and pieces from the Baltic; quite a little set-to they'd had in the Department over the Russian warship that tried a flit to Sweden and that took a hammering from its own air force and turned back shot up; sub-Desk Military said it was theirs, Charlie claimed it too. Parker Smith sat for half a day on it while nobody spoke in the outer offices, then did his Solomon and gave it to sub-Desk Military. Followed by appeasing Charlie, told him he was doing too much valuable work for him to mess about working on something that was common knowledge to every European NATO set-up. Quite a ripple they'd had over that one. Bit of activity last year down in Georgia; Charlie had liked that because it came right out of the blue. Hadn't expected anything on that sort of scale, not a dozen bombs, quite excited him. He'd wondered what sort of devices they used, where they'd learned the trade. He realized it was the technique, the string and the Sellotape, the timers and detonators, that absorbed him. Should have been ashamed really – and him supposed to be an analyst.

It was interesting work in its way, but Charlie had to pinch himself from time to time to make sure that it was actually important. He'd done enough in his life that was classified as vital, in the 'national interest'. Cyprus had been special, because attitudes were different then, and he was younger, and public opinion accepted that young men would go abroad and die in the sunshine for the preservation of something or other. Aden, too, though nastier there, and the last of its type, and people beginning to bore at the concept of 'our lads overseas', but a serious place where survival took skill if you did Charlie's work. And Ireland wasn't pretty, not in Dublin, and you had to know what the Provies were at, and you spent your nights low down in cars outside the pubs watching for who went in and who came out, and who was talking to whom, and had he done it before. That was important all right if you wanted a man to be able to take his missus for a Friday night jar in the local in Birmingham, or Manchester, or Glasgow or Guildford. Had the '74 campaign and the '75 campaign, and the bombs taking off the arms and legs, and the glass scything the faces, to show for justification of spending his evenings watching the Paddys at their booze. But hard to convince himself that what he did now was of value. Nice to know, of course, that Big Brother was having difficulties as he sat all serene behind his watchtowers, his minefields and barbed-wire fences. Nice to know that the mosquitoes were out and nibbling, that he was scratching a bit, that he'd be turning over in his bed and cursing.

And there was the material that had come in that day. Hadn't gone through the files yet to find out what the pattern was, whether it was new, on-going. But he'd do some typing after lunch, string it all together for Parker Smith's In Tray. Sort of material the Minister liked to have when he was having a hard time at those conferences; it made the man feel that at least he had something up his sleeve. Gave him confidence, Charlie supposed, when he was in for a good kick in the crutch from those humourless bastards. Wouldn't want anything too long, Ministers never did; about half a dozen lines. But a policeman shot and nothing in the Kiev press, that was out of the ordinary. Straight criminals, then there would be no shortage of newsprint. But nothing on this one, not a public whisper – that's why it was different. And someone else thought it interesting, otherwise SIS (External Services) wouldn't have noted it, and the paper wouldn't have been duplicated and categorized so that it might find its way to Charlie's desk. Showed there was a bit of life in the old system after all, if they could pick up pin-pricks like that. So perhaps there was something going on, something for him to think about.

Quite interesting really, if you had the time to look into it. And Charlie Webster had the time.

The source of semi-automatic weapons had been known to David for some months, but he did not reveal it to the others in the group. It was a particular knowledge that he treasured, that he wished to keep to himself. The decision not to spread the information had come a long time before, when he had resolved that if ever there was the possibility he would be cornered then he would sell his life, and well. Being taken alive and put through the courts and the due process of law was an obsession for him, something he told himself he would never accept, whatever the feelings of the others, whatever they would do if the cordon closed tight around them. He would never come out with his hands high, never.

He had come across the old man by accident – had wandered into him in the forest and then been aware of the frightened, primitive eyes that had peered through the trees at him. Faint and sparse hair that was tousled. Clothes that were torn and patched and torn again and were too heavy for the summer weather but were needed for the winter cold of the forest. Hands that were shaking and claw-like and that rose to protect his head lest the intruder should strike him. The bearing of a woodland recluse who forsook company, believed that it brought only danger. David had talked to him and smiled and used soft words and broken down the old man's reluctance to talk. On his visits to their own hut, some three miles away, David would come earlier than the rest, so that he could bring food and, at first, fresh clothes to the old man; the food had been eaten, the trousers and jackets and woollens ignored. David had learned of the man's history, and what kept him in isolation and hiding. And the more he learned the greater the worth of the old man became to the plans he was fashioning for the four-strong cell.

It was a long journey Timofey had travelled. He was from the farmlands south of Moscow that lay behind the German winter line of 1942 running from Zhizdra, through Orel, and on towards Kursk. His town was Sevsk, and in that spring a man called Kaminski had come with a letter in his wallet that bore the signature of Generaloberst Schmidt, commanding the Second Panzer Army. Kaminski became the local governor of all the towns round Sevsk. His authority took in the communities of Navlya, Dmitrovsk, Dmitriev and Lokot; he had the power to appoint civilian officials, and most important of all he was answerable only to Generaloberst Schmidt. Timofey's collective was one of the first that Kaminski 'liberated'. The land was divided, the animals apportioned along with the farm equipment and stock, and in return the workers enlisted in the local militia to fight the communist guerrillas with an expertise that was beyond the alien German troops. It had been Generaloberst Schmidt's brilliance that he had possessed the foresight to realize the potential of men such as Kaminski, and using the carrot of individual land ownership he had derived the benefit of this unexpected source of manpower. Prior to Kaminski's time farmers like Timofey had watched with apathy as the guerrillas came at night to replenish their food stocks from the yards of the collectives; now they were directly affected: they were losing what had been made their own. The life of the guerrilla became harder, his reception at the darkened farmhouse more hostile. The next step was logical enough. The new militia were formed into units for patrolling their property and ultimately for hunting down the guerrillas. As a tactic it was a great success for the Germans; their allies were self-sufficient in abandoned Soviet weapons, anti-tank guns, machine guns and mortars; they became military formations and safe-guarded the access routes. Timofey had a position of rank, commanded a platoon-sized group, was a noticed man. And then the line to the north sagged, and there were bulges and salients before the Germans were gone, pushed back towards the distant Polish frontier. The Red Army reoccupied the towns where Kaminski's word had ruled. There were many now that could name those that had collaborated. Timofey's picture was displayed in the square at Sevsk. There was a reward for his capture.

Three sub-machine guns and a rifle he had taken with him as he had foot-slogged south, moving at night, keeping away from the roads and the towns and the villages all through that long summer of 1943. He had entertained a vague hope that he might assume a new identity in Kiev, that the confusion of war would allow him to reappear without need of explanations. There had been many times when he had thought that the time was ripe for him to throw off his solitary exile in the forests and make the break from the past, but it would have been a great step and he never quite could bring himself to it. Five, six, perhaps seven times he had stood on the edge of the line of trees at the great road that ran towards Kiev and braced himself to step out of his sanctuary . . . but he had never been able to accomplish it. And as the years went by so the task of self-rehabilitation became even harder, till he had made for himself a permanent prison in the forests.

Thirty-five years he had been there now. Through the discomfiture of sores and bruises and spreading scabs, the pain of his ailing teeth, the frustration of his fading sight. He was paid a few kopecks by the dacha owners, who asked nothing more than that he should watch over their properties in the winter, and a few more coins for the wood that he brought them for their fires in the spring and in the autumn. Not that he had any use for the money. And they left him to himself, his memories and his hatreds, seeing him only as a harmless, pathetic, sometimes laughable figure, with a marginal usefulness that protected him from denunciation.

David whistled a warning of his approach when he was still 100 yards from the old man's hut. Then he stood stock still and listened after the harsh notes that Timofey had taught him, and heard the answering call; it had started as a sort of game, but that was before the talk in the group had been of action. After that there had been a difference. New justifications and a seriousness for the precautions. David had not told him of the programme, just prodded his memory, vague and fading, leading the old man to the days in the woods round Sevsk when he had stalked the partisans. Technique, procedure, manoeuvre, tactics – all those Timofey could teach him. Be careful. Be on guard at all times. It is when you relax that they take you. The knife in the back, at the throat, the single shot. Always the same epitaph: that he had relaxed, that he was not careful. A silly thing to bury a man for, that he was casual, Timofey had said.

The hut was not as large as the one the group had found, but big enough for a woodsman to spend a night when his search for dried and fallen branches that were needed for his fires caused him to stray far from his home. Table inside, and chairs, and a mattress on the floor, all had been thrown out from the dachas and disappeared overnight from the rubbish heap. Rabbit snares on the wall, neatly in line, the coils of steel wire suspended from nails, a source of food.

When they were inside David said, 'Timofey, I do not have much time, and I have come to ask something of you. It is of the greatest importance you give me what I ask for. You have suffered greatly at their hands. If you give me what I need you will have the chance to hit them in a way that has not been possible for you. I want guns, Timofey. Not a rifle – I have no need of that – but the machine guns. Two of them, certainly, I must have.'

In the half light of the room David saw the eyes opposite him glint, closing with interest as the old man's attention was captured by the request. Desperate to know what I want them for, the old fox, thought David.

'Timofey, it is not a criminal act, not robbing a bank, not for money. It is against them, the system – it will hurt them whether we succeed or fail. It will punish them for what they have done to you, and to us.'

'What have they done to you?' His voice was hoarse with the strangeness of speaking.

'They have hunted us in the same way as you, only the weapons have changed. They are our enemies as they are yours.'

'You have a house, clothes, work, money – how are they your enemies as they are mine?'

'We do not have the same opportunities, we are second-class citizens. We are not permitted to be part of their world. They reject us because we are Jews.'

'We saw the Jews go in the war. We were on the side of those who exterminated your parents and your relatives. Perhaps we even approved . . . it is difficult . . . it was a long time ago . . . we did nothing. How many millions of your people died then? And now you want guns, and you want to kill people to get a better place in the sun. Is that reason enough? We killed so many of each other at that time; what you now talk of seems a little matter. Perhaps because I am old, but what you seek for yourself seems nothing . . .'

'I have not the time, old man.'

Timofey rose from his stool. 'When you have guns then you will go to war. That is the time when you must learn the wisdom of patience and calm, or you will end as nothing. With the strength of the gun beside you your haste must be tempered, even your haste to be clear of an old man who asks nothing of you, nothing but a few words that can be lies or truth, immaterial.' He moved stiffly because the damp had long been in his knees and movement was hard for him, towards the hanging sacking that marked off the area where he slept. When he emerged again it was with an ageing knapsack coloured the steel grey of the wartime German forces. He placed it with deliberation on the table and unbuckled the straps that held down the top flap. There was pale green mildew on them and the buckles were dark with rust. He saw the way the young man looked at him. 'Have no worry. Inside it is dry. Weapons do not age, not if they have been cared for, if they are cleaned. These have been.' Then the bundle of water-proofed oilskin, a mustard brown, camouflage ground sheet, and that was laid on the table, and there was string to be undone, and finally the guns were revealed. So small, David thought. The tubular steel shoulder rests folded down the stock, magazines separate and detached, just barrel-length basically, insignificant little things such as children play with when they mimic the television pictures of the Red Army at its manoeuvres. But clean, and shining, and as worked on on any of his mother's mantelpiece ornaments.

'The ammunition too I have cared for. It would not be wise to fire a test, but I tell you, my boy, that they will function. They are adequate to kill any who are keeping you as a second-class citizen.' He laughed, his hoarseness giving way to a raven's croak, his face cracking with the humour of his remark, spilling new lines across the log-brown face.

'I need two, Timofey.'

'So there are more than one of you. You have a follower, perhaps an army, and you will be the general?'

'There are no generals. We are together.'

'We all say that when we are young. But do not listen to yourself. When there is danger there must be a leader. You cannot fight by committee, even they found that. And are you the leader, David? Can you take your friends forward? When you have the guns it is changed, you know. You must discover that before you begin the course, whatever it may be, that you have chosen. Later is too late, there is no time.'

David did not reply, and Timofey lapsed to taking the guns in his hands.

For half an hour he showed David the workings of the weapons until the lesson was learned. He showed him the safety mechanism, showed him how to arm them, how to load the magazine, to attach it, explained the drift of automatic fire high and to the right if more than five shots were fired in a burst, showed him what to do if he suffered a jam.

At the door, the load he had come for in a plastic bag, David said, 'What is the call that you taught me, told me to use when I approached?'

'The kingfisher's.'

'Why did you choose that one?'

Timofey pointed past his hut into the tangle of trees. 'You cannot see it from here, but there is a stream, where no-one comes, where I sit. There is the nest of a kingfisher there, and I hear her call, or that of her mate when he has need of her. It is rare for people to see that bird. Most of these swine that live here through the summer would never see one, let alone hear her. So I say that if I hear that call, and I hear it from the path that you use, then it will be you. Another bird, and I could be mistaken, or I might hear it too often. But the kingfisher is the rarity, a princess amongst them.'

'I have never seen one.'

'Because you are from the city. She is fast and swift, and she holds the initiative in her world. None can catch her, few even

44

see her, she is devastating in her attack. She is a lesson to the guerrilla. She is what you must strive after.'

'It is a good name, old man.'

They were walking now, close together because of the narrowness of the track, and the old man was shorter than David, bowed and shrivelled.

'Will you come again?' Timofey asked, his eyes looking up.

'I will not come again. However it goes there will be no return.'

There were no farewells, no hands shaken, no words of comfort or encouragement, just the blunt moment of parting as the old man turned back to his hut. David hurried down the track, his right hand holding the weighted package, his left shielding his face from the low, sharp hazel branches.

Remember what David had said, again and again through Isaac's mind went the phrase as he stood in the centre of the huge marble-veneered floor of the Aeroflot main offices. A bustle of people coming and going around him, and queues at the ticket counters. Just the way they had wanted it. And when it comes to the booking choose a harassed girl, one under pressure with a short temper and a willingness to be done with the business. You didn't want a girl with time to waste and questions to ask. Incredible, really, in a society like ours how people had so much time to ask questions; fear, he thought, fear is what it comes to, fear of being held responsible if there was error. A whole society so consumed with curiosity about the legalities of their fellow citizens' lives.

He had already taken the State airline's timetable and leafed through it till he came to the map that boasted the extent of the international as well as domestic routes. Take the North Sea as the outer limit, going due west. Have to be somewhere inside that orbit that they must be put down, and still be left with a failsafe quantity of fuel in the tanks. Must look at it analytically, that was the way he had been trained at school, and the way they were teaching him at the University. Take a problem and search out the solution. So where to? Where to buy a ticket for?

Leningrad – no good. Equivalent distance to the centre of DDR, and he wasn't to know how much spare fuel they would carry. Would get them to Turkey, but that wasn't safe, not with a fascist military regime, same sort of people as the party here, hard to tell the difference; and they'd run the risk of being shipped back. Needed the 'liberal democracies', as David called them, where they followed the fortunes of Israel with concern, did not genuflect to the Arabs and their oil. North Europe the answer for the refuelling stop. There was a sense of frustration to his thinking that these decisions were being made now, plans that should have moulded days earlier, and would now be rushed and pressurized.

Yalta – too short, same for all the Black Sea resorts. Plenty of flights, but not enough aviation fuel.

Tbilisi – nearer, but whoever went to Georgia? And they must not have to explain the reason for their journey. Miserable, tight bastards down there and everyone in Kiev knew that. Have to explain if he wanted seats to Tbilisi.

He poised the map between his open hands again, running a finger further north. Tomsk and Novosibirsk.

Novosibirsk – opportunities there. God knows why anyone goes there, but that was an intellectual base, Science City. Perhaps a chemistry student could be going and Rebecca with her botany, and David with his working chemistry. The indicator board carried the daily arrivals and departures, covering a whole wall, the flights of the week. Nothing to those two cities for Wednesday. No to Tomsk, no to Novosibirsk, blank, nothing. Disappointment and back to the map.

Tashkent – a flight to Tashkent tomorrow. Flight on Wednesday. 1600 hours, the sort of time they wanted, could have finished their plans by then . . . but if only they had three hours to play with, if Moses gave them that long, and he'd sworn and cursed at Moses when he should have prayed for him, prayed for strength for him. More than two thousand miles to Tashkent, way beyond the distance they needed. Fuel for more than five hours, take them into Europe, into the West. But down into

Tashkent, where the flight was routed, what papers would you need for that? Didn't know. It had been his plan, his idea, the whole thing and the others had accepted it, and he didn't know the answers, and had no way of finding them, only at the counter, only at the ticket counter. Cannot apply logic to regulations, either know the answer or you are ignorant.

He joined the queue to one of the central counters, heavy traffic, more than at the extremes of right and left. Funny how people sought the centre where the delays would be greater. Conformity. Five, ten minutes slipping by, and time for him to sum up the girl in the dowdy blue uniform behind the counter. Customers in front of him being satisfied, queue lengthening behind him. Soon there was only one more man in front – heavy suit of a party worker. Perhaps he wasn't, but Isaac reckoned anybody who wore a heavy suit when it was hot was a party worker, status in showing they had the clothes. Sweat was running down the man's neck on to his collar: so much for the gesture of superiority.

An argument. The man wanted Moscow. She said it was full for two days. He showed her his papers, his documentation and his cards, but she replied by saying it didn't make a damn of difference, that everything was full, although he could go to the airport and try his luck there. Isaac realized that the man couldn't be that important, meant he didn't qualify by his rank for the tickets kept back for senior party officials on all flights. Everyone knew about that.

The girl's cheeks were flushed, and she was looking round her for support when she caught Isaac's eye, and his wink, the lowered lid, was acknowledged. Isaac saw her stifle a giggle and return her gaze to the man whose voice was now raised.

There would be trouble for her, a complaint to the responsible person. His department would lodge a protest at the highest level. What was her name? Blatant obstruction of an official. And he left his place at the counter.

Isaac said, 'I'd like to book three for tomorrow, to Tashkent, student fare, coming back fourteen days from tomorrow. I'd like to go on tomorrow afternoon's flight, return Wednesday fort-night. If it's possible?' and he smiled, boyish, intimate . . . 'silly old fool. You handled him well – you'll not hear from him again.' His right hand had moved from his hip pocket, engulfing the fifty roubles of notes, and the fist opened among the papers in front of her, tickets, timetables, price charts, and without taking her eyes from him she covered the notes, faded and worn, with her booking pad. She didn't reply, just picked up her desk tele-phone – computer not working again – and was talking into it; Isaac waiting for the verdict.

Still holding the phone she asked for the names, and when they had been given to her she repeated them into the receiver, spelling them out letter by letter. It seemed to take a lifetime. She said 'priority', and grinned at him; not bad looking, Isaac thought, but someone should do something about her teeth. He smiled back.

'Confirmed,' she said, and started to make out the tickets themselves. Not much to fill in, not like an international ticket. When she had finished she set to work on her calculator. 'With the student reduction, and the fourteen-day stop reduction, and the ballet festival concession in Tashkent – you're lucky on that one . . . five hundred and twenty-two roubles . . . for the three. You pay over there, on the right at the cash counter, if you haven't a warrant, that is.'

'Our parents have the money,' said Isaac. 'Keep the tickets there beside you and I'll be back with the money . . .'

'I'm not supposed to do that, to make out tickets that aren't immediately paid for.'

'I'll be back. I know when you close. Keep them on one side. I'll be back.'

So the flight was booked, and he found it difficult to walk when he was out on the street again. How easy! It was going to work. The whole thing was going to work. He wanted to shout, to yell the message. David and Rebecca and Isaac, they'd show the bastards. Show them all.

★ ★ ★

48

Isaac's mother was waiting, as he had told her to, outside the Savings Bank nearest to their home. She was a small, sparrow-sized woman, and the lines on her face were devoid of relief. The boy had not explained, given her no reason for her presence there, just told her to bring the payment book. A hard and suffering time she had had, with money not easy to come by; it had been grafted for, worked for and collected with a miser's hand. And he had said he would need most of the deposit that had increased at such pitiful speed over the previous thirty years. He had told her that David and Rebecca's mothers would repay her in part, and she had thought that she barely knew these other persons who were families of her son's friends. But something in the boy's looks had stopped her from remonstrating, and so she now stood and waited for him.

Two per cent per annum they paid – not a way to get rich, not a way that people could lift themselves from the bog of their lives. But what alternative was there? What else could one do with one's money? When he came Isaac took her arm, kissed her on the cheek and together they took their place in the queue. A bright, airy interior. Lace curtains and flowers on the table where the customers could sit and prepare their paperwork Even Lenin, in his wall portrait, seemed content, as he looked the length of the bank across to the photograph of the Ukrainian General Secretary of the Party. At the counter, like a ventrilo-quist's doll, his mother spoke while Isaac a pace behind her primed the old lady's ear as to how much she should withdraw. It was time-consuming but without difficulty, and they maintained a punctilious politeness to the girl, for she could easily hinder them if they aggravated her. And they were Jews, so it was easy to offend.

When the money had passed to his mother and on to Isaac, he said, 'I cannot tell you why, but you will know by tomorrow night, and you must have courage, the courage of our people. Whatever happens you must be brave. Do not bow to them. I will not be home tonight. Do not ask why; be brave.'

There was no emotion displayed by the old lady as she

stepped out on to the street again. She walked away with a brisk and sturdy step.

And he had the money in his pocket. A tight wad of rolled, crisp banknotes, and he was hurrying for the bus that would take him back to the centre of Kiev and the Aeroflot offices. So he had done his part; they could board the plane that would lift off in 23 hours. But had David the guns? Would Rebecca secure access for them? And when would Moses break, when would Moses talk?

Yevsei Allon could barely believe his luck.

First the call by telephone to the freight office, and his being told by the Under Manager that there was a personal message for him, and not to take long because the line carried official business. The voice of the girl that he remembered from school, and who had been too haughty then to acknowledge him, the suggestion that they should meet and talk about the old days in the classroom, the little laugh that mingled with the static of the poor connection, and him thinking of his night classes, and not daring to mention them. They would meet at the subway entrance that was near the small church of Saint Sophia.

Before he had left the airport at the end of the day-shift Yevsei had spent ten full minutes in the washroom, scrubbing his hands and lathering the hard public utilities soap on his face. He wetted and then combed the short hair on his head till the parting was straight and exact, and he had looked at himself in the mirror, and the man who waited behind him to use the basin had quipped, 'You'll need more than soap and a comb to please her.' He'd blushed, crimson over his whitened face, and mumbled an answer before running for the bus.

They had had coffee after they met, sitting at a table away from the bar where the voices of other customers were reduced to a background drone. The girl listened to him as he grew in confidence, and she had asked him about his job, what he did at the airport, and they had talked of their teachers in the low voices of conspiracy and of their friends, and demolished them all. Her white teeth had flashed when he made his jokes, and she had thrown back her head, so that the long black hair trailed away from the slightness of her neck. He could see the shape of her breasts and the outline of her waist till there was a tightness and a sweat inside the ill-fitting trousers that he cursed himself for having chosen to wear that morning. Too much really to believe in. On his way to the toilet he'd stumbled, banging his foot against the leg of the table, rattling the cups. Then he'd scrabbled in his pocket for the kopecks that he needed for the machine, and for the sachet that he would want when the light faded.

She took him in the early evening to the sandbanks of the Dnieper, and they swam in the great river that flows north to south through the city. She was prepared, and wearing a one-piece bathing suit that had been concealed under her dress, he in the blue underpants that bulged and heaved in spite of the cold drift of water round his lower belly. When he touched her in the water, trying to pretend it was an accident, she had not moved away as the other girls did, and when she laughed it was with him, not at him. There were others there, naturally, because it was a warm evening and the authorities prided themselves on the cleanliness of the river, the way they had been able to stave off pollution from the water artery of an industrialized city of more than two million inhabitants. But she seemed oblivious to them, allowing no intruders in the private oasis she was creating for the man who worked at Kiev airport and who had access to the tarmac and the planes.

The parks are numerous in the city, putting those of London and Paris and Frankfurt and Rome to shame. Some are ornamental, with laid out flower beds where the elderly go, others little more than enclosed spaces of bushes and trees where the grass has been permitted to grow, and there are paths that can lead far from the noise of voices. It was to such a place that they walked after the river. His trousers showed a dark and damp stain at the seat from his sodden pants and she, still encased in her costume, hid the shivers she felt. But her trembling was not from any sharp wind, but of what must happen that the guns would go on board

51

the plane; and he mistook the shaking of her hand for an excitement for which he believed he was responsible.

The place they found was some way from the life of the city, hidden and enclosed by undergrowth, and she said to him, 'Don't look, but I can't wear this costume. I'll catch my death if I keep these damp things against my skin.' She had twisted away from where he sat and turned her back on him, and reached behind her to pull down the zip fastener of the dress till it was clear of her shoulders. More contortions and the garment was hanging, straps free, at her waist. Hands now under the skirt of her dress, and the wriggling before it was free and she reached up again to pull the dress back into position. But the zip remained loose and he could see, suntanned by the weather, the knotted outline of her backbone.

'Why don't you take yours off?' she said, matter of fact, as though it were everyday, nothing special.

Though he could feel the clamminess of his pants against his skin he said, 'I'm all right. I think they've just about dried.' There was a huskiness in his voice. The sort of thing the men at work talked about in the canteen during lunch break, and it was happening to him, to Yevsei Allon.

She laid her costume out on the grass neatly and with care as if to prevent it becoming creased, then fell back on to the ground, and with her arms stretched above her head. 'I love it here. So peaceful, so beautiful, so quiet. It makes you forget everything else.' It was a lie; her thoughts were far from the leaves, and the cool grass. What would they do to the boy, if he did as she was to ask? What would be his punishment? Perhaps they'd think that he was one of the group, and if they did that would mean the firing squad, or the execution shed. He'd have to work hard to prove that he wasn't. If he were lucky it would be the cattle trucks to Moldavia and the camp at Potma. The Jews had a hard time there, especially from the fascists – there were still fascists there, from the war days, but they were the 'trusties' and now ran the camps and took their revenge on the newest source of prisoners, on the Jews. Perhaps he would not be linked to them,

52

but that was unlikely. They were thorough people, these pigs, and how could poor Yevsei be warned to cover his tracks? . . . poor Yevsei. God, he wants to kiss me, and there's spittle at the side of his mouth, and how many hours since he shaved? . . . Lucky if he just went to the Labour Camp. He'd be a casualty of the break-out, but there had been casualties before. Six million casualties in the war, and how many since then? And what war was ever won without the ignorant and the innocent standing up in the cross-fire and dying with disbelief on their faces? Isaac had the tickets, only now for David to get the guns. They'll give me one. One of my own to hold.

'I don't think you should do that,' she whispered and smiled bravely. His hand was at her kneecap, and his fingers, cold and bony, were skating patterns on her lower thigh.

'I don't know,' he said. He was panting and his mouth was very close to hers.

'I don't really know either,' she said, and looked into his eyes. Was there a squint or not? She couldn't be sure. God knows he was heavy.

Never done it before, poor boy, she thought. Hadn't an idea. But neither had she – couldn't claim the virtue of experience. Could have with David; but . . . One hand climbing her thigh, the other pushing between her breasts, seeking a nipple to squeeze and hold to, and finding it and not knowing his strength till she cried out, and he believed she encouraged him. The hand higher, searching and brushing gently at her and trying to prise her legs apart, and the one that had been at her breasts gone and the motion of rolling activity as he struggled to release something from the buttoned-down pocket on his buttocks.

'Oh, my God,' she let out. 'The time, it's so late. And I haven't said I'd be out late tonight. Yevsei, I have to go . . . I really must.' But was it too fast, too hurried? Had she merely wound the elastic and in releasing it exploded in him an anger, a teased fury? Out of her orbit, out of her experience. She'd had no need of the casual evenings with stranger boys with a few kopecks in their pockets now that her life was with the group. The anxiety showed in her eyes, the fear that she had damaged the work of the evening. She flitted a hand to his wrist, withdrawing it but consoling. How far along the path must she walk? How deep was the submission required to guarantee the passage of the guns? Hideous, the thought that she had failed them, David and Isaac, that she could not prise apart her thighs for the love of her friends, and Yevsei hovering over her, weight on his knees.

In his confusion she could sit up, disengage, disentangle. 'Another ten minutes, just ten minutes.' Pleading, yet knowing he had lost as she smoothed her dress down her thighs.

'I want to, I desperately want to, Yevsei. But I cannot tonight. You've made the time flee. Tomorrow I could come back. I could come tomorrow evening. If you want me to.'

Yevsei Allon nodded, bewildered by all that had happened to him. But that was a promise, and he had done nothing wrong, had not upset her. Only the tightness and agonizing frustration to tell him how close he had been to the most triumphant success of his twenty-one-year life, and burning in his hip pocket the sachet he had brought from the coin machine in the café.

When they were walking back along the path to the road and the bus stop where they would part she said quickly, 'Yevsei, you're in freight, that is correct?'

'Yes.' He wasn't proud of it. He'd told her earlier what he did – she'd telephoned him there. Why did she need to ask?

'And you go to the planes to load them?'

'That is done by the porters. Rebecca, what time tomorrow, what time will I see you?'

'But you could go to the plane yourself – if it was necessary?'

'Of course. The same time tomorrow, and I will bring my swimming trunks.'

'The same time, Yevsei. But I have something to ask of you. There is a friend of mine who is going tomorrow to Tashkent. He is of our faith, of our people, and he must take a package with him. There are some books that he cannot put in his bags in case they are seen. I want you to put them on the plane for him, Yevsei.' She had linked her arm through his, and walked close to him, her hip bouncing against his. 'I want you to tell me where they are placed so that he can collect them during the flight. When he gets off at Tashkent there are no searches and he can carry them off.'

Still the suppressed, flattened pain fighting the coldness of his pants, but tomorrow there would be only liberation. It was a promise. She had promised. He asked, 'Is it dangerous?' and was immediately ashamed at his reaction as she smiled and shook her head.

'We would not ask anything dangerous of a school friend, much less of one of our faith, one who worships with us.' He could not remember that he had seen her at the synagogue that he visited with his family each week. He felt his arm, encircling her waist, being pushed higher, so that his hand could cup her breast. 'Which flight?'

'The flight to Tashkent. The one that leaves at four o'clock in the afternoon.'

'Bring the package to me at midday when I take my lunch-break, at the outer door of the freight offices. Then you will need to telephone me at three, the same number that you used today. I will be able to tell you by then in what seat your friend should sit to recover his books. I can do it for you.'

She kissed him on the cheek, and did not fight when he moved her mouth to his and explored behind her gums and teeth with his tongue. He saw that she was still smiling, a radiant, consuming smile.

Parker Smith was never at his desk before ten in the morning, claiming with a shrug that he could never survive the stampede of the rush hour, but he stayed late to clear his In Tray, load the Out. He let it be known amongst the men who worked for him that he was most receptive to discussion and exchange of viewpoints after the general office hours had been terminated, when the telephones had stopped ringing, when no secretaries were left on the premises to harry him.

Around seven in the evening he would put his head out

through the door to his office and see if anyone was waiting in the outer section. It was a house rule that after five o'clock nothing short of the death of Stalin, the chopping of Krushchev or the declaration of war between the Union of Soviet Socialist Republics and the People's Republic of China should cause him to be interrupted before he indicated his willingness to receive visitors. Parker Smith was keen on rules, had learned them in his army days and not forgotten them when he transferred from Intelligence Corps, Ministry of Defence, to the civilian wing of the government's espionage service, the SIS.

With his jacket left in his own office, and his tie loosened, collar button undone, Charlie Webster was waiting, far back in an armchair, and idling through the previous day's *Financial Times*. Not really the type we're used to, and more's the pity, thought Parker Smith. The totally committed man, and with more experience up front than the rest of the Section put together. He'd noticed the way the others kept their distance from Charlie Webster, didn't mix with the older man from the different background, put him on the outside. Hadn't read his personal file, had they? Would have treated him like a king if they had.

'Come on in, Charlie.' He liked the way the man straightened in his chair, left the newspaper folded on the coffee table, pushed up his tie before entering the inner sanctum. 'Take a chair, and what can I do for you?' It was a good office for talking. Parker Smith had the rank and the Civil Service grading to be able to choose, within a stipulated budget, his colour schemes – kept them soft, a gentle sky blue and a rich cream, full-length net curtains, two quietly abstract paintings, and a sprouting philodendron in the corner; none of your Annigoni prints of HM in Garter robes, nor any 'Myself Meeting Winston Churchill' photographs.

'It's this, sir. Something or nothing, I'm not sure yet, but could be amusing. I put in a "B" category to you this afternoon, about Kiev. Perhaps I shouldn't have bothered you . . . It's just that a policeman has been shot, and there's silence in the local rags and on the wireless. External picked it up and pushed it in my direction. If the Soviets had been trumpeting it I wouldn't

56

have bothered. But they haven't, and that's what made it a bit unusual to me. Seemed it could mean there's something political there.'

'I read it,' said Parker Smith. 'What's the source evaluation?'

'Not bad. One of the businessmen's pick-ups from a long-termer, passed on by the handlers. We've had this chap's stuff before, and not had reason to doubt it.'

Parker Smith bowed his head faintly in acknowledgement. One of the crosses the Department had to bear was that its source of hard news came more often than not courtesy of the active wing of SIS that occupied floors below.

'There's not much to add to the report I handed in, except that a bit more has come in from the Moscow end. It's a bit convoluted, but it's moved fast. Seems a British student on exchange post-grad studies at the University got into a bit of a panic, left his passport on a bus in Kiev, and rang into the Embassy in Moscow for guidance. Seems he told them that the talk there was of truckloads of militia moving into the city late this afternoon and that there'd been an attack on a policeman. It's very fresh this: he was only talking to the Embassy a couple of hours ago. He said all this was mixed up with a rumour running the rounds at the University, and only a rumour, that a Jewish youth had been taken into custody. The kid said that the students were saying all these three factors were related. He's just an ordinary student, nothing special, not one of ours. But it all comes at the right time to go with the other stuff.'

'Interesting, Charlie. But still doesn't up it to "A" category.'

'Be pretty hard for anything the bloody dissidents do to manage "A" quality, sir.'

'But it's nice to know. Nice to know the bastards have their own little bit of Belfast. I don't envy the little blighters up the sharp end if they get their hands on them.'

'That's not really why I wanted to see you this evening. It's just that if what we have already is genuine, then we could be into something much deeper.' Parker Smith was listening. It was what he wanted to hear, what the Department existed for, drew the

Treasury funds to discover. 'Ever since I came to work here it's struck me that one day the Soviet Jews are going to get lively. We've been through all the primary stages – press conferences, hunger strikes, trying to stir the pot up to get themselves shipped out to Israel, the botched-up job of the Leningrad hi-jack when they didn't have a gun between them and were riddled with informers and didn't even make it on to the plane before they were picked up. We've had all that kind of thing, but that was the older generation at work. It's the same the world over. All these things start with the thinkers and not the hard boys running the show, and they're too fragmented to have any unity, and there's failure. But there comes a change, when the toughies get involved. I've damn all of nothing to base this on, but if you have – and it's only an assumption – but if you have a specific target – shooting, and you have troops coming in – para-military anyway – and you have a Jewish boy picked up, then you have a pattern. There's a load of "ifs" about the whole scene, but should there be the connection that I'm drawing, then things could get very interesting.'

'I think what you're saying, Charlie, is that it doesn't really matter how the Ukrainians and the Georgians and that crowd up in the Baltic spend their evenings, but that if it was Jewish, then the flavour would be richer, the spices would be in the pot. We'd have an international scene.'

'Something like that, sir. And I thought you'd like to know.'

The conversation was over. Anyone else and Parker Smith would have given him more encouragement, but it didn't work like that with Charlie Webster. Always at his best when he had to convince people, and seemed to lose interest once he had. Strange chap, not really part of them, but a good man to have around.

Charlie let himself out and walked back to his office to collect his coat and briefcase. The bag had nothing in it beyond the morning paper, and he'd long done the crossword, but his wife liked him to carry it, had the EIIR monogram on it and she liked that to be seen. Couldn't take any of the office papers home – all classified and restricted – but he liked to humour her. He'd be in time for the 8.52 from Waterloo.

4

A tin of stewed meat, sliced open and the contents eaten cold and messily, dribbling on to their shirt fronts, and a loaf of bread were their food as the two men waited out the night hours in the forest hut. They also had a litre of beer to wash it down with, to deaden the taste, but this they left unfinished. They needed a clear head in the morning, David had said, and Isaac had watched as the screw-top was replaced on the bottle-head. But the beer had been good, had chilled their bodies and soothed their throats, sore from their incessant talking. Like talismen they had laid out, where both could see them, their achievements of the afternoon. Close to David's right hip lay the bundle in which he had brought the guns, the protective wrapping artfully pulled back so that the metal shapes could be properly admired. By Isaac's crossed ankles was the thin paper envelope that bore the Aeroflot insignia, and in which were placed the strips of paper, printed and Biro-scrawled, that were their tickets to Tashkent. Both packets were worthy of study, comprising the power and the subtlety necessary for their escape. And what awaited them now was nothing as tangible as they had accomplished, just a promise: Yevsei's promise.

With the end of the meal they were left with nothing to succour them but the sight of each other's face, the sound of each other's words. Frequently Isaac looked at the door, as if anticipating that it could open without warning, that the girl would be back, spilling out her success. It was irritating to David, who preferred to keep his own company, and who sat quite still, breaking the mood only once to throw the empty meat tin into a darkened corner, far into the shadows made by the single, flickering candle.

'How long do you think, how long till she comes?'

David shrugged, disinterested.

'Can she came in the night?'

'You know the bus times as well as I do. There is no other way she can reach us.'

'It's just this waiting. Everything we have done today, and still not knowing whether it's meaningless . . .'

'There is nothing we can do but wait.'

'Doesn't make it any easier.' Isaac laughed, nervous, cramped.

'Why should it be easy?'

'I didn't say it should be easy. I just meant . . .'

'There is nothing in a fight such as ours that can be easy. If it were then there would be many like us. We would not be alone.'

David spoke with almost a drawl, his eyes closed, seeming to ignore Isaac.

'Is that why you began? Is that why you started, because it wouldn't be easy?'

'Someone had to, after everything that our people have gone through . . .'

'But that's just jargon, David.'

'The fight had to be started . . .'

'More jargon.'

'If you didn't believe in it why did you come? Why are you part of us?'

'Different to the words you use, a different reason. Revenge, perhaps – revenge for what has happened.'

'We are no different. We are of like mind, the same body. We hate with the same depth.'

Isaac shifted his position, mindful of the nails in the floor-board, poorly hammered and whose heads bit at his buttocks.

'What was your vision of victory, David?' He saw the other man start, the eyes flash, a warning curl of anger at his mouth.

'What do you mean?'

'A campaign must have an aim, there must be a possibility of victory. If we are to fight them . . .'

'We have to hurt them – is that not enough?'

'It's never enough, just to hurt. We could go on hurting them for weeks and months and the achievement would be nothing.'

'You think that it's nothing we have achieved? A policeman shot, an organization formed, a commitment, and you call that nothing?' David stared at Isaac, intense, chin jutting, spitting out his words.

'It was a start to something.' Isaac sought to catch a tone of reason and rationality. 'But it could not be the end. You must have thought of how what we did would develop, lead on. I can't find the words to express quite what I want to say ... Just that – what did you hope for, what did you expect?'

'You say to hurt them is not enough. Well, who else has hurt them? Tell me that. Who else has filled their coffins? Has wounded and angered and insulted them? And what would you have us do? Send another telegram to the President of the United States? Call a press conference for the foreigners to attend and tell them our problems? Sit down in the street and wait for the militia to carry you away? Does that hurt them? Has anything changed in the years of the passive people, the clever people, those who relish the banner of 'non-violence'? Have they won any battles? Do visas flow because their names are broadcast on the outside radio? Does it, shit. They win nothing, only a mindless and valueless moment of attention before they are forgotten and taken to rot in the camps.'

Startled and quieter, fearful of the passion that had been laid before him, Isaac said, 'But you knew, David, you knew that it could not just continue. They have organized themselves, they will since they have a target. You yourself have said that in all probability they have taken Moses. If we cannot escape then they will close around us ...'

'They would never take me.'

'But is that what you foresaw? David, is that what you thought would happen, that one morning they would surround us ...'

'They would never take me.'

Isaac was shouting now, changing his voice, believing he had secured the truth. 'It's a bloody death-wish, isn't it? You want to play the martyr. Spread out like a hero, and your name on the song sheet. Is that what you want, a tree on a hill outside Jerusalem . . .'

'I don't want to die.'

'. . . and a crowd of people to come each Shebat, and stand in silence? . . .'

'I don't want to die.'

'. . . the weeds will grow over you. You'll be nothing, just a bloody symbol. Is that what it was all for, to satisfy your bloody death-wish?'

'The door, Isaac. It's behind you. You can open it, you can walk through it, you can walk away, make your own path.'

Isaac looked into his face, blinked at the unmoving eyes of the friend he had known since he played with a tennis ball in the dust of his street. Saw that the composure had taken root again, and would not falter whatever the provocation he offered.

'I'm sorry, David. I mean it, I'm sorry.'

Just a whisper, competing with the light wind in the high trees. 'If you think it has been easy, Isaac, it is because you have not listened, you have not watched.'

For many minutes neither spoke, both their faces in shadow, so that neither could sense the brooding mood that gripped them. When would the girl come? thought Isaac. How much longer? Would she come in darkness and in secrecy or in the public light of dawn? They'd be able to read it, written over her, whether she had succeeded or failed them. They wouldn't need words, or explanations: they would see it in her face. David had won his battle, had found the guns, and Isaac had fulfilled his share. Was she capable, the girl, of meeting her commitment? Hours Isaac had spent with her over the last years, and yet he hardly knew her, understood little about her. Just a façade, not why she was a part of them, not why she had cradled the policeman's gun in the brief moments she had handled it, or why she had declared her intention to execute a man who was unknown to her, or why on this evening she would be wheedling her sexuality on a stupid, oafish youth. What did she owe them, that she risked her life to be part of a strange and demented crusade, a

62

witness to David's death-wish, an accessory to Isaac's vengeance? He'd noted that she kept silent through David's monologues, seldom joined the others in questioning, seemed to float with them, a piece of driftwood. It would be different and straightforward if she were David's girl, but the moments, hidden or open, of gentle affection were not present – not that he had seen, anyway; never entwined fingers, never the hidden jokes and intimacies of lovers, nothing to give them away. But she was not relegated to the rôle of follower, to provide the boys of the group with the services they needed; she was an equal, as much a part of the 'programme' as he, Isaac, was. And now they depended on her: there was no flight without her, no salvation. If she failed them it would be the police cells and the beginning of David's yearning for the martyr's lime pit, and the end of Isaac's vengeance. He pictured her in his mind. The awkward and ungainly chopping stride that was too long for a girl that cared to draw attention, the teeth that were too prominent, almost like a rabbit's, the hair that was not tended, the clothes that were husbanded. It was difficult to imagine her in David's front line, fighting his battles, setting out for combat where the intellectuals of their people had lost their way.

What would they do if she had not won Yevsei, if there were no escape?

It was a hot, perspiring night, but Isaac shuddered, and hunched forward with his body as if to draw towards himself the fragile heat of the shrinking flame.

Rebecca was haggard with exhaustion by the time she reached the hut. It was the first light of the morning, Wednesday morning, the day they had chosen for the break-out. The previous night she had spent without sleep. It had been too late by the time that she had ditched Yevsei Allon to get the bus that went far out of the city to the forests, too dangerous to go home in case the police and militia should come. So there was nothing left for her to do but walk the streets, fearful of passing cars, anxious over the noise of footsteps behind, shrinking into shadows and finally collapsing, dazed and nervous, to a park bench. She had taken the first bus of the day out, and then stumbled the long walk through the trees to the hut that had been silent and had seemed deserted till she had knocked softly and said her name and heard the movement inside that told her that Isaac and David were there.

The relief had swept over their faces when she had said flatly, 'It's all right, he'll do it. Someone – it had better be me – has to take the parcel to him at noon. He thinks it is books he is handling. But he'll do it.' Then she had added, 'And you have the guns?'

David had unwrapped them, and laid them out on the floor, and she had seen the killing weapons, and the skin on her face had compressed together.

'Isaac and I will have these,' said David, handling the sub-machine guns. 'We understand them. You can have the policeman's pistol. It is enough for you.'

'Where did you get them?' Rebecca asked, wonder in her voice, built from the uncertainty she had felt through the evening and the night that even if Yevsei agreed to handle the package there might be nothing to give him.

'There is a man who is known to me. In his own way he fought the pigs, but many years ago, and he is now old, and has no need of these things. He would wish them to be used for the purpose that he once had them. He gave them to us.'

'And I have the tickets,' said Isaac, pride on his face, ignoring that he had told her his triumphs the previous evening. 'I thought there would be difficulties, but there were none, and the seats are confirmed. We are going tonight to the West, Rebecca. Tonight we sleep in peace.'

And they stood together in the centre of the small room, holding each other close, kissing each other's faces, and there were tears on their cheeks, and they clung hard to each other's bodies, willing the strength they needed.

'But we were four, we must not forget that,' Rebecca said finally. 'We must not forget Moses. Wherever he is, whatever they have done to him. If we weaken now we betray him.'

64

She had changed their mood, bringing a sombreness to them all. Like abandoning the wounded in battle, thought Isaac, to leave their friend. But what alternative was there? They were turning their backs, though, however they disguised it. David said, 'Rebecca, you must sleep now. If you don't you will be useless to us, half awake. You have time – three hours, four hours – before we go to the airport.'

On the floor she tossed and turned the minutes away, striving for comfort on the uneven boards, and her dreams were of the guns, and the bullets and the blood they might spill. She was alone while she slept, unaware that the others had gone, surreptitiously and with care to their homes and to hers, and that they had collected the personal identity cards that David decreed should not be carried on their person, but which they would need at the airport. Work and school and the morning shopping rounds had emptied the houses, and they came and went unobserved by their families.

It was Isaac who had remembered that they must produce the cards at the barriers at the airport.

Luigi Franconi had lost his suitcase. Or rather the porter's desk at the Hotel Kiev had lost it. All the cases of the delegation had been put outside the room doors, as requested, and had been taken downstairs by the service lifts; all had appeared again beside the main swing doors to be loaded on to the airport bus – all, that is, except the case of Luigi Franconi.

Outside on the street the bus revved its engine and the driver sounded his horn with impatience. The Party representative who acted as the delegation's guide, interpreter and way-smoother attempted to assure the unfortunate Franconi that if he travelled to Tashkent without his bag it would be sure to be found and would be sent on to him on the next flight. A totally unsuccessful effort, as the Partito Communista Italiana's Assistant to the Foreign Policy Committee was not to be budged with mere promises. Not till the other eight members of the PCI delegation touring the Soviet Union had joined in the angry chorus was there a sudden and exultant shout from the far side of the cavernous lobby area: the errant piece of luggage had been discovered nestling among the cases of the Rumanian football team that had just arrived.

There were more delays for a last rechecking of the baggage, and by the time the laden bus was on its way to the airport it was running late. The delegation were in poor humour, and Luigi Franconi, sitting alone at a window seat, was not one to show gratitude that his problem had been solved.

Edward R. Jones Jr and his wife, Felicity Ann, had been more circumspect in their travel arrangements and had left the Hotel Kiev on schedule a full twenty minutes before the Italians. But then when you were on a free trip – and they always travelled on free trips – you went when the car came to collect you. His Russian hosts at the Cultural Section of the city's Party Administration had been puzzled by the use of the word 'Junior' in his name, and found it strange that a man represented to them as a distinguished American poet with more than forty years of writing behind him should bother with such an appendage. That Edward R. Jones Sr had died in 1937 was known to them because the visa applications that the couple had filled in had told them so, but why this ageing son should insist on using what they regarded as a child's title was confusing and baffling.

Edward and Felicity Ann had realized many years before that the best way to travel the world and enjoy their summer holidays was to spend the winter firing off letters that begged in their reply an invitation, and they had found their ploy remarkably successful. Leningrad, Kiev and Tashkent this year. Budapest at the invitation of the Hungarian Socialist International Writers Conference the year before. Two years ago an expenses-paid summons to a poetry seminar at Warsaw. Not that the hotels were that good, and the restaurants were slothful and lifeless, but it was at least a plane ticket across the Atlantic, and a month away from the suffocation of New York in high summer.

As the taxi made its way through the outer suburbs of the city

Felicity Ann mopped her forehead with a scented square of cotton. 'I hope the plane's on time, my dear.'

'If it is, it'll be the first one we've had.'

He did not seek the conversation of his wife. Talk was only a distraction from the task in hand, jotting the iambic pentameters of an ode on the back of a postcard. When it was completed he would type it out with a portable Olivetti he always carried with him, and post it to Valery Guizov who headed the Department of Cultural Studies in the Ukraine. He'd found on earlier journeys that his hosts were quite touched by such a gesture, and sometimes printed the work in a Party periodical.

On the last stretch to the airport now. The fifth-year schoolchildren that packed the coach had had the noise and argument bounced and melted out of them by the 225-mile drive from Lvov on the Polish border. Silent and slumped in their seats, for which their teachers were grateful. Six hours, with thirty-eight children, they'd endured through all the usual gamut of threats and cajolery, and at last the little ones had succumbed to the jerking motion of the coach and the sun that pierced the curtainless windows. In front of them an hour and a half of fractious hanging around at the terminal and then the tedium of the flight to Tashkent. More delays there, inevitably, before there was another coach to take them into the Kazakhstan city.

'If any of them have the strength to appreciate ballet it will be a miracle,' muttered the headmaster, balding, sweating in his dark suit, bright tie knotted high, to his neighbour from the Art Department.

'Well, if they sleep right through it at least the little so-and-so's won't be fidgeting in the seats from half-way through the first act. Remember the ones last year? . . . But you wait and see, they'll sleep on the plane and be as awful as ever by tomorrow morning.'

The headmaster grimaced, then settled once again into his *Pravda*.

* * *

Other passengers for the 16.00 Aeroflot departure to Tashkent were already at the check-in counters, toeing their baggage forward, inching an advance with cloth-wrapped bundles, string bags and rope-fastened cases through a confusion of noise and objection and rancour.

David and Isaac were among them.

Nervous, both of them, and sweaty. Nothing strange in that, nobody in the queue able to keep calm and avoid the perspiration that the minimal air-conditioning system did little to counter. Taking in the scene round them, looking with half-detached interest at the passengers who would share the plane with them, watching their stress and their push and their bloody-mindedness as they struggled to get nearer to the counter, another stage nearer the aircraft. There was a wry smile on Isaac's face as he whispered in David's ear, 'Wouldn't be shoving so hard, not if they knew where they were going.'

For a reply there was just a hushed, 'Shut up, you fool,' that telegraphed to Isaac that David was frightened and fighting to keep his control. Surprising really, thought Isaac; wouldn't have expected that of David – nerves, yes, but not fear. Would have expected him to button it down, shrug off the pressure. Last night that's how he'd thought he'd feel himself now, frightened; but he wasn't. A little tense, fingers stiff, voice hoarse, tight in the guts, but nothing else, almost distant from the whole thing. Not that he was worrying about David; he'd be all right once they had started, once they were in operation.

Isaac wondered how it would be there, what Israel would be like. Just a place that people talked about, dreamed about, but he'd never met anyone who'd been there, nor anyone who had achieved the exit visa. The way they spoke on the foreign radio you'd imagine anyone who applied could get the visa, just filling in a form, and packing up and going. As if they didn't know how many were refused, how they weeded out the ones they wanted to stay, and how if they turned you down the pressures and persecutions built on your shoulders. Didn't know in the West what it was like, the reality of Soviet Jewry. And why was it important, this place Israel? Different things to different people; obvious that, Isaac. Well, for the old ones, for them there was the faith, just a chance to stand at the wall in Jerusalem, stand there and pray to their God. For others it was a place where a man could work and earn his money and live his life and have no fear of the Party commissar and the Party spy. But for you, Isaac? A sort of freedom, that was what he was seeking, a freedom of choice, not that he wanted a society of anarchists, just the freedom to join the system if he wanted to – an end to compulsion. So he didn't really know. He'd have to find out, wouldn't he?

'Get the tickets.' David close to him, hissing the instruction, his face set, controlling his mouth muscles. 'The tickets – come on!'

'Where's Rebecca?' Isaac said as he pulled them from the inside pocket of his lightweight jacket.

'Coming from the far side, from the telephone. Give this girl the tickets.'

Isaac could hear behind him the strident voice with its American accent cutting across the other tongues. Not that he could understand the words – after all, he had studied science at school, not languages – and beyond and just surviving the drowning emphasis of the American was a further babble, European – could be Spanish or French or Italian – but he could not gauge which.

The girl at the counter said, 'Where's your baggage?'

It was something they hadn't thought about; so little time, and so much to think of, but they hadn't considered the need for baggage. Who goes on a plane with no baggage? With a 14-day excursion ticket? They'd gone home for the identity passes, and not thought of clearing a wardrobe, of scattering clothes in a case. People were pushing behind them, the American voice brimming with complaint, while in front the girl was waiting for an explanation.

'Our friend took it,' said Isaac with David still lost and unable to conjure up an explanation, 'when he went earlier in the week.' First thing that came to his head, first thing he could think of saying.

'For three of you? Hope he paid the excess.' She ripped off the top sheet of the tickets, one by one, and gave them the boarding cards. Small and sparse scraps of thickened paper, flight number scrawled on them. 'Gate four you want. Through the departure door, then the security, and you wait in the lounge till they call you.'

'Is the flight on time?' David asked.

But her attention was gone from him, given now to the next passenger in line. She shrugged, and said she didn't know.

The American couple took their places at the counter. Red trousers – well, red with a white check in them and a faded cream jacket. The woman in mauve, her hair a delicate blued tint that caught Isaac's eye by its unfamiliarity. Why do they wear these clothes? Straight out of the cartoons in *Krokodil*.

Just security now and nothing for them to find. Clean. Not a germ among them. Scrubbed and shining and polished, that was the way to go through security. David was talking to Rebecca, arm around her shoulders, heads near to touching and she was showing him a piece of paper. Must have worked, must be where the guns were.

'There's time for coffee. At least ten minutes till we need to go through.' David led and they followed over to the bar – not that any of them were thirsty, but the process of ordering and paying and waiting for the coffees to be brought to the table, and then drinking, all that would use up time, time which they had no use for, which had to be exhausted. Should have told the parents, Isaac thought, should have said something to them, they should know what has happened, and why it has happened, before the time that the police arrive. He excused himself and rose from the table and went to the small shop where there were magazines and newspapers, postcards and cigarettes and souvenirs of Kiev. He asked for some notepaper and an envelope, but the man insisted on selling him a whole pad of notepaper and two dozen envelopes because that was the way they were packaged. There was no option, so he paid for them all and took them back to the table.

'I think we should write something to our people. It will be long over by the time that it reaches them.' There was agreement, and for five minutes no talk at the table, as they wrote out their farewells and justifications.

'Esteemed and respected father and mother and dear sisters,

By the time that you read this you will have heard of our actions. You must forgive us the danger and hurt that they may cause you. We have taken this course because of what we saw as the persecution of our people in this land. If we had stayed the police would have taken us and for what we have done there is only one sentence, and there would have been no possibility of mercy. Our air tickets have been purchased with money from Isaac's mother, who paid for the three of us without knowing for what reason her money was wanted. From the family savings please send her 174 roubles. Rebecca will request her family to do the same. We hope to be in Israel very soon. We hope that it will be possible for you to join us there.

There is much to say and little time. All so difficult to explain. We started because we believed in our actions, but we did not know where they would leave us — we still do not know.

Be brave,

Your loving son, who will not forget you,

David.'

Rebecca took the three envelopes to the post-counter for the stamps while David and Isaac stayed at the table waiting for her. When she came back the three of them walked towards the departure doors leaving the near-filled pad and twenty-one envelopes beside the coffee cups that had remained untouched while they wrote.

Abruptly Rebecca tugged at David's arm, pulled him closer to her as they crossed the concourse.

'What will they do to them, when we have gone?'

He didn't look at her, fastening his eyes on the doorway to the front. 'I don't know.' A lie, and he could not meet her eyes.

'Will they be punished for what we have done?'

'We cannot think of that now.'

'They have punished others . . .'

'What they will do to them will be as nothing to what will happen to us if we stay.'

'Do you care what happens to them, David?'

'I care more for what happens to my parents than you will concern yourself with the fate of Yevsei Allon. Think on that.'

Her hand flew from his sleeve, leaving him free to walk on unimpeded. If Isaac had heard he showed no sign of it – stern faced, regular stride. All three of them continued their way across the tiled floorway.

Beyond the doors there was an airline official, bored and uninterested, who checked their tickets and the boarding passes and matched their names written there against the plastic-coated identity cards, not troubling to marry the Polaroid photographs with the actual likenesses. Further on, the high arch through which passengers had to pass and which showed whether they carried metallic objects in their pockets. This was the realm of the Frontier Guards, pistols hanging on their hips, and clean uniforms with wide-peaked caps. The man in front of them was stopped when the small green light that the guardsman watched changed abruptly to flashing red and his body was searched till a cigarette packet was retrieved from his trousers and he was shown the silver paper wrapping that had caused the detector to activate. Thank God we carried nothing, Isaac said to himself. Then it was their turn, and the light stayed green, and they walked past the guard, and on.

All of them braced themselves, shoulders stiffened as if to ward off a blow, as if they were expecting a shout from behind. But there was none, just a sun-filled lounge, with the ashtrays overflowing and paper on the floor, and dust and grime, and children shouting and running between the wooden benches, and a teacher's command. Across the room from them were the windows through which they could all see the tidy, painted profile of the Ilyushin 18 turbo-prop airliner, due to depart for Tashkent in thirty-five minutes.

In a tight phalanx the little group approached the forward steps of the aircraft. All of them sweating from the slight exertion of the walk across the apron. The captain to the front, straight backed, grey hair thinning, uniform pressed, rank denoted by the gold rings sewn to his tunic sleeve, carrying his cap easily in his hand. A pace behind him the navigator with his briefcase filled with the maps that covered the air routes of the southern area of the Soviet Union over which they would fly to Tashkent. Alone, not seeming to wish to engage in conversation with her male flight deck companions, was the co-pilot. Anna Tashova's skirt rode high on her knees as she maintained their pace. She felt once at the knot of her thin black tie, unnecessary and unfeminine she thought it, but if it were decreed that it should be worn then it was her obligation to make certain that it bisected her collar with precision. The two flight stewardesses, acknowledging they were not part of the cockpit club, came last, handbags on their shoulders, talking of men and prices, and hotels, and the boredom of it all.

At the bottom of the forward steps the captain waited, a fixed smile on his face, for the young technician in overalls to hurry down the stairs. The boy should have waited for them, should not have obstructed and delayed their boarding. He seemed in a rush, and bounced against the captain's shoulder. No apology, just something indistinct mumbled from behind his teeth.

'Dirty little bastard,' the Captain said. 'Soap and water, but perhaps he's never heard of them.'

The navigator laughed cheerfully, all the more for the sneer of distaste on the co-pilot's small mouth as if the retreating, jogging boy had left an odour behind which would contaminate all of them.

'We'll be off on time today, sir.'

'Well, don't blame me for it. Accidents happen even to the best of us.'

More smiles, and a moment of gallantry from the men – stepping aside so that Anna Tashova and the stewardesses should be first on the steps.

The major of the Committee of State Security – KGB – worked from a smaller and less imposing building than his colleague in the militia security police. The address was not listed in the telephone directory, and was known only to those civilians who had a need for the knowledge. The major was a frugal man who seldom took more than thirty minutes for his lunch, but since the arrest of Moses Albyov and his subsequent suicide he had not left his office, sleeping the previous two nights on an army bed that graced one corner of the room.

At half past three the grey telephone on his desk, the direct line that bypassed the switchboard, rang out. A short message and from militia headquarters.

The Jew had been identified.

Quite clever really. The photograph they had taken of him showed indents at the sides of his face from the arms of spectacles, recent enough, but not worn when he had been brought in. One of the patrolmen from the car had said he might have been wearing them when he was taken; and the wounded policeman's description on which the arrest had been made, that had included spectacles. They had found them in the gutter where the street sweeper had pushed them, and the luck was that the lenses were still intact. The major had been kind enough to say that it would be police work that would identify the boy, and that was what it had been. A photograph of the glasses, an analysis of the lenses, a photograph of the boy, and twenty-five detectives touring the city's eye clinics. It was faster than doing it with the boy's teeth: fewer spectacles wearers than those requiring extractions and fillings.

And now they had a name, and were cross-checking with the statutory civil authority dossier. Moses Albyov, residing at 428B Avenue of the First of May; a workers' quarter in the northern suburbs, he was informed, and also that there was no previous record of violence, and that two cars had left for the address and would be there within a quarter of an hour. Smash the little bastards, he thought, smash them till they screamed like the rats they were. Not long till they'd have their hands on them; the Albyov parents would tell of the associates, would have them all in the cells by dawn.

No delays on the departure of Aeroflot flight 927 to Tashkent. On time, on schedule. The passengers walked the 100 yards to the plane, in untidy caterpillar file out across the tarmac, heat streaming back at them from the great, open surface, burning through the soles of their footwear, driving their eyes together with everything beyond the middle distance dissolving into a haze.

'The seats run A-B-C down one side of the aisle, and D-E-F on the other,' David said to Isaac. They were near the plane now and walking to the rear exit where the steps had been wheeled up, and there was an angle of shade thrown by the single high-tail structure. 'Yevsei told Rebecca the package would be on the right-hand side, level with the nineteenth row, and would be under the blankets, the blankets that they store in the luggage shelf at the top. We must get on the plane quickly, before the herd, so that one of us can sit in that row and the rest close by. I will try and see that it is me. When I take the package I will go to the toilet at the back to get the guns assembled. Give me two minutes, then come and knock at the door. Quite soon we will go, after ten minutes, when the seat belt sign is off.'

David was the first of the three on to the steps, Isaac close behind, Rebecca separated by a dozen passengers. David climbed steadily, his speed dictated by the pace of those in front. To any passenger who glanced casually among his fellow travellers David would have aroused no particular interest, his inner tensions successfully masked. He seemed confident and relaxed as he ducked his head through the low doorway. He hesitated for a moment, sizing up the long cigar-like interior of the plane, with the duck-egg decor and green-backed seats stretching away from him to the distant cream-painted door that was half open, so that he could see the silhouettes of the shoulders of pilot and co-pilot. Isaac nudged him, and he walked down the aisle, noting the row numbers. Row 19, aisle seat C. Isaac opposite him, Row 19, aisle seat D. The package would be above Isaac, and the boy hadn't looked for it, was settling in his seat, fastening his safety belt. Rebecca stooped into her place, four rows in front, but not turning to see them, and then David lost sight of her as other passengers surged the length of the cabin in a steady clamour. It was what he had heard, that people always suffer stress before takeoff and before landing; makes them raise their voices, and push aggressively in a way they would not contemplate if their feet were grounded. David fastened his seat belt and looked across at Isaac.

'Courage, my friend,' he said.

'Not courage. It is the time for luck now.' Isaac closed his eyes, waiting for the motion of the plane to tell him they were taxi-ing.

Five minutes they'd been in the house, time enough for them to recognize the stark terror on the faces of the father and mother of Moses Albyov before the truncheon in her lower abdomen and the pistol whipping across his face had delivered up the names of David and Isaac and Rebecca. One policeman stayed in the living room covering with his drawn pistol the woman who cowered in the chair, clutching herself and moaning, and the man lying still on the floor with the blood running from the head wound on to the lino surface. Another had gone to his car to radio to headquarters the fruits of the visit. Six more, packed close together, were speeding towards the home of the one called David, the one the woman had said she had gone to visit the morning before to ask the whereabouts of her son.

Some hundreds of yards short of David's address the driver of the police car silenced the siren he had used to clear a path through the traffic, and when they staggered to a halt, his foot hard on the brake pedal, there was a swift and often-rehearsed routine for them to follow. Two running for the back, jumping the wire fence, then crouching low, their guns aimed at the rear door. Two more at the front, and behind the car, to give themselves cover. The remaining two, an officer and one who was brave, chancing their luck at the door. 'Shoot him if he has a gun. Without hesitation. Remember what Albyov did, and remember this is one of them.'

David's mother, alone in the house, answered the hammering at the door. Her younger children were still at school, her husband at work, so she was without protection as the officer forced her against the old wooden sideboard, his knee hard against her thigh so that the carved angle bit into her skin. There was no reason to hit: she talked without resort to violence. Too much for her, after a year in Treblinka and never called for the showers, no resistance left, not to a man in uniform who carried a gun, and who shouted and who wore boots that reached to his knee. She had submitted before and would do so again. She told them of her son's friends, pointed him out in the family photograph, said he hadn't been home the previous night.

At militia headquarters they believed in the power of routine. Three names, photographs that would illustrate them when the cars came in from the homes, and when Central Records turned up the files. All standard and routine. Just as it was routine to call the airport with the names, and the principal Aeroflot ticket offices, and to send descriptions to the railway station and the bus terminus by the square of the granite war memorial. All routes of exit from the city were notified with 'priority' messages. And because the computer of the central Aeroflot offices was repaired and functioning, that was the source of the first hard information. The message rattled back over the teleprinter – three names, three tickets, flight number, take-off time, destination. All this was controlled from the second floor operations centre of the militia headquarters – fast, quiet, efficient, a trained team that was good at its work, and which had discovered a scent, and believed that the kill was close.

A call to the airport, routed through the offices of the Frontier Guard control point, to the commander of the unit who had responsibility for all matters affecting security. A second call to the control tower.

'Aeroflot flight 927 to Tashkent has been airborne nine minutes, close to ten,' the Frontier Guard commander reported back to the control room. Verified by the tower.

'Then tell the control tower to radio the pilot, order him to return. Tell him the passengers should be informed there is a technical fault. When the plane lands I want every man you have around it. Nobody gets off, not till we arrive.'

'Do you want the pilot to be told that this is a security matter?'
'Why not?'

Down in the yard the black Moskva car had been alerted; it waited with its engine idling for the sprinting figure of the Colonel of Militia.

They were climbing in light cloud when Yuri Zibov, 18 years an Aeroflot pilot and most of them on the lumbering Ilyushin Il18V, and before that Yak bombers in the Air Force, received the recall order. He motioned to his co-pilot – young, feminine, petite, a hint of lipstick, and as many flying qualifications as her male equivalents. Had she understood the message? A nod.

Zibov turned to the navigator sitting behind. He also had understood. Into the microphone that jutted out from his headset and that rested three quarters of an inch from his mouth, he said, 'Bolt the cockpit door. Just a precaution, but fasten it, then we'll swing.'

The navigator started to intone the statistics that would govern their change of course.

David was groping with his arms into the recess of the shelf where he could not see. Even as he stretched upwards he was reliant on the touch of his fingers to tell him if the package were there. Fumbling among the softness of the blankets and the pillows, scratching with his fingers and seeking for the hard shape. Not there, not above row nineteen, and in a driving and frantic motion his hands spilled out to right and left, and he was high on his toes, and the passenger who had the seat beside him was staring, and was interested. Almost at the moment of panic David's hands locked on to the ungiving shape of the parcel. Must have slipped backwards on take-off, he thought. Right over Row 20. He made a low-voiced apology to his neighbour, who was leaning back in his seat with his legs bent sideways to give David room. He lifted the package down, just as they had wrapped it, right down to the knots in the string; not tampered with. Tucking it under his arm he lurched his way through to the rear, to the bolted security of the lavatories, and a half-turn to be certain that Isaac was watching him; the gleam of recognition that told him Isaac was ready, coiled, anticipating. Had to push past the two stewardesses, blue uniforms, crumpled shirts, hair wisping from buns, minimum of make-up, preparing the food trolley and drinks. No alcohol on board – mineral water and orange juice and coffee, reluctant to step aside and let him pass, an obstruction when they were trying to work, seeming to say why couldn't he have gone in the terminal lavatories.

He slammed the door shut behind him and ran the catch across. Then he began to tear at the paper and the string binding, pulling at the cardboard that had given the parcel the rectangular shape, that had made Yevsei believe it was indeed a mass of books that he had handled. The parcel spilled open, pitched the hand-gun on to the floor beside the pan where he let it lie while he unravelled the further protection around the two sub-machine guns. Lovely babies. Sweet, keen, pretty things, but already taking on the ugliness of their trade as the barrel symmetry was broken when he fastened the magazines at right angles to the bodies. One at a time and take it slowly, remember the drill with the old man, with Timofey. Never hurry in the preparation of weapons, he had said. The loud rasping of the cocking mechanism – devastating how the noise reverberated inside the confined space then check the safety catch is on. Same for the pistol. No accidents, not in a capacity-filled airliner, not when the pressure of the cabin will soon be at risk.

Abruptly he lunged to the side, cannoning into the

wall-fitted basin, knee ramming against the rim of the pan seat, thrown off balance by the sudden shift in direction of the plane as the pilot banked to begin the long turn that would bring the aircraft back to Kiev. David's mind was razor-sharp, honed by suspicion . . . He was still regaining his balance when there was Isaac's voice muffled by the closed door, dispute with the stewardesses, and them retorting angrily that the seat-belt signs were illuminated again, that he should return to his place. Over the loudspeaker which had its own amplifier in the lavatory . . . 'This is Captain Zibov, your pilot. Sorry, but we seem to have some minor technical problem, but it means we must return to Kiev. It is nothing that should concern you, but we have to land again and get the fault repaired. Please fasten your belts again, and no more smoking. I hope the delay will be short. Thank you.' Warning bells, cymbal loud. Not good enough, you pigs. Has to be wrong; too controlled, too much of a coincidence. Must not land, not at any cost.

David pulled the door open. Sub-machine gun in each hand, pistol in the belt of his trousers, he careered, straight into the grey-metalled drinks trolley, heaved with desperation to rid himself of the impediment, saw the faces turning, the necks twisting. Then he was clear and sprinting. Isaac in front of him, standing, waiting, sharing his anxiety, had read the same message from the pilot's announcement and the tilting of the plane, ready to receive with outstretched arm the weapon that would be his. Unaware of everything now, of the passengers, of cabin crew, everything except the door of the cockpit. David's right shoulder cannoned into it, expecting it to give, face wreathed in amazement as it flung him back. The old David, the man of decision and fight, who had brought them together, armed and aimed them. The old David, who should have told Rebecca to go and scratch herself with her bloody twigs, who should have vetoed the use of Moses in the attack. The old David, that Isaac would follow as far as he was led. Sub-machine gun held low and away from his body and the flash and explosion that drove at their eardrums as he fired into the centre of the door.

'Open or it's machine-gun fire. Open, or I kill the whole fucking lot of you.' Voice at screaming pitch. 'Open the fucking thing.' There was a hesitation, seeming endless, but in fact little more than three seconds, then the bolt was withdrawn, the door opened.

So small in the cockpit, a tiny space, like the lavatory, a box room, and three persons already strapped and harnessed in their seats. Saw the pilot, saw the co-pilot. A woman: David noticed that because she was the one who had turned her head towards them, then his eyes were riveted to the maze of dials and buttons, the instrument boards. Find the altimeter, that was the first thing, had to be certain they weren't losing height, had to climb, had to get up . . . after that the time to set a course.

'Take the bloody thing up,' he yelled, and pushed sideways with the gun barrel at the pilot's shoulder, aware there had been no response, still staring at the labyrinth of controls, searching for the magic of the altimeter.

Isaac said, his voice very quiet, 'You're wasting your time, David. No point shouting at him. You've killed him.'

David stepped back, peering at the pilot held upright in his cockpit straps, then took in the neat expertise of the drilled hole at the back of the skull where the circumference showed clear against the short-cropped greying hair, and the path of blood that ran down to the uniform collar and the white shirt. David arched his body round towards the hole in the door where the woodwork had been forced out by his bullet. Then his eyes rolled back again, via the instrument panels to the co-pilot. The noise and the venom gone, replaced by a vague aloofness, like a schoolmaster in a laboratory talking to students.

'What's your name?' he asked, almost conversationally.

'Anna Tashova, pilot officer.'

'You will ignore all instructions. Get the plane up now, get it high, and set a course to the West. We want a course to the nearest frontier of the West. And know this. I am ignorant about flying, I have never piloted an aircraft, but I think I would know if you deceive me. If you seek to trick us, Miss Tashova, then I will kill you, and if you die so does everyone on board the air-craft. We are Jews, Miss Tashova, and the days when we could be told that we were going for a warm shower to shed ourselves of lice are long gone. Do not test us, Miss Tashova; today we are a harder people.'

She did not fight him, recognizing her responsibilities. 'The tower is talking to us. They direct us to return to Kiev. What do you want me to tell them?' Calm, with a brusqueness in her voice, as in a committee meeting.

'You say nothing, ignore them. Let them shout. They can do nothing.'

He watched her hands, moving deftly over the scores of but-tons and switches in front of and beside her, never allowing herself a glance towards the dead captain. Saw the preparation until she was ready to move her hands, both together, onto the control lever that bisected her knees, heard the navigator beside him calling his lists of numbers and figures that represented a path through the airways. And there the sensation at his feet – the sensation that they were climbing.

It was possible for him to look now. Possible for him to gape at the occasionally lolling, drifting head of the first man he had killed. He had bickered with Isaac that first evening, snapped at him because he had used the word 'easy'. What was easier than this? Not a moment's thought demanded, no intention, no pro-gramme, no plot, just the pulling in of a finger knuckle. A man died that David might go free. The pilot officer involved in the work he had set her, the navigator concerned by his task. Only David and the captain who had no immediate function. But it had not been intended, not to kill him. Yet he is removed from your apology, David. Now you must live with it.

Meanwhile, soaring upwards, the Kingfisher bird was escap-ing from her enemies. Full power given to the four Ivchenko A1-20 engines, reaching for her operational altitude of 27,000 feet, fuel tanks loaded to a capacity of 5,200 Imperial gallons, offering a range of minimally less than two thousand miles with the cover of one hour's clear reserve.

5

In the control tower that dwarfs the whitened form of the air-port terminal buildings the traffic controllers were quick to observe the change of course. For a full minute the Frontier Guard commander demanded of the man who wore the head-phones and who had been talking to the crew of Aeroflot 927 that he should continue repeating the instruction that the air-craft respond to its order and return to Kiev.

The controller did not turn to his superior, hovering at his shoulder, but just repeated, 'There is nothing, sir. No response. They ignore us. Nothing since the second pilot reported the shooting, that the captain had been hit and incapacitated.'

'But the plane is still operational, it is not flying on automatic controls?'

To a man of lesser importance than the Frontier Guard com-mander the controller would have been scornful of such lack of knowledge, but he answered with politeness, 'There can be no question of that, sir. The manoeuvres it has made are not those of a plane flying remote. It must be the co-pilot who is handling the aircraft, and she is working now to orders – that must be the assumption. The planes are dual; she would have no difficulty in piloting on her own . . . only if she has to land by herself, and if she were tired and under stress.'

'What is the course?' The Frontier Guard commander could feel the initiative slipping from him, losing whatever tenuous control he had once had on the aircraft.

'Towards southern Poland, and climbing. Ultimately such a line as they now hold will bring them into the airspace of the BDR. Perhaps two hours' flying time.' He was the uninvolved

83

one, cocooned from responsibility, and in the grandstand seat to watch what his betters would make of it.

'And again, what was the last message?'

'As I told you, sir. They reported the bolting of the door. They reported they were responding to instructions to return. They reported a shot being fired at the door, that the bullet penetrated the door and struck the captain – that is, Captain Zibov. They reported the impression that he was killed instantly. They reported that they were being threatened with machine gun fire unless they opened the door, and they reacted to that threat. There is no option, you must understand that, sir.' As if fearful that the military would have no knowledge of the reality of an aircraft cockpit, and the weight of the burden of the lives of a cabin full of passengers, he went on: 'Not when you have such a confined space as the flight deck; the damage could have been very great. Since the opening of the door we have had vague shouts, which I could not distinguish. That will be on the tapes, but to us they were not clear – perhaps you will be able to decipher them. Pilot Officer Tashova has identified herself to the hijackers, if that is what they are, and has told them that we are talking to her and requesting her to return. There has been nothing since that.'

The Guard commander finished the scribbled note, reached for the desk telephone and dialled the militia headquarters. Operations room patched the call through to the telephone in the back of the car that was bringing the militia colonel towards the airport. The situation was relayed, the number of the nearest direct line to the Guard commander was passed on, the call was terminated.

The communications of the Russian internal security services had long been a source of justifiable pride, much admired by their opposite numbers in the West; the colonel was able to reach within seconds a senior official of the Ministry of the Interior in Central Moscow. He was connected directly to the Minister, one of the four most important personages in the Soviet Union, and the one who at that moment had the power

84

and the full authority to make decisions on the future flying of Aeroflot 927. The colonel's rôle in the immediate course of the incident was completed. During the subsequent two minutes radio and telephone conversations were activated from the seat of government to the airforce base that lies close to the small town of Chernigov, due north of Kiev. The order for the moment was short, and very clear. The Ilyushin II-18V should be forced to land within Russian territory.

In a flight of four the Mig 23s lifted off. Two pairs, matching and racing each other down the runway till they had achieved take-off speed, then airborne in an explosion of aviation fuel fumes, and with sheets of flame spewing from the rear engine vents. These were not the low-level ground-support aircraft with the North European theatre camouflage motif but the sil-ver-fuselaged altitude interceptors that were held far to the rear of the Cold War front.

Closing into diamond formation as they climbed, capable of eighteen hundred miles an hour in flight, code-named by NATO planners as 'Foxbat', they made an unmercifully unequal match for the lumbering, hesitant airliner which those same planners had titled 'Coot'. Four sharks thrusting their way into the upper atmosphere where they would poise themselves, biding their time till ground control gave them the precious radar bearings that they would need to lock themselves on their quarry. At the controls were young men little older than David or Isaac, but the élite of the society that they served, on whom money and exper-tise and time had been lavished that their effectiveness would be guaranteed. The sun burnished a reflection off the cropped, sharpened delta wings as they banked to take up the level flight that meant they had achieved the necessary altitude, in excess of forty-five thousand feet, that when they came for the airliner they would be diving. Cannon belt loaded in the wings, and slung below the snap-down missiles. Lethal and vicious, with no morality of their own, without an opinion on their orders, and now responding to instructions, feeding the information into their transistorized computer workings. Beginning the search for a creature that by comparison was unworthy of their strength, a lamed and limping prey.

David was still in the cockpit.

Isaac shooed the stewardesses back towards the main passenger cabin, gesturing them towards vacant seats with his sub-machine gun, telling them to sit and to fasten their belts. Time now to see who they had on board, to evaluate the passengers. Stunned they seemed, most of them; all staring at him till he caught the individual pairs of eyes that then looked away as if terrified by what they saw.

He shouted the length of the cabin, that those at the back, 75 feet from him, might hear and understand and have no doubt as to his intent. 'All your hands on your heads. If you do as you are instructed no harm will come to you, but you must obey our orders, and without hesitation. All hands on your heads.' He felt a curious thrill at the depth of his voice as it echoed back at him, drowning the monotonous roar of the engine. Some reacting immediately, some so confused that they had to have the instruction repeated by those who sat beside them. Old hands that were weather-beaten and vein-ribbed and on which there were heavy gold rings, hands that were used to manual work and which showed callouses and worn skin as they were lifted. Hands that were manicured and had no bruises, hands that were young and pink and undeveloped. The small hands of the children reaching up to the well-washed hair of their heads. That was how he was first aware of the school party. He hadn't seen them before, not so as to register, hidden away behind their seats till their hands came up, with the popping eyes and the wide-opened mouths.

He was surprised in a way that there wasn't more hostility on the faces – but not once he'd thought about it – it was not him they were frightened of, not little Isaac, not a student with a hole in his shoe, and underpants changed once a week, and the shirt with the collar button off. It was the gun in his hands that brought the submission and the respect for his orders. Not for yourself – kick your balls half-way to Khabarovsk if you gave them the chance. The gun, that was his protection.

Isaac moved warily down the aisle, Rebecca walking backwards behind him, covering the passengers who could have turned to face his retreating back. About sixty of them in all, he reckoned, not an exact count, but good enough for his needs. All of them waiting on him, waiting for the explanation that would clarify the gunshot, and the lurches in the direction of the plane, and the sight of the young man with the curly hair and the shabby clothes, and who carried the sub-machine gun at his hip, whose thumb was on 'safety', whose forefinger was abreast the trigger guard. He walked the full length of the plane, reaching with his free hand sometimes to steady himself as the aircraft pitched and fell away. His arm then close to heads that shrivelled away from him. He checked the lavatories, both empty, bar the one strewn with the wrapping paper that had parcelled the firearms. A good precaution, necessary to make certain no hero of the Soviet Union was hiding there looking for a Red Star to be pinned posthumously on his coffin. Clean at the back of the plane. Everyone in their seats and where they should be, neat and tidy and packaged. He called Rebecca forward, so that she could stand in the stewardesses' province, away from the passengers and close to the rear exit door. He pulled the soft drinks trolley across the aisle where the rear row of seats ended and the galley area began. This gave a free space in which Rebecca could stand, and a degree of protection if he left her there. It made a barricade for her to shelter behind, the bottles rattling and chinking together in protest as he moved the obstacle into position.

'You're going to be at this end, Rebecca, and for much of the flight. I'll be at the front with David, him in the cockpit, and me mostly watching the passengers. If they turn round to stare at you order them back, to look at the front. Don't talk to them; don't start speaking to them – nothing at least till we are over the West.'

'What's at the front . . . David was shouting?'

'Nothing now. The shot that he fired to get the door opened, it's killed the pilot. The co-pilot is flying now.'

'Oh, my God, oh, God . . .'

'He didn't mean to, it was an accident.' Her head was down on her chest. Exhausted, all in, beaten. And David half out of his mind and screaming up there in the front. On your own, Isaac, and where to turn to for the reinforcements? 'Take a grip, Rebecca,' he snarled at her. 'Remember why we are here, what we came for, and if another of the pigs gets in the way, tries anything, attempts what the pilot did, then you shoot him. You understand?' Saw his failure, and the unreasoned rejection of what he said. And then more gently, and with the smile. 'It's not long from now, just a few hours, two or three, and then we land. Then it's the petrol, the refuel and on to Israel.' He took her left hand, closed it in his own, small and buried and cold and without response, trying to impart his own strength, trying to hide his own fear, then walked down the length of the aisle again towards the cockpit. Forty-eight paces, that was the length of their castle, battened down and with the hatches fastened, wondering again how David was. He turned to face the passengers.

'Ladies and gentlemen, you have nothing to be afraid of from us. We are taking this plane to the West. We will be there soon, and then you will be rid of us, free to return wherever you may wish. I must tell you that my friends and myself have no life left inside the Soviet Union – we have nothing to return to except a death sentence. I must tell you that because you have to know that we will die in this plane rather than return to Kiev. If there is any resistance, any attempt to disarm us, we will shoot and that will endanger the safety of the aircraft – and of you, of all of you. Later in the flight we will tell you more. For now you must remain seated, your hands on your heads, and you must not talk. That is all.' Another speech, Isaac, another audience. Seemed so inadequate, so divorced from the wood hut, and the faint light of evening when they met there, and the plans to conquer the system that they hated. But then there were so many things that had not been prepared; free-wheeling really, with the engine dis-engaged, but the hill was steep and there was no braking now.

No murmur greeted his words, not of appreciation, not of condemnation; the passengers just soaked them up, as they stayed in their seats, hands on their heads. Nothing to please him, nothing to anger him. Nothing.

A brisk little face she had. Pale and smooth-skinned, with a pittance of make-up, a severe bobbed cut to her hair and eyes that flitted over her instruments and that were sharp and a deep honey brown. When Anna Tashova smiled the lines at her mouth were clearly drawn, not a smile of pleasure nor of satisfaction but a smile of triumph. David saw it, saw the way she half-turned, and broke his concentration on the hazed horizon to the front, turned instead to follow her glance to the starboard cock-pit window. They were flying very close, the Migs. The nearest were some fifty feet from the Ilyushin's wing, had crept their way forward with a stealth that had deceived him, and beyond the nearest of the fighters lay another, so close that the two seemed to nestle together. They were near enough for David to see the pilots, to identify the numbers of their machines painted on the slender nose, to witness the menace of the rockets hung beneath their wings.

The pilot officer pushed the microphone mouthpiece away from her lips. 'They are on the other side as well. They have come to take us home.'

David could see the gestures of the nearest pilot on the port side, the motions of his gloved hand, that they should swing again, retrace their path towards Kiev.

'They will have orders,' Anna Tashova said. 'They will bring us down if we do not comply. What do you want? A plane full of dead passengers? Does that serve your cause?'

The lead port side plane, the one whose pilot had made the arm movement, inched its way forward. Strange really, and the effect upon David was hypnotic, compulsive, the way it could move so delicately, a beast of such power yet held to a fingertip control that permitted it to nudge, foot by foot, into the airspace almost immediately in front of the Ilyushin.

'He will slow now, force me to lose thrust and altitude if I am to avoid him. It is an accepted procedure.' Jet interceptor and airliner, the gap closing between them. An inevitable course they were following, collision course, mid-air, fragmentation, break-up. Fascinating for him to watch, crawling towards the impact. A distant shriek, then Isaac beating at his shoulder.

'David, what are we doing? What are you telling the pilot? The Migs have come.'

A deeper, more general noise from behind, that took him a moment to understand and then was clear as the hysteria of the passengers. Predictable, and he knew the course he would take.

'You fly on,' flat and without emotion, speaking to the pilot officer, ignoring Isaac.

'Then you have collision, is that what you want?' Strain in her voice – the first time. Turning hesitantly from the cockpit window and the great shape that masked her view to the pallid, closed features of the young man at her back, with the gun loose in his hands.

'There will be no collision. Fly on. Remember your responsibilities, and they are to your passengers.' He turned to Isaac. 'They are trying to force us down, and we will not respond. I believe they will not risk more, and soon we shall see.' They were so close now both men could see the huge chasm of the interceptor's rear exhaust, blackened and flame-charred. And the distance narrowing the whole time, second by second, foot by foot, and the pilot officer's hands beginning to waver above her controls. 'Do not touch them. Touch them and I shoot.'

'If they have orders to bring us down that will be sufficient. They have rockets, you can see for yourself. They can bring us down if . . .'

'Who is listening on our radio? Who can hear us?' The lustre back in his voice; he, too, rejoicing in the power he had accumulated, as Isaac had done moments before, drinking deep in the new sensation of being at the centre of events.

She paused. 'Half the world can listen to you when you talk from an airplane cockpit.' The moment of triumph lost, dissipated by her assessment of the man with the gun, and of his fanaticism, his determination. At the briefings in Moscow, the anti-hijack briefings, they had spoken of the two types, those seeking a ride out, those yearning for a wider audience. The second grouping they had said was the one to be feared. 'At this speed we collide; ten seconds more, that is all. I must reduce speed. I have to . . .'

'It will be they who increase speed. I want to use the radio. I want to speak.' Radio silence so far, he had noted that much, not even talking to the navigator. No conversation with the airliner from the jets – serve to make it all public, wouldn't it? Confirmed what she's said, that half the world could hear him now, half the world listening, and wondering why a plane was off route, out of the air lanes. One hundred and fifty feet in front and fractionally above was the tail of the lead Mig, and the escorts closer to the wings, crowding them, boxing them in, and at three hundred and thirty miles an hour as they flew four clear miles above the Russian plains.

Headphones pushed down into his hair, microphone across his mouth, he instructed her to activate it, all the time the barrel of the gun close to her side and his finger by the trigger.

'This plane is now under the command of a Jewish Resistance Commando. We have taken the Aeroflot Flight 927, Kiev to Tashkent, and we go to the West. Our final destination is Israel. The pilot of the aircraft is dead, and his colleague, Pilot Officer Anna Tashova, is flying. I hold a sub machine gun to her body. We have an escort of Mig 23 fighters who are trying to make us land. We have told Miss Tashova that if she follows their instructions then we shoot her. We are prepared to die, and if we shoot her then the plane will surely crash. There are many passengers on board. We call this flight the "Kingfisher" that is our name for it. There will be no more broadcasts from the aircraft until we are beyond the borders of the Soviet Union and her Socialist allies.' Short and staccato sentences, but the whole spoken slowly,

91

mindful of radio operators bowing over their sets in many countries, ensuring the message was clear – understood.

The Mig immediately ahead abruptly surged clear of their path, climbing beyond David's vision, and the wing-tip escort banked away.

'They are not finished,' Anna Tashova said, 'they manoeuvre to shoot at us.'

The screaming in the cabin behind David and Isaac had not lasted for many seconds, stifled by the very helplessness the passengers felt. What was the point of pleading when there was no-one to answer? The girl was far back, at the rear of the plane, and no-one dared turn to see her. The man, the short one, the one who had addressed them, hovered half in and half out of the cockpit. The other man had long gone from view and was busying himself with the direction of the aircraft. Those at the windows had the best view of the gleaming Migs, and saw from the gestures of the pilots that this was a time of crisis.

Luigi Franconi had won the courage to ignore the instruction that his hands should be on his head. They covered his eyes as he crouched low in the seat, shutting out the fantasy nightmare of the killing machines that cruised so calmly, and that displayed with such ostentation their rockets. He knew what they were for, and saw also the determination in the young man's face, the one who covered them with the gun, always watching with the gun, always ready, as if some ludicrous intervention were possible. A test of wills, that was what was involved, and though the young man might at some time submit this was not the hour; the mere presence of the fighters was insufficient. That was the reasoning of the Italian, was why he buried his head from it, and thought of his wife and his children and the flat on Via Aurelia. At home, he reflected, the government did not fill the cells of the Regina Caeli with the terrorists they held at Fiumicino; they shipped them out by military aircraft, unmindful of whether there was a decent lapse of time between arrest and release, but concerning themselves with the safety of the Alitalia fleet, and the avoidance of reprisals; the Western world called them cowards for it. Franconi could only surmise as he peeped between the clenched fingers across his scalp that the Russian approach would be different, and that his life was as irrelevant as the safety of a wooden chess figure – a humble pawn – to the generals and senior politicians who would make their decisions in deep-set operations rooms and bright office suites.

Edward R. Jones Jr and Felicity Ann understood their future less dramatically. She too had removed her hands from her thinly waved hair and they operated the couple's Agfamatic 3000, the camera that they took on all their travels and which aided him in his notes for the lecture tours of the Mid-west that followed the summer journeys. His own hands still embedded in his winter-white hair, he called the stop changes to his wife as she alternated between interiors and film of the fighters through the porthole. A fortune to be made, and what an auction! Associated Press against United Press International for the world exclusive rights. His optimism about the immediate outcome was not based on any specialized knowledge of Russian thinking, rather on a lack of it. American and conditioned to reading that the pilots of his own country had orders to fall in with hi jackers' demands, he could not conceive that the interceptors had any rôle other than one of bluff.

The schoolchildren whose ages spanned their eleventh and twelfth birthdays had lived too sheltered an upbringing to realize the dangers to which their young lives were now exposed. Most rigidly obeyed the instruction to keep their arms raised, only a few grumbling to those who sat beside them at the discomfiture. No question, the headmaster thought, of querying the order, not with the girl and the two men so preoccupied. Necessary to maintain calm among these people, and any interruption, however trivial, however well-founded, would only lead to anger, only harm the position of the children. He kept silent.

Twenty-five others. Some praying through closed eyes and clenched hands, some stolid and defiant and gazing straight ahead, some fascinated by what they saw beyond the reinforced windows, some crying quietly. Even the baby, half-way back, snuggled in a mother's shawl, sat hushed.

Wandering with his eyes, restless, Isaac fastened on the two stewardesses, sitting together, holding hands, watching him, following his movements. The pretty one in the centre seat, with the red hair, smoothed her skirt down her thighs. Isaac winked at her, just a flash, and saw her blush and twist her head away. All of them sitting there, inanimate, straining away the minutes.

Would the jets open fire? Quite a way to go if they do, thought Isaac.

From Moscow the orders were transmitted to Air Force Headquarters, West Ukraine, and from there relayed to the major who commanded the Mig pilots. He led the formation, four planes in line, separated by a half mile, across the path of the Ilyushin, spitting long bursts of cannon fire 200 yards in front of the airliner. For pilots as highly trained as these it was a simple manoeuvre. Climbing again and leaning back across the space of his cramped cockpit he radioed that there was no apparent deviation of the Ilyushin. Once more, he was told, he should fire across the nose, again with the cannon, but closer. If that were not successful he should return to station and await further instructions.

Inside the cockpit and the passenger cabin, hemmed in by the hermetically-sealed fuselage, the noise of the cannon fire was considerable. Isaac had joined David in the cockpit and they stood together, huddled in the limited space as they watched the contortions of the fighter planes. Dive, level off, pull out. Vicious hammering of fire from the wings – so close that it made them draw back and wince, instinctive and involuntary, seeking safety from the threat. The slipstream of the jets jolted and rumbled the Ilyushin, and both men clung to the back of Anna Tashova's seat.

And then they were gone, and the airliner was still on course, and it was as if there had been nothing, except that David's knuckles were white as he held himself upright and his face was drawn and old beyond his years, and Isaac saw that there were tears in the pilot officer's eyes that she fought to suppress. She thought they were going to kill us, herself as well, and all of her passengers, that was what she would have preferred, that was the depth of her hate for us.

The navigator in his seat behind them broke the silence. A forgotten man, who had stayed quiet and unobtrusive since they had swarmed into the cockpit, contenting himself with plotting their course, identifying their position on his maps. 'We have perhaps half a minute to turn. The next time it will be the missiles. They know they cannot damage us, sufficiently to force us to land, but so that we can land successfully. If they damage us we crash, and so they will make it fast for us, they will destroy us in the air. The pilot who tried to land the Libyan plane that the Israelis fired on, the Frenchman, he tried and he failed. A passenger liner cannot withstand any damage, not at this altitude.'

'We fly on,' said David. 'The Kingfisher bird is on course. They will not come again.'

'Are you blind to it, you crazed fool? Can you not see the signs with your own eyes? That was the warning, the final warning. The next time it is over.' Anna Tashova's words lapped around David, rippling and eddying at him, but without the conviction to strike him, leaving him unmoved. Isaac put his arm around the taller man's waist and hugged and pulled their two bodies together. 'I did not know it would be like that,' David said. 'I had no idea . . .'

'But you found the strength to fight them,' encouraged Isaac.

'Never again, not like that . . . never again,' David whispered, and he trembled, his whole frame consumed by the convulsions as Isaac held him. And he no longer stared out through the small cockpit windows, but was again magnetized by the captain's slowly moving head, its inverted pendulum motion.

'He still fights me . . .'

'Don't be so stupid. You weren't to know. It was only one bullet. You weren't to know.'

'He still fights me . . .'

'Keep the bloody plane on course,' said Isaac wearily.

Radio chatter amongst the Migs.

'Eagle 4 to Sunray. What do they want us to do now?'

'Eagle 3 to Sunray. We cross the Polish border in under a minute.'

'Eagle 2 to Sunray. Do we shoot to bring them down or not?'

'Sunray to Eagle Flight. You hear the orders as I do. The order is to wait – they are checking something out. Maintain course.'

'Eagle 4 to Sunray. What is there to check out?'

'Eagle 3 to Sunray. Did you see the children at the windows? Quite clearly you can see them.'

'Eagle 2 to Sunray. There is the man in the cockpit. I saw him . . . with the gun.'

'Sunray to Eagle Flight. Stop the bloody talking. I know where we are, so does Ground. I have eyes too – I have seen the children – I have seen the man. They will be checking the passenger list. They want to know who is on board.'

'Eagle 4 to Sunray. If there is no-one important we shoot – is that why they want to know who is on board?'

'Sunray to Eagle 4. Keep the airwaves clear. Keep your opinions to yourself. Observe the order.'

The Migs overflew Polish airspace for two minutes then peeled away.

Three years previously a hi-jacked aircraft had mysteriously disappeared from the radar screens of Western military forces stationed in Germany, and was presumed to have been shot down. That Aeroflot Flight 927 was permitted to continue its progress was determined by the composition of the passenger manifest. The matter of the children on their way to the ballet festival at Tashkent did not sway the issue, nor did the question of the survival of the Russian adult passengers and the Russian crew count in any degree toward the final decision. It was the knowledge that among the passengers was the delegation of the

Italian Communist Party, senior men all of them and belonging to a Party with whom the Soviet Union was trying to heal ideological rifts. Luigi Franconi and his comrades ensured the safety of all on board. If the only foreigners to have taken the Tashkent flight had been Edward R. Jones Jr and Felicity Ann then the Ilyushin would have been a mess of wreckage, burning and disintegrated, scattered over a half mile square, scorching the summer stubble of a collective field. Perhaps the Italians would have been flattered had they known their lives were held in such esteem, but their ignorance was total, as was that of David and Isaac. Both stood in the cockpit above Anna Tashova as the plane powered on, content in the belief that their determination, their power had won them a great victory, that their greatest test was behind them.

The defining of the problem and the taking of the decision not to shoot down the Ilyushin had involved two of the Soviet Union's most senior officials in a bitter and protracted argument fought out over the telephone lines between their respective ministry buildings. Defence was for the strong arm of physical prevention of the aircraft leaving Russian air-space. Foreign Affairs held out a calmer option, and pledged a massive diplomatic campaign by telephone 'hot-line' and teleprinter to persuade all governments in whose territory a landing might be attempted to offer the terrorists neither refuge nor succour for their onward journey to Israel. From the moment that David had broadcast over the aircraft radio that the group was Jewish he had played into the hands of those who saw, with sharp clarity because they had only bare minutes in which to reach their conclusion, that a great diplomatic coup was offered for the taking should the three be returned to Russia to face trial. The discussion had ultimately been three-pronged – Defence, Foreign Affairs, and the omnipotent Secretary General of the Party who would ultimately influence events – and the argument of the Foreign Minister had been the most persuasive to the ears of the ruler of the country.

'If we destroy the plane in the air we have achieved the aim of the Jewish terrorists. We will highlight what they call their "cause". The whole world will talk of our brutality. We will make these three into martyrs and none will remember the crimes from which they are fleeing. Problems from Italy, problems from the PCI. All this can be avoided. It is the suggestion of this ministry that we let them fly to the West and that we precede their landing by messages to the heads of government in all the countries in which they might come to rest that we expect these people to be disarmed immediately and returned to face the charges that can be brought against them.'

There was more that he could have said but insufficient time. The Migs were in the air, pilots' hands close to the shooting triggers that would release the cones of cannon fire and the projectiles that would seek out the heat of the Ivchenko engine exhausts. The airspace was being eroded as they talked.

'And among the passengers, who do we have?' The Secretary General, seeking time before his decision.

'We have children. We have the delegation of comrades from Italy, from the Central Administration of the Party, and the effect there could be catastrophic. Also to be considered is the fact that they have broadcast from the plane. In the West it is now known what has happened. The incident is no longer confined inside our own frontiers.'

'We are all agreed that the plane could only be brought down over our own territory. You have very few seconds to make up your minds.' The final intervention of the Defence Minister, certain by this stage that he had lost the day, certain too that the time of the hard men who had mobilized the great wartime defence of the country, whatever the cost, was now a thing of the past.

'Let the plane fly on.' The order of the Secretary General. 'And the message that goes to the Foreign Governments, I will want it read to me before it is released. It will bear my name.'

Three o'clock and a London afternoon. Charlie Webster at his desk and with precious short of nothing with which to entertain himself. Usually like that after lunch; worked fast enough in the morning to clear his desk, didn't space it out like the others who seemed to have something to get round to, to keep them busy, all eight hours that God gave for working. Too hot, and the bloody air-conditioner still up the spout. Typical, really: put them all in a damn great tower block with all that glass to soak up the sun, and not a window that could be opened in the whole place. Must be some sort of breeze flying about this high up, if only the window could be opened and we could tempt the little blighter in.

Trouble is, Charlie, you're not really an inside man. Never were and never will be. Not the temperament, not the patience, not any of the things to believe shuffling paper is worthwhile. Wrap it, Charlie, becoming a grumpy old goat. Stop worrying about yourself, worrying about what happens to old soldiers too ancient for anything useful and too young to fade away.

He'd changed from the Cyprus boy and the Aden boy, when he hadn't cared, when he was with military intelligence, not thirty, not married, and not a doubt to trouble him. Ireland was the undoing, the greyed, opaque fight, the tedium of procedure and rule books. The danger, too. Something he hadn't thought of before, hadn't concerned himself with.

Not worth getting your arse shot off, Charlie, he'd told himself. Not worth getting blasted into the gutter in Monaghan or Clones or Ballyshannon. Not worth bumping across the churchyard with the Union Jack to keep the sun off the box and eight blanks to give the rooks a fright. And so he had said that he would like to come inside, and everyone had seemed very pleased, and said he'd be a big asset to the team. He'd told them he didn't want anything connected with his previous work, wanted a change, and pointed to his Russian course qualifications, taken years ago on national service before he'd decided to go for Regular. So out of military intelligence he'd popped, demobbed, bought a grey suit – nothing special and off the peg, and they sent him over to SIS, Soviet Desk. Probably bloody glad to see the back of you, Charlie.

One of the chaps from sub-Desk Military coming in without

knocking. Didn't do that normally, observed protocol. A flimsy in his hand and couldn't keep it to himself, not till he reached Charlie's desk.

'There's a hi-jack, Charlie. Over Russia. All hell broken out, fighters up and everything.'

Day-dreams gone. Feeling-sorry-for-self time over. All attention. Charlie said, 'Out of Kiev, is it?'

'How do you know? How did you know that?' Looking blank, stopped in his tracks, puzzled.

'You mean it really is?' said Charlie. 'Really Kiev? Just a guess and something we were talking about yesterday. Let's have a look.'

Eight teletype lines, and telling him all he needed to know. Aeroflot internal, pilot dead, Jewish group, broadcast from the aircraft, unsuccessful attempt by Air Force to turn it round, shots across the nose, now over Poland, still escorted at a distance. Too good to be true, thought Charlie. They'll have me down as fortune-teller at the next Christmas binge.

'Any more?'

'Well, that's not bad for starters. There's something coming through. The Russians are putting out a long screed. In essence it demands that the plane and the passengers and the hi-jackers be returned to them forthwith after landing. It's pretty hard stuff. They're saying it was only for humanitarian reasons and in the interest of the passengers that they didn't shoot the aircraft down. But they want them back. Say they're gangsters and attempted to murder a policeman.'

Bloody amazing, Charlie. 'Boobed it though, haven't they?' he said. 'Shouldn't have dropped the pilot. That's not the way to earn a nice jolly welcome, not when there's blood sloshing round the joystick. Someone's going to have a packet of trouble when that little bird . . .'

'Fuel isn't its problem. It's a long-range Ilyushin II-18, and well tanked. It was on a run to Tashkent, and was lifted straight after take-off. There's enough juice to go anywhere in Europe, including here. They've all of Europe to choose from. Anywhere they want, except Israel – that's off-limits to this plane, out of fuel range. But they can take their pick round these parts.'

'All the makings of a very cheery scene.' Charlie thanked him, and sat alone in his office. It was a bit confusing when he started to think about it. Terrorist hi-jack or freedom fighters' break-out. Square pegs in round holes. What did you greet them with at the airport – a bouquet and a speech of welcome, or a Saracen and a pair of handcuffs? Been rabbiting on long enough, hadn't they, our political masters, about the state of Soviet Jewry, so what were they going to do with this one? Only one thing to do, he thought. Pray God it doesn't come here.

6

While the big Ilyushin purred its way across the airspace of
Poland and the German Democratic Republic – with its
now more discreet escort of Migs, scrambled from more forward Warsaw Pact airfields – frantic meetings were being
convened throughout Western Europe.

All the continent's countries can now call on the services of
'crisis committees' of politicians, civil servants and senior police
and army officers who are on call to advise the heads of government on what course they should take if confronted with a major
guerrilla action. It is the task of these committees to evaluate the
threat and the implications of involvement with the new breed
of warfare that since the start of the decade had proved so costly
in terms of money and prestige to the old world. The lesson of
preparation had been learned the hard way, with cabinets ill-
briefed and security forces poorly trained to do battle with the
new militia playing by their own rules of warfare who descend
in their capitals and airports with the AK47s and RPGs and
who spread mayhem and disgrace and disfigurement with minimal discrimination.

Meetings in Bonn, in Copenhagen, and Stockholm and Oslo
and Helsinki. Ministers and officials hurrying to their chauffeur-driven cars in Brussels, Paris and The Hague. Policemen
being called by telephone to the Cabinet offices in Madrid and
Rome and Lisbon and Berne. In all these capitals, as in London,
it was recognized that speed was of the essence, that a policy
must be formulated and agreed before the Ilyushin attempted
its inevitable landing. Dominating the discussions was the Russian note, now being studied in a dozen languages, none of

which could blunt the harsh message that it had been the intention of the Secretary General of the Russian Communist Party to convey. They have something in common, the politicians of Europe who are answerable to an electorate; the constant factor is the determination not to lay their backs open to the rod that can strike and wound them. To permit the plane to land when it had fuel to fly on, that was only begging for difficulties, for diplomatic furore and dangers in the high echelons of international relations. Those countries most keenly affected, in that their airports lay within easy striking range of the present flight-path of the Aeroflot airliner, had the least discussion time available to their committees, and reached their decision first.

In Bonn the advice to the Chancellor was without equivocation. Under no circumstances should the aircraft be allowed to land. Any airport that the Ilyushin approached should immediately be closed; if necessary, trucks should be driven across the runways to prevent their being used. A drastic solution, it was agreed by all who took part in the evaluation, but then so were the alternatives horrifying. Let the plane land and offer yourselves to the whim and hazard of a full-blown hi-jack siege; there could be no question of allowing the airliner to refuel and fly on in the face of the Russian demands, and no possibility with the pilot still warm in his seat of offering safe conduct. Far better to skirt the issue, and pass the problem outside the Federal frontiers. The embassies of West Germany were instructed to pass on the government decision to other interested parties. Including the Soviet Union.

It was Isaac who stayed close to the navigator watching the pencil lines that he drew across the green heavily overscored map surface on the small pull-out table that acted as his workbench. Slow and painstaking, the plotting of the course. A few more minutes and they would have crossed the dark and shaded line that marked the barricade between the cultures of East and West. Just a line on a map at that height, and hazed squares of toned brown and yellow beneath them. Nothing to demonstrate the wire, and the mines and the watchtowers, and the fear and the clinging helplessness that the frontier meant 27,000 feet beneath. Soon the descent would start, and the ground shades would sharpen, and then it would be over, and they would have achieved the impossible. Escape, something that could not have been contemplated two short days before. And now it was achieved, bar a few miles, a few minutes' flying time.

'We are nearly there,' he called softly to David. Why is the man still so tense, why is it necessary to hold the gun so close to the girl? The Migs have gone, been defeated, seen off. 'It is over now, friend. We have beaten the pigs, hammered them, destroyed them. Relax, David.' Still the stress etched across David's face, still the suspicion there, nothing to show that he was convinced of their victory. Impatience now from Isaac, 'Can't you see, David, we are there?' He pulled the map from the navigator's table and thrust it under David's face. 'It's over, we are there. What was it you called it? The Kingfisher flight? The Kingfisher flight is over. The breakout of the Kingfisher, and we have done it.'

David did not speak to him, but said quietly with strain eating at his voice to the pilot officer, 'Which airport should we land at?'

Disinterest on her face, not her concern, she jerked her head back in the direction of the navigator. 'You should ask him. He is the one who will tell you that.'

'Which airport do we go to?' David asked his question of the navigator, and the man in the blue uniform with twin rings of gold braid on his wrists waved away the question. 'I am talking to the ground. They have contacted us. They say they have a message for us and are awaiting the responsible person who will read it. The nearest airport should be Hanover, that is the civil airport, also in that area are many of the military bases of the NATO forces of the British . . . It's unlikely they would permit us to use an Air Force camp. There are many options that are open if they give us permission to land. But you must be quiet, because I do not have much English and that is the language they will use to me – the pilot officer has very little, insufficient to talk to the controllers. The man that you killed was the one who spoke English.'

'How far are we from the border?'

A momentary calculation by the navigator, a deviation from his main task of awaiting the message from the ground, pencil and ruler on the map. 'We are there.'

Isaac turned away from the cockpit, walked past the forward exit door and the lavatories and the cupboard space for the winter coats, came to the entrance of the passenger cabin, machine gun still at the ready, held low across his thighs. Looked at the faces, saw only the drained and exhausted stares that faltered back at him. He realized the ordeal to which they had subjected this passive, muted collection of strangers – only one thing in common, all of them, that they wanted to sleep tonight in Tashkent. Time to relieve their misery, and time too, to demonstrate the power of three young Jews, and what faith could win.

'Ladies and gentlemen, I have news for you that I hope will prove welcome. We are now crossing the frontier between the two Germanys. We are awaiting the instructions of the government of the BDR as to which airport they wish us to use for a landing. You should be aware of our descent very soon. It has not been our intention to cause you any hurt, but you must stay in your seats and observe our orders. That is all.' And as an afterthought – and he laughed like a child when he said it – 'Perhaps some of you would care to leave the plane with us?' His humour was met by the sad, tired eyes that offered no flicker of response. Separated from him by the full length of the cabin, half-hidden by the drinks trolley that was her protection from the rear passengers, Rebecca, flagging in her strength and leaning on the trolley top for relief and showing the pistol; he smiled to her, saw her return the greeting. Funny girl, he thought, but she'd done them well. There hadn't been the time, not the opportunity to talk to her of Yevsei. The little bugger must have been on a hope and prayer to have put the guns aboard, but he couldn't have made it with her, could he? Not if David wasn't getting it . . . No chance for Yevsei. If she wasn't round David so much, then there could have been the opportunity, roll of drums for Isaac. David just didn't understand – too busy with his war games to see what was there on a plate. But she couldn't have kept her legs crossed all night, must have let old Yevsei get his hand in somewhere – stands to reason, if he was going to take a risk like that. Take a girl to persuade a man to put guns on Aeroflot, only a girl . . .

David was tugging at his shoulder, pulling at him, wrenching him backwards and off balance as he was swung towards the cockpit. 'Shut up, you fool. Shut up and come in here.' A moment to see the relief sucked from the faces of those passengers closest to him, and David had dragged him too deep for them to follow his whispered words. 'The Germans say we cannot land. They forbid us to use their airfields.'

'It's a bluff . . . like the Migs.' Even as Isaac spoke the cold sweat that comes from chronic uncertainty, comes when the mast is broken, when the ladder slips, was spearing its way across his stomach, into his groin, an awful chill. 'They don't mean it . . .'

'How do you know they don't mean it? They say they will prevent us from landing.'

'Perhaps it's just an airport official, someone who had not been notified about us. Do they know who we are? Do they know we are Jews?'

'They know everything about us. They know we are Jews. They know our names. They know we have passengers on board. They say that they know we have fuel, and they say we must fly on.'

'Which is the nearest airport to our present position?' Isaac snapped at the navigator, seeking to regain the initiative.

'Still Hanover.'

'Tell them that we are going to Hanover. Tell them we are going to land at Hanover.' Isaac was shouting; they were coming to the West, they were coming to freedom, they were coming to the democracies. 'Tell them that, and hold the course for Hanover.'

'Only one person that can give orders in the cockpit, Isaac, and that is me.' David, animated, creased in anger.

'Well, give some orders then. Take the plane down to Hanover.'

'Take the plane to Hanover,' David told Anna Tashova. The transfusion of energy from his fury was short-lived, and he seemed to crumple again, the belief in the outcome slipping. The girl's hands moved to the instruments to make the changes and deviations that were called for by the navigator. Checking altitude, checking airspeed, asking him to seek a talk-down into the airspace, and with her face set tight as she shrugged and said they would give no co-operation, that they could only repeat the message already passed to the airliner, that they were sorry.

'How long?' David asked the navigator.

'Ten minutes and we will see the airfield. I will tell them again that we are coming. But you should know that they were very definite. They said they would prevent us from landing.'

Because he was a big man and sat high in his seat Edward R. Jones Jr had seen David pull Isaac back towards the entrance to the cockpit. All the passengers, adult and children, were susceptible to the changes of mood in their captors, studied and analyzed them, because they had little else to do, and because these were the only clues they possessed as to the future of the flight. Every smile, every furrowed forehead was noticed and evaluated as the passengers sought for information. It was as if the act were mimed, because the voices of David and Isaac were far removed, and were lowered, and the yowling of that bloody baby obliterated any possibility for even the keenest ears to eavesdrop. But Edward R. Jones Jr was not totally disappointed by his inability to hear the words that were spoken; his eyes had not betrayed him. They reported a new mood, a new urgency, a new tension at the front of the aircraft. He and his wife were seated at the back of the plane, among the last rows of the cabin, while the mass had herded towards the front because they had not read, as the American had, that the only possibility of survival in an air disaster is to be sitting in the rear. He and Felicity Ann always sat at the back, and it was that which put him in easy conversational range of Rebecca, as she stood with the gun still unfamiliar in her hand watching her charges and as ill-informed about what was happening in the cockpit as they were.

'Miss,' he said, hands still on his head, 'Miss, do you speak English?'

'You have heard the orders, it is forbidden to speak.' Clipped, hostile, shunning the contact; but an answer in the language that he sought.

'Forget that crap, Miss, if you'll excuse me. The question was, "do you speak English?" and the answer was that you do.'

'It is not permitted for you to talk.' Halting and styled by school classrooms, but she could understand what he said, and reply in a fashion.

'It strikes me, Miss, and I'm only a passenger here, but it strikes me your friends up the front have a problem. You get that impression?' She ignored him, wondered what else she could do. Couldn't hit him, not without coming from behind her barricade, and she couldn't call David or Isaac because they were at the cockpit, and she had seen what the American had, and the two men had looked anxious. 'Perhaps the problem is, Miss, that no-one is that keen to have you. Thought of that one, have you? That there won't be a red carpet down there waiting for you.'

'We are Jews, we are persecuted. We are fleeing from a system of intolerance, and so we go to Israel. In the West they are the enemy of the Soviets – you tell me they will not help us?'

Edward R. Jones Jr turned full towards her, eye to eye, face to face. Quite a pretty girl really, if she did something about her hair, bit of make-up, little eye shadow – not a beauty but presentable, dreadful frock, but they all wore things like that over here.

'Have you thought, Miss, that it could all be a bit harder than that, that people this side of the line might not be quite as cosy, quite as friendly as you thought they would?' A rhythm in his voice, monotonous like the drip of a tap that needs a new washer, hypnotizing in its way, and dulling and wasting. 'When the Palestinians fly the planes into Arab countries they get locked up now, you know. No more garlands and a big villa to lie around till the heat cools. They shove them in the cells. Times move on, Miss.'

'We are not Palestinians, we are not terrorists. We are Jews and we have been oppressed, we have been persecuted, and now we have fought back . . .' She too had now raised her voice, the last of the group to do so, but responding in her own way to a strain that was becoming intolerable, crippled all the time by the isolation of her position, divorced from the others, wanting comfort, reassurance.

'They all say that, Miss. All reckon that their God is on their side, that he looks with a friendly eye on their cause. You're not the first to join this merry-go-round, Miss; there are plenty before you. Proper all-sorts they are – Weathermen, Puerto Ricans, Tupamaros, Zeepa, Provos, Baader-Meinhof, ETA 5, PFLP. They're all in your line of business. And one problem they all face – they need somewhere to go, somewhere to sleep, somewhere where they aren't going to be hunted. Rest houses are short on the ground, Miss. If you can't put this bird down in Tel Aviv you're lost, you'll be like all the other lepers and pariahs. No-one will want you . . .'

'We are going to land, Isaac told you so. Isaac told you we were going to land. And the plane is now descending.'

Close to shrieking, and the words carrying the length of the cabin, enough to rouse Isaac from far away so that he ran the distance of the aisle, and when she pointed to Edward R. Jones Jr she could not speak because the tears choked in her throat. He seemed to dare the boy, to taunt and anger him in the very defiance of his steadied, aged eyes. Not even the hands raised in self-defence across his face, nor his body turned away that a blow might be warded off. Isaac swung the barrel of his gun in a short, chopping arc on to the apex of the American's skull, one blow to submerge it under the protection of Felicity Ann's arms, and there was blood on her dress and the sound of the distress of an old man for protest.

'Rebecca, it will be over very soon. We are nearly there. We are losing height. Courage for a few more moments. Courage.'

Isaac's was the only voice in the great hushed cigar of the cabin. But he had not told her of the message from the ground, had not thought to. Flaps moving and arresting the progress of the plane, causing it to yaw from side to side, thrust sound changed to a higher pitch, and the rumbling of the extraction of the undercarriage.

The movement of the plane made it difficult for David to stand in the cockpit, but there was nowhere else for him to go. The pilot officer in her seat, the navigator in his, and only the captain's place with the strapped-down body available to him. Couldn't bring himself to touch the man, different if they'd meant to kill him, if he had been an enemy and his death had been reached by decision. But it was just an accident, an empty and hollow accident to a man whose status represented no threat to them. Not like killing the policeman. And so the captain reserved his seat, his head rolling with the motion of the aircraft and the blood trail congealed and darkened.

'We are talking again with the tower at Hanover. They repeat that we are not permitted to land there. They call it a blanket order for the whole of the Federal Republic. They are emphatic that we will not be permitted to land there.' The navigator seemingly calm, unaffected by the bow-string tension around him, and repeated his messages as if uncaring as to who heard them, all the time interrupting his recital of instructions from the ground with the minutiae of course adjustments that the pilot officer required of him.

'Another few seconds and we will be through the haze, then we will see the runway, then we will see if they mean to stop us, or whether as your friend says it is just a bluff.' Five years' flying she had had, three more before that at the training school, sufficient experience solo for her to be able to handle the Ilyushin on her own. Too senior really for her to be flying co-pilot, especially a creature like this, but the rosters were not logically drawn and did not always recognize her logbook of flying hours. They taught you how to pilot an aircraft, and gave you lectures on emergencies – but those were concerning the technical problems that might be faced – fire in an engine, undercarriage that would not retract, fracture of pressurization, loss of flap control. They did not know how you would react if there was a sub-machine gun at your ribs with a thirty-round magazine attached, and a class of schoolchildren that you must bring to safety. No way they could know that when they gave you command of an aircraft. Lectures and courses, but this . . .

'There is the runway,' she snapped, peering high over the bottom lip of her windscreen at the dun-coloured strip of concrete thousands of feet beneath her. The city was laid out like a toy town further away. Neat gardens, high chimneys of the factories, rising office blocks. But closer – and this held her attention – the shape of the airfield, runway placed straight ahead for her by the skill of the navigator.

'There are trucks across it. See them? Petrol lorries, armoured cars, suicide, suicide if we go down there.' Without the order from David that had preceded her every previous move she had pulled on the instrument column, and was scrambling to complete the job she would have shared with her captain, to reset the mass of dials and switches that were necessary if the plane were to climb again. David had seen it all, seen it as she had. And he too recognized the impossibility of a successful landing. Every three hundred metres the variation between the yellow and white petrol tankers and the green and olive armoured cars, clear and silhouetted against the background of the tarmac.

'Do not answer any calls for us from the ground, and circle the airport, low enough so that they can see us.' David moved out of the cockpit, the first time that he had left it in more than two hours, stepping into the corridor, the passageway between the flight deck and the passenger cabin. He reached forward to pull the curtain across that the watchers might not observe him as he spoke to Isaac. He spoke in a quiet and sombre voice, and with a resignation about him that unnerved Isaac, and with his shoulders seemingly shrunken by the enormity of the problem. 'What do we do now? In God's name, Isaac, what do we do now?'

'We can tell them we are coming in to land, and see what . . .'

'And if they do not move the trucks, and if we are committed to landing, and cannot climb again – then we are dead.'

'Perhaps it is because they know we have fuel.'

'And how many countries will follow the lead of the Germans?'

'If we crash the plane that is by our hand. They know the fuel that we have, they know when we can go no further. It will not be at our hand, David.' Isaac spoke feverishly, searching to build again the momentum that had taken them to the flight. 'When the fuel is expended what government will refuse us permission to land when they know we have children on our flight? This is not the crisis, not yet. Time for "Masada", the time for suicide is later. When we have landed, then it will be different.' Again Isaac had his arm round him, the gesture of friendship and support. 'David, you are down, and that is how they would wish you. They want us to dispute with each other, they want your depression because that helps them. We always knew it would not be easy, that it would not be simple. There are other countries that we can reach, many others. Not all are like the Germans. We too have friends, David.'

'Less than two hours now, that is the fuel position. After that it will be settled for us.'

As he went back into the cockpit David wondered at the new turn in their fortunes. He realized that he was bemused they should meet with opposition at this time, and after they had won so much. Like a betrayal, like a boy feels when he knows his father has told him a lie. He had not known that Isaac possessed such inner reservoirs of stamina; they would come to lean on him, both of them, Rebecca as much as himself. He felt such a great tiredness now, just a longing to be shed of it, to walk again on the ground, to escape this box of confusions that he did not understand. The joy of walking again on grass, and of not running, and of not listening at night for the footsteps that might follow.

He repeated it over in his own mind. Lean on Isaac, lean on him till his own strength returned. Could any of them understand the awful wearying, endless conflict in the cockpit? The pilot dead, the shape that would not respond, would not forgive. The fighters, modern, technological killing soldiers that he had stood his ground against and beaten. The cool proficiency of the girl pilot. He had stood against them, stood against them and seen them off. But it had sapped and weakened him and now he should rest on Isaac, let the boy carry the load till he was ready again. And the boy was good, better than you expected, David, and there was comfort there. The only comfort he had.

'Give me a course for Holland,' David said. Again the Ilyushin banked and began to turn, roused by the new thrust of power, searching once more for the Kingfisher's landfall.

The airport at Hanover is categorized as 'international', but the trade that it handles is not considerable, and certainly minor in comparison with Frankfurt or Munich or Cologne-Bonn. So the groups of delayed passengers and crew and idle airport staff were sparsely scattered on the concrete terminal roof. Clusters of multinational businessmen, a party of British war veterans who had come again to relive the triumph and the misery of 1945, some Scandinavians in search of fresh hiking pastures, mingled amongst the Lufthansa men and girls.

All could see the Ilyushin, alone in the azure, late afternoon sky. They watched its flight around the far perimeter of the airfield, occasionally stealing their glance away to the rock-steady armoured cars and trucks that were the runway obstructions. A transistor radio chattered a report from a local broadcaster who described the scene and could tell of no more than their own eyes could take in. It was the only sound to compete with the lowpitched, incessant drone of the engines set far forward on the wings from which the Aeroflot flight's markings could be read by those with clear eyesight.

And the watchers realized that the plane would not come, that the confrontation was not sought. They saw the new course set, and watched the diminishing silhouette and were left with a feeling of emptiness and inadequacy, because they were part of something that would not be completed. Only when the plane was telescoped to their vision, small and hard to see, and its engine noise was faint, did a new sound spring forward, powerful and dominating, as the armoured cars and tankers revved their engines and started to move clear of the tarmac.

There was a woman from Stockholm who cried, and said again and again, 'I don't know why. I don't know why.' And her husband was embarrassed and gave her his handkerchief and tried to shield her from view as she dabbed her eyes.

The tolerance of the men with dark suits and attaché cases and schedules to maintain was waning. There was much checking of watches and loud discussion on how long it would take to get things moving again, to fly them on to their homes or belated meetings.

The ground staff were first to leave the roof, beckoned by the work and organization that now awaited them, the businessmen hard on their heels, the hikers needing to make up lost time if they were to reach their chalets by nightfall.

The old army men stayed on. They'd no hurry; it was known where they were, and they were confident of being called when their flight was ready. Men in their sixties and seventies, at the fade of their lives, who for a week had recalled 'machine-gun platoon', and 'mortar platoon', and 'Monty', and 'knocking the Hun for six'. A great deal of wine and beer and sausage and reminiscence they'd been through in the last few days, and they did not seek to end it by returning more quickly than necessary to the polished cleanliness of the departure hall.

'Should have come on in, shouldn't they?' Cyril from mechanized infantry.

'Then there'd have been the risk of pranging her.' Bertie, HQ Staff.

'If you're to win in that sort of game you have to take a few chances, like it was when we crossed . . .' Jim, Pioneer Assault.

'They won't have come this far if they haven't taken some risks. You don't knock an aircraft off and get this far without chancing your arm a bit. I wouldn't fancy doing what they've done.' Herbie, Armoured Corps Maintenance.

'Cyril's right, though. Whatever they've done up to now, they chickened this time. Should have come on in, like Cyril said. The Hun always buckles. Pressure him enough and he buckles.' Dave, General Staff, Batman.

'What do you bloody know about it, Dave? You were so far back, they never even bothered to give you a rifle. Never even saw a bloody Hun with a gun in his hand, you didn't.' Harry, Airborne machine-gunner.

And they all laughed, and Dave looked pained, and they slapped his back. 'Time for another beer,' someone said.

Harry Smith had been a sergeant when they'd all been in uniform a lifetime ago. Para too, and they admired that. Gave him a sort of leadership over the rest, that and his Military Medal, and the fact that he now had a sweet shop in Kilburn and was 'self-employed'. 'I heard a bit of what the chappie said on the radio, picked up a bit of the language when I was here. They're Jewish boys up here. I don't know whether that makes it all different. But it's not for us to call them cowards. We had a bloody great back-up scene behind us. Stores, supplies and orders, some other bugger to tell us what to do. So what have they got? Sweet Fanny Adams, not much else. If they're Jewish they'll have thought it was all over by the time they reached here. Thought they were home and dry. Think of it as they'll be seeing it now, think of it and you'll know why that bird over there was crying.'

'They're still bloody terrorists, Sarge,' said Dave.

'If you say so,' said Harry Smith. He stared hard into the lowering light, searching through his spectacles for the aircraft.

But the haze and mist of distance had wrapped around the Kingfisher flight, lifting it beyond his reach.

Had David but known it, the West German 'Crisis Committee' had anticipated that an attempt might be made to land the plane in spite of the precautions taken. The petrol tankers and the armoured cars all had members of the green-uniformed *Bundesgrenzshutz* at their controls. If the word had come from the tower that the Aeroflot plane was on irreversible landing approach then the order would have been transmitted to the cabs of the vehicles that they should drive onto the grass verges of the runway and allow the aircraft to land without further hindrance. In the first-floor offices of the Federal Ministry of the Interior in Bonn there was much congratulation and back-slapping among the team of politicians and civil servants who had directed the operation as the news was brought to them that the plane was climbing, and had taken a flight plan that ran to the south of Hamburg and to the north of Bonn, Cologne and Düsseldorf. A bottle of Scotch was broached. It was the opinion of the aviation experts that the course was for Schiphol, Amsterdam.

'I had not thought,' said the Minister, 'that we would accomplish the plan so easily.'

'It was a new tactic for these people. Their protests have been verbal before; they have not attempted anything of this intensity. But it is surprising, as you say, that they could be so easily deflected. I think we will find when the business is completed that they were very young.' It was the contribution of the senior police officer present who had been on the ground in the chaos of the Munich police ambush of Black September at Fürstenfeldbruck airbase, who had laid out the bodies of nine Israeli athletes and coaches, and who never wanted to be part of a similar confrontation again. 'But because they are young, and because we have turned them, that does not mean that the problem for someone else is in any way diminished. What we have done is temporarily to depress them. My forecast is that this setback will, in the long term, serve only to harden their resolve.'

The policeman spoke with distaste, unimpressed at the enthusiasm with which the unresolved problem had been shuffled elsewhere.

Parker Smith had left in a hurry, his departure preceded by a confusion of ringing telephones, summoned messengers with paperwork and shouting through opened office doors. He had just time to push his head round Charlie's door. He was excited, and did not care who saw it. Call from the Big Boys, from Whitehall, beckoned to the presence, to attend the Emergency Group meeting. He might send for Charlie later, and would he have his files at hand, and be ready to bring them if it was required that he should come? Charlie noticed he hadn't cared to comb his hair, a mess without the ruler-straight parting, and that was unusual for him; meant the flap was building.

'Getting a bit nervy are they, sir? Our masters?'

'Decidedly so, Charlie. You've seen the Russian note, and it's very tough. You've seen what the Hun's reaction is. Pass-the-parcel games, and it's with the Dutch next, and FO are trying to establish what position they will take. If they don't come down in Holland and they keep going then we're next in line, and not much fuel to play with. If we send for you, look snappy.'

'I'm not a counter hi-jack expert, sir. Home Office do that . . .' Caution from Charlie. Long time now since he'd been involved in anything fresher than stacking paper.

'Course you're not. But you're supposed to know these bastards, that is what we'll be requiring from you, every damned little thing about them. So don't shift off that telephone.'

Parker Smith was gone, not finding the time to close Charlie's door, lost in a welter of shouted farewells. And the word that the section was involved spread through the offices like a grass fire. Huddles in the corridors, and voices raised in anticipation, and pleasure that the 'old man' had been sent for. Charlie went to his steel-grey cabinet, fished in his pocket for the keys, discarding those of his front door, his car, his office door, his garage. He unlocked the combination fastener and began to riffle through the buff-coloured folders. Kept a good system, did Charlie, something he'd learned in his old army days. Extracted seven – two of them marked with a red sticky-tape 'X' diagonally across, denoting the classification 'Secret', five with blue-tape crosses that were simply denoted as 'Restricted'.

Time for some fast reading, Charlie.

The helicopter that carried the Israeli Prime Minister had left the Golan Heights in a swirl of choking, rasping dirt, saturating all those who had gathered at the stone-cleared landing-pad to see him off.

His tour of forward positions on the Syrian front that over-looked the ruined and war-broken city of Kuneitra had been scheduled to last for three more hours, but the radio transmission from Jerusalem had caused it to be cut short. And there was enough for him to be concerned about with the burden of new-fashioned crises; in his mind he was attempting to obliterate the problems of perpetual argument between Defence, who sought more planes and more missiles and more anti-tank weapons and more cement for fortifications, and on the other side Finance, who bleated at every Cabinet meeting at the cost of it all and the effect on civilian morale of the creeping taxation that was the corollary of sophisticated and modern fire-power. Shut it out, block it, as the helicopter staggered off the ground and hovered before seeking its route. The Prime Minister had been a military man before entering politics, and prided himself that he had spanned the gulf, that he understood both points of view, but that in itself made it no simpler for him. Three devaluations, and that inside the last nine months, and no change in the precari-ousness of the national budget, and still the army demanding more hardware and showing no interest in where the money should come from. The visit to the Golan and its strongpoints was long-planned and was supposed to have been a sweetener to his generals. He was to have walked around behind the sand-bags and the barbed wire and laugh and joke with them in the slang they had used when they were together as lieutenants and captains, and look serious and understanding when that was required of him, and sympathize with their complaints and shortages, and make promises that would be vague and that would not sustain analysis, but that would mollify and placate.

And now the effect of the day was wasted.

The summons had come from his offices on the hill in Jerusalem that he should return forthwith, and there had been no time for explanations and excuses, just the opportunity to shake the hands of men who showed their disappointment, and who had the look in their eyes of soldiers who do not trust the commitment of their political leaders.

An hour and twenty minutes he sat in the helicopter. They'd brought an Alouette in from Rosh Pinah to ferry him back, a maintenance problem, fractured oil-feed pipe, denying him the use of the faster, more comfortable Sikorski that had made the morning journey from the capital. Room for only three passengers once the army fliers had taken their seats – ADC and a bodyguard. No-one to talk to, and he'd left the majority of his party on the bare, stripped ground of the Heights, to follow on by car. There was a radio in the helicopter but that must be kept clear for operational messages, so that effectively he would be out of contact for the duration of the flight. Little enough information to consider at this stage. Russian aircraft hi-jacked, internal flight, on its way to the West, that the involvement was Jewish, that the Soviets would take a hard line. Not much to chew on in that.

No contour flying, not with the Prime Minister on board. Up to three thousand feet where the sharp winds that gathered on the hills behind Tiberias buffeted and pitched at the helicopter, causing him to steady himself in his canvas seat and feel for the safety harness that he wore. Not a time for thinking, for weighing alternatives. Dead time, lost time, that would duly add up till inevitably the pressure on the decision-makers would increase. Not the way it should be, but the way it always was; the penalty of living in a country perpetually in a state of war.

Flying south of the hills and towns and villages where the

Palestinians liked to work, the settlements close to the Lebanese border fence. The targets the Palestinians sought out. Hard, fanatical killing teams who came to Israel to test their muscle against the might of a modern and sophisticated society, and who were broken on the anvil of gunfire and grenade explosions, and who kept coming. This was the ground they came to, bright in the harsh sunlight below him, to the little communities that nestled close to the cultivated fields and the orange groves that were burned and dry in the heat. Men who came in their groups of four, having let their blood run together in the symbolic farewells in the Fatahland of South Lebanon, and who died horribly and brutally at the hands of Squad 101, the élite of the Israeli army, the counter-terrorist storm squad. 'Terrorists' they called them in his country – could find no other title for them, shunning the acceptance of such words as 'guerrilla' and 'commando' because that would bestow a certain fractional legality on their actions. He was musing to himself, not thinking with the speed and clarity he was capable of, just wafting the ideas in his head as the helicopter powered its bumping way towards Jerusalem. And what was it Gadhafi had said? Moammar Gadhafi, President of Libya, paymaster of the assassins, organizer of their plans, harbourer of their escapes. Gadhafi said there were terrorists and freedom fighters, that if the cause is right then so too the action is justified. Any action against the State of Israel is justified, any attack could be supported if it bore the name of Palestine, that was the message of the Libyan. And the response of the Prime Minister's government had been fierce and consistent; that the international community should succour no sympathy for the gangs and cells of armed men, that there should be no condoning of the terrorist, that he should be fought and brought to justice. There must be no weakening.

The helicopter yawed its way down the scale of the altimeter, dropping sharply and without ceremony into the city, the sun's flat beams splintering light on to the golden dome of Al Aqsa. Was a Jew with a gun held to a pilot's head a different flower, to be watered and husbanded from the Palestinian weed that they chopped and hoed when he took his grenades and explosives to the cockpit of the El Al plane? Did the Jew fight for freedom or for terror? Principle or self-interest? There was no precedent from which to take comfort. The decision of Entebbe had been easy by comparison, the decision to loose the killer squads in Europe to seek out their Palestinian counterparts had been simple. But this was fraught with dangers. Principle and expediency, principle and emotion; all cavorting inside him as the machine lurched the final feet to the ground.

He hurried to the grey-green Pontiac with its curtained rear windows and chassis that strained low under the weight of the armour-plated body. Men around him with unshielded Uzis and walkie-talkie radios, and police who saluted him and who wore pistols at their belts in holsters of which the top restraining flap was unfastened. And why were they all there? One reason, one reason only: because of the threat of the small groups, the men who stood apart from the shouting, chanting abusive crowds of protest. Four hundred yards from the helicopter pad to his offices, and a lift to the third floor. More men in slacks and light summer shirts that they wore outside the waist of their trousers that their hand-guns should be concealed and not frighten the stream of foreign visitors who came to pay their respects and tell him how his government should conduct its affairs.

The Security Committee was waiting for him, gathered round the table by the window, opposite his wide-topped desk. Piled in front of the chair that he would use were the papers that would tell him the story of the hi-jacking so far, what was known of the participants, the statements of the Russians, and the decisions that had been made by the West European governments in whose territory the plane might attempt a landing. Sombre reading, no light in the darkness, no crack through which optimism might wear a path.

He shuffled the papers together, waved his colleagues into chairs, understood the pain in their faces and knew they had read all that he had seen. Fools, he thought, three idiots wallowing in their own stupidity.

'One decision at least can be made,' the Prime Minister said. 'We cannot condemn and we cannot condone. The world will be watching for our reaction, our friends and our enemies. We cannot support these three, not publicly, and at the same time we cannot be seen to be abandoning them. Our movement must be through the passive channels, through suggestion.'

'But that does not confront the issue.' It was the senior civil servant of the Ministry of Foreign Affairs, still in his thirties with the aggression of youth and the high brow of intellect. 'The Russians are asking for the return of these people once they have landed; they are telling the Europeans that these three are criminals and must be sent back to stand trial for murder. They are accused of shooting a policeman in Kiev, and we hear now that the pilot of the aircraft has been killed. The penalty for those offences in the Soviet Union is death. There are many in our country who would believe in such a sentence if the rôles were reversed. For any Western government to permit the plane to land and refuel and facilitate its onward flight is unthinkable. That is why the Germans refused to become involved. The country to which the plane comes must disarm these three and then will have to consider its options, will have to decide whether to send them back, to their executions. Whether we do it privately or publicly this is the issue on which we must clear our position.'

'You have pre-empted me,' said the Prime Minister. 'I too see the problem. You are not alone in identifying the difficulty. All of us can see it.'

'We have spoken much in the past of the need for solidarity to fight the aerial warfare of the Arab groups . . .'

'You say the obvious,' interjected the Prime Minister wearily, his ears still ringing with the hammer of the rotor blades. 'We know that, we know what we have said. So what do you ask me to do? Do you ask me to tell the British, or the Dutch, or the Danes, or the French . . . do you ask me to tell them to disarm these people and put them on a flight to Moscow?'

The silence was broken by the scraping of chair legs on the

tiled floor. All except the Prime Minister began pacing, searching for a clear way forward, while the smoke rose up in grey-blue columns, and coffee was poured . . . The evening of the Middle East comes fast, running across the sandstone houses, and the cement towers and the grey roads, but it was many minutes after the shadows had infiltrated the room before the lights were switched on; that seemed to change the mood and break the stillness in which those present had cocooned themselves, and emphasized the passing of time. The Prime Minister rapped the desk top with his pen.

'When the plane lands we must offer our services to the government concerned. We must make an offer to help in all ways possible to ensure that there is no further bloodshed, no siege. Perhaps we could send one of our people to talk to these three youngsters, to persuade them to surrender. We would demand one thing in return, and require a solemn promise on this, that the three should be tried in whatever country they land for whatever offences they have committed. There are no death sentences in Europe. We would accept a period of imprisonment . . .'

'And in Western Europe who has the greatest sway?' The scepticism of the Minister of Defence. 'Is it us, or is it the Soviet Union? What if our appeal is rejected?'

'What is your solution, then?' said the Prime Minister, angry that his reasoning so carefully arrived at should face challenge so soon.

'I have no "solution", as you call it. Perhaps there is none. But we must be clear in our minds what we are looking for. When the French took Abu Daoud then we called for his extradition. We made noises and we flexed what muscle we possessed. It is irrelevant that it was not sufficient. On the same basis the Soviets will want the return of these children, but that is something that we cannot permit, that is unspeakable. There would be the deepest shame on ourselves and our people if we failed to use every artifice available to us to prevent the young ones being sent back to execution. I accept, of course, that we cannot associate our government with their actions, but at the same time I say that we cannot disassociate ourselves to the extent of permitting them to go to their deaths in a Soviet prison . . .'

'What would you have me do? Fly in the paratroopers again, recreate Entebbe? Lift them from whatever airfield they land?'

'I say that we cannot hold our heads high as the representatives of the people of the Jewish State if we tolerate the sending back—'

'What do you seek to tell me?'

'For years now we have fought and struggled to rid our people in Russia of persecution. We cannot allow – must not allow – them to be sent back. The humiliation would be unacceptable.'

'What then do you think I am suggesting? Do you believe I look towards a craven retreat? This is why I offer to send a man.'

He broke off, thankful for the softened knock at the door that precluded further argument and would only take them deeper into confusion. A single sheet of paper was handed over to him, and while he read it he took in the sound of the door closing behind the messenger. A deep sigh, from far down in his chest, then the Prime Minister shrugged, irritated, as if to throw off the constriction of a burden.

'Gentlemen, there is little time now. The Dutch government has informed our Embassy in The Hague that they have decided – and they say it is with regret – that they have made certain conditions which must be met if the plane is allowed to land. They must have the word of the three that they will disarm themselves and surrender. I note that our Ambassador makes no mention of what would happen to the three should they comply with the instructions. But it would seem that the question is irrelevant. The demand has been rejected, the plane is flying on. They will be over the United Kingdom in less than three quarters of an hour, they have enough fuel to get there, but not for a further diversion. It seems it is the British with whom we have to deal.'

The Defence Minister leaned across the table, his hand outstretched, and reaching for that of the Prime Minister. 'I agree to what you propose. It is right for the first step. We must win more time to talk of alternatives. You have my support. You have my word.'

There was a pale moon of gratification at the Prime Minister's mouth. He said, 'You must find a man that you think of, who could talk to the three, someone young, someone they will admire and accept, who can convince them. A man of our strength, of the strength of our people.' And then he added, as an afterthought, half to himself and yet not caring who heard, 'I would rather it had not been the British.'

7

The closing of Schiphol Airport represented a huge task to the dozen air traffic controllers on duty in the tower. All flights on the ground were to be indefinitely delayed – simple enough that, with only the passengers' fury and the carriers' frustration to contend with – but harder and more complex to handle the fifteen aircraft in various stages of final approach. Diversions to Brussels for those closest, to Rotterdam for those that came from the North, and for those that were further afield there were requests for information on fuel loads and suggestions that they put down at Lille, or Charles de Gaulle and Orly on the outskirts of Paris. Short-haul flights coming from North Germany and Heathrow were advised to delay take-off until the situation had clarified. Within a matter of minutes of the order being given the intricate and complicated process of planning the controlled flights of some scores of aircraft across Northern Europe was in apparent chaos. In the terminals there was confusion, passengers struggling into queues at the check-in counters where the abused staff could neither accept their baggage nor award them with boarding cards.

Out on the runways of Schiphol Dutch troops had taken to their lumbering armoured personnel carriers. Blue-uniformed members of the police airport squad with steel helmets and MI carbines drove their jeeps alongside them to augment the effect of the APCs. The blocking programme successfully used by the Germans was aped till the runways offered no scope for landing, only for disaster. But the Dutch government faced greater emotional problems than the Germans. Ever since the Yom Kippur war of 1973 when the support of the Netherlands for

Israel had been unqualified through the clouds of bitter invective from the Arab oil producers, the small nation had acquired a reputation of providing a solid staff on which the Zionist State could lean. For this reason the Dutch cabinet had felt the need to offer landing permission to the Ilyushin, but had attached such riders that they felt confident they would deflect the Aeroflot's route beyond their airspace. It was by now academic what line the cabinet would have taken in response to the demand of the Soviet Union that the three should be returned to their jurisdiction. The plane had circled the airport twice, watched by huge crowds of transistor-toting passengers and mechanics and ground staff, before heading towards the dykes and the sea wall and the cold evening waters of the North Sea.

Although on their circuits of Schiphol David and Isaac had been able to identify the faint and indistinct shapes of the blocking vehicles, their feelings were much changed from those above Hanover when they had first realized that the West was reluctant to play host to their errant migration from the East.

The navigator had provided them with the piece of paper on which was written in his neat hand the brief message from the Dutch authorities that listed the conditions of landing. They had studied it, read it perhaps three times each, trying to win the nuances of the carefully prepared government statement of policy, and known, both of them, that they would fly on.

'Where can we go?' David had asked the navigator, quietly and with respect, as if accepting that in spite of their guns and their proven willingness to kill they had still needed the man's expertise.

'We can go south. Try Belgium, perhaps, or the French. We can go north towards Denmark, or back into the Federal Republic. If we continue we will reach Britain. But if they make us circle, if there is more waiting, then we have no further alternatives. We would not be able to regain the European continent. If we go to Britain that is where we must land.' The pilot officer supported him, wordlessly pointing to the quivering fuel counters that now edged past the vertical towards the wing of the measurement arc and that hustled closer to the red warning line.

The navigator waited for them. He did not interfere, sensing perhaps that at this moment they relied heavily on him and that in their dependence on his skills he might exert, subtly and imperceptibly, at least some influence. If he antagonized them or disputed with them then the relationship could be destroyed. He knew that at this moment there was no possibility of abject surrender, that it was not the time for him to begin the gentle and clandestine process of wearing down the resolve of the two men who shared the cockpit with himself and the pilot officer, knew that that time would come later when the lives of the passengers were not at such direct risk. He was just past his twenty-seventh birthday, tanned from his holiday on the Bulgarian coast, engaged to be married and flushed with the confidence that came from the knowledge that he did his job well, that he would advance. The men who stood behind him and looked over his shoulder at the air routes and tried to decipher the meaning of his lines and paths and to assess the distances he talked of and weigh them against their scant knowledge of the different implications of reception in the north, in the south, or the west, were only a little younger than himself. They were similar to the people he saw in the streets of Moscow and Leningrad and Kiev when he was on stop-over. A great ordinariness about them, he thought, nothing to distinguish them from the wallowing, compliant herd, nothing in their faces, their hands, their clothes, nothing to make them stand out . . . only the guns. He suppressed the slow smile, their only claim on him, on his interest, his attention, his curiosity . . . the guns, and the fact that if they were fired then a planeload of people would perish. But such ordinariness surprised him, and he wondered how they could have chosen this course, and why, why they were there, why they had started, just why.

'We will go to Britain.' David speaking, evenly and in his own voice, calmed now. 'I want it made clear that this time we land.

You must tell them of our fuel position, but not till we are near their airfields, till they cannot move us on, parcel us up, send us elsewhere.' He was going to say more, but clamped on his tongue. He had to talk to Isaac more, had to have consensus, had to draw again on the strength of his friend.

Again the nose of the plane rose, climbing once more.

Out in the passageway between the cockpit and the passenger cabin, where there was storage space and the cupboards and the forward toilet and privacy, the two men huddled together. David stood facing the flight deck crew, Isaac the passengers, both studying their charges and speaking from the sides of their mouths, bodies close, and still the guns aimed at their charges.

'I had thought it would be finished by now,' said David.

'They have made it difficult for us. They will not change now.'

'I did not think it possible . . .'

'And we do not make it easy for them. It is not they alone who can hurt.'

'You have heard the stories of the Arabs on the radio . . .'

'It will be difficult, but they can be made to soften.'

'They give in to threats.'

'We have to take the philosophy of the Arabs, David.'

'And we have hostages, and we must use them.'

'If we want to see Israel, David.'

'If we are to force them, if they must bow to us . . . but then it will be a long road . . .'

'It has been a long road already.'

'You know what it means, Isaac? If we are to go on, if we are to succeed?'

'I know what it means. I understand.'

'We must use the passengers . . .'

'I understand that.'

How docile they sit, how quiet, and they do not know what I have talked of, what David has accepted, what I know. Like the Jews of old. Do not know they are no longer just human beings, that their destiny has forsaken them, that they have become casualties that will fall if our will does not rise supreme over that of the people that we will face. Expendable . . . and how many of them? How many to be taken before we convince the people on the ground that we are travelling to Israel? One? Perhaps the Italian, the man who sits in the middle of the front row of the group, who cannot look at me, who has the capped teeth and the silk tie; would he be enough to convince them? Perhaps the schoolmaster – perhaps we will need two? With his glasses that do not hide the way he stares back at me, not because he is brave and has courage but because he is afraid to lose face in the presence of the children. If we kill him, will that bend them? Take a third, and why not? The American with his bleeding head and the handkerchief that his wife has wrapped around it, who seems like a farmer now in the field with his hay who must stop the sweat coming from his scalp to his eyes. Why not him also, if they hesitate, if they wish to test us? And the children, what of the children, Isaac? A wave of nausea rose up from his stomach. A terrible shame, a humiliation that the thought should even come to him. He had made David say it first, led him to the cliff face, defiled him, nagged him, pressured him, till they had come together to the ultimate – the children. And what if their will is stronger than ours, if they do not bend? How many do we kill to find out the temper of their resolution? He seemed to shrug to himself, disengaging from David. It will not be so, we will have the fuel. They will give us the fuel.

A full-measured, slowed, leaden-paced hour since they last came to the back of the plane to see her. Only the seat tops to look at, and the hands on people's heads, and the occasional stolen glance over the shoulder to see that she was still there – that the pistol was in her hand. There was hatred on some faces when they looked back, something they would not dare when Isaac was watching them, not since he had struck the American. But that was an hour back, and they looked differently at Rebecca, because she was a girl, just a girl, and had no right to be feared. But they do not come and talk with me, leave me here, isolated, ignored, searching the length of the plane to lip-read their whispers far away as they meet in the corridor outside the cockpit. Because I screamed, is that why I am not to be trusted? she thought. Have I less strength than the others, and is that the only currency they value, strength whatever that may be, man's strength, their stupid, ignorant puerile virility? David has screamed too, and I heard it, heard it the length of the plane, heard it with all the passengers and seen their heads jump up like those of jerked marionettes and subside cautiously again when calm returned to the cockpit area. They loathe me, these people, they would like to stamp and kick and pummel the life out of me, beat and beat till each bone is broken, that is the revenge they seek, and only the gun prevents it. Only the squat and polished security of the gun holds them back, because that is what they fear.

The headmaster's hand raised.

Like all the teachers she'd ever known. In his best clothes because he was taking the children somewhere, would have polished his shoes, selected his best shirt. A compilation of Soviet virtues, preaching the Love of the Motherland, Industriousness and Frugality, Friendship and Comradeship, Love of Studies and Consciousness. Teacher's hand raised. Ludicrous, the classroom table turned.

'The children want to relieve themselves, Miss.'

Of course they do. Don't we all?

'The children have been very patient, Miss. They have waited a long time.'

Just like the American. Called her 'Miss' because she had the gun, put his sharp bony knee in her crutch if she didn't have it, and kick her, and kick her, and kick her. She looked for Isaac, but he was lost from sight again. Lost in the bloody cockpit where with David he spent all his time, time when he should have come and told her what was happening, what the descents had meant, why they had not landed, why they had flown on. Was it like the American had said – that there wasn't a red carpet, that nobody would want them? What was the word he'd used? 'Pariah', that was it. A beast that fed off the scraps, that turned the nose of people, an outcast, something set aside. Could have called her a Jew, couldn't he? Same thing, what he meant, but nobody said what they meant, not while she held the pistol.

'Miss, the children have been very patient, most patient. There can be no harm in their going to the lavatory.'

No sign of Isaac, and anyway what harm could there be from it? That was what they had left her there for, because they had problems to wrestle with in the cockpit. It was not out of choice that they had left her there, but for a reason. David must have had a reason, Isaac, too. She was being stupid, playing the idiot, and they had left her in charge and given her responsibility. Above the droning power of the engines that permeated the insulated cabin she shouted her answer to the schoolmaster.

'They can come in threes. Just the children to start with. They must come from each block of seats at a time, and the next will follow only when the previous three have finished.'

She pushed the soft drinks trolley end-on to the aisle so that there was a gap through which the children could pass, and the first three rose and hurried towards her, relief written on their faces.

'Thank you, Miss,' the headmaster called to her from his seat, craning round, watching the procedure, watching her.

Disciplined children. The product of the System and the Pioneers, taught at school to conform and to show respect, bobbing their heads with acknowledgement as they passed her on their way to the three rear toilets, and another conveyor-belt expression of gratitude when they came back into the cabin and moved to their seats. Bright faces, scrubbed with soap and short hair for the boys, neat ribbon-tied pigtails for the girls. A few years back, and that's what she had been, not different, not separated – until she had met David, before she had known Isaac and learned the power of a policeman's pistol, the pistol that was in her hand. They regarded the gun as they passed but were too well-mannered to stare at it, too well-schooled to give it more than a glance. Eleven years old most of them, twelve a few, and now regimented and able to hide their fear of the gun under the umbrella of childish curiosity. Doing what they had been told to do.

The headmaster was out of his seat and walking towards her holding loosely the hand of a child, leading him and coaxing him towards the gap between the trolley and the galley wall.

He said quietly, a voice that would not embarrass and attract attention, 'This one, Miss, he has a kidney problem. There is equipment under his clothes, and I must help him.'

She let him pass, scenting the damp perspiration of his body under his suit as he pushed through the narrow entrance that was available. She turned to watch them disappear inside the toilet door, saw the 'Engaged' sign light up, and twisted herself back again, easy and relaxed so that she faced the front, dominating her passengers.

She was not aware of him as he came close to her back, had no sense of his proximity, was concerned only with the woman and the mewling baby who was rising from her seat far to the front. She understood nothing of his plan till his hands were on her.

The baby crying, always that bloody child crying . . . and then the sudden, panic-stricken fear, coming alive in a single moment. One hand across her mouth and fingers squeezing against her lips so that she could not scream, shovelling the ends with the clipped dirt-tasting nails between her teeth so that she could not bite, and the other hand clawing for her right wrist and seeking to break the grip that held the gun. Had to get the hand from her mouth, had to scream, had to give warning, tumbling through her mind the need to arouse the others who were at the front, and all the time the fingers in her mouth choking at her, denying her air, and the grip on her wrist was vice-tight and closing so that the blood could not pass, her muscles not respond. Others in front of her, coming from their seats, gigantic, looming, fearsome . . . and she was falling . . . another of the schoolmasters, one that she took for a farmer, and a boot caught

133

her flush to the bone of the shin causing her to buckle and collapse to the carpet of the aisle.

It was the fall that broke the headmaster's grip on her arm, the jerk with which her body collapsed was not anticipated, the sudden shift of her balance and weight was too great for the pliant fingers, not used to physical action. When she hit the floor the gun exploded in a blast of noise and cordite fumes, and she winced from the flash burn to her chest that seemed to sear a way through the fabric of her dress. Hands all round her now, pummelling and driving to reach under her body to where the gun was, pulling at her thighs, at the slight softness of her breasts, frantic in their haste now that the noise of the discharged bullet had sounded the alarm.

And then there was no-one. Liberation. The hands withdrawn. She wiped the hair from her face front and looked up. She saw the feet that were edging back from her, moving away, and tilted her head further. Their hands were on their heads again, faces of guilt and fear, the boys found out, and half-way down the aisle was Isaac with the sub-machine gun at his shoulder and far past him and guarding his back was David. Just the droning pull of the engines and the fractional swaying in the air currents of the plane on steady course: no words. The men who had left their seats making their way back, ashamed, caught out, a girl to disarm and they had failed, and now they faced the wrath of the young man with the chill in his eyes. He would not have made the mistakes that she had, and their faces showed their concern at the retribution he would exact, the toll he would take.

Deep throbbing pain in her leg where the man had kicked her, and an aching through her shoulders where a knee had pressured downwards against her spine, and a place on her forehead where there would be a bruise from the impact against the metal stanchion of a seat support.

Interrogation in Isaac's voice, questioning. 'How were they out of their seats?'

Difficult to speak at first, had to get the air back into her pinched lungs.

'They said the children should go to the toilet, they said there was one who needed help, who was ill, that was how they came behind me.'

'Nobody was to move.'

'But they said the children wanted to go . . .'

'You were given an instruction. You disobeyed it. You've jeopardized the whole of our mission.'

'But the children have to pee, Isaac. It was not . . . how was I to know?'

'If they wanted to pee they could have used their knickers. You nearly destroyed everything, the whole plan, and you alone could have destroyed it.' No anger, not the burning in his eyes, but something else. She had never seen him like this before, not with the contempt turning the lines of his mouth and the single reddened patches on the high points of his cheeks, and the hands that were white and bloodless in their grip of the machine gun.

'Which one was it? Which one attacked you?'

As if in a limbo of loyalties she hesitated, the struggle warring inside her as to whether she should identify the headmaster. What would Isaac do? Would he kill him? Had she the power to sentence the man, to cause his execution? He was closer to her than to Isaac, with his head bowed, and she could see the bald top of his scalp, and the places where the grey hair still grew, and the places where the revealed skin was blotched and discoloured, and . . . and he had tried to kill her, that man, that was why he had struggled with her, to kill her and to kill David and Isaac.

'It was the one in the aisle seat, four rows from you, on the left.'

'Louder,' said Isaac, but his voice was hushed and low, competing with the aircraft's power. 'Do not be afraid. Do not believe that these people will save you. They'll cut your throat, Rebecca, bleed you like an animal. If they could they would have bludgeoned you to death, if the gun had not fired, and I not come. Which one was it?'

135

'It was the one in the aisle seat, four rows from you, on the left.' She looked away as Isaac advanced up the aisle between the avenue of passengers, no heads turning to watch him, just the shuffle of his canvas shoes on the carpet.

'Listen to what I say,' Isaac said to the headmaster. His voice as in a conversation, a tone of mutated friendship, bizarre to her, obscene. 'The Germans have prevented us from landing, and the Dutch too. They have driven lorries and army trucks across the runways of their airports to make it impossible for us to land. And now we are going to England. We have fuel to get there and no further, and they will let us land for that reason. But we have not come this far to finish in England: we go to Israel. Perhaps we will have to show the English that we have the will to fly to Israel, that we are not as the Jews were, that we are a new generation, as the "sabras" are. If it is necessary we will shoot you, one by one, to prove to the English that we have determination. If that should happen then I make a promise to you, a promise that I shall keep. If anyone dies on this plane to convince the English of our will then it will be you, you will be the first, you will be the one that we call for.'

Isaac walked on till he reached Rebecca. Held out his hand for her to give him the pistol, checked the mechanism, ensured there was a bullet in the breech, that the gun was live. 'The mistake must not be repeated, Rebecca.' He turned on his heel and strode back down the length of the cabin. And the Ilyushin continued its course across the smooth unruffled waters of the North Sea towards the coastline of England and the Kingfisher's landfall.

The news that the Dutch landing conditions had not been accepted was sufficient for the summons to Charlie Webster to attend the Emergency Committee meeting in the offices of the Home Secretary in Whitehall.

The Home Secretary was in the Chair, flanked by one of his junior ministers, two civil servants of the Department both with the grading of Principal Under-Secretaries, a lowly Foreign

Office minister in order that the deliberations of the two giant bureaucracies could be dovetailed through liaison, and the Commissioner of the Metropolitan Police from Scotland Yard. At the far end of the polished mahogany table was Parker Smith, whose suggestion it had been that they call for the man in his section who specialized in the study of Russian dissident groups. The windows were open because it was a warm and windless evening, and the murmur of the London rush hour traffic came up to them from the courtyard. Coffee cups on the table, and filled ashtrays, and the paraphernalia of the meeting – torn up scraps of paper, others crumpled and discarded, some with the artistic and intricate doodles of the Foreign Office man, brief-cases and maps, and telephone on an extended wire at the Home Secretary's elbow.

A messenger in the blue livery of the Home Office had been waiting in the wide and high-roofed lobby for Charlie to arrive. They hadn't bothered with the formality of signing him in, and together they had taken the sweeping staircase two at a time till they were on the first floor and walking briskly along the central corridor flanked by the uncleaned oil portraits of the Minister's predecessors in office. A brief knock and the messenger opened the door. Charlie spluttered involuntarily as the smoke wall hit him, fogging his nostrils and his eyes.

'Mr Charles Webster, gentlemen.'

The Home Secretary waved him towards a seat, the only one vacant and half-way down the table on the right-hand side. Interest on the faces of all except Parker Smith. Different type of fellow to the ones that the politicians and civil servants of rank were accustomed to doing business with, suit not pressed as keenly, and shirt looking as though it had done service the day before by way of bonus, the shave wearing fine because he had not slipped to the men's room at lunchtime as these more public men were accustomed to do.

Parker Smith, sitting easily in the company, anxious to put Charlie at ease, and overdoing it, sounding patronizing, sort of speak-up-boy-they-won't-bite. 'Charlie, I've told the Minister and his colleagues here of your background. Told them of your experience overseas and in Dublin, and I've sketched through the work you do now, with emphasis on your predictions of last night.'

The Home Secretary cut him short.

'Mr Webster, the Aeroflot flight is perhaps a quarter of an hour off our coastline. We can keep it circling for a bit, but there will not be much opportunity for prevarication. We are advised that it has enough fuel for perhaps a further forty minutes' flying time, three quarters of an hour at the most. It is our intention to put it down at Stansted in Essex. We do not have the luxury of our European colleagues of being able to pass the buck. The buck stops here; the fuel load of the plane determines that. We will obviously attempt to persuade the hi-jackers to surrender without further recourse to needless and stupid bloodshed, but we have to know from the time that the wheels hit the ground what sort of people we are dealing with. We want you to put some flesh on them, Mr Webster. I don't mind conjecture, provided that it's based on very sound background, but what you tell us may have to be acted upon very quickly so I'd prefer caution in your analysis.'

Civil servants and junior ministers with their sharpened pencils and gold-coated pens poised, only the Home Secretary and Parker Smith looking at him. And what do they want to hear? What can you give them, Charlie? Tell them about the kids who have learned that you don't walk through Hyde Park shouting anymore; you get yourself a nice shiny Armalite and shoot a copper in Belfast, you get dished out an AK and blow a Brit squaddie to kingdom come in Crater, you get an RPG and cuddle up to an airport fence to bag yourself an El Al jumbo. They're waiting for you, Charlie, so go slowly, and don't use long words.

'There have been two confirmed hi-jack attempts out of the Soviet Union in the last few years. A family took a light aircraft to Turkey. Insignificant and a one-off incident. Then there was the Leningrad plan that aborted and never got off the ground, a group of Jews who wanted to take over a plane, unarmed, and fly it to Finland. It was a short-haul flight and the whole thing was a disaster, the group hopelessly infiltrated by KGB. All arrested at the airport, and some still inside. There is a third incident but it's less hard and we have fewer details, even through "I" channels – Israeli announcement that a hi-jacked internal flight was coming out, and it never came, '74 or '75, I think. From the East bloc there have been a series of chaps jumping a plane and coming over, but not Russians. There hasn't been a major Russian one before, so that's the first bit of new ground. Now the second one: these people up there are apparently Jews. In the past the Jewish dissidents have for the most part contented themselves with media protests, clandestine interviews, press conferences, civil disobedience where they'll be noticed by foreigners and it will get reported, trying to get pressure on the local authorities and most of their efforts aimed at the United States. Chief contention has been emigration either to Israel or to the West generally, followed by complaints of racial discrimination. That's very broad and very brief, but probably sufficient.'

There was the click of a cigarette lighter, the noise of nibs scratching on paper.

'These people however are different. We've had a policeman shot in Kiev, wounded, apparently seriously and nothing in the media. That indicates it was neither criminal nor casual. The one thing that would really concern the people over there is if they consider this a target shooting, an attempt at a gesture, though a botched one for all that. A gesture they will equate with conspiracy and organizations. That would concern them. There have been terror attacks put down to minority nationalist groups but nothing that we have been able to identify as internally aggressive and specifically Jewish. As I said we had the shooting of the policeman. We've also heard of rumours round the university site that a Jewish student was arrested a few days ago, and that militia reinforcements were seen moving into the city. Perhaps he talked, the one they picked up, and the assumption has to be that the security people were on the point of staging a large-scale arrest sweep. And then we have a hi-jack.'

Charlie paused. Not for effect, just to clear his mind again. He didn't make speeches – not in his line of work. The difficult bit starts now though, he thought, where we lose the facts, where we start jogging along with the theory.

'There are two types of hi-jacking or hostage-taking operations. When the Palestinians do it, along with the people associated with them, it's usually what we call a "leverage operation" – designed to get some of the comrades out of prison, and usually an Israeli prison. Doubled with that is the publicity factor of attention being turned on their operation with all the attendant explanations as to who they are and what their grievance is. That was Dawson's Field in Jordan, OPEC in Vienna, the Air France to Entebbe. All well documented. That's one type, then there's the other sort – what we call a "break-out job", which is what I think this one is. Kids who felt that time was running out back at home and were looking for the fastest and most successful bolt they could manage. Difficult place to go underground, the Soviet Union, especially if it all starts falling round your ears quickly. You'd need months to set an underground situation up, just for the paperwork of changed identity. They didn't reckon they were capable of that, so they've tried the bunk. I doubt if it was planned more than a few hours before take-off, and their major success was very simply to get the guns on to the aircraft. They're probably young, early twenties at the most, naïve politically by the standards that we are familiar with, and by this stage they'll be frightened and dangerous.'

Waiting for someone to interrupt, get him off the hook, but nobody did.

'Keep going, Mr Webster' – the gentle rebuke from the Home Secretary – 'Please remember that if we have any advantages at this stage time is not one of them.'

'I say "dangerous" because they will have believed that they would be permitted to put down anywhere in the West. They've tried twice now, and as you explained this is their last chance. They'll know that if they are still to get to Israel then they've a fair amount of shouting to get through first. You have to be

140

pre-prepared for them to shift from break-out to leverage, if and when they discover that the fuel wagons aren't going to be beside the plane and filling her up.'

'There is no possibility that the plane will be permitted to fly to Israel. Both from the diplomatic side and the question of the principle involved that eventuality has not been considered.' The basic approach had been agreed long before Charlie had arrived, relayed to the Prime Minister at his holiday retreat in the South of England, sanctioned by him without dispute. So that's the policy, Charlie, taking a hard line. Easy to be tough with this one, he thought; one-off job.

'I can't be definite,' Charlie said, 'but I would expect these people to go hard once they find that things aren't that rosy. They'll know the case histories of previous hi-jacks, they can take in BBC, VOA, plenty of radio sets that can pick that kind of thing up in the Ukraine, no problem of jamming now, reception's not difficult. I wouldn't think they'll have a stamina fallback, they won't be able to keep the pressure up for long, forty-eight hours or so, but in the meantime expect them to play it rough.'

'Will they be intelligent?' enquired the Under-Secretary with responsibility for co-ordinating and implementing the decisions of the Emergency Committee. The high pitch of the Public School and private means that Charlie detested, but it was a good and important question.

'Academically they'll be bright. They'll have an ideology at any rate that won't be political, but will stem from their breeding, their position in Soviet society. Committed people. Probably they'll believe they are prepared to die for it all, providing the moment isn't too close at hand. They'll be similar enough to all the other groups. When you get down to it – start trading, that is – you'll find them the same breed as all the other groups, same breed as the Palestinians, Baader-Meinhof, Tupamaros, Monteneros, Provos. They'll be speaking a different language, that's all you'll notice.'

'Do you call the Provos intellectuals, Mr Webster?' queried the Under-Secretary.

'You asked me a different question. You asked me whether these people were intelligent. You don't need a university degree to be good at this game, but you have to be sharp, know your way round and keep your thinking cap on. I say again, these people have done bloody well to get this far; it takes a bit more than luck, you know.'

'Is there anything you'd like to say in conclusion, Charlie?' Parker Smith was filling his briefcase with assorted papers, cigarettes were being stubbed out, pens removed to inside pockets, ties straightened.

'Only this. They've come a long way, these three. But they think they've a fair old mileage still to come. Don't underestimate them. Take them very carefully to start with.'

Charlie sat back in his seat, felt tired, hadn't the old resilience. The man next to him – there had been no introductions and Charlie didn't know his name – pushed three photographs across the table to where Charlie could see them. Snapshots, and they hadn't travelled well on the photofax machine from Moscow to the Foreign Office. Blurred and creased from the printing apparatus but still the recognizable features. Names printed in Russian and English across the bottom of each picture. Straight out of the bloody Bible.

'Mr Webster, I'm going to Stansted now by car. I'd like you to accompany me.'

The Home Secretary had risen, gestured to Charlie to lead through the door, followed him out to the corridor and the rear staircase that led to the car park. The Minister's black Humber waited there, with a chauffeur and his personal detective, and with its engine idling was a three-litre Rover that would drive behind them. Three in the back they managed, Minister, Under-Secretary and Charlie.

Out into the traffic, swinging east from Whitehall towards the City. End of a routine commercial day, and the pavements thronged with the last shifts of commuters, only hesitating for their evening papers, succumbing to the propaganda of the billboards – OUR HI-JACK ALERT   BRITAIN PREPARED FOR RED HI-JACK

CRISIS. The Ilyushin would be at Stansted when they arrived, and Charlie pictured again the three faces that they'd shown him. Stupid little bastards, and don't know what they've bitten off, and who'll wish when this is over they'd stayed at home and played kids' games. And now you're deep down in the pit, Charlie, and after you'd said you didn't want to see the ladder anymore and wanted a desk job. Should have been franker months ago, told them that you were sick of the killing, of being a guardian of the right of the middle-aged, middle classes, middle-brows to sleep in their beds at night. Should have spoken then and you didn't. Kept your speech till tonight, till you impressed the big men, and they wanted you as part of the team, want you to help screw these three, help con them – help kill them. Stupid little bastards.

'Too slow! Too slow! What do you think they'll be doing, sitting around chewing betel? They'll be ready for you. They know what time we come, can set their watches by it. Always we come at dawn. They know and they are ready for you, and you've got to be quicker than them. If not then it is you that are dead, not them.'

He stood watching the soldiers as they trooped sheepishly back to their starting line, the top of the cement staircase. Eight soldiers, all of them deflated by his criticisms, and the air was heavy with the reek of fumes from the flash grenades they had thrown and the blank cartridges they had fired.

'You must remember this for us is a rehearsed drill, simple and straightforward. You will have experienced it many times so that it has no strangeness to you. But for them it will be the first time. However much they are ready if you are fast enough you will have the time. When you hear the machine gun fire outside then you must *explode*. You have to be faster, or you are worm-food. We shall now do it again.'

Thirty-one years old, Arie Benitz, and wearing on his denimed shoulder, black against the olive green, the insignia of lieutenant colonel. He commanded the most specialized force in the Israeli armed services, the anti-terrorist storm squad. Akin with both his predecessors, who had died leading their men on operations, he was a draftee from the Parachute Brigade. One who had held the rank had died in the assault on the beach-front Savoy Hotel in Tel Aviv after Palestinians had sprinted with their hostages to the top-floor rooms, the other from a random sniper during the mopping up stages of the Entebbe rescue mission. Any new commander will insist that the training of his men bears his own hallmark, his own stamp, especially when the expertise called for is the ability to prise out dedicated and determined fighters from the cramped rooms where they had chosen to die, and die if possible in the company of their hostages.

The building that Benitz and his front-line section used for training was a three-floor block of discused sleeping quarters in the big army barracks on the Beersheba road out of Ashdod. They were working on the top floor, because that was where the enemy usually sheltered with their prey of terrified and hushed civilians, where the space for movement of the attack force was limited, the opportunity for varying the direction of assault minimal.

Hand on his stopwatch, he gave a blast on the whistle clamped between his teeth. The long hammering chant of the outside machine guns that would be aimed for the windows of the last bunker the Palestinians would creep to. High fire aimed to pass into the rooms and then impact against the ceilings, fire to make a man hesitate in his desire to win courage, to force him to the floor where he would cringe, to gain the precious seconds that the attackers must have.

At the first echo of the firing he screamed at the pitch of his voice. 'Go, you bastards, *go!*' First man raking the door, flattening himself against the wall adjacent to its hinges. Number Two crashing into it with his weight, a second's fraction after the firing stopped, Number Three with the grenade pins already pulled and hurling them into the opened space. Fourth, fifth, sixth and seventh and eighth, bullocking through the smoke in the moments after the explosions and firing for the corners as they entered each room, where the man who already knows that he is doomed will hide for an illusion of protection. When the next group came from Fatahland Arie Benitz would be fourth in line, fourth man, but the first through the door. It was traditional that the commander led from the front, not in practice when the men worked on the drills, but when it was for real.

'Better,' he said, as they emerged. Smiles now from proud men who valued his accolade. 'Better. Three and a half seconds from the machine gun fire to the grenade explosions. Seven seconds till the last of you was inside. At that speed you have a chance, perhaps only two hairy arses shot off.' Low murmur of laughter from the squad. Hard, battle-tested young men all of them, born and raised inside the State of Israel. Helmets covered in camouflage cloth and netting, denims that were not encumbered with any webbing that might encumber the rush forward, and on their backs a weird and incomprehensible series of fluorescent strips, all in varying patterns, the one different to the other, but which told the trained soldier which man was in front of him, what was his job, essential in the demi-light in which they would fight.

'We do it once more.'

He went inside the rooms beyond the flapping and damaged door, rearranged the target dummies of beaten straw wound about with sacking and adorned with the grotesque masks that his men had fashioned, moved them from where they had been the last time – placed them under beds, behind chairs, deep in shadow – and lit a candle in the inner hallway that would serve as the only illumination for the soldiers. This was the way it was learned, the killing game. None of the long-range marksmen crap that the Germans had tried at Munich; but close-quarters work, body to body, point-blank range, near enough for the nose to find them, the eyes to see them, the ears to catch the sob for mercy as you fired.

When he came back out of the flat and slammed the door shut behind him he saw the stranger among the troops. Not one of the unshaven, dirt-smeared soldiers gangling and lolling in apparent semi-sleep but a ranking officer in office uniform. Could have cursed the men, not one of them stiffened, not one of them erect, not a salute among them. No recognition of the deputy-commander of the barracks. Because they were para-troopers and had now been elevated to anti-terrorist stand-by, and the outsider was just an admin man.

'Colonel, my apologies for the interruption. There are men from the Ministry of Defence, from Tel Aviv. They are in my office to see you.'

'We have one more run, then we are completed. My respects and I will be with them in ten minutes.'

'I do not think, Colonel, they would appreciate such a delay.'

Pleasure on his men's faces. Knowledge that the shouting and hectoring was over for another day. Time for a shower and something to eat, time to get out of the sweat-sodden fatigues they had worn through the day and half the night.

'Don't look so bloody lively,' the Colonel snapped at them as he followed his escort to the stairs. 'Tomorrow we're back here, and all day, till we lose at least a second off the entry time.'

But for the men of the storm squad stationed in the Central Military Zone of Israel there was waiting a long sleep, no early call in the morning, no immediate repetition of the assault tech-niques. From a briefing by two military intelligence officers and a senior official of the Foreign Ministry Colonel Arie Benitz was driven to an Israeli Air Force base. Under the mantle of dark-ness he was strapped into the navigator's seat of a Phantom fighter bomber and flown at many hundreds of miles an hour to the Royal Air Force base at Akrotiri, Cyprus. At the airfield, denuded of activity by successive Defence White Papers, he was transferred without formality to a VC10 of Support Command. He sat far to the rear of the aircraft and separated himself from the small groups of service personnel and their families. During the five and a half-hour flight to Brize Norton, the transport base in Oxfordshire, he would have a chance to mull over, to evaluate, the direction that had been given him, to concern himself with the rôle that the Prime Minister of his country had asked him to play. No passport, only his IDF identity card, and the uniform still splendid with the twin flashes of fluorescent light on the back. At Akrotiri they'd assured him that he'd have five minutes in the wash house at Brize Norton before the helicopter flight to Stansted, enough to change into borrowed and less conspicuous clothes.

At the time that the Colonel was flying out of Israel Aeroflot flight 927 scheduled for Tashkent was beginning its final approach to the Essex airfield of Stansted.

The original course plotted by her navigator had taken Pilot Officer Tashova towards Heathrow, London's principal airport and one of the busiest in the world. Paris, thankful that the ultimate responsibility was not hers, had guided the plane in accented English along Green One, leading her to the fan markers, the radio beacons that drove a high, shrill whistle into her earphones and flashed sharp lights at her control panel. Paris signed off, with gratitude, offering as final consolation the London airways frequency of 128.45. The Ilyushin should begin to call for further instructions. That the navigator had brought the plane south before beginning the short drop across the English Channel was not out of error but deliberate. There was a determination that whatever authorities now had jurisdiction over the plane should have no doubts from their calculations that the fuel tanks were drying out and parched, that the flight time was exhausted. From the cockpit on the Eastern approach to London they saw the distant hazed lights of the lit-up city that merged into the ink-dark horizon, and then the instruction had come for the diversion to Stansted, an airfield that neither Tashova nor her navigator had heard of. There was no reason why they should – it was not an international strip, but dealt with the trade of holiday charters and offered facilities to virgin British Airways pilots and crew on their take-offs and bumps.

The instructions on flight level, squawk ident, course degree numerals, VOR locations were incomprehensible to David – a foreign tongue, a foreign science. It was not possible for him to know that Stansted had been chosen as the airfield in Britain most suitable to receive a hi-jacked airliner – that the studies had been made by Security and Board of Trade a full three years earlier. It was remote, could easily be sealed, and if it had to be shut down because of an alien presence on the runways then the disruption to the massive traffic using British air space would be minimal.

As the Ilyushin headed away from London, its red indicator lights flashing the message of its traverse over the Essex countryside, three companies of the Third Royal Regiment of Fusiliers were beating a path down the country lanes from Colchester, the barracks town to which they had returned thirty-six hours earlier from four months' duty in Londonderry. Leave abruptly cancelled, and orders to the commanding officer to provide a military cordon. The Fusiliers travelled in the high-powered whining Saracen armoured cars and in the clumsy three-ton Bedfords; men disappointed in the cancellation of the reunions with their families, but for all that thrusting the adrenaline through their bodies at the prospect of seeing for themselves, watching, guarding over the plane that had come from Russia, the plane that dominated the television screens . . .

Further away, but closing with greater velocity on Stansted, were a formation of Puma troop-carrying helicopters, bringing a Special Air Service detachment from their distant camp on the Welsh borders. These were the men specifically trained in anti-hi-jack operations, and the lack of talk among the eighteen being ferried across Southern England reflected their frustration at being summoned late, due to arrive only minutes before the airliner, little time for reconnoitring, preparation, before they slipped to their planned and practised positions.

From divisional police stations in the country FN rifles and Smith and Wesson pistols were distributed to men of the Regional Crime Squad. Uniformed police were dispatched to set up roadblocks on the approaches, on the roads from Saffron Walden and Thaxted and Great Dunmow and Bishop's

Stortford. Keep the rubberneckers back, hasten the arrival of the various agencies, civilian and military, now speeding towards Stansted to greet the arrival of the Ilyushin.

David knew none of this, just watched the cold, unspeaking skills of Anna Tashova as she alternately cudgelled and caressed her controls, followed her instructions that came from over her shoulder. He knew nothing of the guns and the armour and the tensions that were amassing and that would await him.

Flaps moving again, change in the engine pitch, deep-throat rumble of the undercarriage dropping, and the passengers were craning at the cabin windows searching out the lights on the ground.

Would take more than a blow from a gun barrel to depress the inherent cheerfulness of Edward R. Jones Jr, and besides his wife had managed a picture of his head and the blood-stained handkerchief, right after she'd attached it, when the blood was really red, before the wound dried out.

'Hey, Miss,' he said, turning again in his seat, looking back to Rebecca, 'and you don't have to get that gorilla to belt me this time, but is this it? Are we really going in this time?'

She did not understand the American with his bright plumage clothes and his bravado, could not come to terms with the man, and so said nothing.

'Have it your way, Miss. But I hope you know where the ball game goes from here. It could be awfully disappointing, Miss, awfully messy.'

Still no response, and he smiled at her, two and a half thousand dollars of capped teeth, and turned back to the window.

The Italians, talking fast and excitedly among themselves, tightening their seatbelts, leaning sometimes forwards, sometimes backwards to spread their conversation among the whole group.

The children sat subdued in their seats. They were tired and hungry and had not been taught what their reaction should be to this situation. They had looked for a lead and received none, and were unable to digest the new noises of the engine and closing lights of the farmhouses and villages below.

Alone on the plane, bound in his own deep and introverted mood, was the headmaster. No-one had spoken to him since his attempt to disarm the girl. He was shunned by those who had not matched his own unreasoned moment of courage.

And as the aircraft dipped and the pressure levels changed and the engines throttled their power so too increased the fevered screaming of the baby, unnoticed, irrelevant to all on board as the ground slipped and lurched towards them.

8

Remember that she'll be close to exhaustion, nerves frayed on a hacksaw, that she doesn't understand English, that everything must go through the navigator. Nurse her down, not condescending, not patronizing, but take it ever so gently. Those were the instructions given by telephone from London to the air traffic controller in the Stansted tower who would talk Anna Tashova on to the runway. Encourage them to query anything, make it 100 per cent certain, hundred and one. No risks, not at this stage. Policemen, army officers, airport manager, senior air traffic supervisor, all crowded into the dim-lit space behind the young man who was now in direct contact with the Ilyushin. Full runway lights blazing out in the half-gloom of the evening, marking the tarmac that stretched 3,000 yards beyond the battery of red 'line-up' lights upon which she would straighten trim, make the final calculations.

'We'd like you to tell her that everyone here is with her, that everyone thinks she's done very well, that it's nearly over.'

'Roger, I will explain to her what you say.' Voice of the navigator booming inside the glass cased tower.

'About a hundred too high. She should drop 20 knots. Otherwise she's fine. We'd like to see her landing lights.'

'Roger. She is making the adjustments you require.' Pause. 'The pilot officer apologizes for the lights.'

Just like they are in the books you read, thought the controller. Not an iota different. Formal, correct, like it's a training run, as though there isn't a sub-machine gun six inches from her. Apologizes for not having switched her lights on. Pilot dead beside her, or on the floor somewhere, planeload of people to think about, three mad bastards with guns, and she's saying she's sorry.

'Just tell her not to worry. She's doing fine. We're all with her.' Pause again. Silence in the tower, all eyes peering at the sky for the lights. 'No wind problems, surface westerly fifteen knots, you'll be landing right into them. There is no other traffic, nothing else to concern yourself with. Still a little high, drop the speed down ten. Call at the outer marker.'

'Roger, thank you, 927 outer marker, inbound. Your instructions are very clear. We appreciate your help.'

'You're not going to need them, but there are emergency services ready. Everything is prepared.'

The controller wondered what it must be like in the cockpit, checked the flight plan they'd given to him, saw the take-off and mentally equated it with the British time difference. Five hours the girl had been flying the bloody thing now. He knew about the Migs, knew about Hanover and Schiphol. Poor little bitch; must be like having a guardian angel all dolled up in haloes and wings and white sheets hovering alongside to have a sympathetic voice talking from the control tower to her. Not that she'd know what he was saying, just get the feel, the togetherness . . . Could see the lights now, the men behind him pointing out to his right. He looked away from the green-tinted radar screen from which he had been working, turned for a moment from the bright grass-green blip that was the Ilyushin. Two huge and powerful beams scything into the night from the elevated angle of the aircraft's approach.

'927, we can see you, and you're doing very nicely. Take it calmly. No problems. Speed's right, height's right, line's right. Doing very well.'

Nothing more to say now. Time just to watch and pray that the tiredness of the girl did not force her into error. No reason why it should, only male chauvinism that made him worry, he thought. Chance of a woman flying a plane in the West was next to minus nil. One or two of them, of course, but so extraordinary that they had their pictures in the papers each week

– nothing like the Russian system, where the girls had the same opportunities as the men. Wondered what she'd look like. Funny not being able to talk to her, only the distant voice of the man who sat behind her, and who switched off his radio each time he relayed the instructions to his pilot, as if they didn't want anyone else to hear the backchat of the flight deck. Meant you couldn't evaluate her state of mind, didn't know what her condition was.

'Trim's right. Height right. Speed right.'

'Roger.'

'No problems, take it steady.'

'Roger.'

Don't give anything away, the buggers.

The shape of the plane eclipsed the lights at the far end of the runway, and in the tower they heard the roar of the reverse thrust being applied: that meant she was down, the big bird had made her landfall. The tower's rotating searchlight caught the Ilyushin half-way down the runway, flooding the white and red and silver of the fuselage as it began to slow for the taxi-ing run, and in a moment as the beam moved on the plane was lost, and there was only the noise and to the front the lights by which the men in the control tower could follow its progress.

All eyes fixed on the plane.

Like men who've seen a topless swimmer for the first time, and stare on unashamed – voyeurs, that's what we are, thought the controller. Fascinated by it, and it looks no different from any other plane, not from the scores he talked down each week. But they stared at it, as if hoping by their very persistence to see men with guns, or the passengers, unwilling to accept the shroud of night and that the Ilyushin was still a full six hundred yards away. They'd plotted on the airfield map where they wanted him to direct the aircraft to take its stand; the position had been carefully worked out, not for this flight, but years back when the hi-jack plan for Stansted had first been rehearsed.

'Turn her through 180, and back the way you came. Two hundred yards up on the starboard side you'll see a "Follow Me" van, with yellow lights. He'll take you to the stand. And well done to the pilot officer. Pass that to her, please, from all of us in here.'

'Roger.'

The controller saw the plane turn in the distance and begin a sedate progress back up the runway towards where the truck with the flashing amber lights waited. The searchlight on its pass picked out the two Saracens that crawled in pursuit – invisible to anyone on board.

'I'll stay with them till they douse the engines, then it's your problem, gentlemen.' Half a minute more, and wringing in sweat and knowing he'd slipped half the procedure rules but feeling for once in his life he'd achieved something, the controller eased out of his chair.

The Assistant Commissioner of Police for the country had taken his place beside him, looking warily at the equipment. Too bloody right, he thought, now it's our problem. Till the heavies get down from London.

Three green and white petrol tankers parked close to each other and forming a half-moon barricade. A little to the right of them a squat single-level building. Close to here that the Ilyushin should taxi and come to rest. Simple, logical, as all military plans should be, cover for the troops close to the aircraft, offering no risk of detection. Ten of the SAS team here, with their control radio set, their chests heaving slightly from the exertion of running to their hide with their equipment as the plane was readying for its approach. A hundred yards from it, perhaps less, certainly no more. They wore no badges of rank, were dressed in dark-blue, boiler-suit overalls and had covered their faces with the newly-developed lotion that turned the brightness of their skin into an indistinct mess. Stirlings, rifles, machine guns, an anti-tank rocket launcher, a crate each of the incapacitating CS gas canisters and smoke grenades. Via his elaborate radio net Major George Davies, 22nd Regiment of the Special Air Service, learned that the first stage of the planning blueprint had worked as had been hoped. But he was not a man who suffered from self-delusion, and he could recognize that this was a small bonus, trivial. Out beyond them, quiet, hidden and silent, lay the cordon of armoured cars and the prone and crouching soldiers of the Fusiliers.

The passengers' reaction to the successful touchdown was a great and spontaneous burst of applause. Shouts in Russian and Italian, and one in the English language, and all carrying the same message of admiration for Anna Tashova, a desperate gratitude for her skill and stamina. As the plane slowed some gave way to tears, noisily, silently, publicly and behind clenched fingers. Others hugged those who sat next to them, total strangers embracing and pressing their cheeks together, and there were smiles on the faces of the children who took their cue from their elders and realized that this was a moment of celebration. The experts who have studied the subject of hi-jacking, and who sit in the offices of the Secret Services or Defence Ministries of those countries that regard the problem with care, would have said that this was a totally predictable emotion for the passengers to be showing. They would point out that the morale of men and women and children who have travelled for many hours at gunpoint and at risk is a very fickle matter, that they are constantly seeking for the sign that their ordeal is over. On Aeroflot 927 there was a general feeling that their troubles were now gone. They had forgotten, because they wished to forget, the words spoken by Isaac in the passenger aisle a bare hour earlier.

Silly, helpless, laughing tears on the face of Luigi Franconi, something they would never have believed in his office in Vla Botteghe Oscure; not little Luigi, not the silent one. He found he could barely talk, not with coherence, and felt the muscles of his stomach slacken, his legs lapping hopelessly together. The arm of his friend round him, the comfort of Aldo Genti, who supervised in party headquarters the world of economic affairs, and who was a man who chose not to show his emotion.

'I did not believe it possible.'

'It is not finished yet, Luigi.'

'It cannot be worse than it has been. They will see reason now. The worst must be over.'

Further back towards the rear Edward R. Jones Jr swivelled his backside in the confines of his seat more to face Rebecca.

'What now, Miss? Where do we go from here?'

'We refuel. Then we go to Israel.'

It was an involuntary reply, and she knew that she was not supposed to talk, and hated herself for the weakness and loathing the moment because there was no-one with whom she could share the joy of the landing that was all around her. An outcast, her link with the general pleasure severed.

'Might not be easy, Miss. Like I said earlier.'

She bit at her tongue, stifling the desire to argue. Who was he to tell her what would happen? Sneering at her, contemptuous of her.

'What happens if they don't give you the fuel? What happens then?'

She did not reply, only stared back at him, trying to outlast his clear and unwavering gaze till she accepted defeat and focused again down the line of the cabin, unable to look back at where he sat. She heard him say to his wife, his voice loud and unrepentant, 'They haven't an idea in hell, these kids. It's what makes them so damned dangerous. If they were a bit more pragmatic about it all you could assess what they were going to do. But they're out of this world, don't know what it's about, and Christ only knows what they'll do when the truth sinks in.'

The art teacher leaned over from his window seat towards the headmaster, sandwiching the boy who sat between them. It was the first time anyone had spoken to him, first time for a life-span and his face was haggard with the strain of the silence, lines at his eyes, age at his mouth.

'Headmaster, we will support you. We believe in what you did. It was right what you attempted.' What they would all say. But who had joined him when they needed his strength, who had come to him with anything more than a medley of desultory kicks at the little bitch? Held their ground, hadn't they? Waiting to see the outcome, fearful of committing themselves till they knew who would win, who would stand condemned.

Forward in the cockpit Anna Tashova sat immobilized in her flying harness, head flopped on to her chest, eyes closed as if she were asleep. A very great tiredness she felt, and a desire only to immure herself behind any barricade that would protect her from the talk of the two men who had dictated her route and from the eyes and fingers of the dials and switches that peered back at her from the control panels. For her too the flight had seemed an infinite nightmare of darkened, cloying turnings chased and harried by endless closing pursuit with the only sedative to block out the images found in the mechanics of the aircraft, the occupation of controlling the insensate instruments. Like the American passenger whose existence she did not know of, she too wondered what would happen next. But unlike him, now that she had shut down the four Ivchenko engines, she cared not a damn.

The navigator – she had been briefly introduced to him before take-off by the captain because they had not flown together before, and she had forgotten his name – was shuffling his papers and maps. Methodical, a tidy man, and putting them quietly in his briefcase, as if they might be of further use. Yet the scope of the maps had long since been exhausted. To the border of the BDR, and everything after that on instruments and from the chorus of ground controllers who had passed them on, like a ship that flies the yellow flag and cannot find a welcoming port.

Both of them in their various ways ignored David's presence. The pilot officer who had not spoken since the landing, and the navigator who did not meet his eyes and who busied himself with trivia. And the captain too. Not a movement from him. Five hours dead now, and not a wavering of his posture; the ultimate act of defiance, sitting there, trapped, head bowed down. Face whitening, the mouth clamped fast as if in determination not to show the pain that would have come too fast for him to know it.

157

Isaac stood behind him at the end of the corridor, the mouth of the cabin, studying the passengers, relentless and with total concentration after the attempt to overpower Rebecca. Suspicious and hostile and watchful, seeming to crouch his body as though among the facing mass of people there was a missile or weapon that could damage him if he presented the broader target. He stood out in the centre of the aisle where all could see him if they stretched up from their seats and took note of the rock-firm grip on the handle of the sub-machine gun. The passengers would know that the inhibitions of the pressurization of the cabin had now deserted him. The plane was on the ground: he would have no hesitation in shooting now.

'I am going to talk to the tower on the radio. I want all the people to remain in their seats. No-one is to move, not for any reason.'

Isaac did not look away. His eyes were sweeping over the passengers like a prison tower searchlight, and nodded his agreement.

It seemed natural that David should resume the initiative, take up the leadership again. David waved – an afterthought – to the girl at the far end of the cabin, caught her attention and waved again and stayed long enough to see the thankfulness on her face.

'When you are ready, Isaac, take her place. She has been away from us too long.'

Inside the cockpit the navigator made way for him, but David declined the small, low-set seat, not wishing to box himself in, seeking the freedom of movement from which he could dominate. He held the gun in his left hand now, away from the pilot officer and the navigator, and with his right he began to pull at the head-set that was fastened to the ceiling of the flight deck.

'You waste your time,' the navigator said. 'Unless you speak in English there is no-one there who can talk to you.'

The navigator saw the disappointment cloud over the young man's face. So far, so much at stake for him, and no-one to speak his bloody language. Half a smile, little more than a suspicion, and covert, as David backed out of the cockpit, petulant anger rising.

He strode down the corridor, almost marching in his speed when he reached the passenger cabin aisle. For many of them it was their first clear glimpse of the man they took to be the leader of the group, the man most directly responsible for their position. Good-looking, those who could be remotely objective would have conceded, but they were few and from the majority there was only loathing, hidden in their turned-away faces. Edward R. Jones Jr took a surreptitious picture but doubted whether it would expose well in the dull, interior light. All the way to Rebecca, pushing past the drinks trolley, till he reached her and took her slowly and gently in his arms, the greeting of a brother, of a friend. An arm round her shoulders, and another pressing her head against his chest, the one that held his machine gun, and the gesture was awkward till he sensed the intensity of her response.

David felt the ripple of her breath playing on the skin of his neck, heard her say, 'Are we free now, David? Is it over, is it finished?'

'The crewman says there is no-one there who will speak in our language. You can speak some of their English; in a moment you must talk to them.'

'How will they be to us, after the Germans and the Dutch? How will the British be?'

He found that all he wished for was to hold the girl, keep her close, continue the contact. Her words now a distraction. He sensed the softness of her body, the pliant pull of her weight.

'Was it a great crime, the shooting of one policeman, and him not dead?' she continued. 'They know why we fight, they have told us on the radio of their sympathy. Does the wounding of one policeman outweigh all their statements?'

Tighter, closer, pressing her frailty against him. Silly, stupid girl. Lovely girl. Squeezing, hugging, her to him.

'You forget, Rebecca, you forget the captain in his cockpit. You have put him from your mind. But they know of it. At

Hanover they had the knowledge, and at Amsterdam, and these people here will know of it. I have killed the captain, and to these people he will be the martyr and we will be the animals. One shot only I fired. One shot. It was I who fired it, not Isaac. The door would not open, and I fired. I did not angle the gun, Rebecca, I did not fire for the floor. I killed him, Rebecca, and to them that will be murder . . .'

'You are wrong, David. Too tired to think.'

'Where can there be rest now?'

'You must calm yourself.'

'I should have been calm when I fired at the door.'

To the girl he seemed to sag, forcing her to grip at his waist to steady him. A terrible pain in his eyes, a great hurt. He hung on to her a full minute, then jolted awake.

'You are the one who speaks English, you must come and talk to them.' But he made no move to loosen her, just stood, rocking slowly, feeling her body against his own.

The words of the navigator barked over the loudspeaker system of the tower. Volume turned to maximum and the listeners knew from the sound of his breathing that the Russian was whispering.

'They are all out of the cockpit now. Three of them. The two men have machine pistols. There is also a girl, but she is always with the passengers and we have not seen her. I think they have gone for her, because they do not speak English, the men. I have said there are no Russian speakers. Sometimes they are calm, sometimes they shout. They believe they will get fuel for Israel, and . . . they are returning.'

Nothing more came from the loudspeakers. There was an opportunity for the second tape recorder to be switched on, while the spool of the first was lifted off and hurried for transcription. There had been a shorthand note, but every word spoken from the control tower would, as usual, be recorded.

'A very switched-on boy, that one,' the Assistant Chief Constable said. 'Be a star hanging on his chest when this lot's over.'

He'd done the courses and seminars, Home Office-organized, and attended the Special Study Groups, because Stansted was in his 'manor', and if the fiction became reality then he was designated as having a part to play. He fancied he knew his subject, and liked the fact known. It put him a cut above administering CID and Regional Crime Squad and investigating the corruption allegations.

'The fact that there's only three of them, and that one is a girl, where does that put things?' The question was from the Fusiliers Colonel, familiar enough with urban guerrilla fighting across the Irish Sea, inexperienced in this particular field.

The Assistant Chief Constable warmed, revelling in the deference shown him by the army officer. 'I think the fellow knew what we wanted to hear. Took his opportunity well and gave us the bones of it. Didn't mention explosives. On the Middle East jobs they try and booby-trap the doors, but he didn't say anything about that. Could be that he just doesn't know, but if they haven't then it has to be easier for us if we go heavy. The fact that there are three means it's not likely to last long. But I didn't like what he said about the shouting: infinitely more dangerous to everyone if they become unstable. Then anything can happen.'

There was much more the policeman could have said, a longer and more elaborate assessment. But the voices behind him cut him short, and the bustle of activity behind him, and the drift of the attention that he had held veered towards the door. The familiar TV features of the Home Secretary who grinned thinly at the stiff salute. There was a man at his right shoulder that he had not seen before, not present at the weekend courses – worn, pale, autumn face, and baggy under the eyes. There were handshakes and he caught a name. 'Webster, Charlie Webster,' no explanation of rank or department. Had they started talking yet from the plane? And he'd scarcely begun to answer before the newcomer was in the chair where he'd been sitting and close to the extended microphone and was gathering together rough paper and drawing a Biro from his pocket. Wouldn't say that he was unhappy that someone else had come to do the chat, but he'd like to have been asked, to have known the pedigree.

Charlie slid his jacket from his shoulders, slung it over the back of the seat-rest, loosened his tie, and settled himself to wait for the contact. Sort of been drawn into it, hadn't he? Never really been asked. Just expected of him, taken for granted. Charlie Webster, terrorist hunter back on the job, keeping people safe in their beds, letting the great unwashed fornicate in peace, and by-the-by chopping a few kids who'd been sold some crap ideology and thought they could change the world on the strength of it.

The transcript was placed in front of him; he read it briefly – three to chop this time. Shouldn't be too difficult, Charlie. Not unless they played stupid.

The Parliamentary Private Secretary was at the cabinet administering the ice cubes, pouring out the gin.

'Plenty of that, and not too much tonic.' The Foreign Secretary always said that and it didn't affect the same weak mixture that was always surrendered to him. He had hated the drive back from Dorneywood, detested the speed. It should have been one of the privileges of his rank that he didn't have to submit to those bloody siren-paced races up the M4. Generally he was able to instruct the driver that he wanted a steady ride, forty-five miles an hour, but events hadn't waited on him that evening. The Russian would be waiting outside, in the ante-room, but time first for a stiff one – not that it would be. Some of the blighters you couldn't talk to, the Russians, not a spark of contact, dead as the Sargasso. But at least this fellow was out of the ordinary, quite human, and good enough English to ditch the interpreter which always seemed to smooth the way. He downed his drink in a single gulp, leaving the ice and the lemon slice unsullied, then handed the glass back to his PPS; the man knew the drill, put it out of sight in the cabinet and closed the doors on the array of bottles.

'Let's have him,' the Foreign Secretary said.

Decent-looking chap, in his way, hair well cut, and not a bad suit. First impressions of the Foreign Secretary at the entrance at the far end of the 40 foot office of the Russian Ambassador at the Court of St James. He offered him a seat on the sofa and took his own place in the armchair at the side. PPS behind them both with the scribbling pad and the pencil. Not really form, not having an FO man in here with them, but the Russian hadn't brought anyone either. There were times for an official, minuted record, times when it wasn't suitable; and neither was seeking to preserve this particular conversation for posterity.

'I would like to say first,' the Ambassador began – flawless English, marginal accent – 'that my government sends a message of gratitude to the British government for permitting the Aeroflot flight to land.' With a gesture of his hand the Foreign Secretary acknowledged the formalities. 'But I think, Minister, that we both understand that we have reached a most difficult and complex stage in the handling of this criminal incident. I am informed by my government that prior to the murderous hijacking of the aircraft this gang of thugs had attempted to kill a policeman in the city of Kiev. For this they were being sought at the very time that they took over the Aeroflot flight from that city to Tashkent, and by doing so endangered the lives of many innocent passengers. During their capture of the aircraft – which had no armed security men on board – they killed the captain at his seat in the cockpit – we have been told by the young pilot officer who successfully flew the plane to Britain that her captain was executed as the assassins took over the flight deck. All of this you know, Foreign Secretary. Also you will have had by now the communication of my government, personally signed by the Comrade Secretary General of the Party, and sent to all heads of government in the countries in which we thought it possible that the aircraft might land.'

He had the admiration of the British politician. So many of them would have taken half an hour to get to the point, but they were already there, and the first cigarette in the Russian's hand not half-smoked.

'My government look upon these three not as political refugees but as murderers and criminals. We regard them as you regard the terrorists of the Irish Republican Army that bomb your cities. When you arrested the men and women of Birmingham and Guildford, the terrorists of your central London campaign, you put them through the courts and you sentenced them as your law permits. I venture to say that if these men had taken refuge in any European country you would have sought their arrest and extradition. We cannot believe that the British government would contemplate the refuelling of the aircraft to facilitate its flight to Israel.' There was a nod of acquiescence from the Foreign Secretary. 'And after your authorities have disarmed these people we will require that they be sent back forthwith to the Ukraine to face justice in Kiev. I am also informed – and this may help you arrive at your final decision – that the position of the aircraft at the moment the captain was shot places the crime within the jurisdiction of the courts of that city.

'That is what I have been asked by the senior personalities of the Soviet Foreign Ministry to pass to your Excellency in addition to the communication of the Comrade Secretary General. I have also been asked to furnish some indication of the attitude that the British government will take in this matter.'

Right between the eyes, and where he'd expected it. Been dealing with them long enough to know that the sting was always in the tail. Used a hard word, for the language of diplomacy that was: 'require', nearest thing to an ultimatum you could get, not a friendly word, not leaving much room for manoeuvre. And wanting some sort of answer off the cuff. He knew the problems just like everyone else did, but was piling on the pressure from the start, getting his foot in the door. He'd done it well.

'I can assure you – and you may pass this on to your government and to the Comrade Secretary General – that it is not the intention of the British security forces and officials who are currently at Stansted that the aircraft should leave there except as a free flight and without passengers and crew being held at gun point. There is no question while the plane is under the command of armed men that it will be refuelled for an onward flight to Israel. That is a solemn guarantee.' The easy section, obvious and would satisfy nobody. The next leg was harder. 'I am advised by the British government's legal officers that the hi-jackers have already contravened various sections of the British criminal code, certainly illegal possession of firearms, possibly kidnapping, and it is likely that should they surrender they would be required to face the due process of United Kingdom law . . .'

'I do not wish to have to report to my government that in my opinion the British would use minor charges to protect these three criminals from the Soviet courts. Perhaps I have not made myself clear, Excellency: we want these people back. We want them quickly. We would take procrastination on this point as a most serious matter.'

'Threats will not be conducive to settling our problems.' It was quietly said by the Foreign Secretary, but with the acting and the politeness vanishing from the soft-lit room.

'It is not a threat.'

'Then I misunderstand your choice of words. We must be most careful in the choice of words that we use, otherwise we will have misunderstandings, which would be unfortunate.'

'What then should I inform my government concerning the extradition of these people?' A fractional retreat, but tactical only, and the Foreign Secretary knew it would mean as little at the end of the day as his answer.

'You should tell your government that the British Foreign Secretary has undertaken to pass on the details of this conversation personally to the Prime Minister. You should also say that the first priority of the British government is to ensure the safe release of all the passengers and crew of the plane. In the short term we regard that as the more important issue.'

The Soviet Ambassador rose, smile back on his face, firm grip in his handshake, a word about future meetings and he was through the door and into the ante-room. He had time as he walked across the Isfahan carpet to recognize the short and stubbed presence, buried in an easy chair, of the Israeli Ambassador, now waiting for his appointment.

There was no greeting, no acknowledgement from either.

From where he sat Charlie Webster had as good a view as any of the Ilyushin.

Static and immobilized, it was swathed in light from the portable floodlights that the military had put in place within a hundred yards of its towering, crab-like form.

Behind Charlie were the Emergency Committee who would dictate his replies once the hi-jackers chose to begin transmissions. The Home Secretary, there at the Prime Minister's request to assume overall political control of the affair, with the covey of civil servants hovering near to him, to advise and to caution. The Assistant Chief Constable, spruced and neat and boasting the thin multi-coloured ribbons of war service and police work on his chest. Two army officers who had made a separate journey from London, coming from Ministry of Defence. One civilian, as different from the rest of them in his own right as was Charlie; check shirt and the collar stiffeners bent in too many washes so that they rode up his sports coat lapels, a tie that had shields on it that were lost and disfigured by the many times it had been knotted, hair that was long and had not known the benefit of comb and water and that hung loosely from the body of his head, rounded brown corduroy trousers and scuffed brown shoes: not a man who was kept, not a man who owed allegiance to conformity, stiff bold cheekbones and a ferret nose that poked and pried into the conversations around him. Not somebody who was accepted but tolerated, because he was the psychiatrist in the team, with a special rôle to play: the man with experience of psychopaths, of the deranged, who had advised on the siege at Balcombe Street, and the Spaghetti House stake-out in London's West End. The Dutch with their knowledge of the prison and train hostage-taking operations had proved the value of a medical man in the team, and the Home Office had drafted Anthony Clitheroe into their plans, placing him on call so that he could be summoned from his Wimpole Street practice whenever the need arose.

Later the group would disperse to the offices of the airport management but at that moment all of them wanted to witness the initial contact, sought to hear the timbre of the voices of the opposition still hidden from them by the sleek, wind-wiped walls of the Ilyushin's fuselage.

In front of him Charlie had placed the three photographs he had been given in London: he could see the faces, study them, learn from them. Further to his right, as if denoting its lesser importance, he had laid the diagram of the interior of the 11–18. He felt nervous, tense in his stomach, waiting for them to begin, longing for them to do so. But had to let them take the initiative, that was the procedure; the young people should not be hurried, all the privileges of the bride.

It was the girl who spoke first.

'To the authorities, do you hear us . . . do you hear us?'

'We hear you very clearly.'

'Do you hear us : . .' The girl had forgotten, or never known, that she had to take her finger off the depress switch when she'd finished speaking, otherwise she couldn't hear the replies. Stupid cow.

'We hear you very clearly.'

Her memory of the technicalities jolted, or someone had told her, but now she had mastered the equipment. 'We call ourselves the Kingfisher group. We wish to talk to the responsible persons. Have they come yet?'

Not bad English, out of the classroom – like your Russian, Charlie. She was speaking too close to the microphone so that she distorted and he could not gauge the strength of her spirits, her morale.

'Hello, Kingfisher group.' Where had they dug that one up? Out of the norm – Black September, Black June, First of April movement, Struggle group of any wet November Thursday, that was what they'd come to expect. 'My name is Webster,

Charlie Webster. We can talk in Russian or English, whichever you prefer. If you want to talk in Russian you must accept that there will be pauses while I translate to the people that are with me what you are saying.'

Silence, while they worked it out. Decide whether the big man in the group wants to do the talking for himself, which means Russian, or whether they delegate to the girl. A handwritten note was passed in front of him. Charlie should not let it be known the Emergency Committee had already assembled at the airport. Going for the stall game and delay; Clitheroe's advice was clear on this, adamant.

In Russian, and a man speaking. Sounded an age away, more distant than the girl, subdued, unsure; perhaps just the angle to the microphone.

'My name is David. I wish to speak to the persons in charge.'

Charlie in Russian too. Couldn't match his dialect, softer, less cruel to the ear than the harsher speech of the north, of Moscow. Wouldn't try to ape him, just speak the way he had been taught, the way they were all taught in 'I' Corps where it was assumed that any Russian they would need to interrogate had done his secondary school in the Kremlin's shadow. Not easy, not at first. Seemed a long time since he'd spoken the language conversationally. One thing to read newspapers and official reports, even to write it, but quite another to chat in the tongue and summon up the persuasiveness to win confidence.

'Webster, Charlie Webster here. I'm the Russian language speaker, but as I explained to your colleague there will be delays while I tell my colleagues what you are saying, and what I am telling you.' Take all night at this rate. He flicked the transmission button to 'off' on the console in front of him, told the men who stood behind what he had said. Back to 'on'. Live again.

'We should say who we are. The Kingfisher group is Jewish. We are of a people who have long been oppressed and persecuted. We are political persons. We have flown out of the Soviet Union because we seek to arrive in Israel, and now we need fuel

168

to continue our journey. We mean no harm to anyone, but we demand the fuel. Have you understood that?'

'I have understood that, David. I am going to tell my colleagues what you have said.' Charlie repeated the drill on the console, turned in the swing chair and explained the message.

The Home Secretary said, 'You know, Mr Webster, that there is no possibility of them having fuel. The question is, do they find that out now or later?'

Anthony Clitheroe was an eminent man in his field, accustomed to delivering detailed and lengthy speeches to his colleagues, with a considerable list of major studies to his name and a quarter of a column of *Who's Who* to back up his claims to be heard out. But he had learned from his two previous encounters with security forces that they required the shortest of responses from him in such situations.

'Find an excuse, put him off, tell him the people necessary to make such a decision are not here, and won't be till the morning.'

Finger back to the console, Charlie speaking again to the flight deck.

'David, this is a very important request that you are making, and one which would have to be considered very carefully by the British government. The problem is that we're in the middle of the holiday season here. Many of the most senior men are away on their vacations. There is no-one here who could give that sort of authorization. Probably we won't be able to get a decision till the morning.'

'Don't make a fool of me.' The inanimate, detached voice cracked back from the loudspeaker high on the back wall of the control tower. Pitch rising, and hostility communicated.

'I'm not making a fool of you, David.'

'Don't take me for an idiot. The Germans were able to make a decision that we should not land, the Dutch were able to offer us impossible conditions knowing that we would not accept. We are not peasants. Your people facilitated this landing; that was not authorized by a junior official. Do not tell me that the responsible people cannot now be contacted. Do not play a game with me. We are very tired, we are impatient now. Do you know why I say that . . . ?'

'Of course you are tired, and that is the more reason why you should sleep, and the pilot too must have a chance to sleep, and then we can talk in the morning.'

'Not in the morning. We want the fuel tonight. In the morning we fly.'

'It is not possible . . .'

'It must be possible. Tell your people that, whoever they are. Tell them.'

Clocks ticking, a subdued cough, the shuffling of feet. Charlie sighed, loosened his collar further and turned once more to his audience; but they didn't need him – not to give them the bones, at any rate. They'd picked that up from the voices – David's anger, Charlie's wheedling. But he went through the drama and the explanation.

The Assistant Chief Constable had manoeuvred till he was at the Home Secretary's shoulder. 'With respect, sir – and I acknowledge that there are others better qualified in these matters than myself – but it's dangerous this way round, codding them along. I suggest we make it plain, right from the start, that they are not flying on, that it's not negotiable.'

'I want to lead them to the realization gradually.' Clitheroe held his ground, not seeking proximity to their political master, aloof and with his hands in his pockets. 'You have heard the man's voice; it didn't need Mr Webster's translation to tell you he's near-hysterical. He is exhausted, and may become totally irrational. If you push him you could have a suicide situation, at best a collapse, at worst mayhem among the passengers.'

First conflict, Charlie thought to himself. Haven't been here forty-five minutes and they're swapping punches already. Always the same when you try and do things by committee.

'You have to take a firm line . . .'

'Not for its own sake, only if that helps the end result.'

The Home Secretary looked beyond his protagonists. Then he went to the man who had impressed him in London, who seemed to know and who had the humility of caution in his assessments.

'Mr Webster. Stall them, or give it to them straight?'

Charlie closed his eyes, tried to think, to see his way into the minds of the three young Russians. Just photographs and distant voices. How in God's name did you answer that one? 'I think I'd go with the doctor,' he said, noting the anticipation of the Assistant Chief Constable blend into his set, uniformed, clipped moustache face. 'With respect to all who might disagree with me, we should not underestimate what they've been through, to put it crudely. The stress they've been under, the strain . . .' What do you know about strain, Charlie? Well, more than any of these buggers. 'They could go mad if we rapped them down right now.'

Clitheroe didn't acknowledge Charlie's support, just walked away and jangled the coins in his pocket. The policeman was gazing through the windows.

'Stall them, Mr Webster,' said the Home Secretary. He looked hard at Charlie, seeking rapport, trying to share the loneliness of taking decisions on conflicting advice. Sorry, can't help you, sir. You say what happens, I just march up and down and do as I'm told.

'David, it's Charlie here. Now you've got to listen to me.' Trying to get colloquial, trying to find the phrases that create understanding. 'David, listen. We've spoken to London by telephone, and we are told that the ministers of the British government will be meeting later tonight or in the early hours of the morning. They have to talk about this thing, David. You have to believe me, they must be allowed some time. We'll have an answer by dawn. That's the best I can offer you, David. It's a very important matter, this. They must have time to talk about it. They promise an answer by the morning.' They'll have an answer by the time you've had a good night's sleep, by the time you've calmed yourself, by the time the SAS boys have it all worked out.

'You are trying to confuse us, Charlie. You do not think that

171

we are serious people.' But the doubt was registering – that much was clear from the inflection. Don't know what to do, what to say. Had the set speech worked out for the 'yes' or 'no' answer, and they're thrown by the 'wait and see'.

'I'm not trying to confuse you, David. Just explaining things the way they are.'

'You do not deceive me?'

'I don't deceive you, David. You'll have the answer in the morning, good and early.' Like pinching pocket money out of a blind school. First-timers – no briefing, no plan, just showed up and hoped for the best.

'Good night, Charlie. And you will tell us early the reply of your government. Tell us about the fuel and the onward flight to Israel.'

'Good night, David. We'll talk in the morning.'

Believe that lot and you'll believe anything. Charlie tucked the console button back to the 'off' position, stretched up out of his chair and braced his legs stiff from the long period crouched at his desk.

To no-one in particular he said, 'I thought they'd be better than that.'

9

The Foreign Secretary would dearly have liked another of his PPS's mixtures from the cabinet, but it was hardly the suitable time for that – not with the night stretching ahead, the threat increasing.

For this senior politician with a lifetime of manoeuvring and negotiating in the fraught and deceptive world of diplomacy the problem was totally straightforward – so clear-cut indeed, that the area for compromise was minimal. He had a fair idea of the appeal that the Israeli would make to him, knew it would be impassioned and emotional and difficult to deflect. His rôle would thus not be easy. He still carried the burden of the one-time superpower, one-time member of the Big Five, but the world had moved on, and the weight in affairs abroad of the government he now represented had diminished to a startling degree in the previous two decades. And if the cloth had shrunk so had the muscle of the wearer. Circumspection was required if he were to avoid the unnecessary pitfalls of winning the hostility of those who had usurped the influence that had once been Britain's. Forget the principle, take the practical way out. And why not, with these silly children to concern himself with? The Russians would want them back, the Israelis would accept almost anything other than that course. Three idiot children, and because of them he wrestled with a dilemma that should not have existed, who to offend, who to hurt – the monolith of the Soviet Union, or the massive voice of the Jewish lobby across the free world. Damned ridiculous. And both of them, Russians and Israelis alike, would be wanting one thing in common from him that evening, a binding commitment on a course of action. Only card he held, and he'd see both went home without it.

He'd stayed in his armchair after the Russian had gone, musing, turning the problem over slowly in his mind. When he rose to greet the Israeli Ambassador it was with some awkwardness, the legacy of the war-time shrapnel embedded in his hip. It was not usual for the Foreign Secretary himself to greet ambassadors, not when the issue at stake was the future of three juveniles, killers, but then the situation was not usual; no point on an evening such as this in sticking to protocol. Another circumspect bottom sinking into the comfort of the settee's soft cushions, a moment's pleasantries, and then the starting gun.

'Our position is sensitive, Foreign Secretary, in that we do not have any direct connection with these people, we knew nothing of them before their action became public knowledge. I begin with that, but my government believes it carries a responsibility to all the Jewish peoples, not just to those who reside in the State of Israel, a responsibility that we must discharge within the boundaries of acceptable international conduct.' The Ambassador was leaning forward, and having difficulty making his point with the emphasis he strove for as his small body had sufficiently depressed the cushions that he was unable to gain the height and stature suitable for his address. 'That these young people have committed crimes we accept – serious crimes, we accept that also. In our country there have been no executions since the mass-murderer Eichmann was put to death, in Great Britain there have been none for close to fifteen years. We have both abolished the death penalty for humanitarian reasons. Neither of us believes in judicial killings.' The Foreign Secretary raised an eyebrow; an art he had, only the right eyebrow, and its intention was to signify scepticism. He did it very well. A popular vote in either Britain or Israel would, he thought, have endorsed with enthusiasm a return of capital punishment if directed against the IRA men who bombed the British cities, or the Black September gangs that assaulted the northern Israeli settlements. But the Ambassador was not to be deterred by the movement of a hair line. 'In the Soviet Union these three will face the supreme penalty . . .' and that would be so wrong? . . . 'I would suggest that you could assume with near certainty that these three will be put to death if they are returned to Russia . . .' and would the world be a poorer place in their absence? . . . 'My government could not countenance the sending of these three young people to a death they would not have faced if their crimes had been committed in your territory or in ours . . .' serve the little blighters right . . . 'I am instructed by my Prime Minister to ask of you an immediate guarantee that these people will not be returned to Kiev.'

'What would you suggest happens to them?'

'I am instructed by my government that we would accept their appearance before British courts, and that should they be convicted then they would serve terms of imprisonment inside the United Kingdom.'

'And what charges would they face in Britain?'

'They would face the charges that would have been laid against them in Kiev.'

The Foreign Secretary drew a long breath. An audacious approach, but then that was to be expected. Same as the damned Russians, seeking the propaganda coup – that much was clear to him, even through the pain that meant tiredness and that the fragments of metal still bit at the encasing gristle deep in his body. Concern for advantage, paramount; concern for the lives at stake, minimal. 'I am reminded – though I do not have the exact text at hand – of the eloquent statement made recently by your Ambassador to the United Nations General Assembly. It was a call, if I recollect, for a rule of law to combat aerial piracy, a demand that nations should band together to stamp out this contemporary evil. Are we to assume that the religious faith of these three young people excludes them from the type of justice you would wish to see exacted upon men of other creeds?'

The Ambassador did not answer him. It came as no surprise to the Foreign Secretary: diplomats seldom replied to each other's points of debate. It failed to get them anywhere if they did.

'As you know, with the co-operation of your government, we are sending a personal representative of the government of Israel to Britain. This man is a fighter, he holds a substantive rank in those units of our armed forces that deal exclusively with the terrorist threat. If you were to find it possible to commit your government not to return the young people to their deaths then we would order the officer to use his utmost influence to persuade them to surrender without further bloodshed. We have chosen this man with care. It is not accidental that he is the one who has been sent. In our society were his name and his achievements able to be published he would be a hero among us. We believe he is the man to appeal to these youngsters, to gain much from them, more than you can achieve.'

No longer audacious, damned arrogant now.

'What makes you think we need help . . . ?'

'We have the experience.'

'And no-one else?'

'Not to the same degree, no. Ask the Germans who were responsible at Munich, ask your friend the President of Uganda.'

'You know, of course, that the government of the United Kingdom does not have an extradition treaty with the Soviet Union.'

'I know that military aircraft can take off under cover of darkness, and that politicians can justify their actions at a future date.'

'The Ambassador of the Soviet Union has just departed after telling me *his* government required an immediate answer on the same question that you ask. I told him that we were considering the situation.'

'From which he would have assumed,' said the Ambassador, 'that the British require time.'

'If that was his assumption then it would have been a correct one. Your officer will indeed be taken to Stansted, but whether there is any part for him to play, while conditions are attached to his presence, remains a matter of debate.'

Termination of the conversation. The need that was much

more pressing was to speak with the Prime Minister. Worthless and predictable this, a mere swapping of words now that the battle-lines had been drawn.

Alone, while the PPS led the Ambassador through outer offices and empty corridors, the Foreign Secretary sat still in his chair. What if they were not his concern, what if the ministry of another country were in turmoil over the problem, what if he were exonerated of anxiety? Would his feelings on the fate of three young people be different then? How many speeches had he made in the constituency . . . the Russian threat – the need for vigilance – not to lower our guard – persecution – the tanks of the Warsaw pact – how many war planes, how many missiles, divisions, chemical-gas batteries of artillery . . . always went down damn well, those speeches, particularly at the mid-July garden fête. Three children had taken the System to battle, thrown a tatty unlined glove at it, and looked for a champion to ride to their rescue. Well, they'd have to look elsewhere, wouldn't they? Silly little blighters.

Wouldn't bother the switchboard, dial it himself, the number that was personal and restricted, the Prime Minister's holiday home.

In the forward corridor of the aircraft, where they could achieve privacy, straddled between the cockpit and the passenger cabin, David and Isaac and Rebecca talked of the radio conversation with the man who called himself Charlie. None of them had ever met an Englishman before, which made their attempts at assessing what had been told them difficult, almost impossible. There had been English students on the campus that both Isaac and Rebecca had seen since they had started their studies at Kiev University, but they had not been in their classes. There had been no point of contact.

David had said it was better to wait till the morning before talking again. Isaac had not challenged him, realized the depth of exhaustion to which his friend succumbed, saw the need he had for sleep and reassurance. Get no sense out of David, not till he was rested. Wished he'd been there, in the cockpit, to hear at first hand the message from the ground, but his persistent, clinging anxiety about their security at the hands of the passengers following the incident with Rebecca had prevented that. While David was talking behind him in the flight deck he had hovered in the doorway of the cabin, attention bound to his charges, watching them, a chicken with its brood when the fox is close to the coop. Told later of the conversation he had laughed to himself, amused at David's faith, convinced of his own suspicions.

Many hours now since either had lain in a bed; the last sleep reduced to a few tossing and restless minutes on the floor of the forest hut. Both were unshaven, and the new growth tickling and irritating at their collars, and their eyes large and reddened, slow and sluggish in their movements. The girl was worse than both of them, hardly able to keep her lids from closing and vague in what she said when they spoke to her. Had to sleep, all of them, had to devise a rota for resting. And now circling, aimlessly and without direction, around the conversation that David had made with the tower, and him defensive about what he had said, and the girl uncomprehending and repeating only that the man they spoke to was called Charlie, and that he had *promised*. Had to get them to sleep, both of them, and summon for himself the strength to outlast and out-fight his own great weariness. A few more minutes, then they could go, could be excused, could seek the deliverance they needed. But first the passengers, the currency, valuable, without price, first he should concern himself with the passengers. Voice a little hoarse now, but clear and to those who listened these were the words of a man who had usurped command, who had filled the vacuum of leadership.

'We have requested that the English give us fuel. We are told that their government is meeting in London tonight to discuss our request. They will tell us their answer by the early morning. In the meantime we will all sleep on the aircraft.' He paused and there was the vaguest of smiles, a suspicion, and he corrected himself. 'In the meantime you will all sleep on the aircraft. There is no food for you, and there will be no drinks. You must not talk and nobody on any pretext must leave their seat. The lights will remain on through the night, and all of you who sit at the windows must draw their blinds. We will shoot if anyone moves. That must be understood. When I say we will shoot, you should not take it just as a threat. You should not seek to prove me.'

Isaac walked half-way down the aisle to where the legroom was greatest, to the seats by the passage to the emergency doors with the escape route on to the wings. Luigi Franconi and Aldo Genti were on his right, three of the schoolchildren from Lvov to the left. He beckoned to them with his gun barrel, the motioning gesture drawing them from their seats as if he had discarded the possibility that they would understand his speech. The children were simple, absorbed immediately among their friends, but the Italians were harder and he had to lead them down the aisle to where there were vacant places and stifled protests from those who were comfortable and settled. Both had to climb over knees and bags and passengers that were already settled and unyielding and heavy with hostility at the disturbance, Franconi two rows in front of Genti, separated from their camaraderie and nervous and fiddling with their spectacles. Isaac checked the doors till he was satisfied they had not been tampered with, were as secure as they had been when they were airborne. He walked on down the aisle, the sub-machine gun swinging easily in his hand, turning neither to right nor left, as if ignoring those who sat to either side of him. He walked to where the drinks trolley still blocked the rear passageway to the far exit, and bent down to rummage under the final row of seats till his hands emerged with two life jackets, brilliant orange and with their straps sagging. A few moments work and he had lashed the trolley to the nearest seat legs, pulling on the knots he had made with the straps till he was satisfied that they would hold. A slight and primitive barricade, an obstruction between the body of the plane and the back exit. He returned down the aisle, now staring his way through the passengers, as if his whim had changed and he sought to force his personality over them, but there were no takers, no heroes seeking a dangerous laugh at his expense. Even the American was not talking. And the headmaster looking straight ahead even when Isaac brushed his hip against the shoulder of the sitting man.

Isaac came past David and Rebecca, not stopping, and went on to the cockpit. Again the gesture with the gun, and the pilot officer and the navigator unfastened their harnesses, climbed up from their seats and moved back towards the main cabin. As she came through the passage entrance Anna Tashova dropped her façade of competence and seriousness and grinned, meeting the eyes in front of her, identifying the heads and faces, seeing on them the broad lines of gratitude and thanks. She had heard the clapping when she had landed the Ilyushin, and it had warmed her, a sweetening and sustaining gesture, and now she saw again from these people the trust and regard in which they held her. They were all too frightened to speak to her – yet who was she to call them cowards? She had been told what it was like in the 'Former Times', as the elderly referred to them, when Josef Stalin, who was now a 'non-person', had ruled, when the secret police were rampant, when the prisons were full and the firing squads busy. She knew why they were quiet, and wondered what more she might do to protect them. She found a seat near the front of the plane, the navigator further back.

Isaac lingered near her, interrupting his continuous movement for a moment. He wanted her to speak to him, as if he believed she was part of their plan in some confused and abstract way. Twice he was about to move on his mission of bedding down the passengers, but he faltered, staying close, inviting conversation that she was not prepared to offer.

'Are you comfortable, Miss Tashova?' Almost a request for her acquiescence.

'As comfortable as any of the passengers.'

'I hope you can sleep there, that you will be rested.'

The soft derisive snort in response. 'It is hard to sleep when watched by a gun.'

'It is not of our making, Miss Tashova. We had not believed

we would still be on the aircraft tonight. We had thought to sleep in beds . . .'

'And Yuri, you had thought for him to sleep in a coffin?'

'It was not as we intended.'

'Go tell him that.' Cruel and hurting, spoken low so that those around her could barely hear. 'Go and whisper it in his ear.'

'I tell you it was not intended.' Hardening, his respect cooling. 'You must sleep, Miss Tashova, that you can fly in the morning.'

'There will be no flight from here. Your friend knows it. Have you seen him, have you looked at him? He knows. He knows the penalty for killing Yuri. Only when the jets were with us, when he had so much to think of, only then could he forget our captain. And now he remembers him. Have you not watched your leader? Perhaps you should . . . perhaps you should study him, and absorb what you see.'

She spoke slowly, certain in her words, comforted by the knowledge that he listened.

'It is a trivial, pathetic little army that you have. Banal, insignificant beyond its guns. A leader who is frightened because he kills, a girl that is unsure of her rôle and who you hide at the back lest she should be a part in this and fail you . . .'

'But we have the guns, Miss Tashova. We have the guns and we will use them.' And there was enough in his voice to quieten her, as if at last she believed him. Nothing more to say, and his interest now lost in her, and she responded no further.

Isaac moved away. He checked the forward doors, then slipped back into the cockpit. He closed the door behind him, creating the darkness he needed to see beyond the steep-tilted, angled windows. It would take him time to see through the brilliance of the searchlights that played against the body of the aircraft. He sat himself at the back, where the navigator had been, outside the orbit of the light they could throw on to the flight deck. He kept very still, head motionless, body relaxed and even comfortable in the crewman's seat, steeling himself all the time to resist the tugging and clawing of drowsiness. Would not stay, not more than a few minutes, have to go back into the passage and relieve David and Rebecca; couldn't last, not the way they were, and he must take the burden of the night watch. Not enough of them – that was the fault, not enough for a shift system of watching and guarding. But nowhere you would have found more, Isaac. Not a member of a group, of an organization, with a hydra of cells sprouting, with a recruiting belt in motion, delivering the fodder who could stand and take their positions while others slept. He didn't even know whether others would have followed if they had disseminated their message, who they could have trusted, confided in.

Movement out there. In the space between the searchlights to the left of the cockpit. Shadows at play, flirting and diving and disappearing, but he had seen the men move. And dimmed headlights approaching, and rear lights that were reddened and departing. They came to within two hundred metres of the plane, and he wondered if the men were closer. He watched the lights turn as if unwilling to test whatever strength he possessed with too close a contact, and instantly he was aware of the two soldiers, saw the tripod of the machine gun, and the reflection from the ammunition belt. One man behind the weapon, the other crouched at the side of the barrel, saw it and lost it as the vehicle continued its traverse. Of course there would be soldiers out there, but how many and how close? Another with the silhouette of the rifle at the trail running across the front of the moving lights, hurrying and bent low so that he would be only minimally visible. He thought of precautions he'd taken inside the aircraft; inadequate, hopelessly inadequate if they came. And David believing when the man told him to sleep, told him the message would come in the morning . . . what would their orders be? Take them alive, or kill them? David, the stupid bastard, the one who they followed, and he had drunk in the syrup, taken it right down into his guts, believed what he had been told because he was tired and wanted to sleep and did not understand the trap that had been prepared for them.

No relaxation now, hunched in the seat, and with his back muscles taut and his eyes hurting as he strained into the darkness, seeking more evidence of the perimeter they had placed around the plane. Lights further back this time, on and off, perhaps a couple of seconds, but time enough to understand the gaunt outline of two parked armoured cars. Faintly amused him; all the precautions they would be taking to ensure the watchers from the plane saw nothing of their preparations, and he had outsmarted them. Had seen the machine gun, and the soldier who ran, and now the armoured cars. What did they want the killing apparatus for? Why did they need it if they would supply the petrol in the morning? A mirthless smile, something secret and personal to himself.

As he sat alone with his thoughts in the shadowed cockpit Isaac's resolve hardened. He would fight them all, do battle with the heavy guns and with the tanks they would send, and his hand was steady on the stock of the gun that nestled against his lap. Better here, he thought, than in the cellars with the militia men around him. What did they do to you, Moses? And how did you keep your silence, how did you win us the time to fly out? The pigs are here too, Moses, different only in their clothes and the voices, but they are here, where we did not expect them to have friends.

'If they had told me it would be like this, Moses, I would not have believed them.' There was no-one to hear his words, none for company but the captain. It was an accident, it was not intended, old man. Join the ranks of the casualties – there are many of them. And there will be more, the crossfire will fiercen, the uninvolved who stand between the guns will be many . . .

Isaac came out of the cockpit, moved quietly to where David stood leaning against the wall of the far end of the corridor beyond the cupboard doors.

'Sleep, David. You too, Rebecca. I will watch the first part of the night, then Rebecca can sleep when the passengers are quiet.'

David nodded, numb, unthinking, and slouched away

towards the open cockpit door. They heard him sink into the seat, still warm where Isaac had sat, and they heard him wriggling and turning till he found the position he wanted. Then nothing. Further back in the corridor beside the front exit to the plane were the seats that the cabin crew used for take-off and landing and when the plane was in turbulence. Isaac and Rebecca sat there, the girl on the inside, nearest the door, he leaning outwards so that his vision encompassed the whole of the cabin.

She said quietly, and she was close to his shoulder, 'Some of the old ones, and the children, they want to use the toilet, Isaac.'

'They cannot.'

'But there are old people here, Isaac, they must . . .'

'The Jews grow old. They too have wanted such things, Rebecca. Are there water closets at Potma and Perm, and basins to wash their hands in, to make themselves clean when they are locked in the huts at night? They lie in their filth.'

'David said it was for you to decide. They asked him, and he would not say himself, he said it was for you to decide.'

'And you, Rebecca, what would you do, how much have they weakened you?'

'I would let them go to the toilet, because they must have dignity. If you prevent them from going, if they mess themselves, then they have no dignity. We should not take that from them, whatever they have done to our people. We must show we are different to them. If we are the same, the animal same, then there is no salvation for us.'

Isaac stood up, abruptly, without further comment, and walked forward to the entrance of the cabin.

'There is a toilet here. You may come to it one at a time. You have to be quick, and you have to know what will happen if you exploit the kindness we show to you.' He spoke savagely, soured and resentful at the concession that had been wrung from him. 'And while you are squatting, think of the Jews in your camps, the ones you call "dissidents", whose crime in your eyes is that they want a new life. Think of them, wonder how they are crapping tonight. Think of their spoiled blankets. One at a time you come, and do not forget that the gun is loaded, and cocked.'

For a full hour a procession of passengers moved from their seats to the toilet and back again. Isaac insisted that only one person should be out of his seat at a time, and the process was pained and slow. Some thanked him for his consideration, others ignored him, and he saw those who had not lasted and had already fouled themselves, staining their trousers and dresses and who were ashamed and hated him. They will dance on my body should they kill me, he thought. Dance and sing as if it were a holiday. From the furthest row at the end of the plane came the one who seemed the farmer, he would be the last. As he passed Isaac he spat noisily and with rare force on to the carpet. One at last with balls to him! Isaac laughed out loud and smacked the old man on the back, and saw his face twist in astonishment that the gesture he had spent many minutes thinking over and which was the only protest he could muster should be taken so lightly.

When the man went back, with his bowed shoulders and his worn summer coat and the boots that were heavy and foreign to the aisle carpet, Isaac returned to his seat. He could hear David sleeping. What a mercy sleep was! The time of safety, when all is forgotten, when the dreads and fears are shut out. Lucky bastard. The one that brought us here, and who does not know the cold and the chill and the death that surrounds him. Lucky bastard, David. Dream yourself away, conjure up the wide streets of Israel, the sunshine, green trees that carry oranges, people who laugh and would make you welcome. Lucky David, always the lucky one. And the escape is yours, not ours. You sleep, content in your warmth; and we are left behind with the stink of our own bodies and of another sixty, and the odour of the lavatory.

'What will happen tomorrow?' She was drowsy, eyes half-closed, shoulder against his chest, head against his cheek.

'We will ask for fuel for the aeroplane.'

'And they will give it to us.' Faint voice, and he could not recognize whether she had asked a question or made a statement.

'No.'

'But we must have fuel to reach Israel.'

'They will not give us the fuel. They will not give it to us just because we ask.'

'But . . .'

'But nothing, Rebecca. They are all around our plane. They have machine guns that I have seen, and there are soldiers and light tanks. They are not waiting there to see the fuel loaded at dawn. They are waiting for us to break, Rebecca. They are waiting for our will to snap, fracture, so they can take us.'

'What can we do?' Trying to wake herself, trying to throw off the sleep that had near-engulfed her, bright wide eyes. 'What can we do?'

'We have to surprise them, convince them that we are hard, that we are serious, that we are not easily deflected.' Bored with the sound of his own words, attempting to communicate on a different level. Not something that you can express, only that you can feel. She had no comprehension, the words meant nothing to her. 'They have given in before. They sent the Arab girl back. Leila, Leila something . . . I do not remember her name. They sent her back to her people. If the threat is great enough they will bend. Have we the power to make the threat great enough?'

'Too many questions, Rebecca, and past time you were sleeping.'

Impatience cutting through, and there were too many questions. Too many questions that Isaac himself could not yet summon the answers to.

From behind the barricade of petrol tankers Davies watched the unloading of the equipment that had been brought to him from Science and Forensics, Scotland Yard. Four metal-encased crates, with warnings of 'Fragile' and 'This Way Up' stencilled on their tops and sides, boxes that were handled gingerly and with respect as they were carried from the rear doors of the van. The SAS unit crowded round the cargo, noted the

186

crudely-drawn eye with grotesque lashes that had been painted on the smallest box with the title of 'Cyclops'. Seen it all on exercise, never in the buff, the altogether. Had been at the Spaghetti House and Balcombe Street, but the SAS hadn't been called for – left it on both occasions to the police. But they'd seen the results and reckoned it would make their job way easier if the storm order came.

The Yard had sent their own operators, senior grade men from the civil service union, grey flannel trousers brigade, with buttoned collars and ties that carried the emblem of the single piercing eye, out of place among the denimed soldiers. No contact, no common ground, and a mutual suspicion between those who would operate the equipment and those who would take the risks in placing it in position where it could be best utilized. Some among the new arrivals sought out Davies and closeted with him over diagrams of the Ilyushin interior, fingers stabbing at the cockpit area, at the porthole sections on the flanks, at the windows set into the rear of the aircraft.

They had brought from London three pieces of equipment. Primary among them, pre-eminent, was the 'cyclops', the fisheye lens with its 180-degree visual capability. Relegated to secondary importance by those who now unwrapped the components from their padded cells were the suction adhesive audio devices. It was 'cyclops' that the experts swore by; a lens no bigger than the nail of a man's little finger and that was triggered to a camera via a flexible fibre cable. Had introduced it into the sealed basement of Spaghetti House, down the ventilation shaft, clandestine and silent, to provide the crystal-bright pictures of the siege room, removed the incessant anxiety because you knew what was happening behind the locked and bolted doors. But a greater problem here – the root of the discussion between Davies and the men from London – where to place it, where to gain maximum advantage, where it could be secreted against the outer glass of a window and face the minimum chance of detection? Couldn't just plaster it across the centre of a porthole. And had to go in soon, before it reached dawn.

'We don't know the scene inside,' said Davies. 'They've pulled all the blinds . . . what I'd have done in their boat, but I'd hazard that their central area is toward the front, close to the cockpit.'

'You can have it for the cockpit, or the forward cabin, one or the other,' said the Yard man tetchily. 'We don't have a dozen of them.'

Davies ignored the edge in the other man's voice. 'What's the lighting factor, if we have it forward, outside corner of a window?'

Happier ground for the technician. 'Pretty fair with video. You'll see the faces clear enough. Not into the cockpit, just the passengers and the aisle. Most of that.'

They compromised. 'Cyclops' and one audio circuit at the front of the passenger cabin, the second audio for the cockpit. Further briefings for the soldiers, reminders of how to fasten the suction pads, the angle the camera required, how the cables should be laid. As if the troops hadn't handled the gear before.

'Pretty useless the audio will be,' said one who loathed to see the apparatus out of his personal control. 'With the doors closed you'll hear fuck-all. And the pictures not much better, not going to show through for you. It's not bloody magic.' And the sergeant that he spoke to was patient and explained that though the blinds were drawn now they would probably be raised during the daylight hours. That the people inside weren't fools, that the blinds were down because they needed the lights on in the cabin, and it would be different in daylight, wouldn't it?

Past two in the morning when Davies and four NCOs began their slow and time-consuming leopard-crawl out across the smooth surface of the tarmac. Davies leading, his sergeant the work donkey with the canvas bag that held the fish-eye and the audios and the lightweight 9-foot aluminium ladder, the other three in close fire support. Co-ordinated advance with the searchlights tilting their beams to new elevations, playing on the windows to dazzle and blind any who might look out.

They felt no excitement when they rose to their feet at the belly of the fuselage beneath the various indecipherable words of the Cyrillic alphabet that were printed on the hatches.

Professional soldiers, with the emotion and fervour of their youth long dissipated. Calm and efficient, master artisans, working the practised procedures. Ladder in position, foam rubber upper protection denying the sound of scratch or scrape against the metal of the fuselage. The sergeant climbing and as he went bending the fibre attachment, moulding it to the curve of the plane's exterior, planting the lens itself, upper right corner, third porthole starboard, suction pad and beyond it the shallow protuberance of the cobra head, the lens in place, reaching over the lip of the window fitting, need to be searched for, cursory look insufficient for discovery. The audio close to the next window forward but reservations there, waste of bloody time till the doors were opened. Second audio at the cockpit windows, low down and wrapped among the arms of the rain wipers.

They ran the cables quickly and with discretion across the fuselage, bringing them together where the starboard wheel rested, camera case fastened in the interior of the undercarriage flap. Began to pay out the cables away from the plane, running them in the cracks that separated the concrete segments of the taxi area. Thirty-five minutes it took them till they were back to the cover of the tankers' shadows. David had slept through their visit, Rebecca too, and Isaac who struggled to stay awake had heard no sounds that could have aroused him from his vigil with the passengers.

'Bugs nicely in place, ready to bite,' Davies told the scientist – not a matter to boast of, just the communication of necessary information.

Receivers had been moved into the cement hut behind the tankers. Three men were busying themselves with screwdrivers and transistor circuit diagrams. 'Get a move on lads. I want you out of here by sparrow fart, all tucked up in your beds by morning,' said the major. The civilians worked fast, knew that he joked, knew they were relegated to spend the next day, or two, or three, in the hut. When they had finished with their adjustments they returned to the van, unloaded camp beds, and one carried a Thermos flask, and another spoke of overtime or 'bubble at time and a half', as he called it. 'Not a bloody holiday camp', was Davies's parting thrust. He walked out into the night again. Depended now on the boffins to get the kit into shape, but he'd met them before, believed in them and their equipment. The main thing was the secrecy of the fish-eye: the buggers inside wouldn't know of it, wouldn't look for it.

Davies eased himself into the small gap between cabin and tail of two tankers, where the plane was flush to him. Shouldn't be difficult, not if there's only three of them, and all youngsters. Be in there in no time, if that's what the gods on high decreed. Always the problem though, always the chance that one of the buggers won't see the reason of it, won't want to live, will take his last five seconds on earth blasting all and sundry round him. Plenty of plaudits for the rescue team if he doesn't, if the civvies come out of it in one piece, but sparse on thanks and short on medals for the chaps that pull out twenty stiffs and another fifteen in the ambulances with the sirens going full blast. All a matter of luck, whether one man stands his ground and wants to take people with him before he coughs. Same operation, same tactics, same drills, and you either end up a hero or a miserable bloody failure. Israelis understood that – wouldn't have taken thirty doctors to Entebbe if they hadn't – but Davies's masters, would they understand it? Not a bloody chance.

Behind him the voice said, 'There's nothing to see yet, and no-one talking on the inside loud enough for the mikes, but everything seems to be operational. Should be able to start the peepshow once they lift the curtain.'

Proud and bold, the battleship at her moorings, Aeroflot 927 rode out the night hours. No movement inside her visible to the army of watchers, no sound that was detectable. Splendid and serene and masking her secrets, defying the onlookers to penetrate her inner thoughts. With the darkness had come the dew that caused the soldiers sprawled in the grass to curse and fidget and envy those who owned at least the warmth and dryness of the aircraft seats in which to rest. Over all the turgid throb of the generators for the lights, beating out their own discordant rhythm, sending messages far beyond the circle of men who cradled their rifles and waited.

Charlie would have liked to have gone down from the tower, out into the air and walked close to the plane, sniffed at the atmosphere that surrounded it. But his place was by the radio, and he needed sleep. No point being knackered in the morning, not when the hard work would start. Wondered how they'd take it, how they'd react, when they realized the time was up, come in 927, show's over. Go ape, or take it calmly? Never could say with these kids.

Past two when he came to terms with his camp bed. Not long till dawn, till the time to talk to the plane again. Endless repetition of the same thought. How good would they be? What calibre? Brave? And if they were, how would they use it?

He remembered the kid in Sheik Othman, little bastard, with his shirt-tails flapping, and his futah loosened from the drive of his knees as he sought to clear the soldiers' cordon, and how they'd brought him down and laughed and sat on him, and you'd heard him scream, Charlie, scream for his father, and the captain had come, and the fist had lost itself in the kid's hair and they'd walked him to the corner. One shot you'd heard, you and all the others in the coffee shop, you with the ointment on your face that made you local, made you one of them. And you'd wanted to heave, and had looked around for guidance and for a lead. Not an eyebrow flickering, not a mouth cracking, not a breath drawn in. Called him a grenadier in the communiqué, and the little bugger should have been at school. Defence of the Empire, Charlie, defence of Law and Order. Shook you, Charlie, and you supposed to be a hard man. Never could sleep without a pillow. Remember the night in the officers' mess, infantry battalion down at Plymouth and some bright sod had suggested you go down and talk to a few of the chaps before you went to Dublin the first time? Not that they said anything, anything that might be useful, but crowed like fucking cockerels. How we killed young Paddy, young Sean, young Micky.

Terrorists all of them, seventeen years, eighteen years, nineteen years old. Bloody kids. Chased them round the alleys, up the back entries, closed the net. One shot to slow, one shot to fell, one shot to finish, and get the Saracen up fast and over the body so Dad doesn't come out and whip the Armalite for the next pig-thick ignorant kid with holes in his shoes through to his socks and one pair of jeans to his name who wants burying and thinks he's a freedom fucking fighter. Wrap it, Charlie, time for bloody sleep. Time to kill three more kids, little bright eyes all waiting for you, waiting for you in the morning, Charlie, and with a bit of luck the sun will be shining.

Long time coming, the sleep. Not that a pillow would have helped.

10

Many hours now the group had been meeting. Beyond the closing of the cafés and pubs, beyond the closing anthem of the television stations, beyond the gradual whittling of the drumming traffic noise on the Bayswater streets. At any time of concern this was where they always gathered, not because the cramped flat was in any way suitable for their deliberations but because its tenant was the General Secretary of their movement – in charge of their proud pile of headed notepaper, and the petty cash.

At times as many as twenty had been present, but the size of the group varied, some hurrying away, others coming fretful that they had delayed too long. There were enough, though, to fill all the chairs in the room, and the stools that had been brought from the kitchenette, and the pillows pressed into service from the bedroom. They drank coffee, sharp and gritty, swilled down with tap water and sweetened by spoonfuls of sugar, and they nibbled at supermarket biscuits, and struggled to stay awake lest any should miss the hourly news bulletins that could be found on the World Service of the BBC, and the more atmospheric Voice of America.

The members of the group had many factors in common. All had been born inside the confines of the Soviet Union. All were tarnished with the same labels – 'refugee', 'exile'. All were Jewish, contributors and active members of the London-based 'Committee for Freedom of Soviet Jewry'. All were worried, all anxious, all frustrated that the strand of involvement was stretched so loose. All were attempting to focus their minds and thoughts on a lone aircraft, far away and at an airport none had visited. And all were willing their intellect to transport them across the miles of cityscape and countryside close to the hull of the Ilyushin airliner.

The shared tiredness had long since dulled the clarity of their conversation, so that for long spells the silence hung, burdening, upon the little room. Some it caused to feel unequal to the moment, others the anger of helplessness, and a very few to doze, comforted in the knowledge that they would be awakened at the chime of signature music that would herald the next bulletin. These were kicked and pummelled people. They had experienced the soaring upsurge of spirit that comes from the first breath of freedom at stepping outside their rejected homeland, and now had realized that life was crueller, more savage, and that their visions of liberation had led to the bed-sit land where they lived and the hotel kitchens where they thought themselves fortunate to find work. Little people, whose escape had been quiet and without fanfare and who now fidgeted with their necklaces and their Star-of-David chains, and who searched each other's faces that the next news programme might be hastened, and coughed hesitantly, pulling at their cigarettes and expelling the smoke into the saturated air.

Most Sundays they gathered in a tight knot on the grass of Hyde Park. They took regular turns at making and listening to the familiar speeches, and clapped and cheered, and wondered why the great herd was so uncaring and so indifferent that it passed them by without even pausing to hear the stark message of oppression and humiliation. Most Wednesdays they came to the General Secretary's flat and discussed and argued and made the arrangements for their next public meeting. Always the culmination of the gathering was when the General Secretary's wife drew a single sheet of headed notepaper from the folder, and with pride wrote the requisite and formal letter to Scotland Yard requesting the necessary permission.

All easy, all clean – an absence of blurring obstructions. And if they had not yet roused the dormant wastes of British public opinion then there was always tomorrow, and next year, and a

lifetime. But falling on them now was a cold gust that was foreign, and carried in its wind both fear and confusion.

Yet the evening had started well – back-slapping and jokes
and wide and excited faces. Those that came first brought the
last editions of the afternoon papers with their glaring headlines, and they had stayed, transfixed, beside the television and
radio. Their people were coming out, a flight out of Egypt!
Escape on the grandest and most eloquent scale! Initially they
had discussed a press statement, to be phoned to the agencies
as an expression of solidarity with the young people who were
brave and of their faith . . . Would not their next public meeting
be crowded and packed, would not the masses at last awake to
their cause and struggle? Later had come the flesh that covered the skeleton of the story. A girl flying a plane at gunpoint.
Her captain who had carried no weapon dead beside her. A
party of schoolchildren whose lives were at risk. Damning and
deadening.

When the General Secretary had telephoned the Labour
Member of Parliament who championed their people in the
House of Commons his wife had answered the call. Yes, she
would bring him to the phone, and there had been the scraped
sound of a hand placed over the receiver and camouflaged and
indistinct words. He was not at home, she had said. She was
sorry. Perhaps later. Was there a number she should take down?
Another MP, not Jewish but a long-time sympathizer, was braver
and less anxious to salve their sensibilities.

'It's aerial piracy and it's murder,' he'd said, with a gruffness
that startled the General Secretary. 'You cannot dress it up any
other way. They've killed a defenceless man, endangered a
plane-load of people. I'm sorry, but that's the way I see it. I'm
bloody sorry. Of course I'm sympathetic to you, and to the fight,
but this is different. Take my advice: stay quiet, and don't get
involved.'

They had followed the advice. The drafted statement to the
press was now a torn shambles of paper in the rubbish basket.

Past four in the morning. Time for the lorries to start their

195

trail into the city with the daily load of market fruit and vegetables, and for the street-cleaning trucks to be out on their business. None in the group able to leave now, held and magnetized by the radio reports. Fresh fiddling with the dials, away from World Service seeking again Voice of America. 'Behind the News' reports. Read from the studio, taken from the despatches of the Associated Press Bureau in Moscow. A voice in a cracked, staccato rush so that all in the room had to strain to follow the words. The Bureau had been checking for reaction with those Soviet Jews who were at liberty in the Russian capital but whose opposition to the regime was known. A denial of all knowledge and connection with those who had taken the plane out of Kiev, a condemnation of violence from whatever source. In silence they heard the message, heard the door slammed at any suggestion, however guarded, of complicity. Next, a short voice-track from the network's correspondent in Jerusalem. The Israeli government had no comment, on the record or off the record, to the hi-jacking of the Aeroflot flight. No government official was prepared to speak on the matter. The stance of the cabinet was well known on both terrorism and the plight of Soviet Jewry, the reporter had intoned, and it was the belief of observers in the capital that they were gravely embarrassed by what had happened. From Washington, also, no authorized comment, room only for journalistic speculation, and the expressed belief that the United States administration would not seek to influence the British on the course of action to follow. This incident was regarded as divorced from the President's often-repeated attitude on Human Rights inside . . .

Savagely one of the listeners, galvanized now by his lack of sleep, switched off the set, plunging the room for a moment into an abyss of quiet. Then he shouted, 'The cowards, bloody cowards. Bloody stinking politicos . . .'

An avalanche of contradiction fell on him.

'And what are the people that took the plane, what are they?'

'For years we have suffered in dignity that we might win support, and now that we have succeeded . . .'

'They have betrayed the brave ones, these children . . .'

'In the Kremlin they will be drinking champagne, toasting each other.'

'They can justify anything now. Pogroms, show trials, round-ups, arrests. Anything they wish to do, they are able to now. The children have given it all to them.'

A girl was crying, smearing a handkerchief across her eyes, her voice broken and frail. 'Why did they kill the man? Why did they shoot the pilot? There can have been no need to. If they had not killed the pilot . . .'

'Who are we to speak of what they have done, and what their motives?' said the General Secretary, slowly and with delibera-tion. 'Who are we? We did not even make the journey to Israel. We are not a part of that place. We are the Jews that remain out-side the family, and we are shocked now because a life has been cut short in the name of Israel, perhaps in heat, perhaps in cold blood. We do not know anything of these people . . .'

Interruption from above. The battered protest of an umbrella handle pounding at the ceiling – the upstairs tenant's only recourse to quell the surge of noise and argument.

'. . . whether they have been stupid or wise, brave or cow-ardly, they are of our people. They have stretched us, tested us. Perhaps already they have shamed us, and perhaps also they will destroy us. But they are of our people and they are alone, and they have the right to our prayers.'

Setting aside their weariness, those on the chairs and stools stood up, and those on the carpet and the cushions rose awk-wardly that they could share the moment. As he shuffled his aged legs and felt the pain in the tightness of his joints, the Gen-eral Secretary murmured, 'It would have been better for us if they had not come. But they are here, and they are few, and it should not be us that cast the rocks. There will be many others for that task.'

Each in his own form, and in silence, the members of the group prayed.

* * *

Body strength waning, muscles aching, head throbbing, limbs contorted in the limitations of her resting place, Rebecca sought sleep.

Elusive though, hard to touch. Too many images revolving, denying her the comfort of oblivion. The things that Isaac had spoken of. Tanks. Machine guns. Soldiers. Cold, metallic, functional killing machines that had come for a purpose, that did not wait beyond the arc lights unless their value had been assessed and decided as necessary.

There because of you, Rebecca. There to watch you, pry over you, examine you, and there to eliminate you, Rebecca. Eliminate, if that should be the instruction passed to them.

Subjugated grey shadow in the fuselage, and the fidgeting quiet of the passengers. The only movement, the sporadic prowling guard that Isaac maintained.

Love, Rebecca?

Was that the sensation and the addiction that had brought her this far with the boys, with David and Isaac? Love of one, or love of both? Was that where the answer lay?

And what was love? Not something physical, not body to body, not flesh to flesh, not with the muscles straining and the warmth soft and moist. Had not felt their hands perusing her, wanting her, searching the secret intimacy that she thought of as love.

If not love, then why are you here, Rebecca? What is your purpose?

How can I know? Who now may I ask the question of, and find the answer?

An ordinary girl, Rebecca. Ordinary as cheese and mice, buses and queues, work-shifts and roubles ... Ordinary, predictable. But there are not tanks and machine guns and soldiers deployed through the slow night hours watching and waiting on an ordinary girl, to see what her thoughts and actions will be when the light comes and when she has rested herself.

So easy in the hut, when the battle was just of words. No doubts that the cause was right, certainty. Not in dispute,

Rebecca. But if the cause is right then someone must stand and defend it . . . but why you, Rebecca? Persecution, humiliation, spoliation, all those things have been visited on our people, and they have not stepped forward, have not armed themselves in their defence. So why you, Rebecca? What was different, unique, that made you stand up and plan and conspire? Not enough now, too late, to call to the soldiers that you were just a follower, that it was not of your willing, not your choice. Too many questions, Isaac had said, and Isaac was right. Always right.

And the talk of killing. All the preparations for the death of another. All the plotting, all the reconnaissance. All the hours in the hut used to prepare for the struggle that would be launched against the oppression that sat on their people. All that time, and no thought of this moment, of the trapped incarceration. Brave talk it had been, and Rebecca in the thick of it. Remember? Remember the calling for the choice, haphazard and not by merit, that determined that Moses should go first?

Why, Rebecca?

God, how do I know?

Would David have loved you then, if you had drawn the short straw?

Perhaps.

If you had killed a man, would that have fired, stiffened, strengthened him?

Perhaps.

Did you have to kill a man to win David's love?

But he never came to me, never came to me as a woman. Only as a friend, a colleague . . . an adjunct, never as a woman.

His fault or your fault, Rebecca?

I don't know. God knows it's the truth, but I don't know.

Is it that he cannot, Rebecca? Is it that he is not man enough . . . ?

Let me sleep, please, please.

Did we have to come to this place for your answer, Rebecca, and have we now found it?

I have to sleep. I must sleep.

Is that your answer, Rebecca?

If that is the truth better never to have known, better never to have come. Better to have stayed the ordinary girl. Brave, ignorant and happy.

It was cold in the control tower when Charlie woke and he shivered as he recalled where he was, and why. A policeman grinned down at him from the chair in front of the console that he had occupied, guarding the radio, while Charlie slept. Long time since Charlie had slept rough, not since the family camping holiday outside Aberystwyth when they'd packed it in after four days, conceding second best to the weather and be vowed never again, no more holidays for the mob without confirmed hotel bookings. Have to get ready for when they opened the radio circuit. Should wash his socks through first though, not that anyone else would have, but a standing privilege of a desk job was that a man had the right to clean socks. Quit the rubbish, Charlie, get up and concentrate.

Charlie dressed quickly, just his trousers and shirt, and felt a moment of distaste at the darkened rim of his collar.

'Any chance of a cup of tea and a half-minute with a battery razor?'

The policeman was happy to vacate the chair, said he'd go and look, and that the Committee was dossing down below in the Airport Manager's office, all except the Home Secretary, of course: found him a billet in the Fire Chief's house, a bit away, but inside the perimeter.

'Tell them I'm on the seat, my compliments and remind them that the plane's due to come through any time now.'

Going to have to be careful with this one. This was the crucial conversation: that much had been decided last night. Should be left in no doubt they'd get no petrol, fly nowhere else. Clitheroe had given it his sanction, all right once they'd rested to give them the pill. But didn't really matter how freshened they were, how much they could think things out, labour with the logic; always unpredictable when they flatten into a brick wall for the first time, realize they haven't a safety belt on . . . Shut up, Charlie, shut up and wait for the tea to come.

But the radio call came before the tea.

'Kingfisher here, Kingfisher here. The man we spoke to last night, is he there?'

Charlie waved behind him, the fantasies scattered, alert, in control. There was a shout that echoed away down the stairs, and then the drumming of feet taking the stairs two at a time.

'Charlie to Kingfisher' – humour the silly apes – 'Charlie here. Please identify who is calling. Is that David?' Keep it simple to start with while you tune into the language. What a time in the morning to be fluent in Russian! 'Have you slept well inside the plane? Did you get your heads down?'

'It is immaterial. We are waiting for the answer. We want the fuel. Do you have the authorization for that?' He'd slept all night, the bastard. Didn't sound as if he were back on the ropes like last night – fresher, keener, more determined, and rejecting the request for identification. Someone was tapping on Charlie's shoulder. Assistant Chief Constable there, looking as though they'd pulled him backwards through a hedge and still combing what hair he had, and Clitheroe in his braces and short of his jacket and tie and still breathless from the race up the stairs.

'Don't worry about the translation now, Mr Webster. Give it to them hard and straight.'

Finger to the console, switch to transmission. Deep breath, steeled himself.

'David, this is Charlie. I have a very important statement for you from the British government. I want you to hear it right through, and I don't think you should interrupt me, not till I've finished. Is that understood?'

'We will hear what you have to say.' Concession and a fragment of subservience.

'David, this is the reply of the British government. You are ready to listen? There will be no refuelling of the aircraft. There is no possibility, whatever your reaction, that the plane will be refuelled in order that you can fly to Israel . . .' There was a fast and angry explosion of shouting from the loudspeaker, explanatory, aggressive, yet difficult for Charlie to follow in detail. 'You said you'd hear me out. Shut up and listen. There will be no fuel, there will be no negotiation about flying this or any other plane to Israel. The journey is over, David. Your plane is surrounded by a military force that includes specialist troops of the highest calibre. There are two ways that you can leave the aircraft. You can come off dead, or you can come off alive with your hands over your heads, unarmed and after you've released the passengers. There are no other options. We will sit here as long as you need to make up your minds, but we think that you are all intelligent people, we think you will realize that there is no point in continuing, that you will understand your situation. Look out of any window and you will see the armoured cars. There is nowhere for you to run to, David. That is what the British government says.'

Charlie sat back in his seat, heaving his chest in relief, then half-spun in the chair and gave the men who waited behind him a précis of what had passed. Then he swung back and was writing hard on his pad.

New voice, different accent, devoid of subservience.

'That is all you have to say to us?' Like meeting a penfriend for the first time. Had to be Isaac, and Charlie pointed without comment to the photograph for the benefit of those who watched.

'Yes, Isaac, that is all. There is no room for negotiation, no scope for it. Your position is a hopeless one from any military or physical point of view, and you must surrender unconditionally. If you do that, and have first released the passengers and crew, then I guarantee that no harm will come to you when you give yourselves up.'

'You know what the consequences will be?' Too fast a reply for him to relay an English translation to what he had said, had to hang on, keep up the momentum, hopeless if he broke the spell now.

'There are no "consequences" as you put it, Isaac, that will alter the decision of the British government.'

'You believe that?'

'I know it, Isaac. They will not change their stance.'

'Wait till ten o'clock, ten this morning. Then tell me again.'

'Isaac, there is no point in threats. There is nothing to be gained from them, only the worsening of your situation . . .' No-one listening, the empty, unresponsive echo of discarded headphones far away. Charlie looked up at the digital clock immediately above, saw the numeral flip over – four fifty-two. Five hours till Isaac turned his words into action. More explanations to the men behind and a graveness in their faces as they heard the final stages of the exchange.

Assistant Chief Constable put it with the bluntness that was needed. 'They're threatening to start shooting passengers, executing their hostages, murdering . . .'

'That's about it,' said Charlie, matter of factly. 'And it's Isaac who's coming across as the hard boy. Moved on from the one we have as David.'

'Military won't want to be messing about,' the Assistant Chief Constable went on, as if in ignorance of the interruption, 'not in the light, and that's what we'll have in twenty minutes. Wouldn't have mattered an hour ago when they had some cover. But they have to have cover or it's bloody difficult for them and dangerous for the passengers. If we'd played it straight last night, said what we meant, and they'd reacted this way, then we could have put the military in . . .' In full flow, the staff officer of Agincourt, of Waterloo or Passchendaele, and back from the front with his gunpowder burns.

'The decision was taken by everybody.' Clitheroe rose to his own defence. 'We agreed that they would be more susceptible to the logical working out of their situation and position if they had had some sleep. The first one who spoke, David, he's obviously rested. But his sleep had to be paid for. Presumably the man Isaac has not slept, therefore he is exhausted and temporarily he is the irrational one, but there is much time for the others to work on him and for him to reflect on the measures that he has blurted out to us.'

It was not a new problem for Clitheroe. Early in his working life he had come to accept that the science of psychiatry was not an exact one, that the ill-informed were sceptical and dubious about his expertise.

'We should not take the threat too seriously, there is much time yet.'

Charlie, his attention away from the medical man, focused on the senior policeman, said: 'If it's not vulgar to ask, sir, what's to happen to these people? Assuming we talk them out, or we storm and take them alive, what happens to them?'

The raw nerve. Stamped on it. Pinched it. Off-the-cuff question, and he hadn't thought it out beforehand. The civvies from London looked away. Colour at the Assistant Chief Constable's cheeks.

'I don't think it's been decided yet.'

'They could ship them back, that has to be one of the options?'

'That's only your assumption, Mr Webster.'

'Bad news if they get a wind of it. Not going to come waltzing down the bloody steps and into our open arms. Stands to reason they're going to try and push us about a bit first.'

'Outside your province, Mr Webster.' Putting the clamps down, hiding behind the medal ribbons, climbing on the silver of his epaulettes.

'If I can't put that one out of their minds then not much chance of it all ending in sweetness and light.'

'Don't extend yourself, Mr Webster. You do an excellent job as an intermediary. Quite excellent, and be so good as to confine yourself to those limits.' Bloody martinet, thought Charlie, why can't he come clean, take a dose of the honest johnnie, accept he's outside the confidential circle.

The sun was playing on the aircraft now, burnishing its sides, beating up from the tarmac. Made Charlie squint his eyes together just to look at it. Lonely-looking now, sort of lost and strayed off its path, and doesn't know how to get in the air again. Didn't suit it as well, the daylight, not like the night with its magnification and the floodlights. Seemed to have become shrunken as the sun crept up on it. Didn't have the look of anything deadly, shorn of the melodrama, just another bloody plane sitting on its wheels, waiting for its orders. Blinds were up and some of those behind him had binoculars and gazed intently at the portholes and pointed and passed the glasses from hand to hand, but Charlie couldn't see anything beyond the darkened shapes of the windows – nothing living, nothing moving.

More movement at the back of the control area. Men with cables and a portable television set, the type used by industry with the innards gaping and uncased as the domestic set would be. It was placed on a bench close enough for Charlie to see the screen, far enough for others to watch without disturbing him from his communications on the radio. Further along the controller's work bench they fitted the tape recorders with their attendant headsets and the floor was a net of crazily inscribed wires and junction boxes.

Some twenty seconds of frosting and snow storm as they tuned the set before the clear image came. Not bad, not bad at all, and Charlie joined the others who pressed shoulder to shoulder to identify the greyed soft-shaded shapes of the heads of men and women and children, some lolled as if still asleep, others alert and darting with their eyes around them. He could see some of the children, and across the aisle and in a single-tone suit a man who sat with them and whose face was steady and did not waver.

Behind Charlie someone asked, 'What's the sound quality?'

'Not good, very muzzy. We'd hear something loud, shouting or a shot, but ordinary voice levels won't be satisfactory. Might be better when we put the tapes through the cleaners, wash the backgrounds out a bit. But don't count on it.' They let the audio man get on with it – sound was second best. That the picture was sensational was the general consensus; a new toy, and they were revelling in its versatility.

'That's Isaac,' Charlie broke in. 'The one in the front. The girl's behind him – Rebecca.'

Total attention on the screen now, and hazy in the middle

distance was the figure of Isaac, his chin low on his chest and his hair messed and tangled, shirt creased and floppy and the tail out of his trousers. Watchful and suspicious and minding his charges. Two hands on the gun – World War Two, and Charlie wondered where they'd dug that one up from. He didn't really look at the girl, didn't know anything about her to convince himself that she wasn't there just for the ride; saw she kept close, not more than half a pace behind the man, and that her dress was torn, and that her cheekbone showed the discoloration of bruising. A long way up the aisle the fish-eye followed them before they were lost, cut off by the thick lip of the window's casing.

'That's the one you have to concern yourselves with,' said Charlie to anyone who cared to listen. 'If you can convince him to walk out with his hands up when there's half a chance he'll be shipped back to Kiev, then it'll be champagne all round, and on me.'

Pushing your luck, Charlie, only a cog, and a little one at that, and it's a big wheel you're working in. Steady down, sunshine. Not that anyone was listening to you anyway.

The Foreign Secretary had not slept well. Never did in the Club beds. But the Party had been in office only four months, and the Prime Minister talked that frequently of the impossibility of continuing with so slight a majority and his wish for a snap election that it seemed pointless to make the expensive investment in a central London home. Better to wait and see whether the future was in the chauffeur-driven Foreign Office limousines or the wife-piloted mini of Opposition. The Club was adequate and useful after the welter of official dinners that the Foreign Secretary was obliged to host, and at least it was quiet, with a code of ethics in the smoking lounge that would not tolerate him being accosted by other members and quizzed on government intentions.

In his pyjamas he ate the scrambled eggs that the venerable servant had brought him at five. He glanced fitfully at the morning's screaming headlines. Milking it dry, pulling the udders down, but could hardly blame them. It was the height of the silly season, with parliament not sitting, damn-all going on and now a hi-jack in their back garden. Teams of reporters and teams of photographers, all with the credits above the stories and under the pictures. Even a photograph of himself leaving the Foreign Office by the side entrance that he favoured; shouldn't have smiled, wasn't right for the occasion, but the little devils were everywhere and you never saw them in the dark, only felt the flash against your face. Past midnight when he'd abandoned his desk. Three long telephone sessions with the Prime Minister and not much to chew on as a result of them. Usual story. 'You're the man who knows the implications of it all, as far as foreigners go. You're the man in charge, Home Office will work to you. You act and we'll be behind you.' How far behind? Inside knifing range or out? How many years back was it that socialist chap had called his Ministry 'a bed of nails'? He'd only had Labour and Industrial Relations to worry about – should have tried Foreign Office for a week.

A barely audible knock, and the entry of the PPS. Shaved, suited, clean, and bringing more coffee. Thoughtful lad: good choice.

'Before your solicitations I slept damned badly, feel washed out and would give almost anything to exchange my desk today for a decent morning's fishing.' Smiles all round. 'What have you brought me?'

'Transcripts from the late-night radio and television in Moscow. Going very hard. Meeting the Ambassador had with you last night, spelling out their demands; internal consumption stuff but still a very tough stance.'

'And the Israelis?' Mouthful of toast, and a smear of marmalade to go with it. Beds might be lumpy but the Club at least maintained a good standard with their breakfasts.

'Nothing direct from them, and no commentary on the tail of their bulletins. They're taking it very straight.'

'State Department, and White House, anything there?'

'Secretary of State's office called. Said they didn't want to wake you – I said you'd be in the office by six-fifteen. The Secretary will call you fifteen minutes later. They asked me to say he would be coming out of a function to do so. They describe it as a confidential and clarification matter.'

The lobby getting to work, all its power and all its tentacles beginning to weave into the scene. To be anticipated.

'There was a demonstration outside the British Embassy in Washington late last night their time, a couple of hours ago. Few rocks over the fence and the police broke it up. Fairly Renta-mob, but the law went a bit heavy so there will be pictures that won't be friendly. Banners about not sending them back to their deaths, that sort of thing.'

'Trifle premature, but they don't waste time.' He reached for the new supply of coffee, poured it himself, and the PPS noticed that the hand was not steady, slopped into his saucer. Never at his best in the mornings, not till he'd put himself together. 'What do you think, my young friend? Give me an opinion.'

'You can view the question from three angles. From emotion. From principle. From pragmatism. Take the first and last. If emotion wins the day then we'll find a reason not to return them. If it's the pragmatic we're after then we ship them home because sizeable though the Jewish stroke Israeli scene is it does not compare with the importance of our enjoying the continuing good will of the Soviet Union. Leaves only the principle of the matter. We're signatories to the Hague Aerial Piracy Convention, it's old now and it's gathering dust, but we and everyone else said at the time that we wanted a firm stand taken against hi-jacking. The firmest stand you can take is to send these people back.'

'That's making it all very simple.'

The Foreign Secretary headed towards the bathroom. Once there he turned on the spurting taps, leaving the PPS to compete with the half-closed door and the running water.

'As our chaplain at school used to say, where principle is involved there can be no leeway.'

'And the limit of his concern was you little blighters smoking behind the physics lab and trying to deflower the art master's daughter.'

'If you take those three points you must come out two to one in favour of freighting them. It would only be emotion that would guide you to keep them here.'

'And votes' – a distant reply echoing from the tiled walls of the bathroom, 'and your seat in the House and mine.'

'All it comes down to is a selling matter. News Department can handle that. It's what they're paid for.'

'And if I were to extract a public promise from the Soviet authorities that in view of the youth of these three persons the death sentence would not be exacted should they be found guilty, how would that affect matters?'

'If you pulled that, sir, I'd say you'd wrapped it all up very neatly.'

More water running, topping up from the hot tap. 'Get the Russian chappie in for half seven, and my car here for six.' Would be very tidy if it worked, solve a lot of problems – and not wound too many consciences. Israelis wouldn't like it, but then they didn't like anything, so damned prickly, but it would be a fair solution, and one that he was pleased with.

An RAF staff car had brought Col Arie Benitz from Brize Norton. There had been a shortage of serviced helicopters – that was the excuse given to him on landing for the change of transport. That they were not ready to have him at Stansted was immediately apparent by the initial niggling delays. They had insisted that he should eat something after his long overnight flight, not just a sandwich, but something hot, and the Mess would soon be open, the cooks on duty. There was the problem of the civilian clothes that had to be mustered, a surprise to Benitz because he was medium height with unexceptional contours. It was suggested that he might care to telephone his embassy and more time was consumed while they found the keys to a private office, and then again while the call was routed through to the Ambassador's home.

'The British have a dilemma, Colonel,' the Ambassador had said. 'If they bow to the Soviet pressure then your journey will have been wasted. But if they stand up for themselves – and it might be the first time in many years – then there is a rôle for you. But do not count on it: remember the spare parts for the Centurions in the time of Yom Kippur. At the moment their decision has not been made. I suggest you let the Air Force bring you to London, to the Embassy. There is not the great urgency that we had feared earlier, and the British show they are in no hurry to throw their apple to either side of the fence.'

Two and a half hours it had taken him, first winding and turning on the country roads, then powering along the empty M3, until finally they were catacombed along the half-lit streets of the capital. First visit to London, first to England, and nothing to do but stare at the fleeting sights from the window and with only a taciturn driver for company. When he reached the Embassy he was not surprised at its fortress-like protection. A private road and a message sent ahead by telephone from the Kensington-end gates to warn of his arrival. Floodlights at the front of the building, a remote camera on an arm jutting above him, steel-faced door, an age of identification and explanation before the bolts were withdrawn, the lock turned.

He was taken to the Ambassador's office to read the latest decoded communications from Jerusalem, to hear the most updated reports from Stansted, to study the photographs and biographies that the Russians had supplied to the Foreign Office and which had been passed on to the Israelis in confidence. He said little as he paced his way through the folder of documents, needing to scour the typed words only once, a man who assimilated information without hardship. When Benitz closed the file, signifying that the contents had been digested, the Ambassador spoke, quietly and with concern.

'You have a detestable job, Colonel – not one that should be given to an officer of your experience and ability. If there is a rôle for you in this matter it will be to talk these people into a surrender and will be both wounding and hurtful to many of the

Jews of the world. The position as we see it is this – and you must forgive any repetition of what you may have been told before you left Israel, but I understand the briefing time was short. There is little to no chance that the British will provide fuel for the aircraft. The escape of the three students has ended at Stansted, and it is their future there that concerns us. If they defy the British calls for surrender, if there is more bloodshed, more killing, then – and I do not have to stress this to you – there will be grave embarrassment to our government. We want them out of that plane before they have done more damage, before they have had more opportunity to fuel the propaganda machine of the Soviets. But how, Colonel Benitz, can we wash our hands of them? Jewish children, fighting an oppression that we loudly and frequently condemn. We cannot abandon them. We cannot permit them to be returned to the Soviet Union. Our Defence Minister spoke in the Cabinet last night of our country's shame if they were to be sent back to their deaths. It is a dreadful dilemma that we face. That is my speech, Colonel, but it was necessary that we should all understand the position we find ourselves in. We have offered your services to the British because we believe that the children will hear you, because you are a fighter, and that is how they see themselves. But we make one fundamental precondition for the use of your good offices. Should you help to win this surrender, then the British must guarantee that there will be no question of extradition.'

'Are the British likely to accede to our request?'

'No. It is unlikely in my opinion.'

'And if they do not?'

'I think we have not yet arrived at that point.'

'Most of the men we fight against in the Anti-Terrorist Unit, those that come into our country, have come to terms with the price of their struggle . . . understand that there can be no return . . . know that we will kill them.'

Not articulate, trying to find the words he wanted and disappointed in himself that he could not match the fluency of the diplomat.

'These will be different, without the training, without the discipline . . . their fear and confusion will be great by this time. Yet on their own scale they will believe they have achieved much.' A slow-forming smile on his face. 'Perhaps to them they have won their own Entebbe . . .'

'I said to you, Colonel Benitz, that it was a detestable job that you have been chosen to perform.'

'And there is no chance, no hope whatsoever, that they will be allowed to come to Israel?'

'How can there be? With the pilot dead, it is impossible. And even should the British allow it, could we receive them? When you are unpopular, alone as we are, and you wish to fight back, then your hands must be scrubbed clean. If we falter now, because our kith are involved, then we will have forfeited the right forever to speak out against the terrorism that you know better than I. If we accept that these children can become the heroes of Zionism then we have borrowed the language of the Palestinians.'

With a shrug Benitz said, 'The killing of the pilot has destroyed them.'

'It has critically affected the matter.'

'And would have been the action of a moment.'

'You are charitable, Colonel.'

'Not charitable, just realistic.' He seemed to go far away, beyond the horizons of the room, to have lost interest in the conversation. 'It's so fast, so rushed, there is not time for thinking, not in the moment of assault, not in the seconds that count if you are to succeed . . .'

It was not long before they parted. On his way out the Colonel wrote down a series of telephone numbers, some that ran through the switchboard, others that were connected to direct outside lines.

'We asked,' said the Ambassador with a pleasant smile on his face, one that was rarely revealed, 'we asked that we could send our own communications system to Stansted, to enable you to report to us directly. The British indicated that there would be so much radio traffic that it was impossible for them to accommodate us, they said they regretted this. It would hinder their operations. We are used to these affairs, the British are not, and therefore they are tense and concerned that they will emerge well at the conclusion.'

They had shaken hands and Benitz had returned to the waiting staff car. He dozed for much of the way out of London – not that he was particularly tired, but simply that he was used to taking his rest where he could find it. After a while he woke, aware of the sound of voices and of the car no longer moving. In the demi-light at the outer perimeter road block he could see a policeman scanning the travel authorization with his torch. Three miles further on there was another enforced stop, and again the production of the magic paper, and salutes from men in uniform for the huddled figure sprawled on the car's back seat.

They took him to the control tower building, men gesturing to his driver the direction he should take, to which entrance he should report. He was conscious of the military as he stepped out of the car, bracing himself to the freshness of the morning – the howl of an armoured car accelerating in low gear, the medley of chatter and static on a soldier's radio set, tyres that had gouged tracks in the dried-out summer lawn. Familiar sounds, and sights that he was accustomed to.

Twin pips on the officer's shoulder, but Benitz remained unimpressed with the lieutenant's deference as he was ushered into the hallway, ground floor, of the tower; perhaps a curl of amusement at his mouth at the flamboyance of the Fusilier's cockade, with the hackles of red and white set to the front of the beret. They had allocated a room for him, he was told. But first perhaps he would care to come to the Control Room, where the Emergency Committee had their Operational Centre? Seemed quite proud, this young man, that they had things so sorted out. But it takes more than titles and labels, that was what Benitz had learned.

* * *

It had been slack in the control tower, their anxieties unrewarded, ever since the day's early communication with the Ilyushin, and Charlie had felt free to leave his chair at the console desk and walk around. He remained never more than a few feet from the microphone, but it was still something of an opportunity for him to stretch the perpetual stiffness from his legs, flex his cramped muscles. He was close to the door when the army officer brought in the visitor. Something in the complexion, the tan of the Mediterranean, and the close, quiet confidence of his eyes; Charlie knew from his instinct the origin and homeland of the stranger.

He hung back as the introductions started. The Assistant Chief Constable had his hand out, Clitheroe examining and looking on with interest, new species, Home Office team in a line waiting for the exchange of names and rank.

'Someone to see how things are going. Colonel Arie Benitz of the . . .' the lieutenant tailed away, conscious of the radio and television equipment operators, anxious to avoid indiscretion.

'I think we call it Dixie, don't we? In these circumstances,' Charlie said. 'Colonel Benitz from Dixie.' The usual way of covering embarrassment. Confused Clitheroe though – hadn't an idea what was meant – but the policeman had got the message. Mutual caution in the greetings until it was Charlie's turn. Men of a kind in a way. Charlie still without his wash and brush up, stubble on his chin and the tired, far-away looseness of his eyes, and the trousers that had forgotten their creases and the shoes that had scuffed their shine. Benitz wary, the jut of his jaw showing that he was not prepared to be pushed about; aggressive because he knew that the clothes he had exchanged for his battledress were a poor fit, and a man in clothes not his own is seldom at ease.

'It's been quiet overnight, but it's freshening up a bit out there right now. They have been told this morning that there's no petrol for the onward flight, that they won't see Dixie this afternoon. They're not happy about it, and the one of them who stands out from the mob is threatening dire things for ten hundred this morning. You've seen the pictures that the Russians have sent us?' Charlie motioned to the indifferent snapshots, taking them one at a time. 'This one we know as David; doesn't seem to have much left in him, morale's all over the place. We can talk to him, and work at him. This one's Isaac, and he's the headache; we think he stood watch through the night and is therefore tired, but he's the strong boy, the one who's throwing his weight about. Leaves us the girl, Rebecca; unknown quantity, quality as well. We can't say yet which way she'll fall if the two fellows start arguing. We don't expect them to hold together that long – too few of them, too exhausted, and it's spelled out that there's no future in it for them. David might see reason. Isaac looks as though he's going to try and elbow us.'

Charlie directed Benitz towards the television screen, read the hostility in the other faces at the interloper in the pen. Screw them. He went on: 'I don't know whether you've seen these things before, but they take the pain out of sieges, cut the sweat out. It's a fish-eye lens with a one hundred and eighty degree arc. Means you can watch them and they're blissfully unaware of it. Lets you know when things are heating up and gives you an idea of where everybody is. We haven't seen Isaac for around thirty minutes, hence the assumption he's sleeping. Both David and Rebecca are out of sight at the moment, one at each end of the passenger cabin where they watch from, watch us and the passengers.'

'I heard that similar equipment is being prepared for us; we don't have it yet.'

Charlie denoted the hint of envy, fractional and disguised.

'We rely in these times on the skill of the manpower, not of the equipment.' What you'd expect him to say, a man who did real soldiering, knew what a front line was about and an enemy that hit and slugged with you; not going to be publicly impressed, not by gadgetry. He remembered when he'd been young, and his people had taken him out to Christmas morning drinks, and his own present that day had been a second-hand bike that worked but was short of paint and full of rust, and the kids of the house they'd gone to had shown off their new ones, wheeling them round, bright and shiny and pricey, and he hadn't spoken of his own present. Knew how the Israeli felt.

Charlie said, 'We know it's not the end of the world, but it's useful.'

The Israeli wasn't listening, not giving the appearance of it anyway, and Charlie saw that his cheeks were drawn in and his shoulders hunched low, and turned himself to the screen. The one they called David was in the picture; the girl wasn't with him, and his head was down, and he cradled the snub-nosed gun as a mother might a new-born baby, trying to win strength for herself from the child. In the brief moments that the camera showed the young Jew, caught his expression, he gave to his watchers the impression of deep misery, the caged rat caught in the trap in the barn that knows when morning and the farmer come it will drown in the rain butt.

Still watching the set, Arie Benitz said quietly, 'Do you expect their surrender soon?'

'They're still talking hard, giving us a rough line. There's the ultimatum at ten, and they hint of bad things to the passengers. They're not on the boil yet, but far from cooled down' – Charlie at his shoulder.

'And the tough one, the fighter, the one who makes the threats: you say he is resting?'

'We think so.'

Arie Benitz straightened, looked round the room, said out loud so that all could hear and none could misinterpret, the surgeon who had examined and would now pronounce diagnosis. 'Why don't you go in there and take them, put them out of their shame?'

'What do you mean?' the Assistant Chief Constable spun towards him, pirouetting in his polished shoes, smarting that no-one had informed him of the Israeli's arrival and his rôle.

'I mean, why don't you go and finish the thing?'

'And have half the passengers shot up, have a bloodbath on our hands?'

'If that one is anything to go by it would be over in ten seconds, and you have solved your problem.'

'You can't attack in daylight . . .'

'Rubbish. We had daylight in Tel Aviv when we freed the passengers of the Sabena jet. Even the Egyptians can do it – Luxor two years ago when they took out the Libyans. At Tel Aviv we had four to cope with, grown-ups compared with these children, and the hard one by your own admission is sleeping. Of course it can be done.'

The Assistant Chief Constable fastened on the luckless lieutenant who was Arie Benitz's escort. Fighting for self-control, Charlie saw, hating the eyes that were on him. 'I think we should see if Colonel Benitz has been allocated a room in the building. Certainly he would not want to impede our work in this already crowded space.' Embarrassment, and plenty to spare, hands masking faces, discreet coughs as the Israeli left. Smiling, wasn't he? And a half wink at Charlie.

'What does he think we are, a load of butchers, that we get kicks out of turning machine guns on people?' The policeman had waited till the door was closed tight against further intervention.

'Shortens the agony if all we're going to do is to send them back where they came from at the end of it,' Clitheroe said, playing the marionette, exasperating, and knowing it. 'If all we're here for is to talk them into facing a Russian firing squad . . .'

'It's a politician's decision, not ours, what happens to them.' The Assistant Chief Constable cut short the argument, preventing further contagious growth.

Charlie slid back into his seat. Nothing moving out at the plane. Not a vestige of life, the sun climbing and the plane shadow diminishing, and soon the tarmac would shiver and glaze in the heat.

Then from behind, and a sure sign they didn't take to the waiting. 'Is there any way we can start talking to them on the radio again?'

Charlie shook his head. 'No way at all. It's their privilege, and we have to be patient.'

From his room in the Moscow Hotel Freddie Smyth was shouting at the full range of his voice into the telephone that was connected with the office of the Commercial Attaché of the British Embassy.

Four days he'd been hanging around to sign that contract, worth three and a half million quid, didn't they know? Jobs of five hundred men depending on it. He'd a bloody good export record behind him, and a CBE medal to prove it. So what happens this morning, when he's all dressed up and ready to head to the Ministry with Sales and Technical? Had the phone call, hadn't he? All off, wasn't it? Not using those words, 'course not, 'need for further analysis of the project.' Could cut through that lot, couldn't he? Being fucked about, and they'd gone as far as telling him why. Because of some plane load of bloody hi-jackers. The Attaché should get off his arse and get onto the Ambassador and tell him to get talking with whoever was responsible in London. Tell him that Freddie Smyth, Managing Director, Coventry Cables, stood to have wasted four bloody days in Moscow, and if the factory went broke with half a thousand guys on the dole then Freddie Smyth would make sure every bloody newspaper in Britain knew the reason why.

The Commercial Attaché avoided the Ambassador's office, but went instead to the room on the same floor of the First Secretary. Freddie Smyth's outburst that morning was not unique, only the most vivid. Three other relatively prominent British businessmen had telephoned to report cancellation of morning meetings with Russian officials.

'Just the start of it,' said the First Secretary, flashing the sad smile of a diplomat who has already served two long years in the Russian capital and knew its ways, and had another twelve months of his sentence to run in which to learn them better. 'There'll be a few more of them too. Broad enough hints dropped by their people at the Cuban reception last night, found us out and bashed our ears, and played it coy about the Chancellor's visit – and that doesn't even have a firm date on it. But the factory ought to know about it, and we'll sling them a cable.'

It was a long time since the Kremlin had publicly shown its displeasure with Britain, he reflected. Back to the Lyalin defection and the expulsion from Britain of all the KGB chaps, all the trade men and the chauffeurs, and that was a fair few years back. Taken their time about thawing that one out. Difficult enough to work here, even when relations were comparatively normal, but damned near impossible when you made them angry.

He would put a 'priority' on the cable to Whitehall.

I I

With a sharp, spruce step the Russian Ambassador emerged into the sunlight from the darkness of the Foreign Office corridors. His immense black limousine was at the pavement side, door held open by a uniformed chauffeur. A policeman and a detective from SB Protection Group stood in the background, watching, relaxed and comfortable in the gentle heat. Be a pig of a day later. The Ambassador looked about him and saw the television crew and the reporter struggling to get clear of the camera car in which they had awaited his exit. The cameraman and sound man jogged across the street, connecting the cables as they went, the reporter faster and more anxious lest the quarry should elude him and disappear into the fastnesses of the car. The Ambassador slowed, then stopped, and saw the gratitude on the reporter's face. Lens focused and the recordist asking for sound level, and the reporter explaining the need for it, as if the Ambassador had never seen a camera before, never previously been interviewed. The diplomat smiled, sensing his opportunity. The cameraman called, 'Running. Go in five.'

Q. How would you describe your meeting with the Foreign Secretary?

A. Very fruitful, and I think we have a large measure of agreement on a mutual policy of what our reaction should be to these murderous criminals.

Q. The Russian government has demanded that the hi-jackers should be returned to Russia if they are captured. What are the British saying?

A. The British government and the Soviet government are both determined to put an end to the evil of aerial piracy. I have the impression that the British would wish to return these three to the courts of the Ukraine where they would stand trial for their crimes committed before and after they took over the Aeroflot flight.

Q. If they were returned to Russia, would they face the death penalty?

A. In your country there is no death penalty, and we are most sympathetic to the emotion that the subject arouses. In the Soviet Union we have the death penalty, but it is rarely applied and then only to hardened criminals. I was able to assure the Foreign Secretary that people as young as those concerned in the hi-jacking would be most unlikely to face the supreme penalty of the law.

Q. Are you saying that you have given a guarantee that if these people were returned they would not be executed?

A. We discussed this matter at some length. It was not a guarantee that I gave, because sentence is a matter for the courts. But I was able to indicate that my government would look with great sympathy at this matter. And now you will excuse me. Thank you.

The reporter was astonished at his good fortune, and because of his inexperience unable to assess the extent to which his microphone had been used as a bludgeon upon the Foreign Secretary now sitting in his first-floor office and weighing the results of his most recent conversation beside the transcript of his talk with the American Secretary of State, and the latest digests of world opinion on the issue being fed to the Foreign Office from British Embassies abroad.

Though the camera crew had what they regarded as a minor scoop they had no outlet to broadcast it before the midday news bulletin, but standing beside the interviewer had been a young journalist from the Press Association. Recently arrived in the capital from a Midlands evening paper he had felt too shy to intervene and ask his own questions. He had contented himself instead with taking a verbatim note of questions and answers, and within minutes he had found an unvandalized telephone kiosk and had read his copy to his news editor in Fleet Street. The sub-editors quickly packed the story into shape and context and prepared it for the teleprinters. All the big selling newspapers in Britain, television and radio studios, the Foreign Agencies – Reuters, Associated Press, and United Press International – all had received it before the young man stepped from his taxi at the door of his offices. The quotes he had taken down were recorded as of major significance, an indication of the British policy.

By telephone the contents of the interview were conveyed from the Foreign Ministry in Jerusalem to the Prime Minister's office. And by messenger a photocopy of the 9-inch-long text was taken from News Department to the Foreign Secretary.

It seemed to stun him, the flimsy sheet of paper, the crudity of a coiled fist. Those around him had to wait, unwilling to badger him for the contents. In his own good time he would tell them. The Under-Secretary nearest heard him muttering as if on a loop of tape: 'the swine . . . the swine . . . the swine . . . the swine.' He threw the paper half-crumpled across his desk, available to whoever wished to straighten it out. 'They've taken us for a big ride, those damned people. You have a private conversation. Leave it at a delicate point, nuance and innuendo, nothing signed and sealed, and he walks out and tells the whole damned world about it. Read that and you'll think the British are hand in glove with them. It makes a nonsense of what I told the Secretary of State.'

'Aren't we hand in glove with them, Minister?' queried the Under-Secretary currently in possession of the text.

'Not till they were safely in the air. After that we could be hand in hand, arm in arm, whatever cliché you want, but not till then. That was the deal, and they've reneged . . .'

'And reduced your freedom of action, Minister. Difficult now to change tack. Would seem very strange.'

He realized he'd been outwitted, out-thought. And that all around him knew it.

The 'freedom of action' so beloved by Foreign Secretary and Under-Secretary alike was to be further eroded in the following hour. Home Office press desk telephoning their opposite numbers in News Department: Thought you'd like to know, old boy, that we've had the press chaps on from the 'Street. Seems they have transcripts of tower to cockpit conversations, have translated the Russian, and are asking us for reaction on a hi-jackers' ultimatum scheduled to expire at ten in the morning. Didn't take a brain to work that one out: threats meant government had to respond with the hard line, hard line meant send them back, as the Soviets wanted. Cannot go soft on little blighters who're throwing their weight about.

Can't you have them under Wireless Telegraphy, criminal offence tapping authorized radio channels? asked News Department. Tried it, old boy, responded Press Desk. Told us to get stuffed – more politely, of course, but that was the gist of it.

Explicit instructions had been given: corral the journalists and photographers somewhere where they see nothing, hear nothing, give them a view of the plane and nothing else. The order had been carried out to the letter. A pen was provided, but in such a position that the Ilyushin blocked any view of the SAS command post, and there was an ill-briefed press officer who could in truth report nothing of substance to the hungry observers. But a farm backed on to that section of the perimeter where the press were held, and at dawn the owner's wife, out of a sense of charity and pity had sent her eldest son with three full Thermos flasks of coffee and a plastic bag of sandwiches to the newsmen. The boy brought with him his radio set, an advanced Japanese model, on which he was in the habit of tuning to the conversations between the tower and incoming aircraft; a hobby that he shared with hundreds of other youths who lived close to the noise of the country's major airports.

When the farmer's son returned home with the empty flasks

and plastic bag, he was without the radio, but in his hip pocket were five newly-printed five-pound notes and a promise of the same for each day that the worn, sleep-short men borrowed the set. The family themselves had listened to the talk-down of the Ilyushin the previous night, and the tuning had not been altered. There was disappointment at first when it was realized the early morning exchange was to be conducted in Russian, but these were men paid their monthly salaries for their enterprise. The conversation was recorded on a cassette tape player, and the spool sent back to London by despatch rider to await translation.

It was a sombre gathering in the Foreign Secretary's room. Some standing, some sitting, some watching the window and the crowded pavements, some waiting for the next intervention of the telephone. And the old man in their midst, paled face in his bone-ribbed hands. Poor devil, thought the PPS. Too old for learning new tricks. Should have been out to grass years ago and togged up in his waders and dumped in some river with a hat full of flies to keep him warm. Days that started badly didn't get better, and this was going to be a long and bitter one, and carefully compiled reputations could be demolished by the late summer dusk. And all because of three little bastards from the other side of Europe. Made him want to weep, but there'd be enough tears to be mopped up, enough without him adding to the flood.

The light that poured into the cockpit left Isaac undisturbed. He had curled his sparse body into the seat that had been Anna Tashova's and settled his legs with care so that they would not brush against the floor pedals or the instrument switches of the flight deck. His sleep was dreamless, the exhaustion permitting neither the pleasure of fantasy nor the horror of nightmare. He had checked the safety catch of his gun, made sure that the weapon could not fire if he lurched or reached in a spasm of movement and now held it tight across his chest. The lines of tension round his mouth and on his forehead had softened, as if he had discovered a peace and understanding with himself. He had pulled his knees up to his stomach, and his breathing was calm and regular, marred only by the trace of catarrh from the passing summer cold that had dogged him his last week in Kiev. Not a dangerous-looking creature, not a psychopath or a manic depressive; just a youth who had become extremely tired, and who tried now to regain his strength, to recharge the batteries that powered him. Slight and ineffective he would have seemed if the fish-eye could have found him, far from worthy of all that his actions had brought to Stansted. His stomach rumbled in its desire for food, but even the aching far down behind the stomach wall was insufficient to break the hold of his sleep. The first traces of a beard were showing through, a shadowy mess on the whiteness of his skin. His shirt was dirty now and creased from his own sweat, sleeves carelessly rolled; hands dirty from the oil of the gun that had not left his grip, fingernails too short and clipped to retain the filth that otherwise would have been theirs. Difficult to see as a figure who had created fear, even terror, difficult to take seriously, this boy who had spat his threat into the microphone now idle and propped on the back of his seat. Two hours he'd promised himself, then David should wake him. He was terrified of not sleeping, of not resting and being found inadequate when he sought his best; right from the days of Secondary examinations, and of the tests and interviews for university places. Had to sleep that he would not go pallid and yawning before the tutors. David had promised to wake him. Would rouse him at eight, long before the deadline. He could rely on David.

It was the stench that woke Rebecca.

The heavy, all-invading stench of the forward toilet. The wall of the lavatory was behind the crew seats on which she had slept, small enough to make a bed of, an arm becoming a makeshift pillow. The toilet queue had formed again, but not like the one that Isaac had controlled: people standing up from their

225

seats, and in a line in the centre of the cabin, something different and less fearful than it had been the night before. She lay still, her head motionless, one eye half open, acclimatizing. She had dreamed, she could remember that, images of her home and of her mother and family, nothing vicious in the images she had conjured, soft and warming. But then the harshness of the smell had forced the sleep from her. It was difficult at first to realize where she was, and why, but then she recalled the plane, its trap-like compactness, its arched prison walls. The passengers walked to the toilet, heads erect as if the tumbrils delivered them, and behind her came the constant routine sounds, punctuated by the flushing of the pan and the squirting of water into the basin. One after another they came, edging their way past David as he stood at the entrance of the cabin, some five feet in front of her, showing him deference. He held his gun lightly in his right hand, and that was the termination of her rest, that was reality, the gun and the asymmetry of its magazine from which the old paint had worn and which still showed the oil slicks of its preservation. David did not see that she was awake, concentrating on the passengers and every minute or so breaking away to move to the portholes and peer out, searching for a sign, like someone looking through the windows of his home when a guest is expected but is late.

David, sustaining and comforting, giving strength and help, keeping the wolves clear from the encampment. Ever since she had known him, the bigger boy in the higher class, this had been their point of contact and togetherness. From when he was in short trousers and she in frocks with white ankle socks and they had gone to the Pioneer camps, and he had sought her out, he had been protective and all-knowing. With maturity had come the cementing of their friendship, brother and sister, colleague and comrade. Different to Moses and Isaac, outsiders who had joined: they were the nucleus, the kernel. Always a shoulder to lean on, a chest to rest against, an ear for confidences. Should have loved him, now that he was a man and she a woman. No denial of opportunity, frequent occasions, didn't understand why it had never happened. Seemed to spill through her, the nausea of the awful primitive groping of the fool Yevsei. Thirty-six hours, just a day and a half, nothing in time, and on her back in the grass with that stupid, oafish idiot. Could have been David.

Harvested by her fantasies, the rounded walls of the cabin burgeoned in on her, restricting and claustrophobic. Rebecca was not one to weep, not unless there was a sudden pain, but a deep depression swamped her as she lay on her side on the hardened seats. Always there had been a forest path or a side alley that was good for escape, and now nothing but the barricaded doors with their pressurized locks and the tiny windows with their reinforced glass.

She called to David. 'Have you talked with them? Have you talked with the British?'

'You were sleeping and we did not wish to wake you. We have talked to them.' Had only seen his back since she had woken, and now he turned to face her. The night had not refreshed him. Haggard and unshaven, eyes dulled and deadened. Only the lines of sympathy at his mouth suggested he had news difficult to tell.

'What did they say about the fuel?'

'They said there would be none. That we should surrender. We would fly no further, they said.'

'What do we do, David?' Simple, little more than a whisper, oblivious of the passenger behind who made his way to the lavatory.

'Isaac says we fight them.'

'He said the same last night, before I slept, while you rested. What does that mean?'

'Isaac says we must make them listen to us, that we must show our strength.'

'What strength do we have?'

'Only the passengers. The guns are nothing – against us they have an army. There are only the passengers.'

'Isaac said last night that if we were hard with the passengers then the British would bend. He said they have done so in the past.'

'That is what Isaac believes.' David, remote and lost to her, listened to her questions, but his replies were mechanical.

'What do you believe, David? Not what Isaac says, but what is *your* thought?' Those who are caught in the winter snows, hikers and climbers and those whose cars fail them, and lose the will to go on, and cannot maintain the fight, want only to sleep, the sure and certain way to death. David, uncaring, uninvolved. Had to raise him – lift him again before he was lost. 'You have to know what you want, David. You have your own mind.'

'I don't know. Believe me, I don't know. It was Isaac who thought of the plane as a way of escape. We all agreed and now we must stand with him.'

'And they will kill us here, kill us in the plane?'

'Isaac thinks we can make them surrender to us. He has told them they have till ten o'clock. It is that on your watch now, but you have not allowed for the time difference. They have two more hours.'

'If they do not surrender by the time that you have given?'

'Then we will shoot a passenger, where they can see it, where they will understand.' He motioned to another to come forward in the queue. They were discussing the passengers as would a collective manager and the responsible person from the abattoir. Rebecca sat up, reaching forward so that her fingers were on David's hand.

'And if we shoot one and they still do not surrender?'

'We shoot another. Isaac does not believe it will be easy. He has changed, our Isaac, has made himself of steel. He is the fighter. The last night we were in the hut I was angry; roused by him, because he thought that it was easy. He knows now what we face. A few days back, if you had asked me of Isaac, I would have said he was not capable of this strength . . .'

'And you, David, where is your strength?'

'Perhaps it was never present, perhaps it was just a figment, something we created. Remember when we were in the woods, when we talked, when we planned. It is different here, Rebecca. When we talked did you know it would end like this? Do you believe that I knew that it could end like this? Think, Rebecca, think and tell me if I knew the road that I was leading you on.'

'You told us that we must fight them . . .'

'Nothing but words, slogans, phrases. There was no reality there, nothing of the soldiers, the guns, or what has happened to Moses.'

'Why are you saying this to me now?'

'Because this is no time for deception. Past and gone, that moment. I talked us into coming here, Rebecca. I talked and you listened. You and Isaac and Moses, you all listened to me. That's why we are here.'

'And now that we are here, you will fight?'

He did not answer, as if the tiredness had come again, but just looked at her, as if she were new to him, and a stranger. Then the shrug and the smile, and pushing his fingers in his hair. 'Take your gun, arm it, and go to the back. Check that the seatbelts are fastened, that the passengers not in the queue are strapped in.'

She walked forward, putting a swing in her hips that she told herself was the hallmark of command, face set, measured stride, pistol gripped. Find something to do, occupy yourself, make work and business, hasten the clock hands, that it might cut out the awfulness they had so casually discussed. Right to the back of the aircraft. Check the fastenings that Isaac had made last night and that held the trolley across the aisle, check them and re-check them, absorb time, use it and waste it, bury it and destroy it. What does a man or a woman? . . . Why think of a man, think of a woman, or a girl not yet an adult, not yet opened, penetrated, known . . . what does she do in the basement cells in the hours before they take her out and kneel her in the yard and place the policeman's pistol at the nape of her neck? Tortured, agonized, revolving mind, and how to occupy it, must find something that time shall be lost. Straps secure. Begin on the passengers. Some still with their hands raised because the order was never rescinded. Others ignoring the dictum now that it was not demanded and sitting with their arms folded and fists clenched on their knees. Some seeking comfort from the gesture, some defiance, some just to hide the stains at their trousers and skirts, those for whom the snail-like pace of the toilet queue had been intolerable.

How few of them she knew, how few she would recognize if she walked past them on a pavement tomorrow. The American? Yes, she would remember him. The Italians? Perhaps, but not because of who they were, or what they stood for; only the ornaments, the cut of the clothes, the whispered conspiracy of their chatter. The schoolmasters and the headmaster? They would not fade because she had experience of such people. Would she know the pilot, sitting away to the front, never speaking since she had been ordered back from the flightdeck, know her if they bumped into each other in the street at the bus halt, disputed the right to a purchase of stockings in the store, collided laden with bags at a street crossing? She did not know. Yet a choice must be made among them, that was what Isaac had told David, and he had not disagreed. Academic problem, should have taken it to the professor, perhaps he would have helped them, discussed it at a seminar. The tall one or the thin one, the fat one or the fidgeter, the foreigner or the . . . she pressed her lids tight shut, blocking the sight of the domed head rising above the seat rest. That was the one who had been chosen.

It was the American whose voice she heard.

'Not much going on out there, Miss, just tanks and soldiers. Not much action from the petrol tankers. Not like they're about to refuel you.'

Never had been able to stare him through, she thought, not from the first time, and not now. Couldn't muster the scorn or the indifference, not from the time she'd first been aware of his presence, and the foreign brightness and ebullience of his garments. Handkerchief still at his head – not needed now, but worn proudly as a trophy, stain showing and somewhat awry, so that the wound it was supposed to hide was partly visible. Wife's hand at his arm, counselling caution, and ignored.

'Nearly a dozen hours since we touched down. They'd have filled you by now if they were going to. Don't you think so, Miss?'

A frosted, splintered-ice smile and even with the strangeness of the language and the difficulties she had in following his words she could touch the changing mood, the spirit of aggression and attack. 'They've screwed you, Miss, screwed you proper. I'll take a bet with you, any money you have and give you odds if you know what that means – they're saying the glory ride is over, right? Time to come out with your hands high. Do I have it right, Miss?' Couldn't draw away from him, couldn't detach from the hydra tentacles that kept her listening. 'You're all fucked up, Miss, if you and Felicity Ann will excuse me. Out in the punt and without a paddle. Listen to me now: I couldn't give a damn what you've done back home, what you think your grievances are, if you have any. You've a nice face and you're a good-looking girl, and when you're my age you notice these things. I'd like to give you some advice, Miss.' The pistol in her hand, foolish little appendage, nowhere to put it, nowhere to hide it, felt like a man with his wife's handbag and loath to be seen carrying it, a silly awkward little machine, but which was her lifeline and her survival rope. 'My advice is this, Miss. Find out what the British are going to do with you. I'm an old man and Felicity Ann's no chicken, and no-one gives a damn about us in the States – don't read a word I write, only hire me for the lecture circuit because I'm off-season and cheap – so we're not that interested in how we come out of all this. I'm telling you – and I mean it, it's in your interests – find out what they're going to do to you, and if it doesn't seem too bad, then chuck it, throw the towel in. Don't go playing the martyr because if you give them half a chance they'll chop you, and it won't be fun, it won't be glorious and you won't be around to see if anyone weeps over your box. That's what I wanted to say to you, Miss, and it's meant kindly, and while you're asking them see if you can talk the Brits into sending some food up. People are hungry in here.'

Sent her off on his errand. Rebecca checked none of the

other passengers to see if their straps were fastened, just buffeted the length of the plane, tumbling against the arm-rests of seats, unaware of the impediments, needing to get where David was standing, back to her in the forward corridor and looking out through the cockpit perspex.

'Is Isaac still sleeping?'

Obvious when she saw him, slumped in front of her in the pilot seat, but she sought confirmation and reassurance. David nodded, was watching the stationary armoured cars and the soldiers who lolled beside the mountings for the heavy machine guns. Two hundred yards of open ground separating her from the men the American had said would kill her.

'We have to talk to them, David, you and I. We have to know whether it is necessary, what Isaac wants. Not when he is awake, but now that he sleeps.'

Maddening, driving her to fury, David not reacting. 'We can speak to them again when Isaac is woken. We can wait till then.'

Only served to drive her forward, egg her on deeper into the swamp she had set herself to cross. 'We have to know what will happen to us, what they would do to us.'

'Time enough when Isaac is with us.'

'Can't you see it, David, that you have abrogated to him? There are three of us. He alone does not have the monopoly of negotiation. If we are together then any of us can talk . . .'

'But not behind his back, not when he is sleeping.' But doubt showed on his high line-woven forehead, furrowed with indecision as he hissed his replies, calculated not to disturb the sleep of their colleague.

'Ask them, David. Ask them what they would do with us.'

He wavered, hesitated, then reached forward, weight on the balls of his feet, and lifted the headset from the back of the pilot's seat. He drew it back into the corridor till the cable attachment was bouncing and taut. Rebecca could only hear the questions that David asked.

'Kingfisher. Kingfisher. Do you hear us? The one called Charlie, do you hear us?'

Rebecca listening to David, a draining, sweat-soaked relief overwhelming her. Contact with the outside world, a lifting of the horizon, a breaching of the capsule wall.

'It is David who is here . . . Isaac is sleeping . . . there are questions that we have for you.' Pause and silence, both watching Isaac, furtive and anxious lest he should open his eyes.

'The question is this. If we were to surrender what would you do to us? What would happen to us?'

The words had been said, the Judas sign was fashioned, their faces turned away from each other, the shame not shared.

Charlie had stiffened, pencil alert from the first moment that the call sign had been given. Conversation in the control tower had been broken by the staccato identification over the loudspeaker.

'They say Isaac's sleeping . . . they want clarification on some points.' Intent, and peering down at his papers. Then the mirthless smile. 'They want to know what happens to them if they surrender.' Charlie pushed the microphone button to off position. 'What do you want me to say?'

The Home Secretary was four paces behind the console, summoned late from the bed in which he had slept. Had had time to wash himself and run a cursory wet shave, but showed no benefit from it. Was experienced enough to know that this was the first crisis of morale, and was fretful lest his instructions to Charlie should affect it. 'First repeat the conditions of surrender.' He moved back, the pilot fish formation of aides at his shoulder.

Charlie addressed the microphone. 'The British government are not prepared to enter into negotiations over surrender. That has been made clear to you earlier. The situation remains the same – you must first release all the passengers, and when that is completed you must leave the plane disarmed and with your hands on your heads. I repeat the guarantee that was given to you earlier. You will not be harmed by the British security forces.'

Kids out after dark, he thought, babes in the bloody woods. Three frightened brats – two, anyway – out of their league and wanting to end it all, get back on dry land. He swung round in

233

his chair and said to the policy huddle, 'They say they know the terms of surrender. They want to know what happens to them after that.'

Clitheroe away from the main group, at the Home Secretary's shoulder, a moment of whispered talk, nodded acquiescence from the politician, and he was hurrying to Charlie's side. 'Tell them that you want to speak to them direct . . . that it's difficult over the radio. More you can say if you come to the plane. Tell them it's a very sensitive matter, too many people in the tower, how much better it will be when you talk at the plane, face-to-face stuff.'

Getting like the old days, Charlie. Calling for volunteers. He repeated the message in Russian. Not that they'll buy that one, never in a month of Sundays. First basic of the hi-jacker's bible. Book One, Chapter One, Verse One: never let the opposition near you; keep them at arm's length.

'Keep the pressure on them,' snapped Clitheroe. 'Tell them you're going to come out of the control tower and that you'll be walking to the plane. They'll see you all the way. They'll know there's no trick. But I want to get you to them, face to face, so we can start the confidence phase.' Seemed excited at the prospect. And too bloody right he should be. Wasn't his arse that was going on show. 'See it this way, they've called us up because they're anxious, they want to do some talking. The whole thing is about this answer, this question, the crucial one to them. They want out, and they have to trust somebody, follow someone's guidance. It has to be you, because of the language, Charlie. They won't hurt you, not unless you take them bad news, and you're not going to do that.'

Broke off, allowed Charlie to talk again to the aircraft. 'Don't discuss it with them, don't debate. Just say you're coming.' Charlie speaking, trying to sound calm, organized, casual, efficient, and half the room chuntering in his right ear. Finished, thwacked the transmission button away from him.

'So, what do you want me to tell them when I get there? What's the answer?'

'There is no answer,' Clitheroe said. 'Vague and general, that's how you play it. You're a little man, you don't have that sort of authority. You're not going out there to talk to them, you're going to show yourself, that's all. Most likely you'll be the first Englishman they've ever spoken to. You'll show them that you don't represent a threat, that they'll have nothing to fear from you.'

'But if they want an answer?' Fair enough for these bastards, sitting behind the glass with binoculars. 'If they want the answer, what do I say then?'

'Cover it over, Mr Webster,' the Home Secretary, authoritative, on home territory, used to ploughing through the arguments of committee. 'You've heard the news bulletins, and you know what the Russians are saying. Gives you an idea what's being said in London. Not possible for you to be in any way specific but your own mind can be at rest. Soviets say there's no question of the death penalty for these people, and anyway I wouldn't put too much store by the diplomatic optimism of Moscow at this stage. More likely these people will spend a period in British prisons if no more damage is done.'

Charlie turned to face him, but was denied the politician's features – had walked away, towards the far windows, meandering apparently without purpose. The Home Secretary knew his limitations.

'You'll need some equipment,' chimed the Assistant Chief Constable. Charlie, with a meekness that was not usually evident, followed him through the door.

David hung the headset back on the top of the pilot seat. He felt the lead weight clutching at him, numbing, and Rebecca pestering, pulling at his sleeve and whispering her demand for their final answer, the people in the tower. Isaac still sleeping, innocent of what they had done.

'He is coming to the plane, the one called Charlie. He says the matter is sensitive, that he wishes to talk to us face to face, on the question of what they will do with us if we . . .' Surrender. Capitulation. Couldn't say it, couldn't say the words.

'When will he come?'

'In a few minutes, very soon, he will walk alone to the plane.'

'Is there a danger from this?'

'If one man comes there can be no danger.' And what did it matter, how could it concern them? What further danger could there be at the moment of defeat? But he didn't know, hadn't thought through the possibilities, untuned to those technicalities of defence that had so obsessed Isaac.

'Will you wake him?'

David seemed to shake his head – not a definite movement, just the imperceptible wave of the eyebrows, the flick of the hair across his forehead. They clung together a long time, arms round each other, cheek to cheek, Rebecca stretching upwards to match her height with his. Many times David said, with the tears running on his face, 'I am sorry. I am sorry.' And Rebecca crying too, choking in her throat, unable to reply.

It was a pleasant enough room that had been set aside for Colonel Arie Benitz.

Calendars on the wall – gifts of aviation companies that showed a combination of light aircraft and bikini-clad girls draped on their wings. Photographs, too, of the first airliners that had used Stansted, sepia-toned and looking frail and historic. Flowers on the window ledge. Easy chairs and a desk with a telephone.

When the call came he let it ring several seconds before answering, time to summon his caution and prepare himself. He did not identify with either rank or name, was wary till he heard the Hebrew language that was used.

The Embassy in London. He should know that the Soviet Ambassador had been received at the Foreign Office that morning, that he had made a statement to the press, had spoken of agreement with the British that the three should be returned to Russia. He also should know that there were journalists' reports that an ultimatum had been set on the aircraft, due to expire at ten hundred hours, and that it was the opinion of advice available to the Ambassador that further violence on the part of the three would only strengthen the resolve of the British to fulfil their arrangement with the Soviets.

He should find a public telephone kiosk and immediately contact those designated to liaise with him in London. The number he should call would be the first given him in the small hours. There was a wish of the Foreign Ministry in Jerusalem to clarify his instructions in view of the new circumstances.

Arie Benitz let himself out of the office. There were many civilians and policemen and soldiers who hurried purposefully about their business and who passed him in the corridors, and none had cause to notice him. A cleaning lady, with time on her hands because many of the rooms she normally tidied at this time were occupied, directed him to a telephone in the staff canteen in the building's basement. She even changed for him the fifty-pence piece into the range of coins he would require to make the connection.

As he walked down the stairs Benitz felt the irritation rising in him, fuelled by the ill-shaped and ill-fitting clothes, ignited by the problems of the mission that he had been given. Ill at ease, unwanted, a stranger among the bustle of those who had a task and work that could not wait. Unaccustomed to being a watcher, and on the sidelines.

Arie Benitz was steeped in the history of the State of Israel. He was committed to the defence of its people, had experienced moments when protection came only from the hammering of his Uzi, and the cries of pain from his enemies. He was treated with respect in his own country, called by his given name when spoken to in conference by his Chief of Staff. And these people had declined his help, ignored him.

As he walked into the canteen he was thinking of the three young ones, frightened and alone, in the Ilyushin. And they had said on the telephone to him that they would be returned, that he would not be required by the British to help in the surrender. Arie Benitz had to fight against the thought that came into his mind. Willing them, willing the children, to hit back, attack, show their defiance. Had to suppress it, because that was contrary to his country's interests, and he was a servant of his country.

The hard one, the one they called Isaac, the one who led them now, he was the material of Squad 101, he was fashioned for the Anti-terrorist Unit. Do not lose your courage, children, thought Arie Benitz. There can be no help, there can be no rescue, but do not lose your courage.

Unwatched, unobserved, he dialled the London code.

12

The soldier inclined his rifle and stepped back for Charlie
to pass. Out through the frosted glass door of the control
tower, on to the tarmac. The heat saturated him from the
moment he was clear of the protective air-conditioned blanket,
warm enough to feel it wrap about him, carrying an instant
clamminess to his chest and legs. The staircase had been darkened with venetian blinds, and the brightness reflecting up
from the open concrete wounded his eyes. He had left his
jacket on the back of the seat, and forsaken his tie; Clithcroc
had wanted that. 'Let them see from the start that you have
nothing concealed on you' – those were the psychiatrist's
instructions. Only the radio transmitter and receiver that
bumped against his hip, swinging from the strap he had hooked
over his shoulder. His shoes squelched as he moved, suffering
from the time he'd worn them, and his toes were uncomforta-
ble, irritated, so that he was reminded of the smell and the
shave he had wanted. They'd given it to him very straight
before they'd packed him off – just follow the line we've given,
don't play hero games, don't go promising things that haven't
been authorized or sanctioned.

Don't hurry it, they'd said. They will want to have a good
look at you, size you up, know you're not a threat. We don't want
them jumpy, not now, not with ten o'clock closing. Half-way
there, getting closer, Charlie. Breathing faster, be panting by the
time you arrive. Slow it. Remember the missus, what she says,
no need to hurry, Charlie, we've all night, don't rush, don't
speed up.

He was close enough now to see the outline of some of the

239

faces at the windows – not the expressions, just the basics – eyes and ears and mouths. And how many behind them that were masked from him, and how many in the grass and the rain ditches beside the runway? Half a bloody army out there, and all that shows is a few armoured cars and the men sitting on them. Hands a bit closer to the main armament than when you saw them from the tower, Charlie. All watching and wondering what the hell's going to happen. There'll be concentrated fire-power to support you, that's what they'd said, and he believed them, and he also believed it wouldn't make a damn bit of difference if Isaac or David didn't take a shine to him. Bad place not to be making friends, sonny boy.

Time to start putting it together. Walk round the nose and approach from the far side, with the petrol tankers behind you, where the heavies are, the SAS men. Still be able to see him from the tower, on the outside video camera, and the micro-phone button was permanently up so he could talk if he found anything to say. Colossal the plane looked, damn great predator, 30 tons of it, and the fools called it 'Kingfisher'. Like a great carrion crow. Near to the wing now that he should skirt, should begin to angle his approach so that he would move in front of the hulk and into the empty ground beyond. Charlie didn't look up, resisting the impulse to scan the windows: it might be taken as anxiety. Must walk as if out with the dog for a Sunday morninger down to the pub.

He wiped a smear of sweat from his forehead and with his fingers instinctively tidied his hair. Thirty yards from the aircraft and level with the forward starboard door he stopped. Cockpit to the right, passenger cabin to the left. High above him, domi-nating and impersonal, was the Ilyushin, expression not known, mood uncertain. Difficult to see it that way, but that's how it was, with a mind and pulse of its own.

He shuffled his feet together waiting for a response to his presence. No point shouting, no way anyone inside would hear him through the pressure-resistant windows and doors. Charlie Webster waved, right hand high above his head; as if his wife was shopping on the other side of Woking High Street and he wanted to attract her attention.

Rebecca had spotted him first and called David from his favoured position between cockpit and the passenger cabin. He hurried to where she craned forward across the unprotesting lap of a passenger, her head rammed against the window. With a roughness that was calculated he pulled her back to clear the space and the vision for himself. One man walking towards them, a faint and distant figure, small against the building from which he came, coming with a directness and purpose, his shadow preceding him, running to the front. The man kept far from the armoured cars and chose a path that was not impeded by any obstacle.

'Will you wake Isaac now? Tell him that the man is coming?' Rebecca spoke from behind his head.

'I did not think he would come so fast. I wanted to let Isaac sleep on.' He did not turn from the window.

'You are afraid to wake him. It is because of fear—'

'There is no fear.' He hissed the words from close to the window. 'When I need to wake him, then I will—'

'But the man is coming now.'

'I have eyes, I can see.'

'But are you going to leave Isaac sleeping? Will you let him sleep while you talk with this man?'

This was a moment when both David and Rebecca could have been overpowered without difficulty, for both were so engrossed in Charlie Webster's approach that they had no thought for the passengers. Rebecca was close to David's back, pressing against the muscles beneath his shirt, trying to share the window with him, transfixed by the advance of the lone figure. Several of those who sat behind them were aware of the opportunity but none had the stomach to steel himself and rise out of his seat. The long hours had dulled their initiative and the threat of the guns that now seemed so casually held was too great to encourage those who were closest to take action. Luigi

Franconi was within reach, but his courage had wasted since the time he was in the mountains with the partisans. Aldo Genti had the advantage of an aisle seat, but was further back. The navigator considered the question for a few seconds and then rejected it. The headmaster was too far to the rear to be able to offer effective intervention, and the thought of it faded from his mind when he saw the tousled, shambling, sleep-laden Isaac silhouetted in the cockpit doorway.

Rebecca said again, with greater persistence, 'You will have to tell him, you have to wake him, now that their man is coming.'

'But it was you that asked for the contact to be made. It was you that posed the question that had to be answered. It was you that wanted to know what they would do if we surrendered . . .'

Nobody spoke in the control tower; all were gaping at the television monitor, the flickering 12-inch grey-blue screen.

In the centre of the picture the back torsos of the ones they knew as David and Rebecca – predictable enough that they should be at the window to watch the coming of Charlie Webster. It had been the eyes of the hostages that had drawn attention to the extreme right-hand corner of the picture, as they switched from their two concentrating guards and took on the nervousness and hesitancy of people who have fear and are uncertain, looking only to the entrance from the corridor to the passenger cabin.

A small figure Isaac seemed to those in the control tower, and when they first saw him his face seemed wreathed in sadness, but the change was abrupt and the chin came forward, and the face muscles tightened as the sub-machine gun rose to his shoulder. When the weapon was there he paused for a moment as if to adjust to the comfort and stability of the tubular, extended shoulder rest, then raised the barrel to the low ceiling. He seemed to jolt back fractionally and strangely because it was all enacted in complete silence, and the passengers flattened themselves in their seats while David and Rebecca catapulted back into the aisle.

'We should pull Webster off,' Clitheroe shouted.

'Leave him there' – the sharp response from the Assistant Chief Constable.

The noise of the single shot was ear-blasting inside the confines of the cabin. It burst through the inner thoughts of Rebecca and David, tearing them from their vision of the solitary man who approached across the tarmac; the screaming of the passengers dinned its way into their consciousness, and when they spun to face the centre aisle it took them time to adjust.

The gun was still at Isaac's shoulder, his head steady behind the gunsight and his left fist clenched tight on the upper barrel, his right index finger entwined inside the trigger guard. And there was a depth to his eyes, far down to a blazing molten fury. Rebecca sought an explanation that would justify what was happening, and unable to find it slipped back across the passenger's lap till she stood half-cowed, half-defiant upright in the aisle. David was slower, it taking more effort for him to disentangle himself from among the unmoving and unco-operating legs that held him back. Isaac waited with a humiliating patience until David freed himself.

The passengers' eyes wavered between the seared hole in the cabin roof, close to where the forward life raft is stored, and the man in the passageway. All recognized the crisis, and were afraid to permit themselves even to clear their throats or move their feet. The baby, too, close to suffocation so tightly was it held against its mother's breasts, was silent. An endless, bottomless, quiet as they all waited for the resolution. When Isaac spoke his voice was controlled and they had to strain to hear his words – even David and Rebecca to whom they were directed.

'You did not wake me. You said that you would wake me at eight, and it is past that. You promised and yet I had to wake myself.'

David let out a great sigh, the air in his lungs released in a huge and noisy gust. 'We were going to come, in a few minutes we would have come, believe me, Isaac.'

But Isaac went on as if oblivious to David's words. 'And I wake myself, and I see from the cockpit window that a man is walking close to the plane, and I come to the doorway and I hear the words of surrender.' The sneer and the contempt, scything through the frail and unprepared defences. 'Talk of surrender while I slept, after I stayed the night watch that you might rest, because you begged for it, could last no longer. And when you are refreshed and I take my turn for sleep, what is it that you talk of? What is it that you plan? The talk is of surrender!'

'It was not like that, Isaac, you have to believe us!'

David wondered whether Isaac was about to shoot him. Almost natural, almost logical if he were to. He was not afraid, hoping only that it would come quickly, that he would be spared the games and the play.

'Tell me then. If it was not like that, how was it? Tell me.'

'They are sending a man to talk to us. They say they want to explain things that cannot be said over the radio, that there are too many people in the tower, and they want a more private negotiation with us. We asked them a question, Isaac, a question that we have the right to know the answer to.' Gabbling, believing that with each word he spoke so diminished the chances of his summary execution at the hands of his friend and his comrade.

'What was the question that could only be asked and answered if I was asleep, if I was not a party to it?'

'We have to know what they do with us if we were to release the passengers and follow their demands. We have to know what they would plan for us, where they would send us . . .'

'And that is not talk of surrender? Humiliating, crawling surrender? Don't hurt us, don't kick us, don't punch, and please, please don't send us back from where we came. That is the substance of your negotiation? And all this while I was sleeping?'

'It is finished, Isaac.' Rebecca pushed her way in front of David as if to protect him, provide a shield behind which he might shelter. 'You know that. You know that we go no further. You told me yourself last night that there would be no fuel for the engines, and this morning they have proved you right. They will not let us leave. There will only be killing, killing that leads to nothing. More blood, Isaac. That is what we are talking of, and whether more deaths would advance us.'

Isaac took a firm step forward, all that was necessary for him to be a foot from the girl. With his free left hand he swung hard and sharply. The blow was short and took her without warning, cuffing her semi-stunned to the floor. Had he not worn his grandmother's ring he would probably not have broken the soft skin, but the metal caught against her cheek and by the time she had recovered to stumble upright again a crimson rivulet was flowing towards her neck.

'It is not finished. Not for many more hours, not till we have tested our will against theirs. You understand? It should be simple and clear: there must be no more talk of submission. Our destination is Israel. That is where we go, and we do not permit deflection. Were we stupid and ignorant and useless then we would have been permitted to go, thrown on to the train for Vienna, popped on the flight for Tel Aviv, no difficulties would have obstructed us. But we are the people that they want inside Mother Russia, because we are the technicians that the giant needs to fuel herself from. Who with higher education is allowed to leave? We are the people that they obstruct, that they imprison, that languish on trumped-up charges at Potma and Perm. We have rejected their system, rejected it with blood, because we did not want to be a part of their way. It is not a time to talk of capitulation. We have come a long way. But if this were to be the end then it would have been better we had never started at all.'

Isaac saw the tight laughless smile of Anna Tashova as she sat three rows in front of him, and ignored it. He witnessed too the confusion of the Italian who was closest to him, and who did not understand what was being said and who looked vaguely for an indication from among their gestures and who was to remain uninformed and puzzled. He saw the headmaster who turned away to look through the window the moment their eyes met. Many faces for Isaac to see. Old and young, neat and unclean, educated and stupid, brave and fearful. The passengers were all he possessed with which to fight. Their lives his ammunition. But effective, that he knew, better than the tanks and the machine guns and the infantry that waited in ambush beyond the plane's walls. These were the shells that would carry the weight when battle was joined, would push back the soldiers and their guns. The lives of the men and the women and the children. They would bend, the Britishers, after ten o'clock they would bend. They had lost the will to fight, that was what he had read, that was what he believed.

As if to acknowledge that the episode was over Isaac said, 'The man is close to the plane now. Who is he? What have you arranged?'

'It is the one from the tower. The Russian speaker. They want him to talk to us.'

'I have your word, Rebecca, and yours too, David, that there will be no more talk of surrender? An oath that we fight together?'

He did not hear their replies; they mumbled from far down in their throats, but the movement of the lips was sufficient. He moved into the cockpit, the vantage point, from which he could observe the man who had broken the invisible thread laid across the tarmac and who had entered their territory, forsaking the safety of the armaments of his own people. Isaac looked down at him, noticed that the other never glanced at the windows as if keeping his own counsel, minding his time till the moment for contact was right. Isaac could recognize the mould of experience on his face. A deep man, Isaac thought, not a bureaucrat; someone from security and to be treated with care; someone who came because the persons in authority believed there was advantage to be gained from it, and the fools behind him trusted the promises that had been made, had faith in the words spoken over the radio link. Unarmed – but then there was no reason for him to carry a weapon, nothing gained. His weapons would be in his words, designed to lull and win confidence, and in his eyes that would report back to his masters sheltering in the tower. He had shown weakness in letting this man come close, Isaac knew that, and weakness was dangerous because much had to be sacrificed if the initiative was to be rewon. Isaac had not studied the history and tactics of hi-jacking, but his sensibilities told him that the man in shirt-sleeves and baggy, rounded trousers represented a threat. Yet he knew he wanted to hear what the man had to say, wanted an excuse to break the eighteen hours of isolation, needed some release from the confines of the plane's walls.

A buzz of talk filled the aircraft, a subdued drone, as the passengers with window seats told their neighbours that a man had come close to the Ilyushin. The news stifled thoughts of bulging bladders and empty stomachs, overcame the awareness of the smell of sweat. It was an event, and being the first of the day that offered the possibility of outside interference in their position it was welcome. The children talked more loudly than their elders, and pointed to the man and pushed those with the best view aside. The masters tried to quieten them but accepted they could not be successful.

Huge lenses mounted on cameras and tripods of weight and security had followed Charlie Webster's walk. The uniformed policemen were present to prevent any surge forward by cameramen, and journalists obligingly squatted on their haunches to avoid obstructing the view – the solitary figure barely visible to the naked eye at that range but greatly magnified by film. The static APCs and the resting soldiers had long been exhausted as a source of pictures, and this was recognized as something different. There were many suggestions as to the rôle of the man who strode towards the aircraft. He was 'SAS', he was a 'doctor because some of the passengers were sick', he was 'the leading government negotiator', a 'police chief of rank'. There seemed endless scope for speculation.

'The bastard's going round the far side.'

'Same at Tunis with the BOAC VC10, never saw a damn thing.'

'Shut up. You'll wreck the bloody sound track.'

'Fat lot of sound you're getting at a thousand yards.'

'He's gone, the bastard. Lost him round the nose.'

The advance of Charlie Webster had promised much to the cameramen, and they had been cheated and were angry and bickered among themselves as the film they had taken was canned and labelled and handed to the waiting motorcyclists.

'Always the same, never let you see a damn thing.'

When Colonel Arie Benitz dialled the number he had been given the previous night the response in London was almost immediate: two rings and the connection. He was not told to whom he was speaking, nor did he introduce himself. The conversation was brief.

'We have tried to arrange a meeting this morning at the Foreign Office, and we were put off,' he was told. 'The British Foreign Secretary is in continuous session with his advisors, they say. We are being shut out, and we need to take our own course.'

The soldier of another army would have laughed derisively at that moment, questioning immediately what initiative was possible. But other armies did not fly 2,000 miles across hostile airspace to land at Entebbe, or take their commando squads into territory as hostile as Beirut for the elimination of the men who fought against them, did not force down foreign airliners on scheduled routes because they were thought to be carrying the men who directed and controlled the war against Israel. If a suggestion were made there would be no ridicule at its feasibility from Colonel Arie Benitz. He would listen, evaluate and decide on the best plan available to ensure the possibility of success, however remote.

'Is there a chance that you might get to the plane and talk to those that hold it?'

'It would be difficult. They are suspicious of me, the British, as I was told they would be.'

'We would like a message passed to the plane, to the young people. But it is difficult if we work through the British. They are possessive of this matter . . .'

'They are possessive because they are nervous. It is to be expected. What is the message?'

'I used the wrong word. It is less a message, more a suggestion. Perhaps . . . if they were to offer to surrender now, no more killing, but conditional on their not being sent back? . . . They have asked in Jerusalem that I should say this to you, but it cannot be with the knowledge of the British. I ask again, is it possible for you to reach the plane?'

Patiently and without rancour, Benitz said into the phone, 'They have an army around the aircraft. I cannot just walk to it . . . you understand. And there is little time now. The children have set an ultimatum, you yourself told me that. And you must see that it is difficult for the British to bend at this moment, with the pilot dead, and when they are under duress from threats. If we do not have the co-operation of the security here then it would be difficult for me to reach the aircraft.' Not one to use the word 'impossible', but there was enough in his voice to suggest it. 'I will try, but you must send the reply to the Crisis Committee that I can offer little hope that I will be able to talk with our people.'

'It is understood, Colonel, it is understood what circumstances you find yourself in. Call us please should the position change, but I fear it will not. From London we are still trying for a meeting with the Foreign Secretary, but as I have told you they are not responsive.'

Arie Benitz hung the phone back on its hook, and cursed the noise from the jukebox and the babble of conversation among the airport staff, revelling in their enforced idleness, who gathered for breakfast and cups of tea and chatter of shop prices and housekeeping purses.

He yearned to be back with his own, back with the squad, back at the training school, back near Ashdod. Skirting the tables and chairs he walked slowly towards the door, not caring to glance at the mass of cheerful, laughing, uncaring humanity around him. Dull, miserable little people, who understood nothing, and would be frightened when their livers or their kidneys failed them, and they were close to death. They understood nothing, or else they would be hushed and passive, and thinking of three children, and a plane full of people, and what might be their fate.

Out through the door and moving briskly towards his assigned room; where else to go? What would have triggered them, he thought? An incident, a single episode? Unlikely. It was never straightforward, not with these people, never as simple as the outsider believed. Did not take a kicking, or a rape or injustice to fashion the guerrilla, just an accumulation of circumstances, a construction of despair, a fabrication of hatred. Not a sudden thing, a momentary decision, but a slow-burning, stoked loathing. And courage. Nothing without courage. Even the Palestinians . . .

He flopped down at the desk. Had any of those who passed his door stopped to look at the hunched figure they would have seen a sad and hurt man.

Seventy yards behind Charlie were the petrol tankers, their considerable forward and rear heavy-duty tyres providing cover for the SAS marksmen. Two of them handled the old Lee Enfield bolt action rifle mounted with the tubular telescopic sight now trained on the door of the Ilyushin. Another pair lay beside the standard NATO General Purpose Machine Gun, belt-fed. The rifles would provide accurate shot protection, the GPMG trained on the same target was the fall-back precaution, concentration of fire. Behind the central tanker were men with smoke canisters fitted to the barrel tip of FNs. He was unaware of all this and stood feeling a peculiar loneliness as he waved to the windows and door. Bloody stupid way to be carrying on, Charlie.

It seemed to take an age before the door began to move. A slight shuddering action at first, as if someone was operating the mechanism who had not handled it before. There was a stutter, then a sweeping movement, as the door came away on its arms from the fuselage and swung out before coming to rest. It took

Charlie time to get his eyes tuned to the grey artificial light of the interior, and then the girl was standing there looking down on him, more with curiosity than anything else, her left hand on the edge of the door. Least of her problems, thought Charlie, falling out of the bloody thing. Pistol in her right hand; he prided himself that he knew most makes, but this wasn't one that he recognized, almost hidden amid the folds of her dress. He smiled at her, big and open and friendly, the smile that Parker Smith said would sell sand to the Saudis, ice to the Eskimos, the smile that his wife always giggled at.

'Hello, it's Charlie Webster. You're Rebecca?' Daft really, like a pick-up at a YWCA hop. Had to be some sort of formality. 'I've come to speak with David and Isaac . . . and with you.' Don't count her out, at least not till you've looked at the scene a fair bit closer.

'You can talk to me, they are listening. They would prefer that we talk in Russian. If you speak loud they can hear what you say, and they will tell me what to reply.'

Good thinking, and Charlie always admired that, whether it was from the friendlies or the opposition. If they were thinking well then they should be respected. Keeping out of sight where the guns weren't on them. Particularly Isaac: drop him and the whole thing could be wrapped up, and with all the hardware lying about no way that he would show if he had any sense. Seemed the boy was working it out.

'What I've come here to do is to explain the situation as it stands at this moment.' Time for the big speech, time to calm them down because it gets serious right now if you get them excited. 'The position is very clear really, and since you are all intelligent people we think you will see the only option that is open to you. Your plane has no fuel, and we have said that while the aircraft and the passengers are under your control it will get none. While you are on board the plane goes no further. That is the decision of the British government and it is irreversible.' Working at each sentence before he spoke it, considering the most appropriate Russian words from his comprehensive but rustworn vocabulary. Made him slow but gave an impression of deliberation and authority. 'The aircraft is surrounded by troops who have orders to shoot to kill should there be any attempt to break through our perimeter using the hostages as a shield. There is no escape from the aircraft. You will only leave it when you have disarmed yourselves, when all the passengers have been released. I am instructed to repeat the solemn guarantee of the British government that you will not be harmed by our security forces.'

Clipped to the neck of his shirt, clearly visible, was a small black microphone. From it a thin colourless connection had been threaded, running up his shirt to his collar where it merged with his hair before blending into a plastic moulded earpiece.

'Keep it going, Charlie,' – Clitheroe, slightly distorted, but directing and controlling him – 'Tough stuff first, then on to the message they've put over to the world, and next the freeing of the hostages.' The voice made him lose his concentration for a moment, throwing him fractionally, and he felt a flush on his face as he watched the girl stare back at him, not responding, merely waiting for him to finish.

'We want you to know that your flight out of Russia has been widely reported by the international news media. If it was a protest that you were seeking against any grievances that you may feel you have then you have been widely heard. If publicity was your aim then you have achieved it. We think that any aggressive action you may be considering will only alienate the many millions of people all over the world who are currently sympathetic to you.' Crap, Charlie, but what else to say? How do you get a conversation going at 30 yards? No known way. Bound to stand there exchanging speeches. But it's a load of rubbish you're talking and you know it. He wondered how they knew what he was talking about in the tower; must have brought some of the FO girls down, or one from the Department. Spoke Russian better than he spoke English. Boot-faced ladies with heavy rings on their fingers, gold in their teeth who'd made it out in the '30s and started to work for the British in the war, and were in their sixties now and had to keep going till pension day if they were to afford the bed-sitters of retirement. Hated the Soviets like shit which gave them high security clearance.

'You have many women and children on board. We understand there is a party of schoolchildren. There is no need for you to keep them; all of them could be released now and it would make a great impression on all those people that are following this action.' The girl still looked down at him. He could see her ankles, a little fat, and the solid and muscular shins before the hem of her dress denied him. Face devoid of expression, and Charlie wondered which of them was screwing her – wouldn't get much for his efforts. 'That's what I came to say. There is no point in talking about ultimatums. It's nonsense and it won't work.'

'That is all?' She had a thin, reedy voice, and he had to strain to hear her.

'If there is anything you want me to answer, then I will try to help you.'

She ducked back inside the aircraft, lost to him, and the doorway was emptied. There was just time for him to see the faces of the passengers at their portholes – poor bastards, going through the familiar hoop, and with their hopes raised now because there was a contact.

Charlie said quietly into the microphone, speaking in English, 'That's the first chat over. They're talking about it now.'

'They're all on the monitor,' he was told. 'The open door drives them into the passenger cabin, that's where the three of them are, but the girl seems out of it. It's the two fellows who are involved. Seem calm enough, no arms flying about. Now that the door is open we are getting some sort of sound, but we can't read it right now, only the girl when she spoke to you. They've probably dropped their voices to avoid being overheard by the passengers.'

'Right,' said Charlie. The girl was back in the doorway.

'When you said you would come it was because you wanted to talk to us about our request for information. The question that we asked was what would happen to us if we followed your instructions. What is the answer?'

'I have said that you will not be harmed.'

'That is not an answer. I repeat, what will happen to us?'

'If you have committed offences you will be charged and will face a fair and impartial trial.'

'That is not the answer. Where would the trial be?'

'If you have committed offences inside the United Kingdom you will stand trial in the United Kingdom.' Not much longer, thought Charlie, not much longer this bloody nonsense can go on.

'You are not helpful, you seek to deceive us. Will we be sent back to Russia? Is that your plan?'

'I know of no plan to send you back to Russia.' Lying sod, Charlie, but what else to say? And anyway remember the parting shot of the big political gaffer, nothing sewn up at this stage. And what right have these three to know the truth? Forfeited that, hadn't they, when they took the guns on board? 'I have not heard of such a plan.' Never could lie well, not that many people that can. Only a few, and they're the exception. The girl didn't believe him, agitated and leaning back to be told what to say.

'My friends say that this is a trick, that you will send us back to Kiev. We do not trust you. If you had been able to promise, if there had been a document then we would have believed you, but there has been nothing. Only you, and you are a little person with no authority.'

Now she tells me, thought Charlie. There was a light breeze that fastened to the moisture of his skin and cooled it, giving comfort from the heat. A great clear sky, cloudless, peopled only by the curving seagulls, far off course . . .

'Charlie, Charlie, keep your bloody wits about you' – the message beating through his earpiece – 'The two men have gone half-way down the cabin . . . pulling one of the passengers out . . . down the corridor . . . from among the kids, must be one of staff travelling with them . . . there are hands trying to stop it . . . not a bloody hope, and the guy himself isn't fighting it . . . off the monitor . . .'

The girl was gone, pulled by an arm, roughly and without explanation, replaced by a man, thinly-woven grey suit, masking the shape of another, whose left arm was gripped around the first man's throat and whose right held the snub nose of a sub-machine gun to the captive's jaw. The face of the man in the suit was ashen, and his eyes were pleading and helpless and without fight. The knees shook and trembled, sending eddies down the lower length of his trousers. Charlie could see the summit of black curly hair above the man's shoulder. Isaac was out, Isaac was at the door. Had to break the tension, pacify him, calm him, couldn't shout, not with the barrel an inch from the man's face, not with the finger inside the trigger guard.

'Isaac, it's Charlie Webster. We have been speaking on the radio. You have to understand that we are here to help you. We understand your problems and there is much sympathy through-out the world for the fate of your people. Nothing, nothing can be gained from further bloodshed, only the loss of the sympathy that you have already won.'

All the men that Charlie had hunted when he was active had been young: it had been the common factor, characteristic. No terrorist or urban guerrilla or freedom fighter makes it to middle age. Either dead, locked up or in love with life by then. Youth was the crucial element to see things with the clarity needed to topple windmills, struggle against the sponge of society.

'My friends called to you when I was sleeping. They wanted to surrender. They would have done if you had said to them that they would not have been sent back. But you could not say that. Perhaps you could not tell them the lie that would have made you the victor. But that part of them you have destroyed now – you have made them fighters, you have lost them, Char-lie Webster. Perhaps you do not know the Jews. Perhaps you do not know that we have been turned aside many times, pushed and manipulated and tricked and bent. We know what it is to be trampled over, to be a second class of man. Go to Ukraine one day, Charlie Webster, go to the great synagogue in Kiev. Look at the people there, people who have been deceived and duped. Look at their misery, at the agony of their lives, at their fear. Go and look for yourself then come back and tell me that you expect a Jew to believe you when you say "I have not heard of such a plan." '

No breath left, lungs drained, Isaac paused.

'Isaac, we have to talk about this sensibly . . .'

'The talk of surrender is over. We have told you that we want the petrol to fly to Israel. That is what we came here for, what we will leave with. This man is the headmaster who is travelling with the schoolchildren. He is the one who will die at ten o'clock if the fuel is not loaded. He will stay in this doorway where you can watch him. You have your radio, so you can tell your people what we have decided. You can stay where you are, you can watch and you can think for yourself who has the will, your people or ourselves.' The headmaster stood limp in his hold, almost as if he needed Isaac to hold him up, and all the time his eyes were fastened on Charlie's face, seeking a sign, a reassurance that was not Charlie's to give.

'Isaac, you must understand . . .'

'I understand everything. I want fuel. You at the moment do not wish me to have it. You are playing with the lives of many people on the aircraft – tell your authorities that.'

Clitheroe in Charlie's earpiece, 'Don't move away, Charlie. Stay put and keep quiet. Leave it a few minutes then try to resume the dialogue. We have to keep the conversation moving if we're to save this fellow's life. From what you've seen of Isaac, from his voice – our pick-up is not that good here – is this a real threat or will he soften nearer the time?'

Charlie thought of the face that he had seen, sharper and with a reality because it was now freed from the two-dimension flatness of the photographs and the television tube. And he thought of the strength and the ferocity of the grip on the headmaster. He tilted his head till his mouth was directly over the microphone. 'He means it. The way he is now he'll shoot others afterwards if nothing happens to satisfy him. Right through the whole bloody lot he'll go.' So it would be a killing job, a hard, messy, killing job, and carcasses to be picked up, and thrown on to stretchers.

He eased himself on to the tarmac and sat cross-legged, the hot surface penetrating the fabric of his trousers. They had taken the man back from the doorway and he stood now, blurred and indistinct against the far wall of the aircraft. Charlie reckoned the girl would be watching him, but he could not be certain. Had a headache, not rampant but nagging, chewing at him, always did when he was tired. He looked at his watch: time ebbing away. He hadn't felt it when they were talking, but was aware of it now. Half an hour to go, the minimum, because his watch usually ran fast. Thirty minutes to see what Isaac was made from; only you already know, Charlie, can sense it. Smell it.

13

In the control tower the 'No Smoking' signs had long been ignored, and the fierce pall of smoke was unnoticed as the cigarette butts burned on the edges of tables and in saucers among the debris of coffee cartons and sandwich wrappings. Voices were subdued as if the men there were inside a great and famous cathedral where noise would be deemed irreverent.

The Home Secretary had alternated through the morning between his room below and the operational centre, but since Charlie Webster had walked out on the tarmac he had remained upstairs. Now he talked by telephone to the Prime Minister. Clarification was what he sought, suggested by his aides because they were employed to protect the reputation of their master. Could there be any flexibility in the official stance the government had taken, now that a life was at immediate risk? Not possible, especially at this moment, not after the Soviet statement, not after the leaking by the press that an ultimatum was due to expire: there was to be no suggestion of compromise or weakness under threat. While he listened he pulled at his collar, as if his breathing were constricted, and those who looked to him for some indication of the burden of the conversation saw only anxiety and a slackness about his mouth that spelled dilemma and irresolution. He made his farewells to the Prime Minister, and put back the receiver with circumspection before turning to those around him.

'The Prime Minister has said what I think we all expected him to say. There will be no alteration in our position. The fate of this unfortunate does not affect the decision that we have taken. He wants me to pass to you all that he has the greatest faith in our judgment. He leaves it to us to decide whether the aircraft should be stormed before the expiry of the ultimatum. We do not have very long, gentlemen, and we need to know the options.' His voice tailed away, reflecting a mood that came as no surprise to those who knew him well. His reign at the Home Office had been characterized by a humanity and sympathy that was not always traditional. His concern now was for the passenger they knew only as 'the headmaster', whom he had seen brought to the doorway of the aircraft set inside the squared television frame. A man in a grey suit about whom nothing else was known except that his chin shivered and his hands clenched and straightened again continuously.

'What are the options, gentlemen?'

Clitheroe rose from the stool on which he sat and paced slowly the length of the tower, a few feet only, but a space that gave him room to consider. There was a diffidence about him that they had not seen before.

'It's Webster's opinion – his opinion only on the killing of this man – it is just his assessment that they will go through with it, go to the limit of their threat. Webster is in a very exposed position, probably nervous, perhaps not the best judge. I don't wish to patronize the man, not in any way at all, but we have to remember where he is. He is unarmed, he is within clear range of their guns, he has been close to the intended victim. It is his judgment that they will shoot, but he may not . . .'

'Who is in a better position?' the Home Secretary said.

'I don't know – none of us, I think. All I am trying to do is to remind you of the circumstances that Webster finds himself in: we should not follow his judgment blindly.' But he too had seen the fish-eye pictures, the man pulled from his seat, the hands that rose to his help thrust aside. 'I just don't know. Perhaps they will kill, perhaps not. It is impossible to be certain. And if they kill once it does not follow that Webster is right and that they will begin a wholesale slaughter. The effect of one killing might be to break these three – that has to be considered. We are dealing with the intangible. We cannot draw up a blueprint and say that because one thing has happened then a logical process will ensue. There is another aspect: these people are Jews, but not Israelis, and that may colour the will that they talk so much of.' Clitheroe sat down again, aware of his own limitations.

'If Mr Webster is right, and they intend to kill the man, is it possible to take physical action to pre-empt it? What is the feasibility of attacking the aircraft?' The Home Secretary directed the question without enthusiasm to the Assistant Chief Constable.

'The military would not be happy about it. There are obvious difficulties – open ground, the need to get ladders to the plane. The SAS estimate they would need a minimum of fifteen seconds from the time they leave the tanker till they are entering the cabin. Even with far side diversions it's dangerous, a risk to the troops and to the passengers. At night they could manage it, but by daylight . . . What it comes down to, sir, is this – do we endanger many lives at this stage in the hope of saving one?'

'It would be difficult to sit here and watch a man die and know we have so much strength and not utilize it.'

The politician had expressed the fear that swamped them all. It was a challenge to their virility, to their professions, that they should stand on the sidelines, acknowledge their inadequacy.

'The Dutch did it,' the policeman intoned, 'at the train siege at Beilen, when the Moluccan group took hostages. A passenger was executed and they took a decision not to storm because conditions were unfavourable. They backed off and relied on negotiations; and no more passengers were—'

'We are not the Dutch,' the Home Secretary rasped. 'Because they have taken a course of action it does not mean we follow. We cannot hide from responsibilities behind precedent.'

He paused, seemed to stumble in his words, losing track of his theme, and there was age and unhappiness on his face. He could not have held this high office twenty years earlier when capital punishment was still exercised; he would not have had the strength or the commitment to sign the final authorizations, would not have surmounted the mountain of conscience and refused to recommend that the monarch use her prerogative of reprieve.

'There has to be something that can be done. We cannot just sit here and idle the time away.'

'At times, sir, we are not given freedom of action. Options are not always open to us.' The policeman spoke with respect, understanding the sense of failure that pervaded the room. 'We just have to hope that Webster is wrong.'

The job of guarding the headmaster had been left to Rebecca.

He remained erect and tall, breathing coming fast and in slight gasps, but with his head still and his eyes stretching out beyond the middle distance towards the fields and trees, and the further perimeter fence, and the farm with the white-painted walls and the embossed and dark-stained beams, following the swooping movement of a bird that hunted for food among the migrating swarms of summer insects. When he looked straight ahead he could not see the girl and was only aware of her presence by the occasional shuffled movements as she eased her body into less contorted positions, leaning all the time against the coat cupboard beside him. His thoughts were of classrooms, clean and ordered and where his rule held sway. Of the management of his pupils. His work for the Party. The Party required of him a discipline that he welcomed, gave an outlet for the enthusiasms that he had harboured since his release from the army at the end of the war. The comradeship of the Party, the sense of achievement and accomplishment in his work. Frustrations, yes, but nothing when set against the successes that could be attained. Could take a pride in the way the children had behaved since the taking of the plane, a tribute to his responsibility, and he had not been betrayed by the little ones. Calm and collected and without panic, the children had been impeccable, even with the hunger in their bellies, their fear of the guns. Should be recognized, and reported back to those in authority, whatever became of him; should not be forgotten that they were children under his tutelage and they had not disgraced themselves. He knew what time the men would come for him, when he would pass out of the care of the girl and into their hands, but did not look to his watch. He could hear the two men, talking among themselves, but only faintly, and he could not make out their words. They were behind him and to the left, positioned where they could see past him and down the passenger cabin. Leaving him to what peace he might find.

He saw the man on the tarmac shift his body and settle on his toes with his legs bent out in front of him, squatting as if mounted on a flattened toilet. The man was of his own age, the one who had been sent to talk, and who had been rejected, and who showed now an emptiness of initiative. He had tried – discernible from his voice – to plead with all the reasonableness that he could muster, had tried to save him, and for that the headmaster was grateful; but he was not dealing with people that were reasonable. The stranger no longer looked about him, ranging the length of the plane, and the headmaster gradually became aware that the concentrated gaze of the man on the ground was directed at him. First the man's eyes strained for understanding and comprehension, but then the lips moved as if with a message. Seemed to say one word, one word alone, again and again from the rhythm of the way the mouth moved. The headmaster felt again the weakening of his legs, the trembling of his hands.

One word, one word only, shouted and deafening so that it split into his consciousness, an order, a demand. He fought to follow, struggled to relate the bellowed voice to his movements.

'Jump.'

The noise had been soaring inside Charlie for minutes before he could summon himself to howl the command. Fearful in the moment that his voice would desert him, that it would come as a feeble croak without the incision he needed. From deep in his lungs, far down, reaching for a depth and volume that would make the bastard up there react from instinct.

Charlie saw the headmaster lurch toward the open void of the

262

Ilyushin's doorway, saw him move into the pitching fall with all the expertise of the trainee parachutist who leaves the balloon basket for the first time. Heard the single shot that was an age late. Charlie was on his feet and sprinting. A haze of confusion as the man landed. Awkwardly, agility destroyed by the years, Charlie saw his face rise from the concrete, eyes harrowed and frantic, desperate for new instructions.

'Run, you bugger, run!'

Crazy, slow motion, broken trot, and Charlie was closing with him, and then the first crescendo of gunfire. Ricochets impacting from the tarmac, and exploding pockets of dust to trace the bullets. Charlie turned and saw Isaac standing there, indecisive, then the gun at his shoulder again, steadying his aim. Stupid bastard, he must have fired from the hip the first time. Charlie plunged forward, felt his chest buffet into the other man and sweep him to the right towards the shelter and haven of the wing structure. Had to push him when they were together on the ground, like a bloody sack and whimpering all the time, like he can't believe it, like he thinks they'll still come for him. Together they rolled across the ground, bucking and confused.

'It's all right,' Charlie whispered. 'It's over.' He checked himself, surprised that again he'd spoken in Russian. Spread-eagled over the man's body he could only see his head, pale and with the skin stretched drum-tight, and the reflection where the tears ran.

'You walk at my speed,' Charlie said, louder, and pulled the man up, arms round the flabbiness of his waist. He didn't know whether they'd made the dead ground of the wing or not. Hell of a weight the bugger was, had to carry him really, made him use muscles he'd forgotten. In step, an exhausted dance routine . . . just a few more seconds and they'd be clear, out of range. Charlie didn't look back, his eyes unwavering on the pole in the perimeter fence that he had chosen.

'Not long now,' he said. 'Just a few more yards. Then it's over.'

And endlessly beating through his mind the memory of the hunched and coiled figure in the doorway, the gun clamped to his shoulder, the saucer eyes expanded behind the sight. Be a bloody killing job now. Have to cut you down, Isaac, have to, won't we? Because you're not offering any other way.

Isaac had not lingered in the doorway.

One fierce and uncontrolled burst of gunfire with the barrel pulling high and left and he had realized that the opportunity to cut down the fugitive was lost. Perhaps he could have taken the Briton with an aimed shot, but it would have been a lucky one, and the wing was looming into his orbit. He realized his reactions had been slow, dulled by lack of sleep, but still slow, and sufficient to endanger them all. And the girl had again failed. Pity, really, because she was a part of them, from the same blood, but she had failed when they needed her. Not all her fault, partly his own, had underestimated the man who came, and had been tricked and would suffer for it. It was a calm evaluation that he made, stemming from the same calmness that immediately took him away from the open space, where the rifles that were trained on him could have exacted a revenge.

Could no longer rely on the girl. Obvious, and should have been seen earlier, but proven now. So which of them could be relied on? Rebecca lay slumped on the carpet, the pistol still in her two hands as if the shock of firing it had toppled her. David, quiet and without comment, apart from them, taking refuge at the far end of the aircraft where he could make believe that his work was in watching the passengers. They have lost their faith, the two of them; they do not believe any more in escape.

He shouted to David, 'There is still time till ten o'clock and we will do then as we have promised.'

There was no reply, and he expected none. He did not even bother to gaze down the aisle to witness David's reaction. Like sheep they would follow him, and like sheep they would scatter if he faltered.

George Davies lay on his stomach beside the sniper behind the forward wheel of the central tanker.

'Could you have had him?'

'The one with the curly hair, with the SMG? No problem.'

'There was no instruction, you were right not to fire.'

'Three, four seconds I had him.'

'They haven't clarified on it yet. Up till now it's been not to shoot unless we can get the two men, both of them together. And I have to call in and ask.'

'Take a bloody light year that; they won't hang about for us.'

'Always the same when you bring a coach trip down from London to handle it.'

'Any talk of us going in and busting it open?'

'Not at the moment. Can be done if they want it, but it's not ideal.'

'Make any difference, what the civvie did, pulling that chap out?' The marksman spoke from the side of his mouth, conversationally and without deference to rank. Head never moving, steady on a line down the rifle barrel, searching the greyness of the door's opening.

'Shouldn't think so, there was nothing on the net about it first. Reckon he acted off his own bat, didn't think out the consequences, just couldn't sit there and watch it all in glorious technicolor.'

'Had a point there.'

'We'll have to see.'

All the years they'd trained for this, exercises and rehearsal runs, sometimes thinking it was for real, usually knowing it wasn't. All the alerts, all the false alarms. Living and sleeping the problem for four years since the squad was formed, and he didn't know the answers. 'Expert' he was supposed to be, and he didn't know. Nobody did for that matter, but it didn't make the pill any sweeter.

The television camera with the long lens showed the committee in the tower that Charlie Webster had reached the safety of the cropped grass at the side of the runway. He was on his knees beside the man that he had rescued. The episode was completed.

They waited for him to call in on the radio, and when there had been no transmission presumed that the set was broken.

The Assistant Chief Constable gave rapid orders, content that he was again able to perform a function, and separated from the tiresome world of conjecture and interpretation. A civilian ambulance should be sent to the pair. Under no circumstances should they be allowed to take cover behind the petrol tankers some fifty yards to their left: those in the plane should not have the chance of even a glimpse of the troops, and should continue to believe that the vehicles were abandoned, untenanted. Clitheroe mentioned to any who cared to listen that a major breakthrough had been achieved: they now had in their possession an eyewitness from the aircraft who would be able to furnish an up-to-the-minute description of the state of mind of both hi-jacker and hostage. The Home Secretary remained by the monitor that showed the interior of the aircraft recorded by the fish-eye. Isaac occasionally obliged by coming into view, but David stayed at the far end of the aircraft and was not seen. The girl passed the length of the aisle as if communicating messages. Still no sound from the microphones that were serviced by sheepish and frustrated technicians.

'Has Mr Webster's action helped or hindered us?'

He spoke to the room in general, not turning from the set, his hands clamped on the sides of his cheeks, elbows firmly on the table, feeling the tiredness that was common to all who had spent the last five and a half hours in the tower; a tiredness that came not from lack of sleep but from the frustration of playing the part continuously of voyeurs, unable to alter significantly the course of events.

The Assistant Chief Constable had finished his delivery of instructions.

'It's not yet ten, seven minutes or so to go, and there's seventy more they can pick from. What Mr Webster did may have had the opposite effect to what we have been hoping for. In effect he may have warmed them up.' The policeman knew that his words were not welcome, but time he was heard out and his experience and knowledge realized. 'It's not the sort of thing that is likely to weaken them – quite the reverse. It's a slap in the face for them. I would expect them to try to hit back.'

'I think you're wrong,' said the Home Secretary quietly. 'I hope so. We were all prepared to sit here and watch that poor man die. We had reconciled ourselves to it, justified our non-interference in a way we would have done with an interministerial memorandum. We had passed the buck. That man is now alive because a decisive step was taken. We have a little dignity now. Not much, because it was not we who authorized Mr Webster's action. But we have some, and dignity is important . . .'

'Minister, by the time the day's over we may have some dignity and we may have three or six dead passengers. The two don't equate on my scales.' The back of his neck, clipped and smooth, was reddening where it met with the white laundered shirt above the pressed collar of his tunic. 'I don't give a damn about dignity. I don't give a damn if the whole British cabinet has to crawl on their bended knees to that plane. I don't give a damn whether Mr Webster is the hero of the hour. I want those passengers out, and I want them out safely. When we've done that then we may be able to talk of dignity.'

The Home Secretary came awkwardly to his feet, turned square to the policeman. 'I'm in your way, and you have work to do. I will be below if you need me.' He stopped, as if uncertain as to the wisdom of his gesture, then said quietly and without hurry, 'I apologize for wasting your time, gentlemen. It's an alien world to me, and not one that I relish, nor have any great understanding of. If you think there is need of my presence please do not hesitate to call for me.'

'I really don't think, Minister . . .' the aides were round him, sidling forward, concerned.

'Minister, there is no need . . .'

'It would not be wise . . .'

He smiled to them all and made his way to the door, walked through, and closed it afterwards with care – that it should not bang.

'Dignity, my Christ,' muttered the policeman savagely. 'What does he think we're at, winning a bloody election?'

He crossed the room for support and found it lacking, faces averted, studying the monitors, drawing from the coffee urn, unparcelling the food. Made a mistake, hadn't he? But what did they want? Easy answers, everything's rosy, pound's doing well, balance of payments sensational, exports record-breaking? Did they want that? Or the truth? That we're in a new situation, and it's four minutes to bloody ten o'clock?

And they'd remember that, the smart little arselickers who burrowed in the files and said who was right for promotion to Chief Constable. They'd remember that, and have a little titter behind their hands before they went out to lunch, and a damn good meal they'd have before coming back to pencil out his name.

Luigi Franconi had long been a dreamer.

Back at Party Headquarters, the drab poster-daubed red-brick block behind the Piazza Venezia where he occupied a third-floor room, the secretaries and his colleagues had become used to seeing his concentration drift away from their expositions and briefings. It was almost a joke to those that knew him well, the way he was present and then absent, merely moving his head in agreement or dissent whichever way the argument led. When he was corrected, exposed with much laughing, and irritation from those who were not his friends, then he would assume pained apology and shake himself and indicate that surely it was time for lunch in the trattoria that graced the small square close by. In truth Franconi was a private person, seldom willing to share his day-dreams and not convinced that the words of others conveyed any great importance. He worked from paper, from pile upon pile of mounting typed and printed paper. Only when confronted with the written word or figure did he produce evidence of the ability of which his superiors in the Party were convinced. They realized the value of this man, not a person to be influenced by suavity or glibness or fluency.

The word and statistic had to sustain on its own, without extraneous support. They laughed about him in the office, but only to his face, never behind his back, and told him he must have the blood of the Germans in his veins, because no Italian could put such reliance on silence. Franconi would smile with them, and try to please, and think them fools, and relish their comradeship till the moment came to slip away.

No papers to read now. He had not brought a book with him, not a Garzanti classic, not even a pamphlet draft that needed tidying, nor a notebook in which to jot his more casual impressions of the Soviet Union for the report which they would be awaiting back in Rome. Nothing in the pouch in front of him except a sick-bag and a folder that described the Ilyushin safety procedures, and which was not written in any language that he understood.

The choosing of the headmaster had made little impression on him, a brief flurry of excitement and apprehension as the man had disappeared from the doorway in the moment before the firing of the machine gun. He had not aped the other passengers who had first stared through the windows and then subsided in their seats seeking anonymity as the eyes of Isaac had swept them; the mood of the moment had been quickly lost on him. He had not offended, he was divorced from their struggle, they had no quarrel with him. Before he had been nervous – he would admit that to himself – when they had separated him from his friend, from Aldo. The same fear of the unknown and the unfamiliar that he had known in the hills thirty-five years earlier, and it had passed now as it had then. He had barely glanced from the aircraft porthole to discover the headmaster's fate.

He phased away the exterior world with the dreams of his home. When this was all over, and it would not take much time – the youth and desperation of his captors told him that – when they climbed down the ladder that would be brought, he would bypass the television crews and the journalists. There were enough in the delegation who would be queuing, indeed, jumping forward, to satisfy the needs of the RAI interviewers or whoever else wanted their opinions. He would stand alone at the side, with a half grin on his face, and shrug his shoulders and be polite and shake his head. Just wait till his colleagues had said their fill. They'd send them home by Alitalia; right to travel on the national airline, and an Italian ought to, a gesture to salve an infinitesimal percentage from the annual deficit. Over-manning, the central problem, always had been ... No better at Party Headquarters where they preached organization and control of the workforce and distribution of labour, but still suffered the same malady as the capitalists. Adriana, Maria, Christina, all in the typing pool, all with time for knitting and gossip; any one of them could look after the needs of the section, but how to sack one? – it didn't bear thinking of, the squabbling, the arguing, the challenge over the pension rights. He'd go home on Alitalia. The wife would be there to meet him. Arms round his neck, lipstick on his collar, mascara on his cheek, sobbing in his ear. He'd have to endure all that. They'd drive out from Fiumicino and take the Raccordo Annulare and he'd see the girls beside the bushes and pretend he wasn't looking, and his wife would be coping firmly with the traffic. Be able to drink them in, the girls. Miniskirts and unbuttoned blouses, thighs and breasts and invitations, and he'd be left to his privacy to ponder on it while nodding and agreeing with all that his wife said. Often the cars pulled up sharply, a warning flash of brake lights and a man would jump from the driving seat and the girls were already hurrying for the sanctuary of the undergrowth. Luigi had always wondered what it would be like, just what was said before the removal of the sparse strips of necessary clothing. When did you pay, before or after? And what would there be afterwards – a thanks, an acknowledgement, a wordless wave, or just a grin? He had spent an adult lifetime travelling the Raccordo, seen them, wanted them, lusted in his way after them, his foot near the brake pedal, and never dared. His wife would drive him home, park the car, expansively in the road, and he'd comment on it and she'd dismiss the matter and lead him like an exhibit, a celebrity brought back from the fair, to their fourth-floor home where the gathering would be waiting. Kisses and hugs and back slaps now, a multitude of voices, a swill of chilled wine, a pasta bowl of welcome. All would ask him to relate his experiences, but in concert so that even should he want to speak none would be listening and all talking, chattering, demanding, crying. They'd be there for hours, filling his home, taking up his time, impressing their friendship when all he would seek would be the solace of his wife's arms. Drawn curtains and extinguished lights, the cosmetics to make her no different to the girls still plying their trade by the road kerb. Moving, performing, functioning, that would be his bedroom task on the night of his return; have full run of his domain that night: later would come the denials and the tiredness and the excuses. Not the first night, though.

The hand sunk into the roof of his jacket collar, gripped at the well-woven material, and pulled him upright, splintering his reveries. It was an irrevocable strength that drew him from the seat, dragging him without explanation from the safety of his fellow passengers. Fleetingly he saw the faces around him, saw them twist and turn, aware of their shame and degradation. The one with the curly hair, the short one, that was the one that held him, propelled him out into the aisle, and now there was the thrust of steel against his backbone. The dreams were losing ground, the warmth of the flesh receding, the softened arms on him no longer gave hope. A cry came, hoarse and splitting into his consciousness, his name shouted at the pitch of hysteria, and the voice was Aldo's. Just his name, and an agony in the voice, and the sound of it hammered at him till his knees buckled and his bowels weakened, till his eyes glazed to a mist and he was blinded by the flood and could not tell where he was going, only reacting to the pressure at the nape of his neck that drove him forward.

It came late, but there was a moment of total clarity before the brightness of the intruding sun through the opened aircraft door obliterated all images in front of him. And there was the memory of the face of the headmaster who had taken the similar path minutes before, as he had been led down the route that separated him from the rest, from the bovine accepting herd. Had Luigi Franconi looked like that? Had he showed the broken fear, the collapsed chin, the nerveless sagged cheeks, the faltering walk? Had he screamed inside without sound as the other must have done?

The power of the gun barrel was no longer at his back. Gone, lost for a moment, giving the fractional hope of salvation, before he found it again, found it where he knew he must, found its chill and symmetry against the gentle skin that slid back from his earlobe towards the base of his neck.

They all heard the single, echoing refrain of the shot.

The reverberations were fierce inside the aircraft, quieting the frenzied shouts from the remaining members of the PCI delegation; an empty hollowed thud where Charlie Webster lay on the shortened grass, that caused the man he still protected to shudder underneath him and squirm as if trying to bury himself in the hardened soil; a faint popping noise, a distant car door slammed to those immured inside the plate glass of the control tower windows.

Inside the press corral where the journalists were screened from the open door of the Ilyushin the solitary report was noted. Quizzical eyes, a margin of excitement, a switching-on of cameras, that their synchronized sound systems would record any further gunfire, a scribbling in notebooks.

'What time do you make it?' A man from the Agencies asked the reporter who stood next to him; he was required to log the day's events with accuracy.

The other kept his eyes fastened on that flank of the aircraft that was visible. 'Just on ten o'clock.'

'Not much we can say then. At ten o'clock a single shot was heard from the far side of Aeroflot 927. That's it. Nothing else we can say.'

With more powerful binoculars than they possessed the journalists and cameramen might have been able to distinguish the lifeless body of Luigi Franconi where it rested close to the starboard undercarriage wheels. But at the distance between where they stood and the Ilyushin the wheels only merged, shimmering in their stillness, with the unnoticed corpse.

A sound recordist, a large man who prided himself equally on his wit and the perfection of his trimmed beard, made a joke, weak to those that heard it, but his own chorus of laughter was picked up by all in the pen; a palliative to the suppressed tension carried by the unexplained shot. The zephyr of laughter swept out across the scorched concrete, rippling its way towards the aircraft and the control tower till it settled on the faraway ears of those who lay in the grass with their rifles and machine guns.

There were a score of impotent obscenities from the troops who had watched the small Italian die.

14

Charlie had not looked back towards the tarmac. He knew what he would see if he turned his head, could picture the exact position in which the body would be lying. No need to look, not when death no longer held a fascination. He'd seen many before: the corpses of men who had 'died well', who had 'died badly', whatever that meant – of men who had been killed judicially, and those who had gone without the solace of legality, of men who had screamed and of men who had prayed. It made little difference to the poor bastards, not now, not when it was over.

And this one, this nameless one down by the wheels, why had he taken the trip? Pretty straightforward, when you think about it, Charlie. One was going to go. Those were the rules they were playing by: take a mouse from a cat and she'll go find another. Made you wonder whether it was worth it, worth all the adrenaline surge, the scream and the gunfire. Can't play heroics seventy times, Charlie.

He could hear the approach of the ambulance, creeping carefully forward, low gear, on the outer perimeter road. It stopped a full hundred yards from him, as if nobody had told the driver the range of an SMG. Couldn't blame him, couldn't blame anybody who didn't want his head blasted. Not an ambulance driver's quarrel. Jews and Israelis and Russians, so where did a driver from Bishop's Stortford on forty-five pounds a week and struggling fit into that pattern? Charlie raised his right hand and gave the thumbs-up signal – put the poor blighter out of his misery and let him know he didn't have to come closer.

Gently Charlie pulled the Russian to his feet and eased him

into a position where his own body still gave protection from the aircraft. Together they shuffled forward, slowly and without precision because the headmaster's legs were still weak and unresponsive.

'We're well clear of range. We'll just get to the truck, then you can forget it.'

Without turning, the Russian said through the tremor of his voice, 'The last shot. They have killed another?'

'I think so.' Charlie knew the inadequacy of his answer. Brusque and with a suggestion of authority, he said, 'There's nothing we can do. Not our problem any more.'

'They have killed him because you have taken me from them.'

'Perhaps.'

'I had not thought it would be that way.'

Close to the ambulance now, a few more steps, and the moment for Charlie to conceal his impatience. But he led with his tongue, lashing and aggressive.

'Well, what do you want to bloody-well do? Do you want to go and stand by the door and shout, "Hey, there, I'm sorry I escaped. I've come back to ask you to forgive me. I didn't want the other bugger killed. It was all a big mistake, and if you shoot me can we have the other guy back, give him his life again, because I want to play the bloody hero?" Cut the crap out and get down on your knees and thank whatever God you have in uptown Kiev that an idiot like Charlie Webster was sitting on his arse on the tarmac with nothing better to do on a sunny morning than stick his neck on the block so that if anyone has to go in the box it wouldn't be you. Course you didn't know it would happen like this, no bugger did. The whole lot may go on that plane, every last one of them. You may be the only one that walks out of it, and if that happens don't be in a corner and blubbering that you wanted to share it with them.'

Charlie loosened his grip around the waist of the Russian as they reached the twin rear doors of the ambulance, and the other man turned and faced him.

'I am sorry, truly sorry. I have to thank you because of what you have done for me. But it is frightening for a man to know that he has lived and then another . . . In the war . . .'

'Get in and shut up,' Charlie said.

'In the war there were endless columns of men who went to their deaths, with no hope of rescue, nothing to help them beyond the comradeship of dying together.'

Charlie opened the doors, pushed him into the interior, so that he stumbled and tripped forward across a red-blanketed stretcher bed.

'Shut up, forget it.'

The ambulance swung through one hundred and eighty degrees, causing Charlie to grab at a wall-attached oxygen cylinder, then he leaned out to pull together the two flapping doors. Before he fastened them he saw again the bright and unsullied lines of the Ilyushin, the neatness of its airframe broken only by the opened hatch. In the half light of the ambulance interior, shaded by the smoked glass, he held out his hand.

'I'm Charlie Webster.'

'Dovrobyn, Nikita Dovrobyn, and I am grateful.' Their hands locked together, and Charlie could feel the bony, clasping pressure of the grip.

'Like I said, forget it. Can't ever be as bad again.' They spoke no more on the brief journey to the control tower.

When the ambulance stopped he unfastened the doors and helped the Russian back down into the sunlight. There were other hands now to help and uniformed arms that linked under Dovrobyn's armpits, and one that carried a rug to drape over his back. Bloody stupid, that, thought Charlie, with the temperature where it was. All getting in on the act, fussing round the star turn of the day. Cat with the cream satisfaction on the driver's face, the man who had driven out to the aircraft, who'd done nothing and who would revel his way through a line of pints in the canteen bar at lunchtime on the strength of it.

There was a quiet voice in Charlie's ear.

'What sort of condition is he in, Mr Webster?' Bit of bloody deference there, and not before time.

276

'He's fine,' Charlie said, looking at the pink-faced clean-shaven police inspector with his uniform and neatly knotted half-windsor black tie.

'Will he be able to sustain a de-brief? They're anxious . . .'

'God's sake, how do I know? He's not dead, is he? Not been shot?'

Kill it, Charlie, you're shouting and they're staring at you. Doesn't fit the proper image, not of a hero. Supposed to be calm and collected and organized, and above all modest. Not yelling because an earnest little prig asks a sensible question.

'He'll be fine, just find him some tea and a drop of brandy.'

'There's a great deal of admiration for what you did, Mr Webster.'

Charlie nodded. Would they only leave him alone, stop humiliating him? What did they think it was, a conscious decision? Didn't they know, any of these people, that there weren't risk appraisals and evaluations? You just jumped off your backside and ran. If you were lucky you were a hero, if you were unlucky they'd be scraping you up and wondering how you could be so bloody stupid.

They formed a little cavalcade up the stairs, the Russian in his ridiculous blanket at the front with the retinue around him, Charlie at the tail. As they climbed he leaned forward and tapped the inspector on the shoulder and said, 'I'm sorry, I didn't mean to shout.'

'That's all right, Mr Webster,' said the policeman. 'I know how you must feel.'

A grey Transit van brought George Davies to the control tower. It had driven slowly round the outer road in full view of the aircraft, maintaining a regular speed so that those who watched it from the cockpit and the passenger cabin would not be concerned at its progress. For a few seconds it disappeared behind the barricade of tankers, and it was during those moments that the back doors were flung open and the SAS commander had boarded. When the van emerged again there was nothing to indicate to those on the plane that it had added a passenger to its load, nothing to tell them of the army presence still hidden near the Ilyushin.

As he sat on the metal floor of the van Davies could reflect that there could be only one reason why he had been summoned for conference. The decision must have been taken: the politicians were steeling themselves for the military option.

Inside the control tower there had formed a reception line of grave-faced men with whom Nikita Dovrobyn shook hands.

The Home Secretary had emerged from his lower-floor office to greet the Russian with a public smile and a word of congratulation that was lost on the survivor because Charlie was still trapped by the throng in the doorway and unable to translate the remark. The tight grip of the Assistant Chief Constable, the unwavering gaze into his eyes, the impression of the medal ribbons, all caused Dovrobyn to flinch away, his instinctive reaction to security force authority. By contrast, Clitheroe took the proffered hand with a limpness and led the Russian to a chair that was functional and not comfortable and for which he apologized. Others called the Russian 'sir', some lightly slapped his back, and he wondered why they presumed that he had of his own volition achieved something that made him so worthy of attention. Then, in their impatience, they were all talking to him, a tower of voices that were strange and unknown, and he looked past their heads for the one called Charlie Webster and strained to see him beyond the scrubbed faces and the buttoned collars and the uniforms and the city suits. He just wanted to sleep, to escape from these people. The voice of Charlie Webster cut through his confusion, the same voice of authority that had demanded he jump when his legs were leaden and which he had obeyed.

'Leave the man alone. He doesn't understand a word you're saying. Pack it in, and give him some room to breathe.'

There was a parting of the seas around the chair and Dovrobyn found the one face, the familiar face, that he sought.

Charlie spoke in Russian, gently and without haste, as if there were suddenly time, as if the panic for speed was forgotten. 'We're going to get you some coffee, then we have to talk to you. You must understand that we have to know as much as you can tell us about the interior of the aircraft. We have to know everything that you can remember, every detail. If we are to save other people's lives then you must tell us all you can. We'll hold the questions till we have the coffee, give you time to think and to remember . . .' Charlie broke off and spoke again in English. 'We should get him some coffee. He's dead tired, scared out of his mind and totally disorientated. It's worth waiting.'

They stood in a circle round the Russian, staring, peering, stripping the man, so that he avoided them and focused on his hands that he held together lest they should see the trembling of his fingers. Once when he looked up he saw a soldier in camouflage denims with a webbing belt at his waist and a pistol holster fastened to it, who had not been present when he had first come, and he knew from the murmur of their voices and the way they softened till he turned his head that he was the subject of their talk.

Arrival of the coffee. A single cup set in a chipped white saucer with an alloy spoon and a paper sachet of sugar. Carried to him by a woman who wore black with a little white cloth fixed in her hair and a white apron that showed stains. A panic consumed him as she stretched forward with the cup and saucer – would the shaking of his hands betray him, would he spill and slop the drink? Then Charlie Webster was speaking to her, and taking it from her, holding the saucer himself and shielding him from the gaze of the crowd so that he could grasp the cup with both hands, so they would not see how much dribbled to the floor and fell across his shirt. When he had finished Webster took the cup and with his other hand fiddled in a trouser pocket for a handkerchief and neatly wiped the Russian's chin and coat.

'We need to start now, Nikita. I'll translate the questions for you. If you do not know the answers, then say so. Don't make anything up, just to please us. You must be very exact. That's important, terribly important.'

For ninety minutes Dovrobyn answered their questions. Pausing every few seconds for Charlie to speak, while he found himself all the time growing in confidence. First the narrative of the hi-jacking, then to his own action, through to his assessment of the personality of the Jews. On into the dispositions inside the aircraft. Where were the various groups of passengers? Where did Isaac stand when he was not in the main cabin, out of the range of the fish-eye that they showed him? Where did David stand at the rear? Where did the girl stand? Who had slept the night before, and for how long? Where did they sleep? What weapons had he seen? Did they have grenades? Were there explosives? How had they protected the doors of the aircraft? How was the trolley barrier fastened? What was the morale of the three? Who was the leader now?

The schoolmaster was no fool. He was not a man used to the world of strike and counter-strike, of government ministers and ranking policemen and troops, but he appreciated his purpose in the room. The killing ground was being prepared, the markers and the pegs and the tapes were being laid. He saw it in the face of the soldier, the one with the gun at his waist, who said nothing, wrote nothing, only listened. There would be more men like that, hard and cold-faced and who did not smile, whose attention was held by the task that confronted them. And he thought of his children who sat still and strapped in their upholstered seats, who had no defences, and would hold the middle territory between the troops and David and Isaac and Rebecca. Acceptable that he should die, and the man who had followed him, but the children . . .

'You cannot . . . you cannot . . . what will happen to the children? You will kill the children. On the plane these people will not hurt the children, they are correct to them. But if you go there, and you have to shoot, what will happen to my children?'

Not that any except Charlie understood what he said, just the signs of acute worry, and they moved away from him. It is not pleasant to look on a man who has broken, who can sustain nothing more, who is convulsed in weeping, who has gone beyond his own unexplored limitations.

'Nobody will hurt the children,' Charlie said.

'If you attack the plane and they resist, if Isaac and David resist, then there must be shooting . . . then the children will be hurt. They are in my charge and I am not there.'

'Nobody will hurt the children. All of them will be saved. There is a science in these things and if we know where they are then there is no risk.'

'You confirm my fear. You will attack. There is no other reason for the questions that you have asked me.'

Charlie did not reply. There was nothing to say. He had seen the children on the television screen, their meekness and their submission, and he knew the hopelessness of giving the sort of guarantee he had just delivered. A used Ford and you don't need to service it for twenty years, bullshit. A science in these matters, crap and you know it, Charlie. He knew that when the troops went in the only thing that mattered was luck, a bloody great piece of luck. One good burst of gunfire, and that's all they have to get off, and what do you have? Fiasco, catastrophe, disaster. Put the army in and what becomes the priority? Kill the killers, or save the hostages, or can you even differentiate? All depends on whether they fight. Isaac, the little bugger, he'll fight, perhaps David too if he's caged, and the girl, she might shoot if the hero boys are still standing. So how many lucky bullets do you need to hit those three and no-one else? And how many from the opposition to screw the whole damn thing?

Charlie straightened and rested his hand on the Russian's shoulder.

'I think he's had enough. You should find him a bed and keep him on ice.'

'Express our thanks to him, please, Mr Webster,' the Home Secretary said. Dejected, oppressed by the knowledge that the decision for action was his, and could be passed to neither senior nor subordinate. The circle broke and formed an aisle through which Charlie led Dovrobyn. 'Keep him warm,' he told the Inspector, 'and don't let the quacks give him a shot. We have to have him on tap.'

He walked back to the console and looked out through the glass at the Ilyushin. Same old story, nothing moving, nothing stirring, not a damn thing, just like always. But it was all going to start.

He heard the Home Secretary say to the soldier, 'Well, Major Davies, can it be done, and with reasonable chance of success?'

'A reasonable chance of success, yes, sir. Shouldn't be too difficult. We know all we're going to.'

'When would you attempt it?'

'First light is ideal. But if there's deterioration we could have a go at dusk tonight. We could get in during daylight, but the risk all round is greater.'

A moment of consideration, as if the Home Secretary were rehearsing the sentence, then he said, 'Make the preparations that you deem necessary, Major.'

'Thank you, sir. There's a DC6 over on the far side. Height to the doors is right, width of fuselage about the same, wing cover on approach matches. We'll do a bit of work with it, and you'll be contacted as soon as we're happy.'

'Thank you, Major.'

The session was concluded. Davies bustling on his way. Conversation mounting. A lightening of the atmosphere now that the crucial decision had been taken. Charlie sought out Clitheroe, tugged at his shirtsleeve and took him to the far corner, away from the crowd that now sensed blood and waited for the chase.

'It's a bit early, isn't it?' Charlie urged. 'We've hardly talked to them yet, and now we're ready to plunge in.'

'It wasn't my advice.'

'But the tactic is to wear them down. Nag away at them, starve them out. That's the way it's done. What the Americans do, the Dutch, what we've tried in the past.'

'Correct. That is the traditional way of handling these affairs.

282

As I told you the present course of action is not the one that I recommended.'

'What are you going to do about it?'

'Mr Webster, I'm not here to *do* anything. I'm here to give opinions when they are requested. My brief goes no further.'

'So what's changed, what's put the balls into them?'

'You have, Mr Webster. Your little games out on the tarmac have changed all that. Don't stop me, don't look aggressive. You asked me a question and I'll give you an answer. They were sitting in here watching Mr Dovrobyn, believing he was about to die. They didn't like it, they didn't like the helplessness and impotence – that was a word that was flying round this room a fair bit – and they saw what you did. Probably you shamed them, shamed them into showing what they now regard as courage. They had been led to understand that there was no intervention they could make, and you demonstrated that there are occasions when a physical course of action can be both justified and successful. Now they wish to follow your example. Virility, I suppose, comes into it, they wish to match your virility. Don't look pained, Mr Webster, don't regard me as an idiot. We've been through all this while you were bringing your rescued princess back from the dragon's castle, we've all had our say. Myself, the policeman, army liaison, the civil servants. Mine was a lone voice because I cannot offer exact solutions. I can only surmise what a state of mind will be, given certain deprivation factors. I understand a smattering of Russian, Mr Webster, from my college days. I gather you told Mr Dovrobyn that there was a "science on these matters", referring to the question of storming the aircraft. A "science" implies a solution if a correct procedure is followed. I cannot supply a "science", only an opinion, and that is why I am not listened to. And you must allow for the death of the second hostage: it has deeply shocked our masters. They were not prepared for it, and therefore their anger is all the greater. And they are fearful now of seeming weak.'

'It's bloody nonsense,' said Charlie quietly.

'Not so much nonsense as cowardice, Mr Webster. They are unwilling to repeat an experience. They do not have the courage. The previous two occasions when they have been confronted with this type of situation there had been no killing of hostages. Neither in Knightsbridge nor in Balcombe Street. They could afford to be patient then; there were no corpses for the world to see, to bear witness to their inability to intervene with a strong hand. You have to comprehend and perhaps you do already that the basis for the respect held by the Western democracies for the urban guerrilla is that so few persons can appear to ridicule the power of an established and elected government. By your own assessment only one of the persons on the aircraft is, as we would say, the hardliner, with the other two his followers. Yet look around and count up the effort, the ingenuity, the technology, the striking power that has been assembled to eliminate this threat. All of this concentration was sitting on its collective backside, wondering what to do. They think now that unarmed, unprepared, you showed them a course of action.'

'If they go in there shooting then there has to be risk to the children, like the headmaster said, and he's right. What do they want? Another bloody Maalot?'

'Perhaps they consider the risk to the children less substantive than the risk that they will see another man brought to the door of the aircraft, and after him another, and another after that . . .'

'But that's not your opinion. You know and I know that perhaps they will kill one more, but they're human beings in there. They're not animals, they won't be able to go on chopping like a slaughter-house foreman. They couldn't sustain it.'

'That's not what you said from the tarmac, Mr Webster. They took great note of what you told them. They remember your every word.' Clitheroe speaking now in a tired, half-amused drawl. 'As I told you, I have offered my advice and it was not accepted.'

He passed Charlie a cigarette, expensive with a gold-papered covering for the filter. Charlie took it instinctively, leaned his head for the light, and blew the smoke into the murk of the room. Without giving any particular thought to it, Charlie said, 'So how do we save them?'

'It depends on who you want to save. If it's the children I suppose they stand an equal chance, and it's a good one, whether Major Davies leads a heroic charge or whether we sit it out and people like myself give advice on a long-drawn-out stand-off. The children will be safe. Or is it the others, my friend? If the soldiers assault the plane then we can guarantee – I use your word – that they are unlikely to take time off for the niceties of capturing able-bodied prisoners. Shoot first, questions later is the doctrine of this type of operation. Is that what concerns you? Perhaps it should concern all of us, three young people who through a chain of circumstance stand condemned to die if the army take the plane. Whether they are evil people, or misguided, or those that in another context we would regard as courageous, they will not survive the visit of Major Davies. And I wouldn't criticize that: his men have wives and children, they too want to survive, and they deserve to. If you wish these three to live then you must persuade them to surrender, and unconditionally because then they will go before the courts, perhaps here, probably in the Soviet Union, and you must believe the words of the Ambassador that were carried on the radio, that they will be unlikely to face the death penalty if indeed they are returned. There can be no happy outcome, yet there was no reason to expect anything else from the moment that the aircraft landed. You've been very patient with me, Mr Webster. I'm not used to such attention.'

Charlie smiled, thanked him and moved without more comment back to the console.

Waste of time trying the radio unless someone was sitting in the cockpit with the earphones on and waiting. Seemed to know that his place was far from here, far from the green-carpeted floor, and the hum of the air-conditioner and the polite laughter, and the deference to seniority. Knew he should be on the tarmac again, sitting on his backside in the sunshine, flicking the flies from his nose and wanting a drink, waiting for something to happen. The pictures were still in front of him, where he'd pinned them in the early morning when the issues had been sharper and the grey fog hadn't blurred the outlines of his faith. Three young faces, ordinary to the point of boredom, and now trapped and vicious and being broken on an anvil by a force they could not combat, only strike against, bloodily and irrelevantly.

Too long on the outside, Charlie, too long living and winning without the back-up of name and rank and number, without legality and authority. As much a terrorist as these little bastards. Had a base camp, sure enough, to come to with the intelligence gained by deceit and stealth, but otherwise a man of his own whims, without a general to direct him and draw lines on his map. Easy for some to hate these three, right Charlie? Easy to label and catalogue them. Easier still if you had a chauffeur and a pennant and a chest of medal ribbons and a swagger stick. But harder if you knew the isolation, and the loneliness and the fear that makes the stomach coil, as you did, Charlie. Disowned if you're caught, that's what they said when he went to Dublin; don't expect the FO to bale you out if the Guarda Síochána lifts you – and when you're caught don't cough, that way you'll keep the pension and we'll see your wife doesn't have to go out to work and the kids get new shoes when they need them. All for a job, all for a way to pay the mortgage. Less motivation than those three. 'Motivation', the fashionable word that meant damn-all, meant you were thick and hadn't thought it out, or too young to know what went on. 'Motivation', the great confidence trick, the public relations target, what they told all the men who formed the starched khaki ranks and lined up to have Herself pin a cross of dulled metal on their chests and went back to barracks to shiver in a corner and wonder how they'd been so bloody stupid.

Years since Charlie had been in uniform, despised it, sneered at the sameness and the identity and the mob instinct of men who needed polished shoes and short haircuts. What did these

people know of the three on the plane? How could they understand them? Called them terrorists, murderers, fanatics ... all
the usual claptrap. But they don't care, not even Clitheroe.
Stuff it, Charlie, you're a raving old bore. You're not paid to
think, to be the referee. Go back to counting the fag ends. Do
something useful.

Charlie stood up from his chair and looked around him.

He attracted no attention, his moment of glory was past. The
Assistant Chief Constable was catnapping, Clitheroe reading,
Home Secretary gone below. Nothing changed on the screen –
David out of sight, Isaac and Rebecca at the forward entrance to
the passenger cabin. Could read the defiance still fashioned on
Isaac's face.

He walked out through the door and began to descend the
stairs, slowly, carefully, aware of the fatigue he felt. He reckoned
he would have about two hours at the plane before the military
had satisfied themselves on the DC6. He realized his hand was
out against the wall, steadying himself as he went down.

Didn't recognize him at first, the man he saw through the
open door of the second landing. Seemed shed of his earlier
confidence and poise that had been on display in the control
tower. Charlie stopped at the entrance, hesitating.

'It's the Israeli isn't it? ... Benitz, Colonel Benitz? The one
who thought our friends were about to surrender.'

'That was me. I remember you too. You were very kind ...'

'Did they dump you in here?' Charlie glanced round the
room. 'Looks like you've a plague or something. Not exactly in
the centre of things, is it?'

'It is not the intention of people here that I should be in the
centre ...'

'What were you sent for?' Charlie said, casting off the small
talk.

'I was sent to help you persuade these people to surrender.'

'Why you?'

'It was thought that an army man might appeal to them.'

'And they just left you sitting here, kicking your heels, our crowd I mean? They haven't talked to you since you were up in the tower first thing? Incredible.'

'I sit here and I wait to be asked.'

'Well, you won't be sitting here much longer. They've just dropped a hostage . . .' He heard the Hebrew obscenity, saw Benitz clench his fist. 'Didn't they tell you? Didn't anyone even tell you that? They dropped one this morning, and there'll be another this afternoon, and then they plan a shooting gallery, with one each hour. We're gearing the heavies up, to go and thump them.'

'You should have gone this morning when the one you call Isaac was asleep.'

'Could have had them all then. Looking back on it, that is. With hindsight we could have wrapped it all up. And saved the hostage, and whoever else gets in the way when the military attack.' Charlie had exhausted his politeness, wanted to be on his way. As an afterthought, he added: 'You think you could still talk them down?'

Benitz forward in his seat, tense and trying to hide his elation. Casual. 'I think it would be possible. If I were at the plane and could talk to them.'

'And what would you be telling them?'

'Surrender, unconditional surrender.'

'Before the next deadline, before the military go in.'

'Surrender, unconditional surrender.'

'Could save a deal of mopping up.'

'Could save lives, Charlie.'

Charlie looked behind him, satisfied himself that the staircase was unused, thumb in his mouth, the nail chewed between his teeth. 'I am going to the plane now. Perhaps . . . if you wanted, you could come with me . . . The message from your government is that there should be immediate and unconditional surrender?'

'Yes, that is the message,' said Benitz looking hard into Charlie's eyes.

'But if they surrender, then perhaps they go back to Russia.'

'If they surrender there will be no more killing. No more of the passengers will be hurt, and they themselves will live. I understand that what happens to them later is not yet decided.'

No opportunity for Benitz to use the telephone, to give explanations to London, to ask for fresh guidance. He prided himself that he had recovered well on the hammer-blow disappointment of the news that a hostage was already dead, that his last instructions were now invalid, inappropriate. Charlie had taken his arm and was hurrying him down the steps, and seemed to stagger and falter, the mark of a man, Benitz recognized, close to exhaustion.

Too late now, too far gone the opportunity for the young people to barter their freedom with the lives of the passengers. Possible before the captain had died, possible before they had taken their hostage. But the moment now lost. Benitz searched in his mind, among the briefings and the messages he had received in Tel Aviv and from London, as to what solution he might fashion that would most please those that he served.

15

David stayed in the dull-lit recess at the back of the aircraft, his body pressed hard against the fastened drinks trolley. Waiting for nothing, passing the minutes away. He had not moved since the Italian had been taken from his seat to the doorway. After the noise of the shot that had sent a shudder through him, involuntary and unsought, barely a muscle or a nerve had functioned. Just stood there, hearing the rhythmic sounds of his wrist watch, willing the progress of its hands. The gun was held loosely across his waist, apparently ready to be fired at a moment of crisis, quickly and expertly, and giving the impression of a man who had found confidence and was his master. David alone realized the deception.

The exact moment when he knew that all was over, that the struggle was hopeless, was not clear even to him. Perhaps it had been on the pavement in Kiev as Moses had stumbled and shuffled through his pockets in search of the balaclava. Perhaps it had been in the woodman's hut when Isaac had first raised the plan for the break-out and in doing so had usurped his own place as innovator and initiator. Perhaps it had been with the words, flat and unemotional, of ground control over Hanover when they had been ordered to fly on. Perhaps it had been as the dawn had risen lighting the cabin and he had witnessed the fear and hatred that alternated on the faces of those who were guarded by the guns. Perhaps the moment had come, the journey been completed, when he had seen the surprise and terror and comprehension merge on the face of the harmless and inoffensive little Italian. Which moment he did not know, but at one of them had come the knowledge that the game was completed, and that he was ready for what Isaac called 'surrender and capitulation'.

They were big and bold words and worthy of a greater occasion. Armies surrendered, governments capitulated. They signified momentous times, nothing as scabrous or as dirty as the collapse in morale of three young Jews far from home. Babi Yar . . . that had been a great wrong, thousands machine-gunned because they were Jewish, for no other reason. A hundred times a thousand people had died in the ravine of Babi Yar. Jews, and not remembered, and the cheap belated monument made no mention of them. And those who came with flowers on the anniversary, on the day in late September, they were stoned and scourged and imprisoned – or 'detained', as the authorities called it. Babi Yar had been the flint that forged the four of them together, a desire to avenge, to tilt the balance of the wrong . . . and now the water had come in its torrent and destroyed the flickering of that small flame.

He had liked Moses, known him better than Isaac, because he was younger and less able and more dependent, and because he laughed more. Remembered him now, untidy, confused, willing to try, willing to become a casualty, a statistic. And Moses was already taken, and had bought them time – at what cost David could not know. And for what?

The Italian should not have died for Babi Yar, nor even the schoolmaster who had jumped. It was not their quarrel. They did not wear the uniform of the authorities, did not carry the badge of office presented by the bullies who would not permit prayers to be said by the ditch where the Jews had fallen, that had become a tip for rubbish. Nor was it they who sent the Jews to the camps, arrested those who sought passage to Israel. They had no guilt, yet one had died and it had been intended another should have fallen in his place.

If that was the cost of avenging Babi Yar and all that it had accumulated in shame, then the price was too high, that was the feeling of David as he stood far from the others at the rear of the cabin aisle. How to surrender? How to conclude his part without destroying what Isaac sought, without betraying his friends? He had thought long and hard behind the unmoving eyes, struggling with his tiredness till the solution came reluctantly upon him. A brutal, desperate solution that brought a chill over his body. And then the decision was made and there followed a calm and a clarity of thought that had been denied him for many hours.

Often the American had looked at him, peering and twisting round in his seat, inviting conversation, still crowned with the knotted handkerchief that he wore across his scalp. While David had wrestled with his problem the man had kept his silence, bided his time. Now Edward R. Jones Jr recognized the lightness in the face, appreciated that he could speak.

'How long do you go on like this? You shoot one, you lose one, but the British aren't talking, they aren't moving, not an inch.' The same nagging, grating voice, primed with aggression. David understood not a word, knew only that behind the deference to the gun and his youth the older man sneered at him. He shrugged his shoulders, and looked on down the aisle.

'I said, how much longer do we have to sit on our backsides here, waiting for you to call it quits?' David turned with the tolerance of one who is irritated by a wasp but cannot gather the energy to swat it, a half smile on his mouth.

'Don't you speak English? Don't you understand me? Was it only the girl that went to school?'

David no longer cared to listen, shut himself apart again, sensing the subsidence of the American in the face of his inability to communicate. Heard him mutter to his wife with her loud clothes and rinsed hair and hands that sought to silence her man, prevent provocation. What did that fool know about Babi Yar, or the labour camps? What did he know of militia headquarters, of the interrogations, of the humiliations?

His eyes rolled over the heads of the passengers. Through the hours he had come to recognize some, to know which were eager for his approval and would cringe from him, which tried to hide their pent-up hatred. He had begun to acknowledge them as individuals, had carved faces and personalities from the initial mass that they had taken on the journey. The children were still quiet, he could not say how or why. The old man with the farm boots bristled with independence as best he could from the confines of his seatbelt. The pilot, Tashova, with her neat and close-cut hair, who held herself above them, superior to their struggle. The navigator, cautiously interested in what happened close to him, but never speaking. The Italians who had screamed, some of whom still cried and held each other's arms. The woman half-way forward, in the widow's clothes, with the baby on her knee and a patch of smell around her and the reddened weather-stained face of the country and who asked each time he passed for milk for the child. The man beside her, who seemed a stranger, and whispered that she should not speak lest she draw attention to herself. Those who were frightened, those who were bold, those who were indifferent, those who rested on their nerves and those whose eyes darted to accumulate each nuance of mood from their captors. He had begun to know them all. But the familiarity had won him no friendship. No warmth, no love, no affection, only the loathing of those who watched him now.

Abruptly, David started to move the length of the aisle. His hands had tightened on the gun barrel, fingers entwined around the trigger guard. In front of him, their faces masked in shadow, were Isaac and Rebecca. Without a victory, he thought, not even there where it had lain waiting. Should have won her by conquest, should have taken her, hours, weeks, months, ago. Isaac had struck her, out there in the full gaze of the passengers, and now she fawned on him and played to him, and was close so that their bodies touched and their voices would be soft with the intimacy of equal conversation. Perhaps that was the defeat that hurt him above all. One could be proud and surrender to an army, capitulate to a government, but when defeat came from the hands of your friend, when the prize at stake was not great but the way between the thighs of a girl, then there was the capacity for wounding. He had hit her and she had come back to him; the bitch that snivels at the ankle when it has been

293

whipped. And Isaac no better, on no higher a pedestal. He had been betrayed by her, yet now he nestled his shoulder close and protectively by hers. But irrelevant now, decision taken. Just a child she had seemed to him, a follower, who was not worth the attention of affection or love, and now that she was taken by his friend regret dominated him, and he fought to hold back the tears that welled in his eyes.

As he passed the woman with the baby arrested his arm.

'Sir, there can be milk for the baby. That cannot hurt you.'

He saw the pleading, and the screwed, torn face of the infant, and the nervousness of the man who counselled quiet.

'I don't know,' he said hollowly.

'But you are the leader,' she persisted. 'If you tell the others to allow it then they will not prevent it. Milk can be sent to the plane.'

'It is not easy . . .'

'It is just for a child. Many hours it has not fed. A child can do you no harm.'

Angrily David wrenched himself clear from the clinging hand and continued down the aisle.

If he had taken the girl then it would not have been as it was now. Could have been in the hut, on the dry and dusty planking, or on the sacking of the window cover if they had first shaken the spiders and cobwebs loose, or in the forest among the leaves and watched by the birds. He looked at her closely, eating into her clothes, his thoughts drifting to the whiteness of her skin, the softness that would be her breasts, the firmness of the hips on which he would have spent himself. Why had it not happened? Why had there never been the moment? And when he had gone would either understand that it was because he loved them, both of them as his sister and brother?

Isaac and Rebecca had ceased to talk and watched curiously as he came awkwardly towards them, sensing in their separate ways that the control he so obviously sought to maintain was a wasted, puny thing.

* * *

There were many contrasts between the two men who walked together across the car park that had been designated for operational traffic only.

Both were trained and expert Counter Insurgency Operators – CIOs in the restricted training manuals – but the methods they had learned to use and that suited their differing temperaments were hugely varied. Charlie Webster, 49, married, two kids, hard-put to meet the bills, keep the garden trim, done it all and seen it all, and opted out, tried to close the file. Arie Benitz, 32, single, devoid of ties and personal relations, a room at the barracks, the seven-days-a-week student, top of the tree and looking for a higher summit. Charlie who had survived to grow old and paunchy through cunning and stealth and the ability to merge into backgrounds. Benitz, the direct, hedonist fighter, faster and dirtier than those they pitted him against. Charlie, who saw all points of argument from whatever side of the spectrum. Benitz under no such disadvantage, his world neatly divided into compartments of right and wrong. Charlie, with the flesh to spare under his chin and the haunted flickering eyes of a man who has been hunted and harried without the strength of military unit comradeship to turn to. Benitz muscled, vibrant, his strength undisguised by the hanging, ill-fitting clothes the Royal Air Force had dressed him in, having to shorten his stride to keep pace with the other.

Charlie had never been part of a spearhead attack team. Benitz had never taken the rôle of the deep-sleeper infiltration agent. Out of the very diversity the men found a respect for each other.

Acting without an order, was Charlie, but then there were many precedents in his career for that, and he didn't give a damn for the inquests his initiative might rain on him. He had made his decision that Benitz alone could help him avoid the mayhem that he believed was the only possible result for a storm assault by the SAS on the Ilyushin. In his conceit – and Charlie was not short of that as befitted a man who had spent an operational life outside the barrack's walls – he had told himself that he alone of the crisis committee, Charlie Webster, understood the capabilities and state of mind of the three young people, and the heart of it was his conviction that Isaac, the little bastard, would stand and shoot it out, and be prepared to die. Across the car park he saw it all – the crossfire, the smoke, the screaming, the children rising from their seats to escape the blasting of the automatics, the bodies cut and ripped by the tempered steel of the shells, and when it was over, just the blood and the moaning, the shock and the pain. Children like his, like the ones in his road, like the ones at the bus stop in the morning, the ones who chased a football across the street. And all because they'd lost their cool up in the control tower clouds, just like Clitheroe said. The big men from London who'd seen a single stiff, and couldn't face the same humiliation again, and would hide behind their bloody outrage, and find the easy exit.

So he walked with Arie Benitz to the Transit van where the driver idled with his morning paper, and toyed with the cigarette that he had tucked into the palm of his hand.

Charlie said, 'Same drill as before. Close to the aircraft are some petrol tankers, where the Special Air Service detachment are holed up. I want to talk to them first, hear their feel of it, and then we'll head out to the plane. When the van is behind the tankers it stops and we jump for it, flick the doors and off she goes. It's what they're doing to ferry the military back and forward.' Benitz listened, well satisfied.

The Israeli climbed inside, Charlie following, both squatting on the van's floor, the closing of the door the cue for the driver.

'You have clearance to take me?' Benitz asked.

'We can do without any more paperwork on this caper.'

'It would not be like this at home.'

Charlie said quietly so that his words were almost lost in the echoed motion of the engine, 'Sometimes you have to kill people like this, but not for the sake of it, and not when you risk the innocent.'

'It is a luxury that is seldom given us, to be able to decide. The tide is not often with us. It is rare for me to have the order that I have been given, that I should help your efforts towards a surrender.'

Won't know what's hit them, thought Charlie. Shining bloody angel climbs the ladder, and then they find he's scaled and tailed and horned, and bringing the news that destroys them, kicking them in the crutch and with interest, then booting them again, just when they're getting used to it. Not a job you'd want, Charlie, not if they were your own people, not telling them it was all over, all down the drain, that they should have stayed home.

'We're just about there,' the driver shouted back. 'Ease the door and go the moment I stop. Don't forget to close it again, and don't stop, don't hang about.'

He crawled forward, brushing against the Israeli's body, scrabbling for the door handle, moved it and waited. The stop was sudden, lurching them together, and Charlie had the door open and slid clumsily, showing his stiffness, to the ground. Benitz out straight after him and both blinking in the sunlight. Charlie fastened the door, banged lightly on it and watched the van pull away.

'Get yourself behind the wheels,' a command, not to be questioned, and the two settled themselves against the warmed rubber of the tyres that soaked up the heat. From his left side Charlie was aware of the blur of camouflage uniform that sprinted to him. A day's growth on the face, dark and mixed with the sweeps of lotion used to banish the whiteness of skin. 'Captain Howard. They didn't tell me anyone was coming out, there's been nothing about you on the radio.' No suspicion, only confusion that protocol had not been observed.

'It's because of him,' Charlie said quickly, 'they didn't want it all over the net. This is Colonel Arie Benitz, Israeli Defence Force, flown in by the RAF. His line at home is this situation. His presence is sensitive.'

Howard acknowledged the explanation. None of his business anyway.

'There's not much here at the moment. The Major and ten others are working on the DC6 over on the far side. Leaves seven of us here, with a basic fire cover rôle. The body's still out there by the wheels, and we gather there's no contact about shifting it. The camera isn't picking up much, but the tall boy has just come down towards the front, so they're all together now where the fish-eye picks them up.'

No more explanation required, and they stood together, the soldier and Israeli waiting for Charlie's lead. But he was quiet, saying nothing, trying to work at the problem that itched somewhere far back in his mind. That did not fit the pattern, that was out of place and therefore annoying and that he should clear up. That Benitz should want them to surrender, and nothing specific and categoric on their future. Wouldn't want them shipped out, couldn't, but there must be more to it, the Russian must have been shooting his mouth, must have been a deal somewhere down the line, a deal that they hadn't been told of in the control tower. Had to be something that was covert, that was being kept from them. But all a bit of a bloody mystery. Nothing new in that. When did anyone ever give you the grand picture? Just packed you off and told you to get on with it. But he'd have to clear it up, sometime, get it all sorted out. People should know where they stood . . .

From the cement hut the top half of a civilian emerged, sweeping his head round, searching for the army officer.

Excitement in his voice, urgency. 'Captain, come and look here. On the fish-eye, they're hanging on to each other like it's goodbye – hugging, kissing, shaking hands, the whole works.'

Everything else erased from Charlie's thoughts. Jesus help us, not a bloody breakout, not a split for it, not a fucking slaughter inside? Captain mirroring him, barking names, and as the soldiers ducked from the hut to their appointed firing positions the young officer was cocking his Ingram sub-machine gun with a single, noise-laden movement.

Rebecca struggling not to cry, Isaac distantly silent and refusing to argue, and David all the time stumbling through his explanation. All holding and clinging to each other as a last link was forged with the past they had known.

'It is treachery, it is a cowardice to you both, but I cannot last any more. I cannot remain, not inside here, closed in here, waiting, for what will happen. Too long it has been for me, and it has broken me . . . not any longer, not trapped in here, looking and waiting through hours and days more, perhaps. There has to be a gesture for me, the only gesture that I am capable of, but I cannot last more. I had never thought it would take so long, that time would creep so slowly, that there would be nothing but existing here and waiting. And perhaps then we die, or we feel the manacles on us. I cannot wait for that. We are doomed, Isaac, damned and finished, and I am afraid. Afraid because I do not know what will happen. I cannot wait any more to be answered.'

He felt the fingers of the girl tight at the back of his neck, holding his shirt collar, and below at his arms the pressure of Isaac, both pinioning him against the lavatory door as if wanting to strengthen him in his purpose. Neither tried to turn him, so that there was no retreat, no backing from his course. 'Isaac, it was brave and courageous, and it might have been successful. But that time is gone, and I can no longer help you. I want to leave you in my own fashion and I do not want to look back. I am only a weakness to you now. Help me, Isaac. Walk away, take Rebecca and go far so that I will not look at you.'

His arm around the waist of Rebecca, Isaac pulled the two of them clear. He saw the deep, nut-brown eyes, felt the hand join with his own, gripped it. 'We showed the bastards, David. We showed them what we could do. Only four, and now they know of us. Moshe and you and me and Rebecca. They will remember us. We are not beaten yet, I promise you, David. We are not beaten yet . . .'

'They will come with the guns tonight . . . they are waiting for the darkness . . . only the darkness, when you are sleeping . . .'

'On your way, David.'

David smiled, and there was the freshness of his youth and the charm of his mouth and the flourish of victory that curled at his nostrils. He reached in his pocket and drew from it the straight stick magazine, and tossed it easily towards Isaac who caught it with his free hand.

'I will only need one. I have no need for another.'

'We will talk to you in Israel . . .'

David was gone from their sight, to the aircraft door, the Kingfisher flown from them. They heard the sound of his body thudding on to the concrete below.

'One out, sir. On the ground and armed.'

A dismembered, disconnected voice to Charlie who crouched by the wheel close to the booted feet of the marksman. Soldiers crawling and scuffing on the ground to gain better vision, a superior aiming point, and the captain wreathed in puzzlement.

'Just one, no hostages?'

'Just the one. Armed. An SMG.'

A pause in time, Charlie and Benitz and the military frozen still.

'Doesn't look like a white flag job. Gun's up now.'

'We'd prefer him alive if we can have him that way. Don't drop him yet.'

'At this range I can take his kneecaps out. Certainty.'

'Hold it, hold it.' In Charlie's ear the captain whispered, 'What in Christ's name do you think he's at?'

'I don't know,' Charlie answered. 'I just don't know.'

Never looking away, speaking from the side of his mouth, and with the quiet of a man who is in church, Arie Benitz said: 'It's very clear, Charlie. He has made his farewells, and now he wants to die. Better they should do it quickly, and kindly.'

Charlie turned to look at the Israeli. Too late. The face averted, the eyes hidden.

Bruised, shaken, grazed at the shins where the cheap cloth of his trousers had been ripped by the fall, David rose first to one knee, then more slowly edged his way upright on to his feet. Had to fight for breath, recapture the air blown from his lungs and combat the ferocity of the sun bursting into his face after the diluted greyness of the Ilyushin interior. A step forward, and another, testing the unfamiliarity of his surroundings, but feeling the warmth on his face, the wind at his back, the exultation at the freedom. Round to his right an armoured car, and the big gun following him, locking on to his body with the sights, repetition to the left with the crew scrabbling on its surface, and to the front the immobile, precious tankers. The tankers that held their salvation, carried the fuel they needed if they were to see the coast and the orange groves and the mountains of Israel; bright, gaudy, abrasive in their paintwork. And a triumph in his eyes when he captured the half-glimpse of the short stubbed barrel of the rifle deep in the darkness beside the forward wheel of the central tanker. That was where they were, hidden, covert, and he had discovered them.

Remember the bird that Timofey had spoken of. Remember the Kingfisher bird, fast and darting, sure in attack, brilliant in retreat, with the colours of a prince and a victor. Remember the dream of the Kingfisher, to be carried to a faraway place safe on the technicolor wings of speed and colour. But the nets had come and the beaters and the men with guns and there were no longer the river banks and bushes of concealment. They have clipped you, my Kingfisher bird, lured you from your sanctuary, broken, violated, trampled you.

The dream would not last. The sleep would soon be lost. Only the clarity of the machine guns and the poking, prying rifle barrel would remain.

Five shots in the first burst, finger snatching at the trigger bar, feeling the throbbing pumping of the recoil against his shoulder, watching the creeping and ineffective gatherings of dust that told him he was short, that he would not reach the man behind the wheel.

Silence.

'Come out you pigs. Come out and fight. Come out and shoot. I'm here for you to kill . . .'

Fire again, whispered the instruction to himself. Dropped down to one knee. Take the aim steadily, don't hurry, there is time now, time to control the shaking of the wrist, time to hold the flight of the barrel till it steadies. Why don't they shoot? Why don't they end it? Don't they know, can they not understand? They must shoot soon, the miserable, cancered pigs, they must shoot soon. How long do they think the gun can be held, how long before it drops, before the hands rise in surrender of their own jurisdiction?

Aim again and fire so that they must shoot back.

'You cannot make me grovel before you, not at the last, not now. You cannot want that, to make me surrender, crawl in capitulation to you.'

Shoot, shoot, hurt the pigs, wound them, anger them. Finger sealed on the trigger, molten to it, the hammering against the muscle of his shoulder. The dirt trail inching forward, creeping to the tyre, hunting the pig in his sty, searching for him, sniffing for him, the long waving line of ricochets and flying bullets closing on his target.

'Find him! Find him!' David screamed.

One shot fired in retaliation. For the marksman it was an easy shot, 70 yards and a static target, better odds than a fairground range and all the time in the world to line the crossed wires of the telescopic sight on the upper chest. Time to reflect too before the captain tapped his shoulder, time to look at the face and its contorted and twisted features, time to see the heaving of the chest. Seemed to be talking to himself, the little bugger, seemed to be saying something, all the time he was firing. Too easy really, not even worth thinking about, never get a pigeon that simple, not even a bloody rook.

David was picked off the ground, hurled a dozen feet backwards and came to rest spread-eagled, arms and legs outstretched, the gaping entry wound a tribute to the marsksman's skill. There were no convulsions, no tremors, no useless lingering of life.

On his hands and knees, low under the chassis of the tanker Charlie Webster saw him fall, seemed to feel himself the power and hitting thrust of the one answering blow, closed his eyes,

302

screwed them shut, muttered a soundless obscenity. He felt the Israeli's arm swathed across his back, and the knot of the fist clamped in the shirt above his shoulder. Heard the man sigh, a low whisper of pain. So, even he feels it, thought Charlie, even he who is hardened and has killed many. Head of the bloody Storm squad, even him.

'But Isaac won't sell himself so cheap,' said Charlie.

They had walked three miles back from the police station.

More than two hours since they had been called from the cells, expecting only another session of interrogation, but instead they had been led up the stairs and then out into the hallway of the building. Their papers had been returned to them and the man in uniform had swung on his heel leaving the couple to fend for themselves with the weight of the heavy swing doors and find their own way back to their home.

Hardly a word had passed between David's parents as they had trudged the length of the streets and along the pitted pavements. Nothing to say, nothing to communicate. Old and wise enough to know the virtue of quiet. There had been hours of questioning, first the mother on her own, then later when the father had been brought from work they had stood side by side. A night spent in the cells, and then more questions through the morning stolidly enduring the repetitions of the officer behind the desk. Always the same point, no deviation from the perpetual question. Who were his friends? Who did he go out with? Again and again. Never a need for them to resort to threats. They were elderly, defenceless, incapable of resistance, and they had answered. Moshe . . . Isaac . . . Rebecca . . . there were no others. They had been shown the police photographs of the dead policeman, they had been told of the seizing of the airliner, of the killing of the pilot, that the aircraft had landed in Britain which was a country too far away and inaccessible for them to conjure the necessary images. The officer said their son would die there in a foreign country or if he surrendered would be brought back to face trial and execution in his own city; he seemed not to mind either course.

Then they had been permitted to go.

There had been a cluster of neighbours outside the house – some Jewish, some not, but all had drifted away as the couple approached their home. Word of plague spreads fast and they were contaminated, this pair, dangerous to touch. They did not speak to those who backed away at their approach; there was no reason to.

David's father opened the front door and put his arm around the shoulders of his wife. It had been a proud household, exemplary in the neatness of the three ground-floor rooms in which they lived. It would take them many hours to clear the debris from the floor, to shift the confusion of the search from the threadbare carpet. They had been thorough in their work, every drawer emptied, every cupboard spilled out, every chest upturned, every ornament split open.

Thrown in the firegrate, the glass smashed, was the large portrait photograph of their son, taken many years back on the day of his Bar Mitzvah – young, radiant, close-cut washed-down hair, promise and hope. David's mother drew it from the resting place on the newspaper that in summer covered the coal and chopped wood. It should not be there when the girls returned.

16

Alone among the passengers who could see from the star-board side-windows Anna Tashova had stood her ground, not flinching during the shooting, staying close to the glass of the window. She had seen everything, heard and relished it all. Her hands had come up from her lap as if she was about to clap them together as David had jerked, then tumbled backwards, but she had desisted just as she had stifled the cheer of exultation within her. She felt no pity, no horror, no sadness at the snuffing out of a life, instead gloried that her captain was at last remembered and avenged. She had noticed long ago the way some of the passengers craved the friendship of their captors, mimicked the collaborators of the old wartime days, and this brought no surprise to her. Despicable, but to be anticipated; of course there would be those without the guts to fight who would wheedle and smile for favours, and hope to win advantage and they would be remembered when the affair was over, named, denounced.

It was to be expected that some would choose to fraternize. At the seminar on hi-jack theory to which she had gone the last summer in Moscow she had heard the lecturer speak of the common practice of passengers in seeking to identify with the men who held the guns. There had been a titter of laughter round the hall but the man on the dais had stamped on that, told them this was not just to be expected: it could be guaranteed. She had talked of this among the cockpit crew with whom she had shared her next flight, and all had agreed that faced with the seizure of an aircraft by force they would never come to terms with terrorists, only play them along for the greatest benefit of their passengers. They were brave words, spoken in safety. Later she had

305

wondered what type of person might confront her; educated or illiterate, young or old, nervous or controlled. But she had found no answer, had not prepared herself for the two young men who had crashed their way through her cockpit door.

For hours, interminably, she had sat upright, staring to the front, trying to shut out the events enacted round her. She had watched the headmaster taken to his death, had not seen and did not know the manner of his escape, watched again as the Italian was pulled to his execution. Now her head moved, bouncing from window to window, swinging round so that she could see behind her, alive and vital because she had seen the man fall and watched the progress of the ribbon of blood that stretched a yard or so from him, highlighted on the pale concrete.

So they did not always win, these people. But the one who called himself Isaac, that was the one she wanted to see demolished. She could wait for that, if it took another day, another week. To hear him scream and plead and collapse with pain. She found her thighs squeezed together, shoulders hunched, her arms rigid, all for the hatred of the young one with his curly hair and his confidence, who stood now at the rear of the aircraft where once his friend had been. She was hungry, thirsty too, longing for a cigarette, yearning to join the lavatory queues; but she would not bend, would not ask. Not of these people.

They had not spoken since David had gone.

Isaac at the back, separated by the length of the cabin from Rebecca, abandoning her, kept his own dark counsel. Neither of them had watched David die, not willing to weaken their own fibre, through seeing the performance of a comrade dedicated to taking his own life because his will had crumbled. But they had been unable to shut out the noise of the gunfire, the little staccato bursts of the handgun, the one report of the heavier, killing rifle.

Where to run now, Isaac, where to hide now that they know that one at least among you was ordinary, human, flesh and blood? Where to go? David had died, uselessly, believing in the value of a gesture. For you too, Isaac? Follow the leader? Follow the Party? No. We fight them, and we hit them.

Oblivious to the passengers he strode down the aisle, gesturing to Rebecca not to come forward to meet him, to hold her position, not to move from her place at the open doorway. Not once did he look behind, never believing that any would dare to rise up against him.

'I give them one more hour. Then there will be another, another for them to watch. One o'clock for the next, and one every hour after that. We will bring them in a line so that all can see them, all who stand out there, they will see them and they can watch with their clocks for the precision with which the next will fall.'

'Why, Isaac? What is there to achieve? After David? What is left for us?'

'Because David was a coward . . .'

'How can you say that? It was he who walked out to face them.'

'Because that was the fool's escape, the quickest path. He was a coward and he was beaten, and he would not stand at our shoulder. We have to show them. One every hour – that will show that we are not defeated.'

'Then they will attack us, they will storm the aircraft.' A breathiness in her words, and she clung to his arm, the little girl again, small and feminine and clinging, who has found her man and will follow. 'They will *kill* us, Isaac.'

As he laughed she saw what she took to be a madness – the fanatical desire for self-immolation, the wish for martyrdom – and she felt the great force that drew her towards him, as if vertigo were dragging her to a cliff face. She had no strength to struggle against it, no willingness to do so.

'If we cannot go to Israel there is nothing left but to die here,' she said.

Isaac broke off from her and went carefully towards the open door. A sharp and darting glance around the corner and to the outside. Time to see Charlie Webster there to the front of the tankers, arms folded, as if he would wait a lifetime, would stay as long as required. Another man behind him, who wore a jacket and who was younger, healthier, carrying the distinctive features of his own people. A bare second Isaac had been visible, and Charlie Webster had reacted to the movement.

'We have to talk to you, Isaac.' The flattened voice, drained of emotion, devoid of tone, patient and carrying across the no-man's land of the tarmac. 'We have to talk again, Isaac.'

Hidden from them and close to the aircraft walls Isaac whispered over his shoulder. 'Cover behind me. And really this time, without mistake.' He stayed watching till he saw her rise, walk to the centre of the aisle, and take up her position, standing where she could see all the passengers. He would miss David. Frightened, abject, pathetic David would at least have stood and presented a reliable front, but the girl . . .

'There is nothing to say,' he shouted. I must keep back from the door, he told himself, no target, give the bastards nothing. 'I told you we wanted the fuel for the plane by ten o'clock or we would punish you for it. The man is there for you to see. At one o'clock there will be another if we have not had the fuel, at two there will be another, at three there will be another. Every hour from one o'clock. What time will you have the darkness you want, Mr Webster? Eight hours after we start? Nine, perhaps? Before it is dark and your troops can come for us, how many will you be able to count down there beside the present one? There is no reason for you to stand there; you gain nothing from it. We will not allow you to repeat what you did earlier.'

The answer was faint and hard for him to hear. 'Isaac, there is much to talk about. It has been a long flight for you, and your cause has been heard. But there is nothing further to be gained for you.'

'There is fuel for the aircraft, that has yet to be gained. If you do not bring it then you must stand there and you must watch, and discover whether you like what you see. Understand this, Mr Webster: we have nothing against you, we want little of you, we want only the petrol. It is a small thing for you, it will not cost you much, not set against the lives you play with.'

Isaac crawled away from the door, and then stood up, brushed the grime from his trousers, and seemed to Rebecca to be laughing.

'If they shout again, you talk to them, let them hear you, let them see you. Perhaps David went too early.' He walked past her, not with haste, but casually, cosseting his gun. Before he reached the drinks trolley where he would again take up his stance he was whistling: a song from the Ukraine, of his people, a cheerful tune.

Behind Charlie's back Arie said, 'You told me he was the hard one, this Isaac. You knew your man.'

'All over it's the same, in every group you find one . . .'

'Can we talk to him, Charlie, can you get him back?'

Never looking behind, watching all the time the windows and the door, Charlie said, 'The little bastard thinks he can win. He doesn't believe in us, doesn't believe we have the will to beat him. That's where he has to be convinced . . .'

'You must tell him I am here, Charlie. This is what I was sent for. It was for this moment.'

'You feel something for the kid, right?' A slow smile at Charlie's mouth.

'As you do, Charlie.'

'And what do you want of him now?'

'That he should not be shamed.'

'And nothing else?'

'If he does as I ask him then he will not be disgraced, and no more harm will come to the passengers. Your masters will be happy with you, Charlie, and will talk of a great victory. For us there can be no victory, only defeat, and if I cannot talk to Isaac then there will be defeat for us, but you will share in it.'

'That's a long old speech, Benitz. Let's cut the crap and get on with it.'

Charlie walked forward three or four paces, isolating himself from the Israeli. Then he raised his voice again.

'Isaac, you must listen to us. A man has come from Tel Aviv. He is the representative of the Israeli government. He is a colonel of the Israeli Defence Force. You have to listen, Isaac, you have to hear what the Israeli government says to you. You must put the past behind you, forget all this rubbish about winning and will-power and strength. You have to talk to this man, for God's sake.'

He could imagine them back in the control tower. Crowded round the television set, picking up his words and searching on the outer camera monitor for the Israeli: be bedlam. Who authorized it? Whose sanction? Deep in now, Charlie, blown yourself, risked the lot, jeopardized the pension, the job, all the same things that mob will be thinking of. No point in saying you didn't reckon it was going to work out like this. Took him there yourself, and you've made it public, broadcast it to the world.

Incessant in his ear were the tribal drums of anger and dissent. 'Come in Webster. Come in immediately. Webster, respond to your call sign. What the hell is going on out there? Did you take the Israeli to the location? It was expressly forbidden that he should reach the plane. Answers must be given.' They seemed to be passing the microphone from one to the other. All climbing on you, Charlie, leaning on your back, pummelling you. Tell them to get stuffed.

'I have one message for you. They will start to shoot hostages again in something less than forty minutes. I repeat, the killing starts again in forty minutes. That is why I am here. I have nothing else to report. Nothing else.' There were further bleated demands for clarification, amplification, justification. He reached to his side for the control console, felt with his fingers for the volume button and turned it slowly, anti-clockwise.

Another step forward. 'Isaac, you have to listen to this man. He comes at the direct instructions of the Israeli government. He's no trick, he's not a stooge. You have to hear him out. You have to listen to him before there is more killing.'

The answer was a long time coming. It seemed fainter to their ears, and there was confusion and hesitancy in the voice.

'It is Rebecca who hears you, Isaac has said that we must have the petrol. Soon he will choose which man stands at the door at one o'clock. You have not much time for the petrol. After one o'clock then perhaps we should hear what your friend has to say.'

Charlie shouted again, and was not heeded. He brushed his hand across his mouth to clear the saliva that had gathered there. They'll have your neck for this, Charlie, right up high they'll swing you. Someone had to get the scene moving, didn't they? But there're ways of doing it, Charlie. Their way and your way. Your way's a loser.

George Davies was well pleased with the training session, as pleased as he would ever be. Eight men approaching the aircraft from the dead ground at the rear. Four for the back door and needing more time because it must be forced from the outside and they would be unfamiliar with the locking devices employed on the Ilyushin. Four more to the front where the hatch was free, and pausing for the dovetailing of the plan, the synchronization of the triple movement that would come from his direction by radio. Three stages and all simultaneous – the opening of the rear door, attack at the front, and the detonation of flash grenades coupled with sustained machine-gun fire on the port side of the aircraft. As much noise as possible, he had said he wanted, create the diversion, get their heads to the wrong windows and rely on the instinctive reaction to gunfire, take cover. He reckoned that if he could get his men inside the plane while the pair were still crouched down, or looking to the port side, orientating themselves to a new situation, then he stood a good chance. But there were imponderables. If the diversion did not drive Isaac and Rebecca down, if their attention was not drawn across the aircraft. If they were standing and shooting. If the hostages panicked and ran from their seats. There were any number of things that could screw it. But you could go only so far in preparation. They had to realize that back in the control tower, had to know that if the military went in then the picnic was over. He did not give the civilians the benefit of his doubt, thought for the most part they hadn't the slightest idea of the consequences of what they now planned.

Timing was working well, and the movement up the ladders could not be bettered. They had reasonable diagrams of the door mechanism to work off, and good photographs of the boy and the girl to imprint on each man's memory. The soldier who would carry the megaphone could handle the Russian language commands to order the passengers to remain seated – atrocious accent, but they'd understand him. Vital that – it was the one continual disturbing worry that obsessed him: that the passengers would start moving.

Five times they worked the manoeuvre – more than that and there was a danger of staleness. Had to keep them hungry, prevent the risk of any blunting familiarity coming into the operation. When they gathered around him, back on the tarmac after the last run, they discussed equipment. They rejected helmets and also the armour-plated 'flak' jackets; too cumbersome, too likely to catch on the ladder, the doorway, between the seats. They peeled their webbing down to a minimum, belt and nothing else. Tennis shoes in place of boots, the short barrelled Ingram in preference to anything that was heavier, larger, whatever the loss of hitting power. Nothing to be taken that could impede the one desperate dash along the aisle.

'Remember,' Davies said to the small group, 'remember, the slightest sign of opposition and you hammer them. Three-round bursts, and angled because we're talking both ends. They have to be bloody fast getting their hands up if they're to live through this little lot. Any chance of them shooting, blast them. If you're impeded, or can't see them, take the ceiling out . . . they only have to get one good burst off and we've wrecked the whole thing.'

'When does the next ultimatum wind up?' One of the group was anxious to know how soon they might be called on to demonstrate before the live audience what they had mastered in rehearsal.

'A little over half an hour. The civvie guy, the spook, is having another go at them at the moment. If he fails and the gaffers think they're about to start chopping again then we go. We won't be waiting for dark.'

Three men were with the Israeli Prime Minister: his Foreign Minister, the head of military intelligence, and the personal adviser to his office on counter-terrorism. All four wore open-necked shirts and light slacks.

It was an inconclusive meeting with little to report. The Prime Minister was assured that the British seemed adamant that in the event of a successful outcome to the siege of the Ilyushin then any surviving hi-jackers would be flown directly to the Soviet Union. It was unlikely, he was told, that the British would even bother to prefer charges for those offences committed inside the jurisdiction of local courts. It would be, the Foreign Minister remarked, the Iranian precedent rather than the Munich one to which the British would turn. When the Prime Minister had raised his eyebrows fractionally, the signal that he wished clarification, it was explained that the Iranians had sent back a Soviet Air Force pilot who had defected in a light aircraft seeking political asylum. The Munich option referred to the West German refusal to hand over a 26-year-old fugitive who had seized an internal Prague-Bratislava flight at gunpoint and flown it to Munich.

'I had hoped for more from the Americans,' said the Prime Minister, turning to the army reserve general, an old friend, one who could be trusted and whom he had brought out of retirement to sit close by his office. 'I had hoped that their influence on the British would be greater.'

'The taste of this business has not been palatable to them. They will stand by us when the danger is greatest, when they believe we are without defences. But they do not like to think of us, or our people, as having a will of our own. The children have shown their claws, they have killed with them. It does not fit the image that our friends have of us.'

'With the hostage dead, with the Americans unwilling to act, then we have lost. They will go back, these two, and there is nothing that we can . . .' He broke off, as if reminded of something distant. Clutching at the straw. 'The man that we sent, Benitz. Has there been communication from him?'

'He spoke to the relevant people by telephone this morning. But his opportunities are limited. The British offer him nothing.'

313

'They have not used him because they wish to send these people back?'

'But he is a resourceful man.'

'A lion, one of the best we have.' The Prime Minister agreed. 'But there are impossibilities, I suppose, even for a man such as this.'

'He has made no contact for some time now, not that has been reported by London. Perhaps—'

'That means nothing. In these circumstances, nothing.'

So often like this, the ill-informed back-seat, while the pursuit of policy remained in the hands of the soldiers. Many times the scene had been enacted; the directions given, the orders made clear, and then the waiting for the cipher cable, the telex, the radio message, always the same men in the room, the same frustration.

Abruptly the Prime Minister curtailed the meeting. Nothing to be gained from further dallying, talking round a situation they no longer directly influenced. The delegation of the Histadrut had been waiting more than twenty minutes in the ante-room outside his office. He should not delay them longer. The problems of the trades unions would be with him long after the affair of the taking of the Ilyushin to Stansted was forgotten.

That he should have closed and refastened the door Isaac knew. He should have shut them in again, barricaded the gate, prepared his defences. But he could not bring himself to return to the bright hole through which the sunlight dazzled, nervous of the danger there. Yet it was weakness not to go to the big lever, plunge it downwards the semicircle of its locking mechanism, it was a weakening of his will that he recognized but felt unable to correct. Not many hours since he had slept, four perhaps and not much more, but the passing of time had been concentrated and had ravaged both his strength and his thinking ability – the escape of the teacher, the killing of the Italian, the death of his friend. Great and cataclysmic events, all far beyond any previous experience he had had, each diluting the importance of the other, till they had taken a toll that he would not have believed possible.

You should have fastened the door, Isaac, if you mean to fight on. The door must be bolted and locked, Isaac. Their entry point. Through there that they will come with machine guns and rifles. They'll be laughing, unable to believe their luck, a door actually left open . . . But the tiredness swept over him, overwhelming, compulsive. If he could only close his eyes . . . A dreamless sleep, without the desperate fear of watching and waiting, and hoping . . .

But the door must be open for one o'clock. Right, Isaac? That was when you told the man Charlie to be watching and waiting if there was no petrol. He allowed himself a slow smile as he remembered the fever in the voice of the Englishman, the anxiety that he sought to suppress. It brought a quiet grin to the side of Isaac's mouth. That was why the door should be left open: so that they could see it, and count the minutes that passed on their watches.

Strange not seeing David at the far end of the aisle, not following his bowed silhouette the length of the aircraft as he had hovered in the cockpit. Had made an abscess in their group, his going. And what for? What for, any of it? The policeman back in Kiev, the captain in his cockpit seat, the passenger misshapen on the tarmac – didn't even know their names. So what for? The path that David had led them to, the road that he had shown them. A road that was safe and secure with the darkened shadows of escape, no blocks, no armed men, no uniformed sentries. David had told them of Babi Yar, and of Potma and Perm, lectured them on the diet of 75 grams of black bread a day and cabbage soup with which to wash it down, harangued them on the young men of their faith who languished in the cells, the injustices, the cruelties, the interrogations. A blow for freedom, David had promised. And where was freedom? Not here, not in this stinking cell, with these animals to be watched and guarded and shepherded. You ran well, David, ran early, and you left us, left us to face the wrath you had brought down. But what if there can be no survival for the fighter, what if he is made for martyrdom? Isaac seemed to laugh to himself, and there was the slow, gentle, smiling shake of his head. Not what you came for, Isaac. Not why you brought the tickets – just to purchase a grave plot. Good enough for David, but not for Isaac. Rambling, you fool, deep in your self-pity. Wonder what they'd said that morning in the lecture hall as they gathered for the first class of the day, the ones he studied with. Would they know now where was the one who always sat in the fifth row, three seats in from the door, the one with the spidery writing, good at practical and poor at theory, who asked no questions and took the 'B' marks, and who was quiet and had nothing to say in the canteen queue at morning break? Would they know? And if they did what would they say? Those who liked him, what would they say if they had stood beside him at ten and watched his fingers tighten on the trigger bar, seen the disintegration of a man's skull, the way he wiped the spattered bone and brain tissue from his arm? Would they have embraced him, or have cowered beyond his reach?

His hands gripped the narrow barrel of the gun. Hurting yourself, Isaac, wounding yourself. But you have to decide now, cannot stall and pass the parcel any longer. Have to close the door if you are going to fight them, Isaac. It's your guts that are fleeing you, draining through the open door, spilling out, splashing on the tarmac, ripening the time for surrender.

Time to move. Isaac pulled himself up from the floor, holding on to the trolley for leverage. So bloody tired, his legs. And the baby still crying. No-one trying to stop the little bugger's fury, letting it scream and yowl as if to batter at him personally. And all of them watching for his reaction to the noise, waiting for him to burst into protest . . . or to capitulate and ask for milk to be sent. They would not wait much longer, but for now the bastards could wait. Even the American was quiet now, the one with the homilies to Rebecca, and the arrogance; should have chosen him, not the little frightened man he had dragged to the doorway: should have been the American. Not that it would have changed anything, only given greater satisfaction.

Down the aisle again, Isaac. Cat in a cage, with a circumscribed path inside the bars. Down the carpet, eyes to the right, eyes to the left, and watch them all squirm, look away, try to hide. He reached Rebecca, and his arm was round her shoulder, not with emotion, more to offer a faint degree of comfort.

They should not have brought her. It chilled him to think what would happen to Rebecca. Perhaps he was strong enough to face the bullets – perhaps. But the girl, never. Without the muscle, without the mind. They should not have allowed her to come. Late in the day for that thought, though. In their eyes she'll be as culpable as the men, would be judged with equality, the same fate. What a screw-up! And how far from where it had started, and what had it started for? A heap of cretins sitting in their excreta, that Babi Yar should be remembered. Babi where? Babi bloody Yar. Isaac laughed to himself, this time out loud.

Rebecca said, 'What you said to the man, Isaac, did you mean that? It is close to one o'clock, do we kill one more then? Do we have to?'

'If we believe that we are going to Israel, then we must kill another, and another till we have the fuel.' His voice was steady, and without anxiety.

'Are we going to Israel, Isaac?'

'Questions, always questions!'

'But now there must be answers, Isaac. David is dead, the Italian, the captain too. There have to be answers.'

'What do you want to hear me say?'

'I have to know what you think. I have the right to know what you will do. Are we going to Israel?'

'And you? What do you think? Do you believe we will fly from here?'

'Don't play with me, Isaac. Not now. We have been here too long for games. We have to have honesty now.'

'So, what do I have to say to you? Do I crawl to you and beg for your forgiveness?' He spat the words at her, and the hate was there again, the loathing not for her but the great sponge that hemmed in on them that they could kick against, but not hurt, not inflict pain. 'Do you want me to plead to you to forgive me and to forget where I have taken you? Of course we will not see Israel . . . There, it is the first time that I have said it . . . I'll say it again for you, only louder, so that all these pigs can hear me . . . *we will not see Israel.* We will never see Israel. We are like the herd of our people, the masses of the camps and the prison cells. No better than them, no worse than them. We are as ineffective as they are. We will never see Israel. You wanted me to say it, and I have satisfied you. It was for nothing, Rebecca. Nothing.'

'So there will be no more killing?' A small voice, almost a whisper, flattened by the enormity of what she had drawn from him. She pushed the hair back from his forehead, a quick movement of the hand so that he barely felt the texture of her fingers against his skin.

'No more of the passengers will die.' The smile regained, promising the girl a present, something she would like and be pleased to accept.

'Who else, who else than the passengers? The soldiers, if they come . . . who else?'

'They will send us back, Rebecca. Remember when you and David talked to them, when he was defeated, when he wanted to end it, and they could not answer you. Remember that: they could not answer the question you asked them. They want to send us back. You understand that, you know what that means. It is not the way I can accept, Rebecca, and you could not go alone. We will not go back, not together, not singly. They will not take us.'

'That was why David went?' She could not use the word that came to her tongue, a betrayal of David as great as if she'd gone to the window and stared down at his broken body. 'That was why David went. Because he knew. That was why you called him a coward . . .'

'Because he could not do it by his own hand. He needed others. We will ask no help. Ourselves, together, we will do it.'

He felt her stiffen against him, driving her body closer to his, pressing with a ferocity as if to mould their two persons into one. 'I will be frightened, Isaac. I will need you.' He kissed her softly, full on the pale and greyed lips, stifling her words.

'We must hear what the man from Tel Aviv has to say to us. First we must hear that.'

He went to the doorway, for a moment was visible to the outside watchers before instinctive caution won through and he backed again to the side and shelter.

'Charlie,' he shouted. 'You can come now. Bring the man from Israel.'

Strong and clear and strident, his voice across the emptiness of the concrete. The burden thrown off, discarded. There were many rifles aimed at the general direction of his body till the hands that held them relaxed and the barrels were dropped. Charlie Webster and Arie Benitz started to walk towards the Ilyushin, a slow and careful step, and all the time the Englishman talking into the microphone close to his chin.

It seemed a great distance they had to go, a chasm to be bridged.

Summoned again from his exile on the lower floor the Home Secretary read the transcript of Charlie Webster's radio message.

'There has been a substantial change of mood on the part of both Isaac and Rebecca. After threatening that executions would recommence at thirteen hundred local, if they were denied fuel for the onward flight to Israel, they have now invited me to bring to the aircraft Col Arie Benitz of the IDF. They want to hear what message he brings them from the Israeli government. The message will be that they should surrender. My assessment is that this represents a considerable weakening of Isaac's position. For personal guidance, is it likely that on surrender they will be returned to face Soviet Courts? Over. Webster.'

The Home Secretary edged his glasses further down his nose. 'Has someone answered Mr Webster's query?'

'Yes,' the Assistant Chief Constable spoke with caution.

'What was the answer?'

'He was given guidance, not specific information.'

319

'Which way did you guide him?'

'We said that the position was not clear, but . . .'

'In heaven's name, man, what did you tell him?'

'He seemed to need some sort of answer, something that would help during the difficult negotiation stage he is embarking on.'

'Don't fool with me.'

'We told Mr Webster that there had been a change of approach by the Foreign Office – we told him they were unlikely to be returned to the Soviet Union.'

'Who told him that?'

'I did.' The Assistant Chief Constable stood his ground, aware the worst was over, that now he had only to confront the puzzlement and confusion of the politician. 'On my own authority. I judged his believing that this was the case would only help Mr Webster at this moment.'

'It's not true, simply not true.'

'Behind them they have a man shot in Kiev. The pilot of the aircraft is dead in the cockpit, a passenger is dead on the tarmac. More stand to die as the afternoon goes on. The truth of what Webster tells these people is frankly unimportant. They've forfeited the right to truth.' He saw the retreat, the change of tack, the Home Secretary backing away from confrontation. Stupid, bloody man, and what did he know of the scene anyway? Better off downstairs and out of the way.

'I hadn't thought it would cave in quite like this.' He had to assert himself in some way, had to say something. Well, let bloody Clitheroe answer him.

'They end with a whimper, these things, that's my experience—' the psychiatrist had joined the group. 'On other occasions we've noted there's an intensification of demands in the final hours before surrender. These two people are undergoing severe nervous strain, loss of sleep, absence of food. They are in a hostile environment, isolated from communication. When they raised their demands it was because they acknowledged their earlier threats had failed. Mr Webster has now confronted them with the Israeli. They are bewildered at the moment and they will want to know what he has to say. The combination of persuasion by Mr Webster and Benitz should be too much for them. I would predict it will be all over today. Shorten that in fact to this afternoon.'

'Extraordinary behaviour of this fellow Webster.' The politician was still perturbed, recognizing his hand was far from the helm. 'Just going off, no instructions, no authorization, taking the Israeli . . .'

'It's quite simple. The last time Mr Webster was present we were engaged in the debrief of the Russian. We were preparing for an attack. Mr Webster was anxious to avoid such an assault.'

'So are we all,' the Home Secretary bridled. 'It's the last thing any of us want.'

'If the military assault the plane Mr Webster believes there would be an inherent risk to the children who are among the passengers, harm a large proportion of them. If I may be indiscreet I think he also believes that it is not necessary to kill the two young people. He would like them to survive. If he is to save them he will be all the better equipped to do so in the knowledge that they will serve a few years in a British gaol before release. He's a complex fellow, Mr Webster, his experiences are outside our own, and I think he's bored with ushering young people to their maker. The only relief I feel at the moment is that it will not be myself who disabuses him of the destination of the two Russians should he prove successful.'

Both in their shirtsleeves, Charlie encumbered only by his radio set, Benitz with the lightweight aluminium ladder that would reach to the bottom of the doorway. Around them a terrible, deafening stillness. Benitz steadied the ladder against the fuselage of the aircraft, noticed its age, the dents of unknown mechanics, the flashes of rust from the vents in the bodywork, the peeling of the weatherworn paintwork of its livery. He put his foot on the bottom step to calm its vibrations.

Charlie began to climb towards the doorway.

17

Isaac was back again in his lair, hugging the drinks trolley, ignoring the sights that he had lived with, the coats and possessions stuffed into the racks, the printed flower patterns on the walls, the terse material covering the seats, the bobbing heads. Rebecca sat huddled in the cockpit doorway, shunning the sight of the body of the captain, unmoving and whitened by the pallor of death. Both from their different positions could see the top of the ladder, saw it buckle and shake before there was Charlie's shoulder for them to fasten on, and his growing height as he climbed into view. He seemed to pause for a moment, to hesitate and look about him, nostrils dilating to the smell of the interior. His eyes roamed about him, and there was a smile of recognition on his face, hasty but still evident, when he saw the girl, followed by a slight inclination of his head and then at his mouth the faint twist of protest, unspoken, at the pistol levelled at his chest. He turned his head, back towards the world beyond the hatch and called in English so that only Rebecca understood him. 'It's fine, Arie. Come on up, the party's ready.'

Isaac, squinting down the length of the aisle, trying to penetrate the face, assess the man: the enemy or the ally? Isaac needing an answer. Didn't fit the image of the enemy. Too old, too careworn, too gross about the waist. An ordinary man such as he would have seen in Kiev, who might work at the railway station or occupy an office in the Bureau of State Pensions. He moved with neither the suspicion nor the aggression of a man who would do them harm. But this was the one who had broken them, who was the spokesman for the great force on the outside, who had not conceded to their demand for fuel. And his weapon had been placid, unyielding reasonableness, the tap that dripped on and on, beating out messages of logic and persuasion in endless repetition. Rebecca had been beaten from the time they first heard his voice, David following her, and now he, Isaac, joining his colleagues in defeat. How many times had he said there would be no fuel before the message slowly and inexorably won through? Not an enemy, but not an ally, not this man with the dirt-stained shirt and the crumpled, rounded trousers. Nothing he had said had carried friendship, sympathy or understanding. He could not be an ally. A functionary, that was what the man Charlie was. The one who had been sent to do the work.

The man that followed him was different, sharper on his feet, quicker in his movements, harder eyes. Poised, intense. He was an opponent, to be watched. But this was the man sent by his own people, the one they had to hear before he took Rebecca past the trolley barricade to the place of privacy in the far end corridor, beside the back toilets, close to the rear door. Not now, Isaac, shut it out: the time comes fast enough.

Charlie began to walk down the aisle of the plane, slowly, gently, so that there could be no doubts about his intentions. Then he stopped where all could see him, reach into contact with him, his hand resting relaxed on a seat-back. Confident, friendly, assured.

The famous smile, winning friends, putting the fears at ease, the man who was in control, looking to the passengers as his priority, avoiding Isaac with his pinched and sprung intensity, and his sub machine gun. Not looking back at the drab girl with the pistol.

'Hello, my name is Charlie Webster. Just "Charlie", they generally call me. I'm with the British Foreign Office and I've come to take you off the plane. It won't be immediately, but it'll be very soon. You just have to be patient for a while longer. I know you've been that already – fantastic – but just a little bit longer while we sort some things out with the gentleman and the lady. Please stay in your seats, don't move at all, and remember that it won't be long now.'

There were some who found his Russian difficult to follow, so there was a chorus of explanation as the word was passed back among the rows of seats till all comprehended. The applause came suddenly and spontaneously, sixty men and women and children hammering their hands together and shouting their support. Charlie blushed and smiled again, and put up his hand without avail to halt the flood of gratitude sweeping down the cabin. He looked for someone to speak to, and was grateful for the presence of the girl pilot, still staring to the front, hands moving in rhythm with the others, tears on her cheeks, losing the fight with her emotions.

Charlie said, 'You are Miss Tashova. I want you to know that everyone in the control tower, all the authorities that are gathered there, have expressed their great admiration for your achievement last night. The landing was brilliant, absolutely bloody brilliant, if you'll excuse me. They are looking forward to congratulating you personally.' Just once she slipped a glance to him, without commitment, without dropping her reserve, then gazing again into the dour material of the seat-back in front of her.

Keep it going, Charlie, keep it moving around, gentle and natural. Make the two of them believe it's all over, that it's finished, out of their control. No negotiation, no concession, just that the game's gone, the whistle's blown. 'Taking the initiative', the boffins would call it, and holding it so that Isaac couldn't wrest it back. Silly little bugger, should have known his bible, rule one, 'Never let the bastards with the open faces and the empty hands on board.' Curtains after that, Isaac, old sunshine.

He moved forward two more rows. Closer to Isaac, closer than he had ever been, where he could see the confused and shadowed face with its sheen of sweat. Able to focus on the gun, understand its cooling system, its front needle sight, its age and peeled paint like a policeman that edges along the windowsill towards the man determined on suicide, and who must talk calmly and be mundane, matter of fact. As he turned to the nursing mother the style of the gun was imprinted on his mind, the knowledge that a flick of the trigger, casual and involuntary or predetermined, and the magazine would be unloading in a cascade of shells hurtling through the trimmed airspace between him and the squat, tensed, curly-haired boy. He tapped the baby's head with his left hand, trying not to draw away from the stench of the unchanged clothes, attempting to weave the web of normality. Just keep it going, Charlie, ever so slow, ever so gradual. In front of him the children, the school kids, still quiet, and waiting for you, Charlie. Had to get beyond them, had to impose himself between the boy with the gun and their soft flesh that would be ripped and carved by a single volley. Winked at a couple of the little brats. Eight or nine more rows, that would be enough, then he'd be a shield for the kids, then he could talk of who left the plane first, then he could believe that it was finished.

All the time moving, edging closer to the boy with the gun, soft voices, controlled smiles, creeping nearer, insidious, and deep inside his heart pounding and his muscles taut and stretched, and his eyes on the gun. Don't lose sight of that gun, Charlie, don't take your bloody eyes off it.

Gently Charlie spoke to Isaac, spanning the few feet of carpet with his words, making the contact. 'I've brought Colonel Benitz to see you, Isaac. He's from the Israeli Defence Force, and he's a fighter, he's like you. Listen to him, Isaac. Listen to what he tells you.'

It took Charlie time to realize that Benitz had begun to speak behind him. A different voice, and words that he could not understand, a language that was strange to him and incomprehensible.

Benitz turned back towards the open door and the cockpit entrance. Gazed down the length of the aisle towards the girl.

'Come here, Rebecca. Come close to us where you can hear what I say.' A cool, spring voice, an instruction in the Yiddish tongue, 'Come nearer, so that I do not shout.' Looking into her eyes, absorbing the creased lines of her tiredness, and her faltering step. The girl who wanted to come to Israel, who wanted to take her place amongst his people, bear her children there.

'Keep coming, Rebecca, keep coming, you have nothing to fear from me.'

He saw the way she looked at him, as if the flood-gates of her misery might now be broken down, saw the relief catch at the curls of her mouth that now, after all the hideousness and pain, she had finally found her friend. And they had told him on the telephone that these young ones would be sent back, would be returned to the land of oppression, and to cells, and to death and to the quicklime pits. He wondered as she came towards him where she had started, where she had begun the journey that had brought her here. In the arms of one of the boys? Or something more rare – had there been the driving inner commitment, the force that sharpened the men that he led, the men of the Storm squad? And he would not know, would never know, because now there was no time.

When she reached him Benitz put his arm around her shoulder, draped loosely and carelessly, glanced once at the pistol held in her hand and mingled with the folds of her dress, worked his fingers into the muscle of her shoulder, the gesture of reassurance, and saw Isaac straighten as if his fear too was waning.

'We know what you sought, we know what you have accomplished,' Arie Benitz spoke with a simplicity, with the humility of the funeral oration at the graveside of a soldier of Squad 101. 'We know of it and we marvel, and are proud. We understand what brought you here, and we understand the depth of despair, the pain and the agony that will have been yours when the welcome was of guns and armed men and tanks. We understand why you felt driven to take the life of a man who now lies outside and dead. We understand.'

Both of them were looking at him, both watching, and the gun barrel of Isaac lowered so that the muzzle aimed at the slight space between his feet. 'In many ways we can struggle against our opponents. The battle may be offensive, it may be passive. There are those that fight in the front line, those that are far to the rear. There are sudden victories that can be won, and there are those that are secret and quiet and without garlands.

'There are times, too, when the victory must be purchased, times when great sacrifice is demanded. Those are the sad times, the times when our people weep upon the coffins . . . The tank commanders who held the Golan at Yom Kippur, when the Syrians came, for them there could be no relief, no reinforcement, no supply. They were pitifully few and they fought till their shells were expended, and then they fought with their machine guns, and when the magazines were empty then they threw their grenades. And they died by their broken tanks. They died because it was required of them. And there was no fear, no terror, no panic. They died because Israel needed their lives, needed them as currency to pay for the ultimate victory. They won us time, and when we returned we stood in awe and understood what these few had achieved for us, and we buried them in the military cemetery on a hill outside Jerusalem, and there are flowers there, and men come with their women and children to stand in silence beside the stones.'

Only Isaac and Rebecca understood his words, but the plane was hushed, as if all were sensitive to the moment.

'We do not share our fight. We do not rely on allies. We stand by ourselves and expect favours from none. It is a hostile, friendless world,' Arie Benitz smiled, not from humour, but a deep sympathy, 'you have found that, you know it as I know it. When you were in the air over Hanover, that was when you would have known it, and when you woke to the dawn this morning and found the guns that circled you. It is a hard and savage place that you have come to.' His hand slipped from the girl's shoulder, and his fingers played now with the sun-dried skin of her upper arm where it was bared beneath her sleeve, pulled gently and squeezed it, and played patterns with his nails. Winning her, comforting her, and all the time edging down towards the limp-held pistol. 'The British have told you that you will not fly from here. If they say that I believe them, and I have no power to alter their decision. And if you surrender the British will send you back . . . back to Kiev, back to the courts . . .'

He felt the girl stiffen at his side, and his hand now gripped her arm, tight, pinioning, pressing it hard against her body, denying her movement.

'What do you want of us?' The peace clearing from Isaac's face, the weariness returning. 'What is the message that you bring us?'

'There is only one course for you, only one that you can contemplate, and I have come to help you.' Said firmly but with resolution, the man who has loved his dog, which now is in pain, and must be killed. 'I will help you. It will be at the hands of a friend.' Benitz's hand had sunk far on Rebecca's arm, below the bony elbow, and his fingers brushed at her waist and close to the butt end of her pistol.

'That is what you came to tell us?' Isaac laughed, throwing back his head. 'That was the message that they flew you here to deliver? Be good little boys, kill yourselves nicely, and we'll send a man to do it with you, to hold the hand, make certain it's a nice clean shot, that it's not messy? . . .'

'You cannot go back, Isaac. Neither of you can go back.'

Isaac now sank to a crouch, the gun barrel up. The passengers fidgeted in their seats.

'There is no other way, Isaac,' Benitz shouting down the aisle.

'From these people, yes, from the British we could expect this. From the Russians, yes, we could expect them to send a killer to us. But that it should be you, of our own people, who can offer us nothing . . .'

'There is nothing else.' The calmness gone, the soldier in uniform. Benitz's fragile patience diminishing.

Slowly and with emphasis, pointing each word, Isaac said, 'But that it should be you.'

'I said it was a hard and savage place that you had come to. I offer you the best, the only way.' And there was a shame in his voice, a humiliation. And banging in his ears the words of the Ambassador. A detestable job. 'I was not ordered to bring you this message, not by my government. They wanted to save you, but you have destroyed yourselves. When you took the man to the doorway, that was when you died, Isaac. Whether at my

328

hand, your hand, or a Russian hand, that was when you died. I only come to make it easier. I can give nothing more. When you took the man to the door you went beyond our reach.'

One hand at the pistol jerking it from the girl's wrist, the other jack-knifing her arm behind her back, so that she shuddered from the pain of the movement. He pulled her across in front of him, protection against Isaac's sub-machine gun that was now at his shoulder, aimed clear and straight down the length of the aisle.

The urgency of his voice scything over the heads of the passengers, Charlie shouted, 'What are you saying, Benitz? What are you telling them?'

'What I have to say. What is obvious to a fool.'

'What is it? Tell me' – the rare anger that Charlie was unused to.

'Keep out, Charlie. This is not your quarrel. Come back here, to behind me.'

A command, spoken with unarguable authority, and Charlie obediently edged his way down the aisle, all the time watching the face of Isaac, watching for the steeling of the eyes that would mean he was preparing to shoot. Backed past the children, past the woman with the baby, away from the American, away from the pilot officer. Benitz's arm came to meet him, grabbed his collar and half-guided, half-hurled him sideways among the legs of the passengers. As he stumbled, trying to regain his balance, pressing into a lap for support, Benitz went past him, using the girl as his protection, advancing with a slow and strange circumspection towards Isaac.

Arie Benitz forced his thighs and knees into the back of the girl's legs, melting their movements into one, compressing his body against hers, and all the time talking in the language that Charlie did not know. Softer now, and using the tactic of persuasion, the same message all the time, till Charlie had no doubts. He wanted the sub-machine gun, wanted it thrown down, wanted it abandoned and harmless. Had the pistol that would be the weapon of execution, raised and cocked and ready.

329

Ten paces from Isaac now, the Israeli and the slight Jewish girl. Ten paces and closing. Charlie could anticipate the way Benitz's mind would run. Work himself close enough to propel the girl against the boy, and in the mêlée hope for the chance to snatch at the sub-machine gun, or just simply shoot into the chaos he would have created. Still closing on Isaac and staring him out all the time. The advance of the predator on the rabbit, and no bolt-hole for Isaac.

One sentence Rebecca shouted.

'Shoot him, Isaac, shoot him!'

Banal, silly, words . . . not those she would have chosen for her epitaph, not the final words she would have wanted to speak to Isaac, the last she would say in her life to the boy who had kissed her lips.

Breaking through Charlie's thoughts – the endless bleating of the machine gun, spitting out its bullets, a single drumming cacophony of noise, on and on, an unbroken rhythm of flashes. It was a low-velocity weapon and the first shots stayed with the girl, beating at her body, hitting, wracking her till she pitched forward. Still the gun fired, as Benitz made a last and forlorn gesture towards the saving of his life. Alone now and without the human wall for security he seemed to try to aim the girl's pistol at the source of his pain. There was a half-face for Charlie to see, bemused and irritated that he had been found out in such trivial company. A man of Entebbe, and the Savoy Hotel, and of Maalot and Kyryat Shmona; a man who had fought with the Storm squad against the best of the Palestinians, and now undone by a boy and a girl who knew nothing but the dream of a country they should never see.

Benitz was a long time falling. Even as the bullets hit him he sought to steady himself, holding grimly onto a seat. Raising the right hand, the fist that held the pistol as each succeeding shell threw back his resolution, forced him to begin again, a man who fights the tide and cannot win. When he was still, on the rumpled carpet of the aisle that his feet had rucked and that soon would be stained by the coursing of his blood, then

330

Isaac pulled his finger from the trigger and lowered the gun barrel.

Scrambling along the aisle, Charlie reached Benitz, knelt by his head, Isaac forgotten, lifted him at the back of his neck as he had been taught to do. Precaution against a man drowning on his own blood, standard and automatic reaction however grave the wounds, however small the chances of salvation.

'It was rubbish you talked, Charlie, silly deceitful rubbish. They go back, and you know that.' A gurgling, panting chant. Charlie's hands under his head, tilting it. 'The little fools did not know, did not know which was the easy way. Dead whatever they do, better at my hand ... better at the hand of a friend.' The death of Arie Benitz came in a last shaking spasm that lifted his head sharply; the cough was barely complete before his life fled him. Charlie eased the weight back on to the carpet, and looked up at Isaac, still motionless, the gun at his knees.

The baby was crying.

'I prefer to believe him, Charlie. Not your newfound promise for us. And we were going to do as he wanted, we did not need to be told. Not by the man that you brought to us, not by anyone. We knew. But it was to be in our time – not with these bastards sitting around us, counting us out. Can you understand, Charlie, Rebecca and I, we were going to do it? We trusted you and you brought this animal to kill us and hang us up by the ankles. You brought him, and because he was with you, because of what you said, we wanted to hear him. He came to execute us, here among the crowd. Not even in Kiev is the firing squad public, Charlie.'

Isaac started to come forward. Lightly, almost delicately, slightly-built and on the balls of his feet. He swung his arm in a lackadaisical way so that as he released the gun it made an arc in the air, almost brushing the roof before Charlie caught it.

'Do it for me, Charlie. Do it quickly.'

In three fast, trained movements Charlie removed the magazine, ejecting the shell in the breech so that it flew from the weapon sideways, falling on to a passenger's trousers. Then he pulled the trigger with the barrel aimed at the ceiling. Harmless.

331

'No, Charlie, no!' Isaac, curious that his request had not been observed. 'You have to do it. You owe it to me, Charlie.'

He had stopped seven, eight feet away, separated by the mingled blockade of the bodies of Rebecca and Arie Benitz. He did not look down, but instead fastened his eyes on Charlie.

'Charlie, you have to do it.' Faint, hard to hear, the first trace of anxiety winning through the trance that had becalmed him since he had killed Rebecca and the Israeli. 'Charlie, you cannot leave me to them. I'm not strong enough, not to be sent back, not to do it here . . . not without Rebecca. Charlie . . .'

'Animals', they called them in the pub where he went at lunchtime from the Department. Swine. Murderers. Communists. Fanatics. All the usual slogans as they chewed at their pork pies, and mouthed through their fat beef-filled sandwiches, and swilled the pints of warmed beer. Should come and face one of their animals, see him at three paces.

'Just keep coming, Isaac. It's all over. You need some food, some sleep. You need to rest. You're not going back, they told me that. Just keep walking.' Nothing else to say, Charlie thought, away from what he knew, away from the papers that would be piling on his desk high in the tower block half a day's drive away.

Now the scream.

'Charlie, you're lying to me. You have to shoot, you have to. You cannot send me back there. Charlie, we believed in you. You were the one we trusted . . .'

There was a scuffling sound behind him, and Charlie spun to see the first of the SAS troopers emerge from the doorway into the interior of the plane. A fast, trained man whose speed was electric and fear-inspiring; the line of the little gun, the Ingram, up to his face traversing with his body. More noise, louder and closer, and Charlie turned back to see the wheeling of the door behind Isaac and the flood of men intervening, scrambling aboard in their camouflage uniforms. The lead man of the group that came from the rear of the Ilyushin was half over the fastened-down drinks trolley when the implications of what was happening swirled though Isaac's dulled comprehension. He seemed to launch himself forward, not at Charlie, but at the space beside the body of the Israeli, the few vacant inches of carpet where Rebecca's gun lay.

Charlie knew the meaning of that last gesture of defiance, could have swung his foot towards the pistol, kicked it clear or trapped it beneath his shoe, and he did nothing. All of the alternatives were there, available to him, but he stayed back, rooted and detached.

Edward R. Jones Jr had understood not a word of the screaming appeal that Isaac addressed to the Englishman. His ears still sung from the explosion of the bullets, and he had seen the entry of the troops from the forward door, was unaware of those who moved behind him. To his own mind the situation was clear-cut. Elbowing his wife hard in the stomach he heaved his considerable frame out of the seat, pitching himself into Isaac's path. Much of his weight landed on the back of the young Jew, sufficient to deter his momentum, cause him to flinch from his target, lose sight for the fractional and vital second of the gun that he stretched for.

Alone the American and the Jew wrestled on the floor, and then, as if a signal had been given, the passengers that flanked them rose from their seats and threw themselves into the mêlée.

Charlie lost sight of Isaac. He saw the face once, one that held terror and shock and surprise, then could not find it. Fists from the teachers; the dark, flying boot of the farmer; the pummelling of a straight arm that wore a suit and had buttons at the cuffs. He was brushed aside, a quick, fast push, and his view of the writhing scrum was obscured by the trim blue uniform that he knew was worn by Anna Tashova. Her flat-soled shoe in her hand, beating without aim, without direction into the mêlée. He made a feeble attempt to pull some of the bodies clear, but he created no impression and soon sagged back on to the armrest of a seat.

The SAS men cleared the aisle. One bellowing into a megaphone that all should stay in their places, the rehearsed drill, others dragging and tearing at the passengers – Russians, Italians, and last of all the American.

His face blooming with a mouth-breaking smile, Edward R. Jones Jr held out his great fist to Charlie. Enveloped in it was the pistol.

'I think I was just about in time for you. Perhaps you'd care to look after it.'

Charlie took the gun without response and looked past the American, already busy manoeuvring himself back over his wife's legs while she reached up and clung with linked hands around his throat. Isaac was there, uncovered now, visible and violated. Angry blotches on his temples, weals where there would soon be blood at his cheeks, his shirt ripped open to expose the reddened patches against his ribs, trousers at his knees to expose the particular vengeance of one. But he was alive, and conscious, and his chest heaved as he struggled to replace the air lost to his lungs.

Nausea rising through him, welling from his stomach, Charlie found he couldn't take his eyes off the boy. He strained to hear what Isaac tried to say.

'Charlie, for the last time, you have to do it. Don't let them send me back. Please, Charlie.'

'It's not like that, Isaac. You're not going back, that's what they told me.'

The boy tried to laugh – bitter and shrill, till the sounds merged with his tears.

'Don't give me that crap, Charlie. Shoot me, for fuck's sake do it!'

The last cry, the last plea, the last moment of faith for a stranger. Charlie felt the pressure of the gun handle where it rested against the softness of his palm, his fingers twined round the trigger guard. He tried to think back to what the control tower had told him, the way the response had been phrased, the words of the policeman, whether they had been specific, whether there was room for interpretation. He couldn't remember the exact words, the phrasing, but the impression had been there: that they wouldn't send them back. Or was that just what you wanted to hear, Charlie? And the little bastard didn't believe him anyway. So what now? He saw that Isaac had closed his eyes, clamped his lids together. It's what he wants, begging you, cringing to you, because he thinks that you alone among all the army of enemies can rescue him. He believes in you, Charlie, believes you can do it. Don't hide, not behind what the control tower told you, don't shelter there. Do you kill him or not? Can't pass the buck any more, no-one else to catch it. Do you kill him, Charlie? He seemed to see a boy in handcuffs pulled by the troops towards a prison wagon and the death cell of Nicosia Central, same height, same youth, same hopelessness, and you'd fingered him, Charlie. And another in Aden who was dead in the gutter with the rubbish, shot in the temple and quivering, and you fingered him, Charlie, told the squaddies where to look. And there are more, who are pushing the weeds up, that you could make a living, earn your shilling. Haven't there been enough, Charlie, haven't you finished sending the bright-eyed kids on their way? But if it isn't Charlie Webster it will be someone else, a bloody Russian, and that only after all he'll go through first. Don't know, do you, Charlie? And you've not time to find out.

The gun was at his side, held loosely, unmoving.

The SAS hauled Isaac to his feet, one on each arm, not unkindly and with only that amount of force that was required to shift him, unprotesting, to the back of the aircraft. He looked back once at Charlie, before the caged face had turned, to be replaced by the matted black hair highlighted by a tremor of blood.

A set of motorized steps was driven to the forward door of the Ilyushin. By the time the first of the passengers clambered uneasily down to the oil-streaked concrete supported by a line of soldiers, their rifles slung, the corpses of David and Luigi Franconi had been covered with the scarlet blankets of the ambulance stretchers.

Anna Tashova, her right shoe still adrift, hobbled the first few steps on the tarmac on the arm of her navigator, before seeming to collect herself, disengage and walk unaided.

The teachers, like worried sheepdogs, penned the children together in a single cohesive group that stood and watched with fascination the bulging heaps that were covered all except the footwear; the one of polished leather still shining and immaculate, the other a tainted, dirt-torn canvas.

The Italian delegation of the Party subdued their traditional ideology and made the gesture of the cross over their chests as they recognized what the blankets hid.

Edward R. Jones Jr had his arm around Felicity Ann and had readjusted his handkerchief bandage so that the coagulation of the scalp blood showed clearly. He remembered to adjust his camera to compensate for the sunshine of the exterior.

The man who might have been a farmer was triumphant.

As best they might they scrambled on to an airport apron bus, and one of the Foreign Office interpreters told them there would be hot meals and beds and baths at a nearby hotel, and that an official from the Russian Embassy in London was waiting there to greet them. There was no shouting, no cheering as the bus pulled away, none believing there were grounds for self-congratulation, and the very smell and filth of their bodies humiliated them.

A Saracen armoured car replaced the bus, but drove closer to the steps. The bodies of Arie Benitz and Rebecca were moved awkwardly down the steps on stretchers by men who sweated but bore the load in silence, and pushed far into the recesses of the vehicle so that they lay among the welter of gas canister boxes, and the coils of machine gun ammunition, and the trenching tools and the emptied cigarette packets and coffee cartons. On top of the Israeli and the girl the soldiers laid David and the Italian, who to those who handled him seemed unmarked except for the scratch on his face from his fall from the plane; no-one looked for the cavity set deep in the sleek and darkened hair.

Then came Isaac's turn. Handcuffed now, his arms locked across the front of his body. To the troops who ushered him from the plane and on to the ramp at the top of the steps he seemed an unworthy opponent. But he intrigued them, a boy who fought without a uniform, in the absence of a commander, and received no wage for it, and they permitted him to pause there, as if to drink in the freedom of the air, accepting and assimilating the surroundings to which he had brought the Ilyushin. Then he saw, deep in the Saracen, the body of David, uncovered, grotesque in the angle of fallen head, and seemed to wilt. He did not travel with David; another armoured car was designated to carry him, and the soldiers hustled Isaac to it, hands under his shoulder pits so that he was near lifted into the back, and then with his escort he was sat upon a cool iron seat. The great, thickened, high-velocity-proof doors were closed on him, exchanging for the boy one prison for another.

From the Foreign Secretary's office overlooking the lunchtime crowds that surged across Horse Guards Parade the news of the conclusion at Stansted spread quickly. Permanent Secretaries wound up their meetings, Under-Secretaries cancelled their lunch appointments. In News Department they prepared themselves for the issue of the statement that would explain the course of action being followed by Her Majesty's Government.

There was no more discussion on whether or not the survivor should be returned to Kiev. That decision had been taken; News Department was concerned with drafting only the justification. There was much fetching and carrying of United Nations debate transcripts, Security Council and General Assembly, that had concerned themselves with aerial piracy. From the Security Council meeting that had followed the Israeli military intervention to Entebbe in July of 1976 there was much to be taken that pleased those who would eventually fashion the Foreign Office release. The red pencils were busy underlining passages from the speech of Chaim Herzog, Israel's ambassador to the United Nations.

'. . . Those countries which fail to take a clear and unequivocal stand against international terrorism for reasons of expediency or cowardice will stand damned by all the decent people in this world and despised in history. There is a time in the affairs of men when even governments must make difficult decisions guided not by considerations of expediency but by considerations of morality . . . It is now for the nations of this world, regardless of political differences which may divide them, to unite against this common enemy which recognizes no authority, knows no borders, respects no sovereignty, ignores all basic human decencies, and places no limits on human bestialities.'

Also coming down from the shelves were the transcripts of the 1970 Hague convention called to discuss the 'Suppression of Unlawful Seizure of Aircraft'. Article 6 was the one that most concerned the drafters.

'. . . Upon being satisfied that the circumstances so warrant, any contracting state in the territory of which the offender or the alleged offender is present shall take him into custody and other measures shall be as provided in the law of that state but may only be continued for such time as is necessary to enable any criminal or extradition proceedings to be instituted.'

It was agreed that a good case could be made out. It would be harder to explain the absence of an appearance before an Essex Magistrates' court, and the speed with which it was intended the surviving hi-jacker should be removed from British soil and begin his journey back to the Soviet Union, but the press conference at Stansted should divert immediate attention from the one point of contention. Get rid of him first was the priority, before the protests were mobilized, before inter-governmental relations were strained.

There were one or two in the labyrinth of Whitehall who voiced concern at the planned culmination of the affair, but they were not overly loud with their anxieties, and were soon muted. Closed ranks and consensus opinion. More dignified that way.

* * *

Charlie was the last to leave the plane. They had let the photographers forward and he saw them in their broken ranks running toward the Ilyushin from the distant perimeter fence, hustling with their pronged tripods and cameras and cables. Those who were least encumbered with equipment, and remembered him as the man who had walked out across their lenses in the early morning had a chance to photograph Charlie. When he recognized their opportunity he raised his hand to cover his face, a reflex gesture. He would have been horrified to know that he had provided the Fleet Street caption writers with one of the day's many bonuses. The 'Shy Hero' was the title they put on the picture of the shambling figure walking away across the tarmac, his shirt-sleeved arm raised, his trousers sagging on his hips.

18

It was late summer afternoon when they flew Isaac out of Stansted.

He had only to walk from the midnight black police van to the stunted steps of the Hawker Siddeley jet. A cluster of men, some in uniform, the majority favouring well-worn civilian suits, were there to see him on his way. No farewells, only a series of curt handshakes between those who were staying and those whose work was not yet finished. They talked around Isaac, pretending to ignore him, not speaking to him as if to demonstrate their relief that the load was to be shed, the burden passed on. No more defiance from the boy, left behind in the small cell in the basement of the airport police station where he had sat and pondered on what awaited him, whiling away the hours for the details of the flight to be arranged. A child again, and not to be equated with the savage hostility that the fish-eye had mirrored. He stumbled on the bottom rung of the ladder, but there were hands on his arms that prevented him from pitching back, and the faces around him were stern and closed, as if unwilling to display their emotions or bare their thoughts to him.

There were five passengers in all. A member of the Russian Embassy staff who had been the first to climb on board; they had checked his name after he had proffered it with the list of Soviet diplomats available to the Foreign Office, found him described as a chauffeur. After him came a uniformed corporal of the Royal Air Force police, immaculate in his starched and pressed battledress, who had a cap with a red ribbon round it and a webbing belt that carried the white-blancoed holster encasing a Browning automatic pistol. Next Isaac, climbing with difficulty as he trailed his right arm that was linked by handcuffs to the wrist of a second Service policeman. Two Foreign Office men, both from security though neither would have admitted it, hurried inside the aircraft before the door was closed and the twin rear engines started.

That was the last Charlie Webster saw of Isaac, the back view of the dark-haired, pale-faced boy illuminated casually by the rotating blue lamp of the police van. Charlie sat slumped in the chair in the control tower from which he had watched the departure. To some he seemed churlish in his rejection of the many congratulations that were showered at him when he was greeted by the politicians and the political aides, the senior policemen, the army officers and civil servants. But Clitheroe had moved among the offended and Charlie had heard the words, hushed and discreet, of 'shock' and 'terrible strain', and 'it was necessary to deceive him, helped him in fact,' and 'what you'd expect in the circumstances' and 'exhaustion' and 'be right as rain once he's had a good sleep.' From where Charlie sat he could see the Hawker Siddeley taxi and then thrust forward in the gathering, closing gloom for take-off, the flashing red lights marking its progress down the runway. He watched it all the way through lift-off, stayed with it till there was just a moving star of light that faded along with the roar of the engines under power.

He reached for a telephone and dialled his home. Told his wife that he'd be home, but late, was irritable when she asked him where he was and where he'd been and didn't he know she'd been worried, didn't answer, and heard her say that the key would be under the front door mat if he'd forgotten to take his own yesterday morning, and there'd be some food on the kitchen table, and please to be quiet when he came in because the children had exams at school tomorrow.

He stayed a long time in the control tower, way after the others had gathered their papers together and made noisy and exultant farewells, after the cleaners had been through with the stiff brushes for the carpet and the complaints about the stubbed cigarettes and the big plastic bags for the debris of rubbish that had accumulated; they worked around him, subdued in their normal exuberance and chatter and gossip by the hunched figure who held his hands over his eyes and who did not move, who had not even a nod of recognition for them.

Tried to blot it out of his mind, the thought of the small jet landing at Templehof, West Berlin. The waiting car and the few courtesies that would be exchanged. Bundled into the back seat of one in the convoy that would not be at the front nor the back, but would be sandwiched against any intervention – not that there were men and women in that city who could even have begun to organize a rescue attempt. Play it by the book, wouldn't they? Because that was easiest, the simple and tried way, and that said five cars for maximum security. Through undefined channels that existed for communication word would be sent that the prisoner was on his way, and a time of arrival would be given. Half an hour, not more at the speed the cars would travel and the column would be at the checkpoint. Barriers would be raised and two groups would meet in the centre of a barren, floodlit road. Brief handshakes and the package handed over. Won't be your checkpoint, Charlie, too public; one of the remote ones, just in case anyone should witness the exchange, ask why, and have no bugger there able to answer. Wondered whether he'd struggle, the boy Isaac, whether he'd be pleading? Didn't think so, wouldn't be his style. He'd be thinking about you, Charlie, stands to reason. Thinking as he stepped forward and alternated captors, thinking why Charlie hadn't fired, thinking of it as the new hands held him. They'd spin on their heels and there'd be a new fleet of cars and a new airport divided from the first by the gorge of ideology, and the wall and the mines and the wire. Should have known, shouldn't you, Charlie, should have seen through the crap they gave you? Would have done if you weren't so bloody stupid. And if you had known would it have been different? Would the boy have been obliged? Can't blot it out, can you, Charlie?

342

The air traffic controllers were less susceptible to his feelings than the cleaning ladies had been. Had to shift now, reopening the airport, needed the chair, all the holiday flights queuing up, Faro, Malaga, Naples, Valetta, Crete. And it was outside regulations for an unauthorized person to remain in the control tower. Mustn't keep the vacationers waiting any longer, sir, put them to enough inconvenience as it is. Polite enough about it, but they wanted him out, and left him in no doubt as to their priorities. None knew who he was, different shift coming on, and some reckoned after they'd seen him through the door that he'd been drunk.

Below a police control post was being dismantled. Charlie put his head round the door, stopping the conversations, cocking the heads inquisitively, and asked whether there was any transport going to London.

'I've been with the Foreign Office people here,' he said.

There'd be a car in about fifteen minutes, Special Branch, he could go with them. He should wait in the canteen, and they'd fetch him when they were ready to leave. So he passed the time with a cup of cooling coffee in front of him till the summons came.

They drove fast and without talk for the first hour along the A11, out through Bishop's Stortford, hammering along the deserted road. It was the driver who broke the long silence.

'Did you see the little bugger?' he asked chattily, uninvolved, wanting to start the dialogue.

'Yes,' said Charlie.

'Didn't look much, did he? Like we could have had him for breakfast.'

'They usually are,' said Charlie. Oncoming headlights lit up the faces of the driver and his companion beside him, relaxed, at ease with themselves.

'I saw him in the cells,' the driver said. 'Meek as they come. Reckon I'd have been going spare if I'd been in his shoes, going back home to face the music and all that. Fair old reception he'll have when they get their hands on him.'

'Yes,' said Charlie.

343

'Wouldn't care to be in his pants. Shitting myself I'd be.'

'Too right,' the front passenger chimed.

'I don't know why we didn't bump him off on the plane. Would have been the easiest thing. His mate's bought it, the girl's dead, could have finished the whole bloody thing then and there. Save the old RAF a mess of trouble. Did you see what he went in? Only a bloody executive jet, like old Onassis, the real red carpet treatment. No, they should have shot him on board.'

'You can't just do that,' the front passenger said. 'It's not as simple as that. We have to show we are prepared to stand up to this business. And the best way to stamp it out is to pack the blighters off home again, let them sort it out there. We don't owe the little rat anything, not a thing. Cost a fortune, this business. Cost the life of the Italian, and he had damn-all to do with what this mob are shouting about. Italian, right? So how does he get his pecker into the state of the Jews in Russia? Doesn't, does he? All he'd done is buy a ticket for a plane flight. You've got to sit on these people. Sit on them hard, that's the way you end it. So the Russkies give him a rough time? Well, that's his problem, not the rest of the world's. Should have thought about that first.'

'You're a hard man,' the driver said, and they both laughed. 'What did you know about sending him back then, squire?'

'I don't know,' said Charlie. 'I just don't know.'

'Keep it tight, you Foreign Office people, don't you?'

'I don't mean that. I'm not avoiding you. I just don't know.'

'Served him right,' said the front passenger. 'If he doesn't like it he should have stayed at home. Should have watched his telly.'

'You're right,' said the driver. 'Course you're right. But doesn't make it any nicer. Not sending him back there. Different if he was a Yank or something, but where he's going, then, that's different, that's something else.'

The car sped on, taking Charlie back to what he knew. His home. His family. His office and his work. Going back to all that was familiar where his attitudes would not be cuffed by a boy half his age. Going back to all that was safe and secure. He wondered what Parker Smith would say. Probably be a sherry on the house, and a slapped back and the word that he'd done the section's name a power of good, and didn't we always know you still had your balls in the right place, and be making damn certain you don't get pinched again by 'operational' after all this.

'I didn't ask you, squire, but where did you see him – in the cells?' the driver, bored with the quiet, had decided to resurrect the conversation.

'I saw him on the plane,' said Charlie.

'I thought it was the SAS blokes that took him off.'

'I was on before them,' Charlie spoke woodenly, without pride, claiming no victory.

'You were the FO guy then?' The front passenger had turned eagerly in his seat, excited, something to tell the lads back in the pub behind the Yard if they made London before closing. 'Were you the one that pulled the hostage clear, then went on board and wrapped it up?'

'I was on board when it ended.'

'Jesus – that must have been something, quite something, when he blasted and all that, when all the heavy stuff was flying about. He shot the girl himself, didn't he?'

'Yes,' said Charlie. He looked at his watch, another hour at least. Felt the noose tightening.

'And the Israeli, he was killed then, was he? When the Jew fired on the girl?'

Where would he be now? High over the north German plains, or perhaps beginning to hear the descent of the engines, the lowering of the undercarriage, feeling the gusting turbulence as the air brakes were applied. Wonder whether they're talking to him, or whether he's just a parcel of bloody freight.

'Shut up, Bill,' said the driver, and as an afterthought that ignored Charlie's presence. 'Pack it in. The poor sod's had enough on his plate today without having to go through it all again with us.'

They talked among themselves for the rest of the journey. Only once did they break into Charlie's private world, when they asked him where he wanted to be dropped. He told them that Waterloo Station would do very well, and that was where they left him. They stayed in the car as he walked across the concourse fumbling in his pocket for a return ticket stub he had bought the previous morning. When he was past the barrier and disappeared through a door of the first carriage of the Woking train, they went on their way.

'Funny sort of blokes you find in the spooks,' said the front passenger as they headed across Westminster Bridge. 'You've done well. If we can find somewhere to park the motor we should be able to get a fast one down.'

The report from the Ambassador in London lay on the Israeli Prime Minister's desk. It was a clinical and well-presented document, devoid of emotion and attempting merely to set out the circumstances in which the hi-jacking of Aeroflot flight 927 had ended. There was a brief description of the death, such as the facts were known, of Col Arie Benitz and as much information as the diplomat could muster on the British thinking that had led them to fly the one survivor of the terrorist team back to Russia. The Prime Minister was more amused than surprised that his representative had chosen the word 'terrorist'. He could reflect that there had been a time, less than three decades ago, when the word had held a respectability now long since discarded. Back in the days of the Haganah and Palmach, the days of Jewish struggle against the British, then there had been no stigma to the label.

But what was in a word? Terrorist or freedom fighter or urban guerrilla were only labels to express the international community's displeasure or acclamation for the men who fought the hidden wars, who belonged to the lonely and unrecognized armies, who shunned the safety of the big battalions. But it was a dangerous thought, impossible beyond the privacy of his office. He could not permit himself to express such a view outside the stout, wooden door, because that would mean acknowledgement of the Palestinians who in their puny groups likewise attempted to overthrow the accepted authority.

His last duty that night was to telephone his Minister of Information. There should be no government reaction, either attributable or non-attributable, by any of the Ministry's spokesmen about the events of the day at Stansted. It was to be regarded as an affair between Britain and the Soviet Union, that was to be the line taken, and any other suggestions should be treated with non-committal answers.

It had been a difficult and trying day for them all, he thought, and his plans that had seemed at best difficult and at worst unfeasible had ended without success. And lost to them was a man they could ill afford to be without. Hard to find again another like the young Benitz. His secretaries were long since gone, and he switched off the lights of his room and of the outer office before walking out to where the bodyguards lounged in the corridor.

You win a few, you lose many, that was what he had learned since he had moved into the office at the end of the north corridor on the third floor.

At his morning meeting the Foreign Secretary was told of the night's developments.

He was briefed on the exchange of Isaac at the least used and least observed checkpoint between West and East Berlin. The cipher teleprinter messages from the Foreign Office men of the transaction being carried out without any unseen difficulties and in strict accordance with the mutually agreed planning. He was informed that the Russian Ambassador had sent a message of congratulation to the British government, thanking them on behalf of the Supreme Soviet for the firm stand that had been taken in the maintenance of the rule of law. There was nothing in the text to bring him to assume that the prisoner would face any penalty other than death. This did not distress him: he knew the habits of the Soviets sufficiently to believe that the fate of the boy would be decided and executed swiftly and without recourse to the beating of drums. He had read two of the day's morning papers in his car on the way to Whitehall, and asked his private

347

secretary if there had been hostile reaction to the Foreign Office statement in those that he had not yet seen.

'Not really, sir. Bit of a quibble in some about the speed of things. But nothing openly antagonistic in the leader pages. They all carried a very good wire picture from the Italian ANSA agency – showed the wife of Franconi, the Italian who was killed, in tears with her children round her. Difficult for Fleet Street to conjure up much of a row when they have a snap like that to use alongside. Seems to me it all went off rather well.'

'I think we sometimes preoccupy ourselves too much with public reaction,' the Foreign Secretary said. 'Every now and then they want a good, firm decision, and that's what we gave them.'

'I doubt if the Israelis are that pleased.'

'Not our concern, young man. We're not elevated to these lofty climes to please the people of Jerusalem and Tel Aviv. They've shouted long enough and loudly enough about the need to teach these people a lesson – and quite right too – they've complained at the softness and the lack of resolution in the West to hi-jacking. Well, we've shown them what we can do . . .'

'But it's not as simple as that, is it, sir?'

'Of course it isn't. Quote me and I'll fire you, too damn right I will. Of course it isn't that simple. The only thing that amazes me is that more people haven't said so.'

What also surprised him was the degree, now that it was completed, that he had enjoyed handling the crisis. True it had not been a major one, but crises and even the little ones were welcomed when you sat in high office. He would miss the briefings, and the hurrying in the corridors and the ambassadors kicking their heels with impatience outside the door. If the opinion polls were correct in their assessment of the popularity of his party then his tenure of the Foreign Office was limited in the extreme.

He would remember these last two days. With affection.

* * *

For an hour now the bird had been still, motionless as a statue, perched on the dark oak root that curved out from the river bank over the clear, fast-flowing water.

Such a small body, with its disproportionate head and the winnowed brown bill that projected with benign aggression from the brilliant mass of the blue and green feathering of the head and back that in turn softened to the reddened brown of the breast. Patient and accepting no limit on the time it must spend before some unwary minnow or stickleback, held in an illusion of safety, might stray beneath the watching eyes.

When it dived it was with a flashing, sudden movement that was too fast for the sight of the old man to follow, leaving him only with the bareness of the root and the wrinkled circling of the water that would soon be lost in the constant eddying. Gone for a second, then the supreme moment of triumph as it broke the water, seeming to float for a moment before thrashing angrily clear of the frail spray and arching up towards the hole that the old man had found many months earlier. That was the reason he came to this place. Mingled with the colours of the bird was the tiny, flapping silver fish, frantic in its death-throes; and they were gone, predator and victim, lost to sight under the lip of the bank that was its home and where he knew the fledglings would be waiting. Most days he came to this spot, crawling on his hands and knees into the thicket that hid him from the kingfisher's view; only heavy rain made him shelter in his hut, or the needs of hunger and a hunting expedition far into the forest would keep him away, prevent him joining the pleasure of the bird as she provided for her little ones. He would not see her for some minutes now as she would break up the meal before consigning it to the hungry throats. Perhaps the male would visit – that would be good reason for a further wait – a heavier, larger bird, its colours more complete and deeply accented, who would swoop low over the stream as he approached and call once in the shrill shriek that was the sign of his coming. The same sound that he had taught the young man, David, who was deep and serious and passionate in his beliefs of something that Timofey did not understand, and who needed the guns for his fulfilment.

It was five days now since David had come. Each day Timofey had remembered him and felt a bolt of loneliness when he thought of their farewell.

His ears were keen to the sound of approaching footsteps and when he first heard the breaking of twigs and the cracking of the parched leaf mould under the policemen's boots he had hoped that it heralded David's return. He waited for the call – silent, hidden, anxious. He had taught the boy well, till his imitation of the kingfisher was perfect. But the barking of the dogs, frantic now with excitement, the scent regained from the hut, aroused him to the danger. Timofey was old, and though his senses were still keen agility of movement was long lost. It took him an age to scramble to his feet, more time to recognize the source and direction of the threat, longer to plot which way he should run. There were voices now, lively with pursuit, and ever closer the yapping of the hounds.

His hands were still scrabbling at the far bank of the stream when they came to the place where he had been concealed. Two dogs, large, well-fed, disciplined to attack and straining at their leashes. Four men, two of them dog handlers, the others carrying light machine guns. All wearing the dun uniform of the Kiev militia. Stupidly, because the chance of escape no longer existed, Timofey tried to pull himself up the slippery and crumbling bank, something instinctive to so old a fugitive. Fighting upwards he fell, rose again and then subsided. Destroyed by the boy who had come, nullified when he had won Timofey's friendship, when he had taken the guns. All clear to the old man as the moss and earth filled his untended fingernails and his movements became more sluggish, more tired.

He did not know of Isaac. He had no way of conjuring in his mind the small hunched figure in a cell corner with the bruises refreshed and alive around his face who had denounced Timofey. The information he had bartered would purchase Isaac a few more hours before they took him from his cell for the last time. A few more hours: that was the value of the old man's life.

Four bullets they fired at him. Three to buckle him in the water, a fourth to be certain the job was completed.

Deep in her hole in the river bank the kingfisher and her family waited for the screams to pass. Half a day she stayed there before hunger overtook her fear and she emerged again into the slanted light of the late afternoon and tripped to her perch to wait and to watch. The water beneath her was stained where the main current had not cleansed it, and though she remained till the dusk the fish did not come again.

'The best practitioner currently working in the UK . . . quite simply the most intelligent and accomplished'
Independent

'In a class of his own'
The Times

'One of the modern masters of the craft'
Daily Mail

'A master of the thriller set on the murky edges of modern war'
i

'A stylish writer'
Observer

'One of the most venerable names of the thriller genre'
Independent

'Richly imagined novels that bristle with authenticity'
Washington Post

'The dabbest hand in the industry . . . a master'
City AM

'The pace leaves you breathless . . . he is the master of the thriller genre'
Edinburgh Evening News

Turn the page to find out more about the thrillers that have earned Gerald Seymour the title of 'best thriller writer in the world today' (*Telegraph*) . . .

THE CORPORAL'S WIFE

'Seymour is, quite simply, one of the finest thriller writers in England, every bit the equal of Frederick Forsyth and Robert Harris.'
Daily Mail

A young woman determined to live her own life in an oppressive society.

A rag-tag team of men sent to bring her out of it against all the odds.

THE CORPORAL'S WIFE is a hugely suspenseful thriller about escaping one of the world's most explosive hostpots – Iran. It is an epic, nail-biting story of courage and betrayal, a brilliant glimpse into a closed society and the way the secret services operate on both sides of the line between politics and morality.

'This is another masterly performance from an author whose recent work turns individual spying missions into ambitious ensemble dramas mixing action scenes and love stories with espionage.'
The Sunday Times

HODDER

THE OUTSIDERS

'Once again demonstrating his ability to probe the moral murki-
ness of the spy trade and create an absorbingly diverse ensemble,
Seymour crafts a sophisticated, reader-teasing tale.'
The Sunday Times

MI5 officer Winnie Monks has never forgotten the death of a young
agent on her team at the hands of a former Russian Army Major-
turned-gangster. Ten years later, she hears the Major is travelling to a
Spanish villa and she asks permission to send in a surveillance unit.

There is an empty property next door, perfect to spy from –
and as a base for Winnie's darker, less official plans.

But this villa isn't deserted: the owners have invited a young
British couple to 'house sit' while they are away.

Jonno and Posie think they are embarking on a carefree holiday in the sun.
But, when the Secret Service arrives in paradise, *everything* changes.

'Those [Seymour] sends off into dangerous territory are, in fact,
his readers. With each book, we enter a dangerous universe, and
are totally involved with utterly plausible characters, faced with
moral choices that are rarely straightforward.'
Independent

HODDER

A DENIABLE DEATH

AN EPIC NOVEL OF HIGH COURAGE AND LOW CUNNING, OF LIFE AND DEATH IN THE MORAL MAZE OF THE POST-9/11 WORLD.

'Gerald Seymour is the grand-master of the contemporary thriller and A DENIABLE DEATH is his greatest work yet. Gripping, revealing and meticulously researched, this is a page-turning masterpiece that will literally leave you breathless.'
Major Chris Hunter, bestselling author of *Extreme Risk*

YOU WATCH. YOU WAIT. THE HOURS SLIDE SLOWLY PAST.

A WHOLE DAY. THEN TWO.

YOU LIE UNDER A MERCILESS SUN IN A MOSQUITO-INFESTED MARSH.

YOU CAN'T MOVE, LEAVE, OR RELAX.

YOUR MUSCLES ACHE FROM CLENCHING TIGHT FOR SO LONG.

IF YOU ARE DISCOVERED, YOU WILL BE TORTURED THEN KILLED.

AND HER MAJESTY'S GOVERNMENT WILL DENY ALL KNOWLEDGE OF YOU.

'Great storytelling . . . you just have to read this novel . . . absolutely gripping'
Eurocrime

HODDER

THE DEALER AND THE DEAD

THE ARMS DEALER BETRAYED THEM.
THE SURVIVORS WANT REVENGE.

'*The Dealer and the Dead* is Seymour firing on all cylinders
and his rivals need, once again, to look to their laurels'
Independent

In a moonlit field near the Serbian border, Croatian villagers waited for an arms shipment that would never come. They
will never forget that night, or the slaughter that followed.

Eighteen years later, a body is discovered in a field, and with it the identity of
the arms dealer who betrayed them. Now the villagers can plot their revenge.

For Harvey Gillott, it was all a long time ago. But now the
hand of the past is reaching out across Europe, to Harvey's house in leafy England. And it's holding a gun . . .

'The final scenes are brilliantly orchestrated . . . Without doubt, *The Dealer
and the Dead* is one of the finest thrillers to be published so far this year'
Yorkshire Evening Post

HODDER

THE COLLABORATOR

CORRUPTION. BETRAYAL. REVENGE.

'A dense, intensely satisfying thriller from one of the modern masters of the craft, Seymour's latest novel will remind the world just how phenomenally accomplished a thriller writer he is.'
Daily Mail

Eddie Deacon has a new girlfriend. She's beautiful, clever and Italian.

And then she disappears.

What Eddie doesn't know is that Immacolata Borelli is the daughter of a merciless Naples gangster. She can no longer live with her conscience and has decided to collaborate with the police to bring down her own family.

But the Borellis will not lose their empire without a fight. They will use or destroy anything and anyone to prevent her from talking.

Including Eddie.

'Tight writing and meticulous research . . . Seymour paints the streets of Naples and their dark denizens with an artist's brush that lingers equally on the grime, the glitter and the blood'
The Times

HODDER